LORD OF THE ISLES

BOOKS BY DONALD BARR CHIDSEY

Novels

Lord of The Isles

Captain Adam

Stronghold

Panama Passage

Nobody Heard the Shot

Each One Was Alone

Weeping is for Women

Pistols in the Morning

Biography

Queen Elizabeth I (*in preparation*)

John the Great: The Times and Life of John L.
      Sullivan

The Gentleman from New York: A Biography of
      Roscoe Conklin

Sir Humphrey Gilbert

Sir Walter Raleigh

Marlborough: The Portrait of a Conqueror

Bonnie Prince Charlie: A Life of the Young
      Pretender

Juvenile

Rod Rides High

LORD
of the
ISLES

DONALD BARR CHIDSEY

WILDSIDE PRESS

To my niece
ANN BARR CHIDSEY

LORD OF THE ISLES

Come, Kiss a Killer

Ann Buttoner awoke with a start, every nerve tingling. She didn't know how long she had been asleep; but she did know, immediately and unmistakably, though she could not have said why, that there was a man in her room.

She lay still. She could not even pray, she was so frightened.

She had not been alone in the house—Mother slept across the hall as usual—but she had been alone in this room she was accustomed to share with her sisters. Helen and Grace were to Middletown, visiting with Mother's sister, Aunt Hawkins; and Orlando the slavey had gone along with them for protection.

The wind moaned. Leaves, falling, clicked against the window-panes, and one of them unexpectedly found the way open for it and tumbled in, turning 'round and 'round until, startled, it came to rest on the floor.

Now Ann began to hear voices of men, back by the pear orchard, or beyond that, in the direction of the river.

She slithered out of bed. She might have screamed, so that Mother would come. But she didn't want to scream; and indeed she wasn't sure that she could, just then.

Her fingers found her shawl. It was knitted, but it only covered shoulders and breast. All she had on otherwise was her nightrail, not even any sleeping drawers. She shivered. It was real cold, especially around her legs.

In the dark, walking sideways, she found the door, examined the latch. It was thrown. Nobody had entered by *that* way.

She heard the voices again, men's voices. She wondered that Mother did not hear them. They were some distance away, calling to one another; but she reckoned that they were getting closer.

She went to the window, not directly but rather she circled half around the room to get there, trying to move in silence, striving to keep her bare feet from shushing on the bare floor.

Another cloud of leaves broke from one of the maples and clip-clicked inquisitively against the windows.

She heard the men again, nearer now. They sounded as if they were hunting something, though she heard no hounds. But they sounded like hunters. Yet this was right in the town, right on Prospect Street; though down toward the river, where the voices were, it was mostly just pasture and pear orchard.

"Please don't scream," said a voice at her feet.

She squinched her eyes shut, stretching herself straight and tight, all but going up on her toes. After a spell she let her breath go out a mite and very cautiously opened her eyes.

"Thank you," said the voice. "You done that first-rate."

It was a roopy voice, slow, with juice in it. It was not taut, twangy, like you might have expected.

Ann could not see him, except as a blur of shadow, fuzzy-edged, just below the window, a place he was crouching in order to be out of sight from the yard.

She looked out. Though there was no moon, there was God's plenty of stars. Another leaf chickered against the window, tried to find the opening, failed, tried again, got in, and spiraled to the floor, where it rested beside the first, both of them looking like wild ducks about to take to the air again at the slightest sound.

A man came out of the orchard, not running but walking mighty fast with long strides, and bent low as he walked. He'd a musket in his hand, and it was nigh onto as long as he was tall. He stopped, looked around, looked up, saw Ann.

"Miss Buttoner, there! You!"

Ann did not stir.

"Don't answer," said the voice at her feet.

10

"You seen anybody pass this way, if you please?"

"Don't say anything," said the voice at her feet.

She didn't say anything. She probably could not have said anything if she'd tried, anyway; though she reckoned later, when she'd had a chance to mull it over, that she might at least have waggled her arms or something; but anyway she didn't; she stood perfectly still.

The man down there nodded. He was one of the river men. He trotted toward Prospect Street, and soon another man came out of the orchard and trotted after him, and then another. They all had guns.

A certain amount of mist had crept up from the river. It trailed each man out of the orchard, twisting and twining around his ankles, pitifully eager to detain him; and now, now that the men had gone, it coiled in sullen ribbons, baffled.

Ann held the shawl tight. Under the nightrail her skin was stippled with goose-pimples.

She guessed she could jump into bed, but that mightn't do any good. She was sure she could not make the door in time.

The shadow at her feet writhed, and rose, becoming real. She could not see his face. He was a tall man, and must have been mighty spry, strong, too, to have climbed up the wooden rainspout and into the window. He stood very close to her, sort of bending over her.

"Thank you," he said again, saying it gravely but at the same time with a hint of a chuckle in the voice, like tiny waves clucking around a piling. "I can leave you now."

"What—was—it?"

"Just a disagreement, down to the ferry tavern."

She shivered again, and not just from the cold. The ferry tavern was the most ungodly place in Hartford.

"Hide high and they'll not find you, way I figure it. Ever notice how landsmen always look *down* when they're searching for something? I'm a seafaring man myself, and I reckon maybe I'd better get back where I belong. There's a whaler down to

11

Saybrook that sails for the Sandwich Islands tomorrow. They'll be needing hands enough to cover me. I hate whaling — but maybe the other side of the world, especially the Sandwich Islands, is the right place for me now, eh?"

He leaned forward and kissed her right smacketty-dab on the mouth. He smelled of rum.

That righted her. She took her hands from the shawl, all regardless, and she slapped his face just as hard as she could, first on one side, then on the other.

She would have started to weep then, feeling better, feeling alive; but the man gave her no chance. Laughing in the darkness, but laughing low and fondly, he reached out. A hand took her shoulder, and she was spun around. Another hand, a large heavy one, thwacked her buttocks. It stung, burning all through her. It set her to staggering.

"One good slap deserves another, eh? Good night—and sweet dreams!"

She whirled, sobbing, choking, tears hot in her eyes, so graveled that she forgot all about the shawl, which fell off; and she flew at him, arms flailing.

But he'd already got a hand on the windowsill, and he vaulted over it before she could get there. She heard him land. A moment later he was running, bending low, heading for the trees. He paused an instant, turning, to wave; and then his figure was swallowed by the shadows of the maples, crispy leaves stirring to mark the place where he had been.

So at last she was free to weep, yet she didn't weep, only stared after him. That was the way she was when Mother knocked.

It was not necessary to evade anything with Mother, who simply assumed that Ann'd heard something but seen nothing. They were at the window together when a man came back from Prospect Street, cutting diagonally across the yard toward the pear orchard. He was stumpy and had a hippy walk, and a hanger slammed foolishly against his knee. Mother called to him.

"Missus Buttoner, ma'am? Miss Buttoner?"

"Who were they chasing?"

"One of them Lamb boys. The one that run away to sea two-three years ago. Johnny. Come back today, and sure as snakes he got in trouble right off. He leaver fight as work, that lad."

"But what did he *do*?"

The stumpy searcher had started off, the hanger whanging back and forth. He called an answer over his shoulder.

"Only killed a man, that's all."

Will You Marry Me?   2

It scraped her. It was well that nobody asked her a direct question about that night—not Mother, nor, when they got back, Helen or Grace, nor yet Orlando—for Ann Buttoner was an honest party and wouldn't have lied. All the same, it scraped her. Johnny the Lamb, as they called him, the most irresponsible member of the town's most irresponsible family, had not been caught. The man he'd killed had been buried, and the fugitive had been indicted by the grand jury on a charge of murder. There were some that said Johnny Lamb had done the only thing a man could do, defending himself against an attacker armed with a knife. Others were not sure. The spectators aren't ever in agreement over an affair like that, which happened fast and amid much excitement, most of them being tolerably well rummed up at the time, too. Anyway, Johnny was wanted by the law. If he had really acted in self-defense, and could prove it, then why did he run away? Or, having run away, which in itself was understandable maybe, why, after thinking it over, didn't he come back and give himself up?

Ann Buttoner did not argue these points, even with herself. She was concerned overwhelmingly with whether she ought to tell anybody what had happened that night. Aside from the disgrace, it could be that she was also an accessory after the fact, or something like that, though of course it was the disgrace she thought of mostly, and the effect it would have on her sisters and on Mother.

Even though nobody asked her, should she speak up? Never mind the State law, which she didn't know much about anyway; but was she breaking a moral law by keeping her mouth shut? Had she ought to at least speak to Reverend Mr. Willets about it?

She was almost glad when the time came, a scant week after the event itself, for her to tell. This was when Jabez Mathewson asked her to marry him.

There he stood, as sad as a turtle, a thin long young man with an abnormally small neck, protuberant eyes, damp hands. He was not attractive, but he was good, and kind: all the Mathewsons were kind folks.

The proposal was by no means unexpected; but two things about it irked Ann.

One: Throughout the carefully prepared and no doubt often rehearsed declaration just finished he had called her "Miss Buttoner." They had been childhood friends, neighbors. Until now they'd always been Jabez and Ann. Just because he was suggesting matrimony and a trip to the Sandwich Islands, that still didn't mean that he had to get so persnicketty all of a sudden, did it? For no reason that she tried to find, Ann resented that "Miss Buttoner." It was that college he'd been going to, she reckoned.

Two: She did not know whether he had proposed to Alice Voorhees first.

14

When Jabez Mathewson had come back from New Haven the previous day with the announcement that he was determined to sail with the first United States church mission to a foreign land, everybody in town knew right off that within a matter of hours he would be asking either Alice Voorhees or Ann Buttoner to be his wife. Normally he would have waited until he finished his studies at Yale. But a wife he must have if he was going to be a member of the mission, scheduled to sail from Boston in a week's time. For various reasons, all good, the newly formed mission board had made it a rule that only married couples should be sent forth to spread the Word.

There were others Jabez Mathewson might ask, if he still had time, in the event that both Ann Buttoner and Alice Voorhees turned him down; but what interested Alice and Ann, not to mention all the rest of Hartford, was: Which of these two would he ask first?

And now here was Ann, not knowing. Jabez had made his declaration sooner than she'd expected. She was flustered.

What disturbed her even more, however, was the realization that unless she refused him point-blank—which she wasn't prepared to do, certainly not until she had found out about Alice anyway—that is, before she let this thing go any further, it was necessary to tell Jabez about what had happened that night last week upstairs. It was only fair. It would hurt him; but it had to be done.

"I—I—"

She turned away, head low.

"There is something you must know about me first," she muttered; and with eyes downcast, hands clasped before her, she walked to the window.

She looked out on the side yard, the maples, the pear orchard. This was directly underneath her bedroom.

Standing there, blinking to keep the tears back, in a low voice she told him about that man in her room.

15

When she had finished, there was a great deal of silence.

The leaves kept falling, turning, turning. Once the leaves start to go, they go fast.

After a while, motionless, she said, "Well?"

"It was a most unfortunate incident. My, uh, my heart goes out to you, Miss Buttoner." Clearly he was confused. "But—you haven't answered my question?"

She understood, then. Angry for an instant, a fleet flare, she felt warm and good and understanding immediately afterward. She turned to him, all but spreading her arms.

Sure, he only wanted a wife now because he wanted so much to go to Hawaii. It was not glory he sought: there'd be little enough of that among naked savages. It wasn't worldly goods: he was the son of the richest merchant in Hartford.

No, the point was that he had grown up. He was a man. No longer was he the diffident tike who had sported with Grace and Helen and her, whom they'd more than once pelted with pine cones and teased because he was afraid to bellywhopper down Sentinel Hill. He had not ceased his theological studies on impulse. He wasn't jeopardizing his chances of a pulpit, simply on a whim. He was utterly in earnest. His eyes shone. He was a man, a dedicated man. That was why he had addressed her as "Miss Buttoner."

She shook her head as she walked toward him. At least, she believed afterward that she had. She'd meant to.

He did not grab her arms or lean to kiss her. Instead he threw back his head, exhaling loudly as though in thankfulness.

"Let us pray—Miss Buttoner," he whispered.

They knelt, facing each other, close, their foreheads touching. Ann loved him then. She could understand how any woman might be willing to go with him and help him on the great and holy errand he was about to perform. Not that she herself intended to do this! She hadn't yet made up her mind. But it was good to be with him, and to feel his clean spiritual strength.

She inhaled tremblingly, and her clasped hands touched his.

16

Somebody started to come in from the kitchen, but promptly and hushedly backed away. It was Grace, Ann knew from the step.

At last he said "Amen," and Ann hastily said, "Amen," and they rose, he helping her solicitously but not acting in a possessive manner.

Eyes downcast, she walked with him to the door.

"I'll give you your answer before supper—Mr. Mathewson," she whispered.

When the door had closed, Mother came into the room, followed by both Grace and Helen. Mrs. Buttoner was a widow of only six months, unaccustomed to authority: her husband had always handled all discipline in this household, and handled it very well indeed.

"Ann, Jabez Mathewson has proposed to you!"

"Only marriage, Mother. Don't you think he has the right to?"

"Do you know what that would mean?"

"Yes."

"Ann, I absolutely forbid you to marry him!"

She couldn't possibly have said anything more stupid.

"Im afraid it's too late, Mother. I have already accepted."

"I tell you, I *forbid* it!"

Chin high, Ann walked past them. She went up to her room and started to pack her chest.

It was an afternoon and night none of them cared afterward to look back at. There were tears and recriminations; there was hysteria. They hated one another as they shrieked at one another, their faces contorted with rage; and then they hated themselves for having hated one another. In time they all became quiet, except for stifled sobs, and indeed some of them even snatched a little sleep. But the step had been taken. Through everything, even when she herself was screeching, Ann Buttoner had gone right on packing her chest, and long before suppertime she had sent Mr. Mathewson, by Orlando, a letter promising to become his wife the next day.

17

For the Sake of the Record 3

There would be a thin high dry long whimpering squeal, as of a soul being tormented in Hell; then a similar squeal, and another and another, until they rose in an ear-splitting chorus, shrill and frantic. Then they'd cease, these sounds, as though at a command from forward—a command in the form of a *"thunk!"* so loud that all the world shivered and shuddered, while water you couldn't see hissed past the battened port, and the deck and ceiling twisted out of line with one another, and the bulwarks leaned out of line with both, and the lamp that hung by a chain spun now this way, again that, flinging specks of light here and there, swirling them, or causing them to jerk and jump.

There'd be a split-second of silence, an excruciating instant when everything except those jiggering flecks of light was still. And then the brig would lurch into another green arching hollow, and there would be a thin high dry long whimpering squeal, as of a soul being tormented in Hell, and then a similar squeal, and another and another . . . as it had been for days, as it would be for days and weeks on end, for months.

Mrs. Jabez Mathewson was reading aloud from her journal.

". . . and so with faith and trust in the goodness and wisdom of the Reverend Mr. Bingham, our leader, who comes from Vermont, and with an even more exalted and fervent trust in that Higher Personage, Our Creator, Who in His Almighty Mercy will not remove His Hand of Protection from us, we are tossed from day to turbulent day 'mid such discomfort as few if any of us ever knew at home could be."

It was poor stuff. Even though she'd revised the first rough draft twice, it still stumbled. She was no author. She was but doing her duty, if doggedly; for they all, but especially the females, had had it impressed upon them that, as a member of the first foreign mission from the United States, each, howsoever humble personally, was an integral part of history and should not fail to keep a journal or diary, in order that posterity might know in what manner it was that they had toiled in the Lord's vineyard.

All of which would be very well if only you had something you dared to write about, or could really describe. Life aboard the *Thaddeus* was so different from anything Ann ever had known or dreamed of, that she found herself unable to put it down in words that would not sting and scald. But no complaints! Miserable as they were, they must not whine on paper! They had been reminded that the letters they wrote home, as well as the diaries and journals they kept, would probably be published, if not now then later, and would in any event certainly be read from a large number of pulpits. From those who read or listened, it was pointed out, must come the recruits who could carry on the Lord's work in the Pacific islands when those of the present group—the Family, as they already called themselves—had fallen by the wayside or been called back to the bosom of the Father. From those members of far audiences, too, must come the money wherewith the good work could be pushed forward. So—no complaints! Yet you must write.

"Daily do we lift our faces toward Heaven and sing the praise of the All-Highest, for that we comprehend undeviatingly that if it should come to pass—does that sound all right, Mr. Mathewson, dear? 'Comprehend undeviatingly.' Should I maybe change that again?"

She paused, peering at the man she had married.

Jabez Mathewson lay motionless, as he did so much of the time these days. Thin always, a thinness his somewhat rubbery lips and protuberant eyes and high out-thrusting cheekbones

19

accentuated, his face was as white as the pillowcase behind it. That face was cretaceous. It seemed flaking away. Ann thought, with a shudder, looking at it, that she might have scratched with a fingernail and got a fine white pile of powder. The eyes were closed. There was no twitch to the mouth.

Jabez Mathewson might well have been a sick man before he boarded the *Thaddeus* in Boston harbor. Had it been fever or the intense emotional excitement yeasting within him, which made his cheeks hectic? Beyond all question, however, he had been sick— and sick in the old-fashioned sense of the word, the stomach sense—so soon as ever the hook was upped and the brig began to roll. His eyes, hitherto unnaturally bright, had gone glazed—and remained so. That frightful, artificial-seeming smear of red on each cheekbone had disappeared. He had taken to his bunk, from which he had never since moved. Though he seldom spoke, and never groaned, they knew he was in pain.

The only physician aboard, their own Dr. Holman — Ann didn't think much of him—confessed his confoundment. "Keep him comfortable" was the best he could suggest. Reverend Mr. Bingham and Reverend Mr. Thurston were doing whatever they could, but necessarily their help was spiritual rather than medical; and spiritually, it was certain, Mr. Mathewson did not suffer, being strong in the faith.

"Are you all right? Can I get you anything?"

There was no answer, and the eyelids did not flutter. She touched his cheek with the back of a hand. It was chill, but not truly cold. She took the hand away hastily. It gave her a queer feeling to touch that skin, a feeling she didn't like, and here alone in the cabin with him she did not have to conceal it. The feeling was worse at night, when she lay beside him in that narrow pitching bunk. She winced.

There was a cacophony of dry timber-squeals; a massive *"thunk"*; an instant of silence while the vessel shuddered.

Horace Crowell came knocking at the door. He had a perfect

20

right to enter without knocking, for he and his wife Abigail, a girl Ann liked, shared the place with Mr. and Mrs. Mathewson and Mr. and Mrs. Sam Whitney. But Brother Crowell was a gentleman, an unobtrusive, earnest young man with watery blue eyes and a fine brow, who had good manners. It was little enough privacy they could contrive in that cramped cabin, six of them, all strangers to one another before the sailing. They used to dress and undress, and do other necessary things, in relays, a man and wife at a time; and even that, some thought, wasn't altogether decent. Brother Crowell in that place was a joy, always the personification of tact.

Now he blinked at her, not entering.

"There's to be a service of praise, Sister Mathewson, in the dining cabin in ten-fifteen minutes. Is he all right?"

"Thank you." She glanced at the man she had married. "He's about the same."

"Should I stay here with him? Or get Abigail?"

"Thank you, no. I'm reading him my journal. But I'll be up soon."

The timbers squealed. She found her place again. Though she had not been sick aboard the *Thaddeus* — not, that is, violently, convulsively sick, as had most of the others, poor bodies — she'd scarcely been an hour without a headache, an ailment she had seldom experienced ashore. Ann was a healthy girl, eighteen, not exuberant, not bouncy, but strong, if smallish. It was of course the lack of air. She would have enjoyed a walk around the deck, cluttered though it was with all manner of crates and coops. But her duty was by the side of her husband — even though he didn't know she was there.

"God has seen fit to send us tumultuous weather, or so, at least, does it seem to us. In all these eleven long days the sea has not been still. Yet beyond here must there be a haven, a refuge where — Maybe I ought to make that 'there must be a haven' instead of 'must there be'? What do you think, Mr. Mathewson?"

21

There was no answer, and she looked at him. She looked at him for a long while, the brig squee-ing and squealing all around them, the lamp twirling to send out a scatter of light-flecks.

Suddenly she reached over and touched his face, as before with the back of a hand. Then she touched it with the palm, then with both hands. It was utterly cold.

She examined him further. She didn't need a physician. She didn't need to be told. She put the journal away, after tying it carefully. She was trembling a little, not much. She knelt for only a moment in prayer.

They all looked up when she entered the dining cabin. They knew that something had happened; and at least Reverend Mr. Bingham, behind the opened Book, his deep eyes burning into her, knew what it was.

"Sister Mathewson?"

"Mr. Mathewson," she said, "is dead."

Stick a Pin in the Queen 4

At a gap in the palisade a sentry, a genial giant who wore a loincloth and a saber, nothing else, saluted.

"The Queen?" she asked in Hawaiian.

"In there," flipping a thumb. "Just go where you hear the most noise."

Ann frowned fleetingly. There could be a misunderstanding, for surely there was no shortage of queens here.

"I mean Kaahumanu."

"Aye, aye, sir," blurted the sentry in all the English he knew. "Aye, aye, sir."

And he beamed, proud of himself.

Ann sighed and went into the court yard. She walked with hands folded, head down; but this does not mean that she saw nothing. She had been taught this walk, this manner; indeed, she had never known another; and since it was natural to her, she could fit it into her human wish to see what was going on. She might appear to be gazing at the ground before her feet, but there was little she missed.

In the court yard, then, from the tail of one eye she glimpsed something that brought her up short, gasping.

She had never seen anything, or known that there could be anything, so hideous. Though clearly a constructed article, it affected her like something alive, a crawling animal, a glittering slithering snake.

This thing was mounted on a pole not much thicker than a broomstick and perhaps eight or nine feet tall. It was a monster's head constructed of red and yellow feathers pasted on a wicker-work frame. Human hair surmounted it and hung in loose dirty dusty hanks along its sides. The eyes, though empty, were tip-tilted and seemed to express a fiendish rage. Worst of all was the mouth, which was wide and voracious: it looked as though it ought to be slobbered with blood. Top and bottom jaws alike were set with sharks' teeth.

She should have felt loathing, and she did. But she felt fear, too. Her body abruptly was sopped with sweat; her mouth went dry; her feet seemed rooted in the packed hard earth; her hands, trembling, rose to her breast.

Afterward, released from the spell, she told herself that she had done well to resist the impulse to topple the thing and stamp it to shapelessness. She'd been so instructed: all of them had. They must restrain themselves. "The simple Sandwich Islanders have overthrown their own gods," the Reverend Mr. Bingham had told them more than once. "We must not smash idols. But we must be alert to replace them with the True Belief once they *are* smashed." All the same, in a little while, after a little reasoning in relief, Ann Mathewson was obliged to admit

23

to herself that she never had known an impulse to mutilate this monstrosity anyway. She'd been too frightened.

This — she recognized it from descriptions — this was Kukai-limoku, commonly called Kaili. It had been the most ferocious, the most bloodthirsty of all the native gods. Officially outlawed, like the others, yet here it still stood — and in the very grounds of the palace.

The stick was a sort of handle, supposedly for carrying Kaili into action. It was said that the monstrous thing, borne high by a priest, shrieked in battle: thousands swore that they had heard it. Ann Mathewson almost could believe this. She was ashamed of herself.

It gave her a start, and jerked her out of her trance, when she saw a serving woman stop before the idol and make the motion of uncovering herself above the waist — actually she wasn't wearing anything there anyway — and bow low.

"You mustn't do that!"

Forgetting herself, she had spoken in English; yet the serving woman caught her meaning from her tone. The serving woman padded off. Ann tore her gaze from the battle god and resolutely refused, as she walked away, to look back.

"The Queen?" she asked another serving woman.

"In there."

Ann went in through the opening of an exceptionally large grass hut. It was a very noisy place.

How different (she thought) from Hartford.

There seemed to be a large number of persons in the hut, but at first she knew this rather by reason of the evidence of her ears than that of her eyes, for she could scarcely see anything at all. There were no windows, and the only light came from the doorway behind her — there was no door — and from occasional vents and openings where the grass of the walls had blown back. After the sun-drenched court, here was gloom. What with the babble of voices, the smoke, the darkness, the shouts and screams of laughter, she thought whimsically, it could even be likened to a descent from Heaven to the Other Place. She hoped that this wasn't irreverent.

She did not move, but stood waiting for her eyes to get used to the dimness. She was not unaccustomed to this. Oahuan houses were all murky. More often than not they were very low, too, or at least the entrance was. She'd become an expert at going down on hands and knees to enter. She never stayed that way, but straightened up as soon as she got inside; and then she would stand awhile, as she was doing now, unwilling to move for fear of stepping on somebody. The islanders, indoors, were customarily horizontal.

Now she saw Kaahumanu first, a fact which was perhaps a tribute to the forceful personality of that dowager, co-ruler of the islands, and indeed the real ruler, since the King even when sober took little interest in government.

The other three women in the center of the hut were, at a glance, exactly similar to Kaahumanu. They were lying on their bellies, propped up on their elbows, pointing in the four directions, each a spoke of a wheel the hub of which was a game of whist. There was no furniture in the room, only mats.

The Queen's companions, Ann saw, were also of high rank. You could always tell anybody born to the chiefly class. They were so much better fed and cared for than the commoners, and so much inbred, that they seemed members of a different race.

All four of these women wore, in addition to many wreaths and ropes of flowers, only the pau and the kihei, the one around the middle, leaving legs and feet bare, the other over one shoulder; and all of them wore this latter garment carelessly, so that each had at least one breast showing.

Yet though this constituted a sort of uniform, and though they were all women of heroic proportions and about the same age, no more than a moment was needed to mark Kaahumanu off from the others. She was massive, almost twice Ann's height, perhaps three times Ann's weight, yet she was symmetrically formed, a Polynesian Juno. She carried herself with a natural grace, and big though she was, there was nothing flabby about her. *Both* of her breasts were showing: they were large and perfectly round, and they didn't wobble.

Contempt, often there, was loud in her eyes when she looked upon Ann Mathewson. Yet they were lovely eyes, huge, long, dark. She grunted with annoyance. She tipped her head back and put the neck of a bottle into her mouth. It made a lot of noise when she swallowed. The bottle was empty when she let it drop, and a servant was fetching another.

"My greetings fly to thee, Long Neck," coldly. "You will wait."

Ann curtsied. The Queen returned to her cards. None of the others had even glanced up. They played very loudly, tittering, screeching like macaws, slamming the cards down.

This was a large hut, and around its walls were ranged many servants. Four of these held kahilis — not the ceremonial kahilis Ann had first seen when she met Kaahumanu and the court, those of nine, ten, even twelve feet length, but smaller, more practicable ones, which the servants were using to fan flies off the ladies. Four others held cuspidors of koa-wood intricately carved. There was one for each lady, who when she wished to spit might or might not remember to call her bearer. It really didn't matter. The bearers were there, that was the important thing. They were living symbols of power. On parade, each of these matrons might have had four or five spittoon-bearers behind her.

Other servants held calabashes of fruits and poi, and a few had armfuls of flowers. They were by no means stiff in deportment. They sniggered and poked one another and sometimes laughed almost as loudly as the ladies. They were evidently talking about Ann Mathewson, who reddened.

Ann cleared her throat, but nobody heard.

"Uh, about that velvet gown, your Majesty — "

Kaahumanu looked up, the smile dropping from her face like a flower dropping from her hair. She said nothing; and in a

26

moment she had resumed her play, a laugh on her lips again; but it was some time before Ann Mathewson ventured to shift her weight to another foot. The servants giggled.

At last the Queen threw her cards down, yawned prodigiously, and rose. She rose without any assistance and with a marvelous swiftness, considering her size. She said something to a few servants, who scurried out; and then, erect, a picture of regal decorum for all her costume, with a nod she summoned Ann Mathewson. She extended a hand, or rather a forefinger; and this Ann accepted, and over it Ann curtsied again.

"It was kind of you to come," Kaahumanu said contemptuously.

"It was kind of your Majesty to ask me."

Queen One-Finger they called her in the Family. She did not like missionaries, and she was not a woman to keep her dislikes to herself. Yet she had a strong sense of the responsibilities of her position, and her rudeness to the Long Necks on occasions of state was purely conventional.

The velvet was brought in, and Ann gasped.

"You like it?"

"It — it's *beautiful!*"

It was Nile green, a double velvet, short-piled, light, and positively fluffy to the feel. One edge was gold-brocaded in a simple foliaceous design. This was rich stuff, the finest Ann ever had seen. She had always loved lovely dress materials. Her own ribbons and bows and rosettes and other bits and scraps of decoration she had stripped from her garments and thrown away, or given away, before she sailed to undertake the Lord's work. This was only proper, and she didn't regret it; but it was hard now, fingering this stuff.

Ann had kept out only one thing — a d'Angoulême poke, a preposterously frivolous headpiece, the inside of the brim lined with pink sarsenet, the crown a mass of parti-colored flowers and fripperies, while a fringe of Mechlin hung from the brim in front. It wasn't real Mechlin, but it was a good imitation. Ann

27

had never worn this bonnet, and now of course she never would; but she had never found the courage, either, to throw it away. She kept it at the bottom of her chest, where it was badly crushed. She hated to think what the Reverend Mr. Bingham would say about it, or Sybil, if ever they came upon it. Nothing, probably. But they had several ways of saying nothing.

The piece of velvet (the gift of some sea captain who had carried it for years awaiting the need for a superlatively enticing bribe) was very long — long enough, Ann estimated, to make five or six gowns of ordinary size. The Queen, to be sure, would not take a gown of ordinary size. Besides, Ann soon learned that the Queen wanted *all* the material used. She wanted it to be draped on her. She wanted to stagger under its weight. If it was good enough for Kaahumanu it was too good for anybody else, even a small snippet left over. The Queen had exquisite arms, shoulders, breasts; but it was no treat for her to expose them, who had done so all her life. Indeed, even now, when it seemed to be in the way, with an impatient yank she tore off the kihei, leaving herself naked to the waist. Ann Mathewson ducked her head over her reticule and with trembling hands found pins, a bit of chalk, scissors, a tape measure. She felt her face hot.

The Queen's mood had changed. All jocularity was gone from her. She seemed to resent the need to cease playing cards and stand before this pasty-faced girl with the pins. She grunted when Ann measured her, and she let out an ear-piercing screech when Ann inadvertently pricked her left buttock.

"I'm so sorry, your Majesty!"

"Nu ke hamau i ka leo!"

Ann blushed but went on measuring and pinning. The three deserted whist players had rolled over on their backs, and there, propped on elbows, they were making remarks about the velvet and passing a bottle back and forth.

There was a great scowl on Kaahumanu's face. Ann, not looking up, nevertheless could see this. There was no knowing what might happen when Kaahumanu felt this way.

28

Then suddenly the Queen gave a guffaw of delight; and Ann Mathewson did look up.

Somebody was coming toward this hut — a man, they could hear him laugh, hear him call greetings to servants.

Ann Buttoner knew that voice.

Her backside burned at the memory.

Gin for the King   5

Johnny Lamb had his hands in the slanty pockets of his breeches, the thumbs outside. His black square-toed shoes were varnished, and there were silver buckles on them. He wore a peaked cap rakishly canted. A long pale cigar jutted upward from a corner of his mouth.

"Hi there, Queen. Good to see you again." He did not remove the cigar. "What was all that screaming just now? That you?"

Kaahumanu gave a cry of delight and fell into his arms.

It would have knocked down a slighter man, that greeting; but Johnny Lamb was well placed, his legs spread wide, his hips and thighs instinctively ready to roll with the rolling of a ship.

His laugh was light. Almost lovingly he disengaged himself, and took the cigar from his mouth, shaking his head, clucking his tongue.

"Good old Kate," he whispered. "It makes my heart warm to see you again."

The Queen smiled. She had a large spontaneous smile, warm and full, showing white teeth.

He leaned toward her and she leaned toward him, each with hands on the other's forearms, and they embraced more formally, rubbing their noses together first on one side, then on the other.

She did not overpower or outshine him; for he, too, was big, firm, strong, straight, with broad straight shoulders and long hard arms, with big feet, big knobby hands. There was nothing slack about him; all, in a sailor's phrase, was a-tauto; there was no fat. He balanced on a thick-corded neck a head that was long and thin. His ears were small, his eyes blue. He'd a wash of light brown, waxy freckles across the bridge of his nose, which had recently been broken, and a few more of these clustered at each end of his mouth. His hair was something between brown and yellow, though in certain lights it could have been thought red: it was short and stiff.

He put the cigar back into his mouth.

"Good old Kate," he said again, around it. "I'm going to call you that after this. Can't be cracking my jaw with a name like Kah-ah-hoo-mah-noo every time I see you."

The Queen giggled. The Nile green velvet, never fastened by more than a few pins, and not designed to survive such an embrace, slipped from her body and tumbled to the mats, leaving her clad in nothing but her skimpy waist-high pa'u. She paid not the slightest attention to this, and neither it seemed did he, as they stood gazing fondly at one another.

Ann knelt to retrieve the velvet. The mats were dusty. She had until this time been careful to keep the velvet held so that it would not touch them. Now fold after fold of it fell, with only Ann to care; for the others were all simpering and sniggering about the Queen and her visitor. Ann gathered the velvet carefully, brushing it, folding it. There was a great deal of it, but it was light stuff. She did not dare to look at the Queen.

"I oughtn't to be here, Kate. I'm a landsman now, and I ought to keep hustling."

"All the time, business, business!"

He shrugged, and put his hands back into his pockets, and rocked on his heels, rubbering his lips out, rolling his eyes.

"I came to these islands to make money," he said. "I don't want you to forget that. But still — I guess a little horua now and then ain't going to ruin me."

"Johnny!"

She pronounced it as if it were "Tony," with a big round "o". The "j" of course she could not possibly have sounded.

"Tony, you can never win on a horua-papa. No haole ever could."

"Listen, Queen. Anything any of your boys around here can do, I can do. That clear?"

"Ten Spanish dollars, Tony."

"Make it twenty."

"Maikai, maikai!"

She called a calabash bearer, and they were both chucking coins into the calabash when Ann Mathewson rose. Ann trembled. She kept brushing and folding the velvet.

"It's a bet then," said Captain Johnny. "You'd better get the best man you know. He'll need to hump it. I used to be dreadful fast, bellywhoppering down Sentinel Hill. And this ain't so different, except there's no snow."

"Your opponent will be worthy of you."

"And say, incidentally your Majesty, put your shirt back on, will you? You make me nervous, standing there like that."

She laughed, and cried, "My funny Tony!" and snatched the cigar from his mouth and thrust it into her own. She spread her feet and tipped the cigar to a steep angle and fisted her hips, grinning, obviously imitating him. Then she trotted out of the room, trailing smoke. She was marvelously light on her feet. She nipped her kihei up from the ground as she went, crying, "I'll be right back. I just go out to make mimi."

When Ann lifted her eyes, very cautiously, she saw Johnny Lamb regarding her. There was no disrespect in his manner, only puzzlement. He shook his head, forefingered his chin.

"Met you somewhere, but I can't remember where. Missus — Missus — "

"Mathewson."

He went on shaking his head.

"I used to be Ann Buttoner. Of Hartford."

31

"Say, of course! I ran away from home so early, y'see. And I didn't often get back."

"Yes."

"Not that I like sailoring. Never did. I'm giving it up — I hope. So you're Mrs. Mathewson now, eh? Hartford boy? Would I know him?"

"Jabez Mathewson. He lived on Prospect Street."

"*That* little rabbit? A fine gal like you?"

"Captain Lamb, you are speaking of the man who was my husband!"

"Well, I'll be swouched!" Then he remembered a word, and caught at it, head cocked. " 'Was'?"

She swallowed, glad to lower her eyes again.

"He knew the call to convert the heathen, but the Society insisted that all sent should be married. I knew what it meant to him, after having heard the call. So I — I married him. It was only two days before they were to sail from Boston. He was horribly sick on board the brig, right from the start. He — he died the eleventh day out. We buried him at sea."

It was quiet in the hut, now that the Queen had gone. At least half the servants had followed her out, and the rest were shifting from foot to foot, bored, unable to understand English. The three remaining card players had fallen asleep. One of them began to snore. The only other sound was the thin, almost whispered click of insects in the thatch.

"Say, I'm sorry. I didn't mean that. Reckon he wasn't so bad, after all. I didn't know him well, really."

"You wouldn't be likely to. He was a good man and a godly one — a very godly man."

"I reckon that's right, at that."

There was gentleness in his voice, and this she resented more than she had resented the former flippancy.

"No, you certainly wouldn't have had a chance to know a man as fine as Mr. Mathewson." She looked up, fixing him, as she hoped, with her gaze. Her mother and father never had

32

thought much of the Lambs, people who lived down near the river and who weren't often seen at the meetinghouse. "Mr. Mathewson, for example, would never have kept his hat on in the presence of a lady."

"Sorry," and he took it off.

"Mr. Mathewson would never have smoked a cigar in the presence of a lady either — or anywhere else."

"Afraid it might choke him?"

"And especially in the presence of a queen!"

"Well, I ain't smoking it now." He nodded toward the door. "*She* is wherever she is, wherever the women go around here."

Ann kept her gaze steady. It was well to be humble, she'd been taught, but not always: in the presence of an enemy it might not be well.

"You don't care much for missionaries, do you, Captain?"

He shrugged.

"Reckon they're all right, in their place."

"Which is at home, I suppose?"

"Well, that's where I'd rather see 'em."

"In order that ruffians like you could have the field clear to sell the poor benighted natives rum and muskets, and to debauch their womenkind?"

"Well, I don't know about the debauchin'. Most of 'em don't seem to need it, really. But liquor and guns, yes. Why not? They're willing to pay, and that's what I came out here for — to make money."

"And you don't care how you make it?"

"I sure do care how I make it! I want to make it honest, so's it won't worry my sleep afterward. And I want to make it fast, so's I can go back to Connecticut where I belong, a rich man."

The Queen returned then, still smoking the cigar, humming.

"Come on, Tony. We will show you the fast horua. *All* come," she commanded. She noticed Ann, standing with the velvet in her arms, afraid to put it down anywhere. "You come, too," she said, and smiled.

33

The court yard was vast, and midway across it they saw moving toward them a plump youngster whose step was unsteady, though it had great dignity. He was almost unattended, scarcely more than twenty men hovering behind him, yet he was instantly recognized. It was his walk. He was tall, and held his fine head erect, the taller for a mass of stiff curly black hair, the broader-seeming of face because of crisp curly black sidewhiskers. He had fine eyes, a loose petulant mouth, a rather absurd mustache. He wore a scarlet silk coat with a high gold-braided military collar, open all down the front, but no shirt or undershirt. He wore electric blue silk breeches with gold buckles at the knee, but no shoes or stockings.

He bowed to Kaahumanu, and she bowed.

"Greetings, Mother. My love goes to thee."

She wasn't his mother, only one of his stepmothers. He was just being royal.

"Greetings, my child. You're drunk again. Love and happiness go to thee."

They rubbed noses formally. Then Kalaninuiliholiho, who was generally called just Liho, and who reigned as King Kamehameha II, with an easy smile extended his hand, his full hand, to Captain Johnny Lamb, who took it. The captain, Ann noticed, had removed his cap.

The King did not salute Ann, but this must have been only because he did not see her, or, seeing her, saw her only indistinctly beyond the pile of velvet she carried in her arms, and mistook her for a serving woman, as well he might. She knew that she was not being snubbed. The King had exquisite manners.

Kaahumanu touched his hand.

"We go to ride the horua-papa. Why not come with us?"

He smiled gently, shaking his head.

"I fancy the sport, as you well know, my mother. But I have pressing matters of state."

"That jug will last," snappishly. "The gin will taste the better for a rest."

34

Still he smiled sleepily and shook his head. He started to bow, but her voice hit his spine.

"No, don't do that. You might fall down."

Though his actual inches were many, in every measurement, there was nothing gross about this young man. Even when he hiccupped, he hiccupped softly. He continued to smile at his stepmother, and perhaps saw nobody else. His eyes were blurred, yet there was melancholy in them.

The dowager sighed.

"Well, I suppose you'd better go on, as long as you've started. But stay indoors, please, eh, my flower, my little bud? Stay in your palace, your Majesty, darling."

He smiled brilliantly at her, more vaguely at the rest of the company, and with an apologetic shrug he turned and walked off, his followers falling in behind him. His walk was unnaturally slow. His feet, large, brown, a trifle toed-out, met the ground with deliberation and left it with the reluctance of uncertainty. Yet he did not stagger. His coattails flapped in a dust-laden breeze.

"A fool," Kaahumanu muttered, "but a sweet one." She took a puff at Captain Johnny's cigar and handed it back to him. She linked an arm into one of his. "Come, Tony. Twenty Spanish dollars, remember."

Faster! Faster!   6

It was a curious procession that wound toward the Punchbowl.

Ahead strode a dozen men with staves with which to beat aside any who might block the passage. There were none such, and the men carried the staves musketwise and affably hailed acquaintances along the line of march. The spectators stayed on either side, mostly in the shade of huts or crouched in doorways.

At least twenty stalwart islanders, ropes of sennit over their shoulders, hauled the Queen's dray. It could only be called that, a dray; for it was no more than a set of wagon wheels with unfinished planks fastened loosely across the axles and tied to one another. It had no dashboard, tailboard, top, or sides. Yet the very wheels were a novelty, and stared at as such.

Four chiefs, two sedately pacing on either side, carried four tremendous aspen-tremulous kahilis, the shortest nine feet tall. These were brave things, like oversized feather dusters, the upper ends being made up principally of the dyed small feathers of the mamo bird, all aflutter, glittering in the sunlight above the swirling dust, aloof and proud. One was black, one dark green, and the other two were scarlet and yellow, the royal colors.

Kaahumanu sat in the rear of the vehicle, facing backward, her bare legs dangling, her bare feet almost scraping the ground. She did not glance at the subjects to right and left, who groveled when she passed. All animation, she chatted with Captain John Lamb, who walked behind the wagon. Johnny had said that he would rather walk than ride in such a contrivance, having regard for his bones. He was often hailed and sometimes he responded. For the most part, though, he devoted himself to the

36

Queen, leaning toward her partly out of deference, partly to avoid the dust.

Johnny had started on a horse, but he had dismounted, explaining that it was difficult to converse with Kate from the saddle. The beast now was led by four delighted chiefs. It attracted almost as much attention as the Queen, being the first horse most of these islanders ever had seen.

Next came a mixed crowd of petty chieftesses, yammering like monkeys, and among them, ignored, the Nile green velvet in her arms, Ann Mathewson.

Ann marched because she had been summoned, though she was sure she'd been forgotten the next instant. Her instructions were to ingratiate herself, if possible, with this powerful dowager who had commanded her to make a gown. It was humiliating; but the ways of God are inscrutable, and the Reverend Mr. Bingham himself had asked her to see what she could do with Kaahumanu. She had refused to leave the velvet behind for the reason that she had not wished to put it on those dirty mats; but now it was so covered with dust that it was all but impossible to tell its true color. Holding it out before her—the only way she could hold it and still keep it from trailing in the road — made her look, inevitably, like a lackey in attendance upon his monarch. Fortunately, she was so hidden by larger, darker women that even her poke was not visible to the crowd. Otherwise that bonnet, and her sleeves and skirt and shoes, surely would have brought about a deal of staring and finger-pointing. The Long Necks had been in this village more than two weeks, but they were still a novelty.

Ann was furious. She wished she dared to weep. She blinked her eyes again and again, and that was not entirely because of the dust. How glad she was, though, that her relatives and friends back in Hartford could not see her striding thus, like a slave, like a Roman captive, behind the cart of a dark fat boisterous conqueror! *That* shame at least she was spared! She stumbled on, coughing.

37

Behind her was a churning mass of servants bearing calabashes, spittoons, flowers, all sorts of things, including the two horua-papas, or land-sleds. And behind them there fell in, uninvited, virtually everybody who had watched the Queen pass, which is to say virtually everybody in Honolulu. The cooking pits were deserted, the babies, too. There was no longer to be heard anywhere the thud of tapa mallets. It was assumed to be a holiday when Kaahumanu rode abroad.

Climbing the side of the Punchbowl was the hardest part of the trip, nor was the view anything notable when they reached the rim of that long-dead volcano. The village below was mean, squalid, the huts, haphazardly scattered, looking for all the world like that many haystacks; the palace was a sprawl of slightly grander but still shabby buildings enclosed in a palisade; the fort, down at the edge of the water, was a rectangle of wall mostly mud, splotched with rusty cannons. None of this could be seen in detail, for a pall of dust kicked up by the movement toward the crater hung uncertainly over it, blurring outlines. The only bright spots were the tops of coconut trees, bunched, which, here and there emerging through the dust, flashed and sparkled in the sun.

Beyond in the harbor, a nobler sight, the water a determined blue, were eight vessels. They were not trig warships, smart with paint, but six whalers and two inter-island schooners, slatternly craft, unkempt. They sagged. Nobody moved aboard or near them. They were dead things.

Ann saw Johnny Lamb stare out at the ships.

"Which boat is yours, Tony?" the Queen asked.

"The last — may she slip her hook and pile up on the reef! It's a miserable business, whaling, Kate. It's a slow, long, sloppy, stinking business, crawling along in a slaughterhouse with everything greasy, and rats and fools and foreigners forward instead of men. I'd never have shipped on a whaler without I was so twitchy to go down to the sea. And the second time it was because I was offered a mate's berth and I hoped the skipper would die, which he did do."

38

"You wanted to make money?"

"I wasn't thinking so much of the money then. And it's just as well I wasn't. Only the owners make money out of whaling."

"The captain?"

"I never shipped as captain. *They* get good enough lays, sometimes. Specially if they're related to the owners. I was only mate on this voyage, until the old man died. And I didn't come in for his lay anyway. His widow got that. I was glad enough to sell my own and set up in business ashore. I'm shut of the sea."

She put a hand on his arm.

"And we are happy to have you here, Tony. We're glad you came back."

"Sure." He turned to her, grinning. "Here come the boys with the papas. Now who is this champion you're going to race against me?"

She took one of the papas, or sleds. It consisted of two runners made of some hard wood highly polished, about nine or ten feet long, and not more than a few inches apart. Cross pieces of hau wood were lashed to these, and to one another, with coconut fiber. The thing was light, and it looked clumsy. Ann didn't see how anybody could balance on it, even going very fast.

"Who else, my Tony?"

"Not you — *yourself?*"

She chuckled.

"You afraid?"

"Well, all I meant was — well, would it be proper?"

"Horua is a sport for kings and great chiefs, no others. I do you honor to race against you, Tony. But if you are afraid —"

"Bless your heart, no! I was just thinking of all those people down there."

The slope they faced, and down which Ann Mathewson behind them peered timidly, was straight and fearfully steep. Its foundation was a sort of pavement of flat stones hammered into the earth so that they made a fairly smooth surface, the labor, Ann supposed, of hundreds of commoners who would never be permitted to use it. Whether so constructed or whether it only followed the contour of the slope, this pavement undulated at places in what Ann, who herself had more than once sledded down Sentinel Hill—though not bellywhopping but rather genteely seated—would have called, there, thank-you-moms. Strewn all over the pavement, in the steepest places tucked in between the stones to prevent it from being blown away, was cut grass in thick dry shiny bunches.

"Three races, Kate, right?"

"Aye, aye, sir," she replied in English, and roared with laughter, slapping him on the back.

All down the hill on both sides of the course, and clustered at the bottom, were natives, men and women alike, children too. There must have been two thousand of them. They jabbered and gesticulated; and though there was no money in sight, and few goods, Ann felt certain that they were making bets.

The racers backed a little, holding their papas high, and Ann skipped aside. The crowd fell silent. Somebody started to count.

"*One!*"

Johnny Lamb crouched, leaning back, his right toe digging the ground. The dowager bent forward, her feet close together, and on her face was an expression of sheer joy. She loved the horua.

"*Two!*"

The race was not to be that in the mainland sense, but rather a contest to see who could go farthest. But if both went the same distance, as often happened, then the one who got there first was the winner; and for this reason a good start was important.

"*Three—Go!*"

They were both running easily and fast, not straining, side by side and about four feet apart. Ann realized with a start that the Queen, who must have weighed at least two hundred and fifty pounds, was in fact more graceful than Captain Johnny. There was something horselike about his running. The Queen did not lift her knees as much. She, too, had an animal fleetness of stride, but it suggested the deer rather than the horse, and seemed effortless.

She flopped first, at the very edge of the slope. She slammed the sled down and threw herself on top of it, full-length. Her grunt when she landed was thunderous.

Johnny Lamb went two strides farther, so that he was literally leaping downhill when he threw himself on his sled.

The crowd began to yell.

With those around her, Ann Mathewson ran to the brink of the slope.

It was like watching a couple of birds fly, except that these flew down instead of up. They soared, nevertheless. Tipping this way and that, for the runners were so close together — it must have been something like skating downhill on one skate, Ann thought hurriedly—they would sometimes, at a thank-you-mom, rise into the air, where they seemed to float for whole minutes together, as though about to do like Elijah the Tishbite and go up to Heaven by a whirlwind. Then they'd strike the course again, wobbling, while all breaths were held; and they'd steady themselves; and once more the cheers would sound.

Johnny Lamb won. He had been a few feet ahead all the way. He came back up the hill on the dray with her, forgetting comfort, and they were both laughing hilariously, like everybody else; but when they grasped their papas and backed away for the start of the second race, Ann detected a certain grimness in the face of Kaahumanu. The Queen did not like to lose.

Ann watched her, fascinated. Here was the person of all persons whom they must bring to the Light. With her political power and her birth, with her popularity, she could twist these childlike people any way she chose. To win her was to win the islands.

Kaahumanu was a jealous woman, also a blunt and forthright one, and stubborn. She would not study English. She did not ask for help.

A bronze statue, she stood poised and silent now, holding her papa high. She no longer panted. Her body gleamed reddish-brown and wet, but no drop of the sweat broke to roll down her skin.

"Three—and GO!"

The Queen won. This time she ran a little past the lip of the crater, as Johnny had done and did again, hurling herself straight down the slope. It was risky, but it paid. Her greater weight carried her almost three feet farther than him at the bottom. The crowd went wild. Even Ann found herself seething with excitement.

The crowd went wilder still during the third race. Here both sledders ran a full four strides down the slope before flopping. They didn't leave their feet until they had to. They would have fallen had they tried to run any farther. So they descended, side by side, a few feet apart, skimming over the dried grass like pigeons who had often practiced together. When one rose at a bump, the other rose. When one came down, down came the other. They might have been fastened together by invisible poles. They teetered, but they stayed on.

The Queen's extra weight did not count this time, and that for a reason apparent to everyone but her. Captain Johnny, as though he did not have enough to do just to keep his close-runnered sled upright, was raising his lower legs and kicking them down together—not steadily, for he had to keep his balance, but every time he dared to do so. It made up the difference.

It was about halfway down that the break came. Nobody ever knew precisely what happened. The Queen swerved a trifle: it seemed probable, afterward, that one or both of her runners passed over a place where a bit of grass had blown away, and briefly touched the bare rock. Whatever the cause, the back of her sled swung toward Johnny, and she moved a leg sideways in an effort to keep her balance, and her foot touched either Johnny or a tip of one of the hau sticks that formed the frame of Johnny's papa.

At that speed, any touch, however slight, was sure to mean a spill for one or both. It happened very fast. The Queen, straightening, struck a thank-you-mom. She flew into the air:

she was still on top of her papa. She landed, wobbled frantically, almost went over, straightened—and swept perfectly down the rest of the course to make what later proved a record.

But Johnny Lamb whirled half around, and he hit the thank-you-mom going sideways. He was turning as he went into the air. He landed on a shoulder and a hip, and the papa was torn from his grasp, and he tumbled over and over to the bottom of the slope.

"Oh, I hope he isn't dead!"

Impulsively Ann started straight forward. Had not somebody grabbed her arm and yanked her back from the verge — she never did learn who it was — she would herself have slid and tumbled the entire length of the course.

A moment later, too worried about him to realize how close to death she had been, she was jostled and shoved to one side of the course, and they all descended, helter-skelter, in a scramble of loose stones.

"I hope he isn't dead!" she cried again, bumped this way and that, stumbling, slipping, getting up, and all the while clutching to her bosom a mass of dusty priceless gold-brocaded velvet.

He was not dead. When she reached the palace at last and was admitted to the enclosure and then to the Queen's hut, Johnny Lamb was lying flat, his head turned from her, while four natives, two on each side, were pounding him furiously but rhythmically with the bases of their fists. He was stark naked. So was the Queen, upon whom four other masseurs were at work.

For an instant even then, coming in out of the sunlight, panicky, Ann thought that he was dead and that they were somehow trying to pound him back to life. But he was only bruised, and there was no blood on his body. He squealed involuntarily when a sore spot was thumped.

"Well, it was worth twenty dollars. Ouch!"

"You like it, Tony?"

"I always have liked my sports rough."

Nobody paid any attention to Ann Mathewson, who after a

43

while straightened the velvet and brushed it and refolded it as best she could, trying not to look at Johnny Lamb where he lay.

Outside, the crowd babbled and sang, but in the hut there was only dimness and the thud of fists on flesh and the sibilant whispering of servants as they passed things back and forth.

The Queen raised her head, and saw Ann. The Queen had been smiling, but the smile vanished.

"My love goes to thee. Come back the day after tomorrow."

Ordinarily at night as she lay listening to the fuss and scrape of grass in the walls, the scurrying of rats among fallen green coconuts outside, the clitter of palm fronds slapped together like thin slats of wood, the pompous bumble of the surf on a reef far out, most of all to the sigh of the trades as they passed this rickety hut, this outpost of God so many thousands of miles from any other, Ann would shiver a little; but though relaxed, she would feel pride, too, and a yeasting of excitement when she thought of the task to which, howsoever humbly, she was helping.

She had nothing to fight against then but lonesomeness.

Tonight it was not so, which dismayed her. For though she tried to push it out, she could see in her mind's eye the sprawled muscular sweat-shiny white figure of the captain from Hartford; and what was more, all the time she could feel in her arms and against her breast the velvet—caressing, insidious, lascivious, soft. She did not move, but still she saw this and felt it. Weeping, she slipped to the floor, where she prayed again. The wind moaned low. A scatter of gritty dust appeared fanwise at the door, and died. A mongrel stood there a moment in silhouette, regarding her; but it prowled away, for there would be pitiful pickings, to be sure, at a mission.

Ann crawled back onto her pallet, and she made the pillow wet with tears. It was no use.

"Wicked . . . wicked," she whispered in agony.

44

Mother So Far Away

". . . that it be *clearly* understood, dear Mother, that this is *distinctly* and *entirely* an epistle to you, not to any other. The days when I used to spend hours making samplers are gone. We have very little time, here in the Family. It is work, work, work, day and night. We have no relaxation at all. We never have time to read; we scarcely ever have time even to pray alone. We have almost no privacy. This ramshackle hut in which I reside with the Reverend and Mrs. Bingham has walls and a roof made of mere dried *grass,* like hay, and this blows away in places, leaving us exposed. We cannot possibly build a fire in it or near it: when these huts catch fire they go up inside of five minutes, *utterly.* The pit where our cooking is done is some distance away. There are no windows. There is a doorway, but no door. *Anybody* can look in, at any time. There is a small enclosure, but the palisade of sticks which encircles this, dear Mother, is a mere strip of slits, through which anybody can peek and practically everybody does. There is hardly an hour of the day, or even of the night, when the outside of that fence is not lined with natives. In the same way, when one goes outside they follow you. They don't *jostle* you. But that constant *snooping!* One holds one's head low, but still they get around in front and peer up under the brim of your bonnet.

"And so you see, dearest Mother, that we have very little time for writing. At night, if there are no sick calls, and nothing special to prepare for the next day's work, Sybil and the Reverend Mr. Bingham and I light up what the sailors call candlenuts, which you hang by a string, a lot of them, and they do

45

not flame for long but they do give out a very good light. We have to be very careful to keep it well away from the walls, roof, etc., lest the whole place go up like an explosion of gunpowder. When we get it lighted we all three write and write, each with his or her own journal, and when the last candlenut goes out (they burn in a sort of series, none lasting long) we take the ashes outside and carefully wet them and stamp on them, and then we say our prayers in the darkness, and go to bed.

"*Those*, you understand, dear Mother so far away, are the journals which we write for the edification of such as seek to know what we do here, what we find here. It is well to read them to friends and even to have the preacher read them at the services on the Sabbath. But I must plead with you again, sweet Mother, not to so consider *this* letter, which is purely and simply addressed to *you*, and to you *only*. The truth is, that I am committing a great crime, here in the Family. I am taking some time for myself, for my own selfish purposes. If the Reverend Mr. Bingham should come back from the palace at this moment and find me so engaged, or even if his wife quit her class in a nearby hut, and came here, I should fairly die of shame. I am fond of them both, and especially of Sybil, who is the very breath of loving kindness. But they *frighten* me."

She sighed, and shook her head, and sanded the page and read what she had written, and shook her head again.

Dust blew in. There were no lawns in Honolulu; there were no gardens or groves. Gawky ludicrous coconut trees stood uncertainly here and there along the shore, but they cast little shadow. With the sandalwood gone, the hills were bare.

When the breeze drooped for a moment, and the dust started to settle, Ann Mathewson could hear from the walls the click-click-clickering of insects. It was a sound, heard only when there was silence elsewhere, which at first had twitched her nerves. Now she troubled about it no more than she had about the

46

crickets, the katydids, and peepers, in the summertime back home.

From another hut within the enclosure, the school hut, she heard the chanting of children:

There is beyond the sky
A heaven of joy and love;
And holy children when they die
Go to that world above.

Their voices were high, quavering. Mrs. Bingham must have interrupted them, though her voice was so gentle that it did not reach the listening Ann a few yards away. Then the voices of the children took up the cantillation:

There is a dreadful hell,
And everlasting pains:
There sinners must with devils dwell,
In darkness, fire, and chains.

Mrs. Bingham — it was difficult to think of her as Sybil — must have been reciting the next stanza for them. Ann heard nothing for a moment. Then, more boldly:

Can such a wretch as I
Escape this cursed end?
And may I hope whene'er I die
I shall to heaven ascend?

Ann loved Sybil Bingham, with her large melancholy nose and her small, grave, light blue eyes, for here was the epitome of goodness, who never censored, never complained, and always did more than her share of the work; and she supposed that she almost loved the Reverend Mr. Bingham: certainly she had the highest admiration for him. Yet it was hard to feel warm with them.

"The truth is, dear Mother, I am *afraid* of them. It is a horrid word to write, and I know not why it should be true; but it is. I *fear* them.

"I would be false, dear Mother, if I denied that my heart

47

has suffered much, and indeed suffers constantly now, worse than ever, from that most penetrating and agonizing of all maladies—homesickness. I feel that I would give all I have or ever hope to have, or to do, for one glimpse of you, my dearest Mother, and of Helen and Grace, and the maples out front, and the yard, the lilac bushes, the neighbors. I *should* not feel like this. It is wicked of me.

"There must be some reason, known only to God our Father, why I am made to suffer so much, in one important sense more than any of the other females in this our missionary family; for *they* have helpmeets to stay at their sides and comfort them. Ah, marriage can mean so much when you see it here, cut off from all the world we knew, where these pairs march with firm step through a howling wilderness of ignorance and sloth, each helping and supporting and encouraging with tender words the person at his or her side—Reverend and Lucy Thurston, Dr. and Mrs. Holman, Horace and Abigail Crowell, Reverend and Sybil Bingham, Mr. and Mrs. Sam Ruggles, Mr. and Mrs. Sam Whitney, Mr. and Mrs. Dan Chamberlain, Mr. and Mrs. Elisha Lommis—all in pairs, all marching two by two, all except me, who stumble alone, sobbing, at the end of the column!

"You suppose that I miss Jabez? Will it jar you to learn that this is not so? I do not miss him, Mother dear, because I never knew him. You were right, my sweet one so far away, when you implored me on your poor knees not to marry Jabez Mathewson—you and dear Grace and dear Helen alike, all three of you. You said that I should know him better first, even though he was a man of God who had heard the call to convert the heathen. You did not question Jabez's *integrity,* and of course you knew his *family,* but he had been away to Yale College for three years, and you said that you did not really know him and that I didn't either. Just being a man of God, you said—with what seemed to me at the time unspeakable callousness—was not *enough.* And he was to sail in a few days for barbarous islands on the other side of the world.

48

"I was angry, and I said things then, dear Mother, which I have many times since regretted from the bottom of my heart. We were all weeping—you remember?—but you and my dear sisters knew only *pity*, whilst I knew *anger*, which is wicked and corrupts the soul.

"I have already asked you to forgive me, in other letters, and I have prayed many times to our Heavenly Father that He may in time cleanse me of the *stain*. This is not why I write now. It is to tell you why I do not truly miss Mr. Mathewson—Jabez.

"How could I miss him, whom I never knew? I *prayed* for my departed husband, of course, but how could I truly *feel the loss of him?*"

From the other end of the enclosure came in a wobbly treble:

> Then will I read and pray,
> While I have life and breath;
> Lest I should be cut off today
> And sent to eternal death.

The class would be dismissed soon, and Sybil Bingham would return. The Reverend Mr. Bingham, too, would come back to this hut in a little while. Ann wrote nervously, jerkily.

"I wish I could read what goes on in the mind of that austere man, Hiram Bingham. *He* is the one who will decide my fate. In all matters, great or small, he makes a show of conferring with the others, men and females alike; and no doubt he he truly *believes* that he has taken all opinions into consideration; but in fact the *final* decision is always as he had originally wished it to be. He is a *very strong-minded man*, Mother.

"It is true that the Mission has an unwritten law, none the less strict for *being* unwritten, that any workers in the field be married and be accompanied by their husbands or wives, as the case may be. This is especially true of females. On the other hand, I could not possibly have returned on the *Thaddeus*, even if I had been willing at that time to desert my companions in the hour of their greatest danger. For the brig stayed here. It is still here. It was sold to the King, who, being the sort of man he is (he drinks, Mother) neglected it, so that it is falling to pieces. Nor has there been any suitable ship since that time.

"But we may assume that there will be one. And I don't know what they are going to do about me. They have as yet said nothing—nothing whatever. I myself would give anything I have to be permitted to go home, but I'd kill myself before I would say such a thing. I shall do whatever Mr. Bingham decides, I hope.

"On the one hand, he is reluctant to have any member of the Family turn back. It might discourage further enlistment. On the other hand, I think he believes that this is no place for an unattached white female; and I declare that I incline to agree with him. Oh, darling Mother, I am so *lonesome!*"

A tear, fat and greasy, shaped like a tadpole, plopped on the page. She blinked at it.

Then there was another tear.

This was shameful! It was a sneaky business! She'd felt a villainess about it from the first. Sobbing, she put away her writing materials and tidied the desk. She took what she had written—to her Mother-so-far-away!—and crumpled it and carried it outside. There was a small fire in the cooking pit, though the man who tended it was not there. She tossed the letter into the fire, and remained long enough to see that it was thoroughly burned. Then she went back to the hut.

She had dried her tears, and was arranging her dress, when she heard a familiar step outside, a familiar cough. Even without these sounds, she would have known who was coming.

The Reverend Mr. Bingham entered.

Will Live to Fight Another Day 8

Johnny Lamb wore a bottle-green coat with slits at the sleeves, with silver buttons and a black velvet collar; and there was a cherry-red velveteen waistcoat showing below it. He wore a white satin stock. He wore long cream-colored kerseymere pantaloons, tight-fitted over Wellingtons. He smoked a cigar. His beaver, broader at the top than at the bottom, was cocked at a rakish angle. He should have felt good; but he didn't.

"They don't know how to defend themselves! That man just now had no right getting his arm broke, if he'd only backed away. And I don't think the bruiser ought to be allowed to jump on him and kick him in the you-know-what when he's down, either. It's mean. And that first one may be dead by this time, for all we know. Is he?"

Kaahumanu shrugged.

They could still hear over the chatter of the crowd the moans of the most recently beaten gladiator, whose friends had pulled him out of the circle only after he'd been mauled while prone. He was somewhere behind the crowd, a cripple, probably, for life.

The victor stood in the center of the circle, not even breathing hard, on his face a sneer as professional, and as meaningless, as an acrobat's simper. His name was Humuhumunukunukuapuaa, which was esteemed uproariously funny, the humuhumunuku-nukuapuaa being a small no-account fish, whereas this man was the biggest man anybody had ever seen. He was usually called Humu; though now his pursuivants, who slapped themselves

51

on the chest as they stalked around the circle, proclaiming at the top of their lungs the superlative, the utterly unbeatable prowess of their champion, gave him his full name fully pronounced, in addition to sundry titles made up on the spur of the moment. On the other hand, these fellows had nothing but contempt for the rest of mankind—mere mice, sick mice at that, when compared with the mighty Humu. Naked except for a malo, *he* stood superb. He must have measured six feet seven, and his arms and legs, and his chest and shoulders, were great lumpy masses of muscle. His face was less arresting. There was no ferocity in it. He seemed rather simple— even, conceivably, an idiot. His hair was thin on top, and it fluffed naturally into a sort of scalplock sticking straight up, which gave him a clownish appearance, an expression of constant astonishment his clamped-on sneer could not hide.

"He's got a might of muscle," Johnny conceded. "But it needs more than that. If they'd only run away from him at first—"

The Queen's voice was a squirt of vinegar.

"In this country we deem it a mark of cowardice to run away."

Johnny looked at her. They were seated close together in two chairs, rarities on the island, and they were in a small boxlike contrivance, a sort of dressing stall, at the very edge of the mokomoko circle. There was no roof. Instead of the tapa which made up the other three walls, there was before them a curtain of dried slit pandanus fronds. Through this, they could see without being seen. Technically Kaahumanu's presence was a secret. In fact, every man there knew that she was behind the pandanus. Her reluctance to reveal herself had nothing to do with shame at attending a mokomoko. She simply was afraid of spoiling the sport. Her popularity was such, and such, too, was the strength of the old belief in the divinity of high chiefs, that it would have been difficult to

52

prevent men from groveling before her. She could always see *that,* always had. She could not always see a good fight.

Looking at her, then, Johnny Lamb thought that here was Polynesia embodied; and what a body! Massive, but beautifully proportioned, if she was every inch a queen, she was every inch a woman as well. She startled him sometimes. He had seen her blow smoke rings and then spit directly up through them, bellowing with laughter, while hundreds of persons, to whom she paid not the slightest attention, pressed their foreheads against the earth. He had seen her freeze a drunken bullyboy in his tracks with no more than a look. Most of the time she was whacking good company, and he liked her, even reckoned he loved her. Some of the time, like now, it was difficult to remember that she wasn't white. Frequently he caught himself switching into English when he spoke to her; and he'd do this without realizing it, and wouldn't know it until he saw her shake her head and frown. She had refused to learn English. This was only in part because of her dislike of the missionaries. She told Johnny that if she could somehow learn the whole language perfectly, complete, with no intervening stages of clumsiness — then she'd learn it. Here wasn't laziness, but dignity: her blood spoke. It was not fitting and proper, perhaps it wasn't even safe, that the descendant of a hundred chiefs, a widow of the great Kamehameha I, should do anything haltingly, awkwardly. She just couldn't afford to.

Right now she was sore about something. Well, he was more than a speck sore himself this morning. He took the cigar out of his mouth and waggled it at her, like a schoolmarm with a ruler.

"Listen here, Kate. Any man who stands up to that bonecrusher is no coward, no matter which way he moves."

He returned the cigar to his mouth, and leaned forward, hands on knees, frowning.

The backers of Humu strode here and strode there, slap-

53

ping themselves on the chest, shouting insults. The gladiator himself stood with arms folded, smiling complacently.

"I'd like it first-rate if somebody lammed that beefwit flat," said Johnny Lamb, and his voice rasped like a peppermill.

"Why don't you do it?"

The Queen should never have said that. Captain Johnny was in a black mood this morning, despite the brightness of his clothes; and when he felt that way he was best left alone.

He handed his cigar and beaver to Kaahumanu, whipped off his coat.

"By God, I will!"

"Tony, you mustn't—I didn't mean—*Tony!*"

He was gone. There was no part of the crowd before the royal box, and when he leapt through the curtain he was inside the circle itself. He wasted no time. He punched one of the pursuivants in the side of the jaw, so that the man whirled completely around before he fell back into the crowd.

"All right. You two get out of here and leave us room."

He started for the other pursuivant, who ran away. The circle was clear. The crowd did not shout, but mumbled and muttered, confused. The idea of a haole fighting in the moko-moko, and against such a killer as Humu, had never been thought of.

The giant himself was astounded. Forgetting his mask of contempt, he blinked and stared at Johnny Lamb.

"Well, what's the matter, ain't you going to fight?" asked Johnny, and slapped him across the mouth.

The watchers began to yell. Their first fear had been that the appearance of a white man from the box meant the breaking-off of their sport. Now they realized that in fact it meant more sport. They were wildly excited, and churned about, making bets, those in the back pushing forward, those in the front squatting on their heels. There were no ropes, no rail or barrier.

Humu raised and lowered his head. He ran his tongue over

54

his lips, opening his eyes very wide at the taste of blood. Then he looked at Johnny, and smirked.

They both put up their fists.

Johnny Lamb knew little about mokomoko, having seen but the two preceding fights, short and one-sided; but apparently there was not much *to* know about it. There was no prize. There was no referee. There were no rules. You could hit or kick, or for that matter butt, anywhere above or below the waist, and this regardless of whether the other man was upright, on his knees, or prone. Gouging, too, was permitted.

One thing only about the two fights Johnny had seen suggested a peculiar skill. It was the custom to block blows not with the elbows or forearms, as a mainland pugilist would do, but with the fists. That was the admired technique, Johnny gathered; but he reckoned that it must make for a heap of splintered bones and for short fights. It was spectacular, but, he thought, dreadful silly.

Another thing. Though there was no scratch to toe, no mark of any sort, the understanding seemed to be that a man should not retreat unless physically forced back by the weight of attack.

Humu held his fists high, palms in, and his elbows were on a line with Johnny's face. When he punched he turned his arm so that the fist was knuckles-up, as indeed Johnny himself did.

It was a glorious morning, with a glorious open sky. The sunlight glanced and sparkled among the fronds of the coconut trees. Far off, surf bumbled impotently upon the reef.

Johnny glanced at the royal box, and saw a curtain of split pandanus, nothing more. No sound came from there.

Thereafter Johnny devoted himself to Humu.

He tried two straight punches, right and left. Both were clacked off by the fists of the giant, who moved with unexpected speed. Johnny's knuckles stung—not as much as they would have done had he not pulled the punches, but enough for warning. If he was going to have any fists left to finish this fight with, he reckoned, he'd better fix it to get past those hands to the face.

The Hawaiian came on with a swift shuffling movement, bending forward as he swung a long high overhand right. It was a clumsy blow, though a strong one. Johnny could have parried it with either forearm, but he jumped back instead. No use getting a bone broken.

It was like having a tree fall just short of you. Humu stopped, teetering, almost off balance, and there was an expression of great astonishment on his face. Johnny instantly jumped in and chopped two short ones to the point of the chin, and jumped back in time to miss a wild heavy hook.

The giant shook a bewildered head. The crowd was jeering, booing. Johnny didn't care. He leaned back, elbows high, chin in.

They were shouting the equivalent of "Stand up and fight!" and "What kind of man are you?" Johnny paid them no mind. He looked only at Humu's face.

In any other circumstances that face would have been comical. There was no craft in it; but neither was there a hint of fear. The small piglike eyes were filled only with puzzlement. The scalplock moved fitfully in the breeze.

The man himself stayed as steady as a rock. The two on the point of the chin seemed to have troubled him no more than flea bites.

He came forward again, more slowly this time, shuffling, guard high. Johnny feinted, backed away. Humu came inexorably on. He tried another long high clumsy right-hander. As before, Johnny had no trouble stepping away from it, and again as before he sprang in with a high one to the face—this time squarely between the eyes. It hurt his fist, the left. It didn't seem to hurt the islander at all. Johnny sprang back.

They stood panting, arms low, regarding one another, the Polynesian as though he found himself face to face with a new kind of animal. Yet though he was perplexed, Humu showed no fear.

It was then that Johnny felt the first sharp thin little twinge of panic. He was not used to fights that lasted this long.

Humu came in again, slowly.

This time Johnny shuffled forward to meet him, guard high; then suddenly Johnny ducked, going almost to his knees, and lurched under the giant's elbows to hook first a right, then a left, into the pit of the stomach. These were hard punches; he put all he had into them, and his heels were firm on the ground at the time. He heard Humu grunt.

Something, an elbow probably, struck the back of Johnny's head, and at the same time a knee came up and caught the side of his jaw. He felt himself spinning. It was like the way he had felt when thrown off his horua-papa the day before yesterday.

He was on hands and knees, but he couldn't hold himself there and toppled to a sitting position. He saw Humu charging, arms wide apart, hands spread open, as though to scoop him up off the ground. Johnny kicked with both feet. A heel caught one of Humu's knees, half-turning him. Humu started swinging his arms to keep his balance. Johnny rolled away, scrambled to his feet. Humu came in again.

It was then that Johnny Lamb lost his head. It was not that the taunts of the crowd goaded him into making a stand. Except in the beginning he had scarcely heard them; and now, anyway, there was a vast hollow wet roaring in his ears. No, it was sheer panic.

He stood cursing, leaning back a little, but not giving ground, not trying to block except with blows. He saw only that preposterous face, which he kept hitting—when he didn't hit fists. He could no longer feel his own fists.

He made no attempt to weave or duck. He was beyond that.

How long this lasted he could not know. He never knew, either, what blow felled him, or whether it was more than one.

57

He could not see the silly face any longer, only a whirling mass of grayish specks that sent off light. He was on the ground, on knees and elbows. Then he was on his back, and he tried to pull his knees up to protect his testicles, and couldn't; and something heavy struck his chest.

He sensed what was coming, and tried to lift his hands to his face. They were swept aside. Sweaty fingers scrabbled up his cheeks toward his eyes.

Through all the roaring, then, and all the rat-tat-tatting of the crowd, he heard Kate scream.

The whirling grayish spheres swam faster, in a madder circle. He tried to toss his head from side to side, but the strong fingers crept on toward his eyes.

Then the bright specks clustered all together into one great bunchy twisting shape, which slowly and without a sound exploded.

Truly an Evil Man   9

Ann's one thought as she passed through the gate, nodding to the sentry, was for the velvet. She hoped that the natives had not pawed it. She knew she should not feel that way about the natives. She should not feel contempt for them, only pity: both Reverend Mr. Bingham and Reverend Mr. Thurston had said so. She would not have the power to influence them if she didn't love them. They, too, were creatures of the Lord, howsoever misguided. All the same, she hoped they hadn't touched the velvet, for it was undeniable that many of them had lice.

It was with a start that she saw the god Kaili still leaning against a sentry box near the entrance to the Queen's hut.

She had reported this to the Family, and she knew that strong remonstrances had been lodged.

Well, she'd complain again. Meanwhile she tore her gaze from the besticked idol, which grinned fiendishly down at her.

The Queen was in a bad humor. Her eyes were all sourness, her lips were intwisted as though she had a mouthful of verjuice. She scarcely noticed Ann Mathewson, but strode up and down the hut, muttering something Ann could not understand, brushing aside all efforts to get her to eat or drink, shaking them off impatiently and with an abrupt violence as a dog emerging from a stream shakes off water, and even refusing new ones when two of the leis around her neck broke and let fall their flowers to the ground, so that when she stalked back and forth Kaahumanu with her bare feet angrily brushed and even kicked aside large lovely fragrant frangipani blossoms—lehuas, gardenias, tuberoses, and hibiscus flowers, white, scarlet, salmon, pink, ivory, yellow, cream.

As though in sympathy with her mood, the sky, dark gray and very low, rumbled borborygmatously. The air was close and taut.

It was dark in the hut, as it darkened outside, and in a little while rain began to chuff into the thatch and to patter on the hard earth of the court yard, kicking up spears of dust.

Ann was frightened, they were all frightened, the servants huddled silent against the far wall, the Queen striding back and forth.

Through the voyage of more than five months from Boston, except when she was at prayer or attending Mr. Mathewson, Ann had been diligent in studying the language of the Sandwich Islands. They had had with them, as part of the mission, four young islanders who for one reason or another had visited the United States and been stranded there. These were to be interpreters, and on the long voyage they were of course language teachers. Ann Mathewson knew a heap of Hawaiian before she ever sighted the snows of Mauna Kea. Then there

59

were further weeks on board, with the brig riding at anchor off Kailua, while King Liho tried to make up his mind whether to permit them to land. There had been natives aboard the *Thaddeus* all this while, garrulous ones. Finally, Ann had now been some weeks in Honolulu itself.

She knew the language; but she was not sure of it. She knew it if somebody looked right at her when talking to her, and said the words slowly and with appropriate gestures, now and then going back a bit to explain, or answering a question or a questioning look.

Only broken fragments of what the Queen was saying now were intelligible to Ann; and they were disquieting. It was something about killing somebody, some man, strangling him.

Kaahumanu was not a woman to use figures of speech.

Ann edged toward the door. Some of the others might have seen her, but not, she thought, the Queen. She had been commanded to appear, to start making the gown, but surely the Queen had forgotten that command. Ann could wait outside. Never mind the rain, which was plopping more multitudinously into the thatch now. She'd rather get wet than stay in this hut any longer, in the presence of a woman she could only think was mad.

She reached the doorway, but did not step outside. This was because of what she saw.

The sentry had quit his post at the gate the other side of the court yard, presumably to seek shelter from the rain, which was whipping itself up to a frenzy now. Through this gateway, as Ann reached the door of the hut, Captain Johnny Lamb came running. He ran right for Kaahumanu's hut, right for Ann.

She was jolted by his appearance. His clothes were good, even foppish, the best she had ever seen. It was the face that frightened her. It was all out of shape. A bandage ran across Johnny's forehead just under the brim of his cream-colored beaver. His mouth was puffed, and the lips were liver. One eye was puffed, too, and the skin above and below it was a dirty dark-purplish blue.

He burst into the hut, brushing past her. If he saw her he gave no sign of it.

"Damn you, Kate! First you interfere in the fight, and now you give orders to murder an innocent man. I just heard of it. And it's got to stop—right now!"

"*Tony!*"

She would have thrown herself upon him, but he stepped to one side, drawing away from her as though from a repulsive animal. He was furious. He shook a fist at her, a swollen fist.

"I suppose I ought to thank you for saving my eyesight, maybe my life. But you call those men back, if you want me to stay alive. D'ye think I'm going to stand by and let you commit murder, in cold blood, in my name? What kind of skunk d'ye think I am?"

She swayed, her mouth open. Rage had gone; incredulity took its place.

"But—but, Tony—*He* would have killed *you!*"

"All right. But that was in fair fight. I knew what I was doing, or anyway I should have. But this is different. This is common ordinary murder." He got closer to her, scowling. "What I heard is right, ain't it? You did order him to be strangled as quick as he's found, didn't you? And you have got hundreds of men back there in the hills searching for the poor devil, ain't that right?"

"But, Tony—"

"Don't 'But, Tony' me! You call those men in! You send out word that Humu won't be touched! And you do it right now!"

She no longer swayed, nor was there any further pleading in her eyes, to which coldness came back. Nobody had ever spoken to Kaahumanu like this—nobody, at least, since the great Kamehameha, the conqueror, who used to beat her, a girl, years ago. Kamehameha the Great had had twenty-odd other wives, two of them sisters of Kaahumanu herself, but he

61

didn't beat them, any of them, only Kaahumanu. He had never cared enough for the others to beat them.

But that had been years ago. Kaahumanu was the kuhina nui now.

"It is not my practice, Captain Lamb, to encourage outside advice on the conduct of the kingdom."

He flung himself away.

"Oh, it's your island all right! I admit that! If you want to get rid of that poor muscle-bound fool—hell, there's nothing I can do to stop you."

"Captain, there are men within whistle who would break both your arms and both your legs if I spoke the word."

"Aye. Listen, Kate. There are men in these parts who would break my back, with or without a word from you. And I'm going to look 'em up and give 'em the chance, if you don't call your bullyboys off that search. There ain't any law here—I know that—except what you make up yourself as you go along. I can't prevent you from murdering that man. You're sure to find him, no matter where he's run to. He can't get off the island. But all I say is this—and I want you to get it right, your Majesty: If Humu is killed, then I'm going to every mokomoko I can find, and when I can't find one, I'm going to start one, and I'm going to meet everyone who'll stand up to me, and I'm going to keep on doing that until somebody kills me. It shouldn't take long—without you there. Now, is that clear?"

She did not answer. She did not even look at him, but past him. He watched her half a minute. Then he bowed a little, mockingly.

"So that's the way it is, Kate? Dreadful sorry. Never did hold with suicide, ordinarily. But—you *will* be the monarch."

She said nothing, didn't move.

He nodded, put his hat on, cocked it, and went out. The rain stopped suddenly, as though his appearance had been an awaited signal.

Queen Kaahumanu whirled, her mouth working, her eyes afire, and in a voice thick as barley clabber began to give orders.

Some of the servants ran out. Others threw themselves face-down before the Queen, who never stopped talking. Still others tumbled in, dropped to their bellies, listened a moment, and ran outside again. The hut was in a turmoil. Ann slipped away.

The court yard, which a moment before had been filled with scurrying figures, was deserted. The rain stood in small bright puddles. The sun was trying to come out. Ann started for the gate.

"Oh, uh, Miss Buttoner—"

Captain Lamb was in the sentry box against which the battle god Kaili leaned. He was but a few feet from the entrance of the Queen's hut. The messengers must have run right past him without seeing him.

"Mrs. Mathewson," she said.

"Of course. I couldn't remember your married name. Will you come here a minute, please? I don't think it would be advisable for me to go out where you are. The old girl's likely still to order that job done on my legs and arms, if she catches me around."

Ann went to him. She was puzzled, and she shook her head. "You should not talk flippantly about such matters."

"Good a way as any to talk about 'em. Tell me—I couldn't quite hear—are those men that were just dashing every-which-way, are they looking for me or for somebody else?"

"They're looking for a small fish, as far as I could make out."

"Oh?"

"Isn't a humuhumunukunukuapuaa a small fish? They were told to see that no harm came to it. But they didn't head for the beach, they all headed for the hills."

"I see," said Johnny Lamb, and stepped out of the sentry box, brushing his clothes. "Well, now that my limbs are safe—"

63

"*Isn't* a humuhumunukunukuapuaa a kind of small fish?"

"It is. But it has another meaning. It is also a kind of big fool. Not, though," and he touched his chest with a bony forefinger, "as great a fool as this one. But I still think I'd better get away from here. I'm fond of Kate and I reckon she's fond of me, but there's no denying she can be dreadful violent sometimes. Hot-headed. It's the way she was fetched up. May I escort you back to the mission house, Mrs. Mathewson?"

"You know where it is, then?"

"I've strolled past. I like to hear the children recite."

He spread his feet, lifted his chin, clasped his hands behind his back, just the way they had been taught to do in school, and singsonged laboriously:

Why should I join with those in play,
In whom I've no delight;
Who curse and swear, but never pray:
Who call ill names and fight?
Away from fools I'll turn my eyes;
Nor with the scoffers go;
I would be walking with the wise,
That wiser I may grow.

"You do it very well," smiling.

"I was brought up on Dr. Watts, too. But of course it's been quite a while—I'd forgotten how much I remembered."

He rubbed his hands together, tugged his coat down, looked around, saw the idol, and smiled.

"Interesting old codger. I'd like to own him."

Kukailimoku, called Kaili, glared with unspeakable ferocity down at them from his stick. Ann stamped her foot.

"Really, Captain, this is disgusting! A heathen god! No matter how depraved you may be, you should at least keep in mind that you are a white man—and supposedly civilized!"

"What's wrong with Kaili? I'm not kowtowing to him. I just like him, that's all. I just wish I owned him. An amusing sou-

64

venir. But the old girl won't even talk about parting from him."

Ann folded her hands and took a place by his side amid loud silence. He offered his arm, but she ignored it.

Near the gate they were approached by a languid handsome young man who had come from the largest hut.

"My love to thee, Capitani. A full measure of happiness."

"And to you, Kaiko. And many of 'em."

They rubbed noses ceremoniously.

"This is Mrs. Mathewson, from the manahini-ma. One of the Long Necks. This is Prince Kaiko, Mrs. Mathewson. Or I guess you'd call him a prince," he added in English. "He's a member of the King's kitchen cabinet. Very close to him."

The Hawaiian, smiling, went to Ann, who stiffened.

"No, no, Kaiko. You just shake hands this time. I don't reckon Mrs. Mathewson would care for that breath of yours. She's not as fond of gin as some people I could name."

"My love goes to thee," the youth said amiably, and shook her hand. "Seas of delight be yours always."

"Well, thank you," said Ann.

Kaiko turned to Johnny.

"I am from his Majesty. He heard that you were here, and he would have the story of how you fought the famous Humu."

"He beat the stuffing out of me."

"His Majesty would have the story."

"Well, I suppose if he would he would. Now?"

Kaiko nodded sleepily, all the while smiling.

"Excuse me," Johnny said to Ann. "This amounts to an order. A command performance. It's different with Kate. *She* can defend herself. But Liho's feelings would be hurt if I didn't go."

"That man has been drinking!"

"Sure has, hasn't he? Matter of fact, he can hardly stand up. That means the King's squiffed again. You can always tell."

65

"You shouldn't go to him! You shouldn't encourage him!"

"Why not? He's one of my best customers. And besides, I like Liholiho. There's something right sweet about him, even when he's fried."

"You—you might even get drunk yourself!"

He regarded her gravely, then nodded.

"You know, now that you mention it, I might at that." He bowed. "You'll forgive me for not walking you home, I trust?"

"*Home!*" bitterly.

"Well."

She put a hand on his sleeve. She trembled while she did it, but she looked up into his face.

"I wish you wouldn't go," she said softly.

"Good day," he said. "It's been a pleasure to meet you again, Mrs. Mathewson."

He linked his arm with Kaiko's as they walked toward the biggest hut, Ann watching them, and Kaiko leaned a bit toward him, doubtless grateful for the support. A great shouting and cheering rose when they arrived at the doorway. They went inside.

"That man's evil, he's evil!" Ann told them passionately at supper.

"I have heard much about him," the Reverend Mr. Bingham said. "The natives have great confidence in him, and so do all the white men of the waterfront."

"He is evil!"

"I must speak to him. It may be that we can bring him into the light. He could be most helpful, if he came to us."

It was nine or ten hours after this conversation, it was in fact at dawn, a dawn flagrantly opalescent, that Captain Lamb emerged from the palace, there being nobody left conscious for him to play with. One hand grasped a lapel of his coat as though for support. His beaver was far back on his head. He was singing.

As I was a-walkin' down Paradise Street,
To me way—aye, blow the man down!
A juicy young damsel I chanced for to meet,
Give me some time to blow the man down!

He was keeping the beat with a cigar, his baton.

She was round in the counter and bluff in the bow.
To me way—aye, blow the man down!
So I took in all sail and I—

He stumbled over something, almost losing his balance, almost dropping his cigar.

"Mercy me," he said. "What in hell's this?"

It was something extremely large, and dim, vague of shape, there on the ground before him. An elephant? A small elephant? Elephants did have babies, didn't they? Of course. He had seen them in India. In Calcutta. That was a dirty trip for you, up that damn' dirty Hooghly! You could spend days at it. Weeks.

The elephant stirred, and Captain Lamb would have leaned over to examine it better, but he was afraid he wouldn't be able to get back. The elephant lifted its head — and it turned out to be a man. It had a foolish, astonished expression, slightly imbecilic, and the hair on its head, fluffed up to a point, suggested a scalplock.

"Oh, it's you," said Captain Lamb. "How d'ye do? Damn' dirty trip, up that Hooghly. Calcut' ain't worth it, you ask me."

Humu burst into speech, confusing Johnny, but the tenor of it was easily grasped. Humu honored and worshipped Johnny Lamb, by gum, his savior. A little earlier he had been palpitating in a cave, prepared to die when found. Now he was free. And who had done this? Who had caused it to happen? Why, Captain Lamb, no other. Johnny the Lamb was a great man. He was the greatest man in the world, by gum, ahoy.

"Hurray," mumbled Captain Lamb, looking at the lighted

67

end of his cigar as if he had never seen anything like it before.

Humu would serve Captain Lamb always. He would be his slave. What could he do for Captain Lamb?

"You mean—now?" asked Johnny, still regarding his cigar, trying to concentrate on it, to steady himself.

"Anything at all! Now? Yes! Aye, aye, sir!"

Johnny removed his gaze from the cigar—and instantly the court yard rocked, and he had to spread his feet, and even then he almost fell. He would have pitched forward, but he put out a hand and grasped the prostrate giant.

"Sure, Humu. Sure. You can take me home."

Folks were getting up, standing or kneeling at the entrances of their huts while they yawned, and they saw Johnny the Lamb being carried home, and chuckled to see it. They were proud of him, a real haole chief. He'd been drinking gin with the King, no doubt. The dear King, such a kind man.

Johnny was singing. His head against Humu's great chest, he had found his beaver in the way, so he'd slammed it on Humu's head. Johnny was waving a cigar, keeping time, more or less, as he lay in Humu's arms.

> Oh, the boys and the girls went a-huckleberry
>   hunting,
> To me way-aye-aye-aye-aye-i-yah!
> Oh, the boys and the girls went a-huckleberry
>   hunting,
> And sing high-low, my Ranzo Ray!

Feathers, Wine, Patchouli   10

It was a stately thing, an Indiaman, Philadelphia-built, as you could tell from the three broad yellow moldings, and the moment Ann saw it her heart gave a bound, for she sensed that this ship meant escape. How she knew this, she could not have said. She knew nothing about the ship. The name on the counter was not visible from where she stood near the fort. She had no way of learning that the ship had come from New York by way of the Cape of Good Hope, the Straits, and Whampoa, and that it carried a cargo of tea, long and short Company nankeens, shalloons, blue gurrah, ivory, rice, ostrich feathers, wine, Gurrapore cossas, coffee, patchouli, and hatchets, and that it would go back soon by way of the Horn. She only knew that somehow her fate might be tied up in it.

This was a grand ship, taller than any she had ever seen before, and cleaner. It showed an aristocrat as well as a giant in that cluttered place, for the company it found itself in was not reputable.

With spring the whalers had gone away to the newly discovered grounds off Japan; to return in September, all of them, and many more besides, more whalers, probably, than had ever before been seen in one place: the inner and outer harbors were choked with them.

Because of these new whaling grounds, Honolulu had become ideal for the buff-bowed waddling ships from New Bedford or Nantucket or wherever—five out of six of them were Yankee ships, and virtually all of the officers were Yankee, though few of the men were. They were not permitted to land in Japan. Canton, the only port in China open to foreign devils, was too restricted and much too far away. The Russian settlements in Alaska, the fur trading posts of Oregon, did not have the things the whalers needed; and neither did the misable little Mexican villages in California. There was nothing, really, between the Japanese whaling grounds, to which the ships would return twice a year until filled with oil, and Valparaiso in Chile—nothing, that is, excepting the Sandwich Islands, and especially Honolulu.

Honolulu had everything—wood, water, women. Not the least of its charms, from the point of view of skippers, was the fact that its white population ashore was small and (except for the missionaries) co-operative. Its natives could often be talked into shipping aboard a short-handed whaler, especially if you bought them enough drinks first, and they could easily be argued out of demanding their full pay afterward. Moreover, if hands deserted, as of course whaler hands did at every opportunity, it was tolerably easy to recover them in Honolulu. The island was not large, and it held no jungle, almost no forest, no caves that were not well known and easily searched. What's more, if a few real seamen were lost, the kind who would be hard to replace, you could always make a deal with Captain Johnny Lamb the trader, himself an ex-whaler, who knew every inch of the waterfront. *He'd* get them back for you.

There were skippers who did not like to go to even this much trouble and expense, or who feared broken bones which would incapacitate seamen for at least a while. These skippers had little difficulty keeping their men aboard. After all, while a few eccentric sailors might long for exercise, or release from the forecastle, and some might even crave tropical scenery close up, by far the greatest number sought only two things — and you could ride at anchor and still get both of these, off Honolulu. The aforementioned Captain Johnny

70

Lamb, for instance, was only one of several traders, albeit the most active, who would send you out all the sandpaper gin your boys could guzzle. As for the other thing—you didn't even have to send for that, you didn't even have to yoohoo for it. It came of its own accord — came swimming, laughing, flowers behind the ears, hair floating behind, and no clothes on at all. The natives of the Sandwich Islands, excepting recently the high chiefs, had no sort of cloth to wear except their own tapa, a beaten bark which would not survive a thunderstorm, much less a swim; so when they went into the water they went naked, which is the way the girls swam to the ships, a convenient arrangement and satisfactory to both parties. The Reverend Mr. Thurston and the Reverend Mr. Bingham made vehement objections, but the girls swam out that way just the same.

However many houris might go to the ships, though, there were still plenty of sailors to come ashore each night of those terrible months, September and October. They came by the dozen, the score, the hundred, rolling arm-in-arm up and down the dusty lanes between the huts, in and out of the groggeries and brothels of the beach.

Of course they stank. The trades, late this year, had not yet sprung up again; and when there was any movement of air at all, it was a sickly slow kona. Whaling was a malodorous business at best, and now Honolulu was oily with fumes from the great deck vats where they were boiling down the blubber Everything you touched was greasy. As for the sailors, you could smell one half a mile away.

These disreputable men came from disreputable ships, sloppy, dirty, badly kept up. Nobody respected a whaler hand. If there was a good seaman in the forecastle of any whaling ship he was either a foreigner or a Negro, glad enough to take any wages, any working conditions; or an impressed hand, probably carried aboard while dead drunk; or else he was, like Johnny Lamb, a boy from an inland town

71

dazzled by the thought of running away to sea, and knowing nothing, as a seaport boy would know, of conditions aboard a whaler.

By nightfall, then, these disgusting creatures would be staggering everywhere, shouting unspeakable things.

Nor were they only vocal. There was hardly a night when at least a few did not visit the mission house—not to receive instruction, not to seek advice, but to jeer. They hated the missionaries, who would have spoiled the only fun they might have a chance to get in years. They gloried in their sin; and it became fashionable among them, the thing to do, to curse the Lord's Anointed. They went further. Not infrequently they threw stones through the doorway or right through the grass walls. Sometimes these fell among the faithful while they were at evening prayer, in the darkness. They had to be careful to keep back from the doorway, to which there was no door. The Reverend Mr. Thurston was hit over the left ear by a stone one time when he was praying; but he went right on, and the others did not learn about it until they rose from their knees.

What was even worse was the fear of fire. More than once the sailors had threatened to burn the God-damned place to the ground, God-damn it. No torch had ever been thrown; but it might happen. Then it would be a matter of minutes, maybe only of seconds.

"We travel twenty thousand miles to a land of savages living in the stone age—and we find that our only real danger is at the hands of folks from home," Lucy Thurston said.

"It's shameful!" Ann had cried. "It's the influence of that man Lamb. He has no conscience at all!"

Reverend Mr. Bingham, as all in the Family knew, had pleaded earnestly with Johnny Lamb, catching him on a succession of nights when Johnny was checking sandalwood bearers at his warehouse. He couldn't possibly have picked a worse time. The King and his principal chiefs, having no sense of money, were deep in debt to a group of Boston merchants,

72

some of them represented in Honolulu by Johnny Lamb. The King, for example, had not yet paid for the brig *Thaddeus*, which lay rotting, unused, but nevertheless he had ordered the magnificent yacht *Cleopatra's Barge*. The King and the chiefs cheerfully acknowledged these debts and ran up more; but how to pay them?

The only answer was sandalwood. They owned all there was, since they owned everything on the islands, and sandalwood was fetching eighteen gold dollars for a picul of 133⅓ pounds in Canton. Very well. The chiefs sent commoners up into the hills with orders to cut sandalwood and bring it down to the beach, where Johnny Lamb, among others, but principally Johnny Lamb, saw that it was weighed and stored and accounted for. This was not an easy job. The natives, having worked hard since dawn, sometimes since the previous day, always came in late, which meant that the work had to be done by torchlight; and they were tired and cantankerous. There was no uniformity to the carriage. The wood, a light yellowish brown, stripped of its bark, had been cut into sticks anywhere from six to eight feet long, a foot to eighteen inches thick, so that they all had to be weighed. A man might carry five or six sticks, or only one or two. They were held on his back by vines passed over the shoulder and under the arms and fastened across the chest. If any man did not bring enough, he must be reported—it was the will of the chiefs—in order that he might be sent back for more instead of being permitted half a week in which to tend his taro. This was not a notably admirable business; and Captain Lamb was nerve-edgy about it.

Hiram Bingham was a man of education and great natural intelligence. Nobody had ever heard him raise his voice. His courage was unquestionable, his patience inexhaustible. He was always willing to listen to the other side, though he was never won over. But he was no diplomat. The most marked thing about him was his intense earnestness, an almost hypnotic sincerity that burned in his dark deep-set eyes. But this was only when you looked at him. Johnny Lamb refused to look at him. Surly, he would step around the missionary, checking figures, muttering to himself, while the overseers chanted, bundles thunked on the platform, the rod of the scales rose and squealingly fell, and against the far wall monstrous shadows of the bearers bobbed, sometimes to swell balloonlike, sometimes to collapse to shapes no bigger than a man's fist.

However, when on the third night Mr. Bingham suddenly fell to his knees and began to pray, there was consternation among the bearers and Captain Lamb spoke in wrath.

"Damn it, Pastor, get out of here! You're scaring these poor men out of their wits!"

Now the ancient gods of the islands all had been evil gods, malevolent; and the islanders still thought of prayer that it was one of two things—either a groveling, a plea for mercy, or else a wheedling of the deity to wreak evil upon an enemy. This latter, called anaana, or praying-to-death, was much the more common, and frequently it did, in fact, suggestion being what it is, end in the death of the bewitched. Thus the prayer was generally a thing to be avoided, a thing of dread. Love in the larger, less intimate sense, love from heaven, pure love, the Polynesians could not conceive.

Captain Lamb knew this. Captain Lamb must also have known, as the missionary was wont to contend afterward, that the anaana was false, whereas the address to the Lord given there on the floor of the warehouse by an ordained minister was demonstrably true.

Perhaps Johnny did not even stop to think about this. Perhaps he only knew that the sight of this gaunt Yankee on his knees, eyes closed, head raised, arms stretched toward the ceiling, was playing the devil with the job on hand. At any rate, he had roughly seized the Reverend Mr. Bingham by a shoulder.

74

"Now this has gone far enough! If you ain't out of here inside half a minute I'm going to toss you out ass-first!"

"I must have done something wrong, I must have offended him in some way," their leader told the Family later. "I must study this."

"He certainly is a most ungodly man," said Sister Thurston.

"He works them even on the Sabbath," said Reverend Mr. Thurston. "It's true there's less gambling now and fewer games, but only because he keeps them working so hard."

"I must ask for guidance," muttered Hiram Bingham.

Ann Mathewson, looking at him then, felt a sudden wave of pity for the leader of the group. Here was a man who never faltered, however unsympathetic he might sometimes seem. She was no longer afraid of him. She could not bring herself to like him, but she had a deep admiration for the man. He fought alone. He must often have been confused—after all, he had no precedent, nothing to fall back on, there had never been a mission like this before—but he did not dare to let that confusion show.

"I must think of another approach," he had said.

Ann Mathewson was thinking of this, among other things, when she stared out at the newly arrived ship. This vessel would mean something. If it had come from home it would have mail, the first in many months. If it was going to the East Coast, Mr. Bingham might send her in it. Would he? Did she want him to? She was weary, discouraged, yet she drove herself, determined to be indispensable. She would endure the life as well as any of them, she told herself.

But the ship was here. Fate was here. She'd know soon.

It was as exciting as the Russian man-o'-war had been, for Ann even more exciting. *That* visit had been good for their spirits as well, making them feel like persons of importance. The mission indisputably was lagging. Everybody in the Family worked hard; but the mission lagged. It was difficult to induce children to come to the school, though it is true that they were well behaved once there. It was even more difficult to get grown-ups. The chiefs had let it be known that they did not favor the idea of commoners getting education—or getting anything else which they, the chiefs, lacked. That way lay rebellion. On the other hand, the chiefs, remonstrated with, themselves made excuses for not attending school, and found unexpected and wholly unreasonable obstacles to the mastery of English. What they really meant was that it took too much time from their sports, their gambling and drinking, in the case of the women their primping and strutting in gauds and new frocks.

The missionaries were not mocked—except by sailors—but neither were they honored. Listened to, yet they were not obeyed. The chiefs were polite; but the chiefs it must be admitted were not interested. Most of the white residents were either apathetic or openly hostile. The United States commercial agent, John C. Jones, Jr., who liked to be called consul, and practically was, was proper but cold. The British official representative, Captain Charlton, was opposed to the mission, which he avowed was no more than the first move in a campaign to annex the islands to the United States. Mr. Hunnewell, who had been mate of the *Thaddeus* and was now doing well for himself in Honolulu, always favored them and encouraged them; but most of the other traders didn't like the missionaries, saying that they were bad for business. Of the four Hawaiian youths they had brought from Connecticut, returning them, converted professing Christians, to their native land, three, alas, already had backslidden; and the fourth was far from stable. No new converts had been made. The natives, who had come out in large numbers for the first Sabbath services, doubtless from sheer curiosity, no longer did this. They insisted that the Sabbath was not a kapu day, that all the kapus had been ruled out by the King before the Long Necks had arrived, and on that day they'd cook their food and dance and play games just as on other days, no matter what the members of the malahini-ma tried to tell them.

It was sufficiently discouraging. But when His Imperial Russian Majesty's ship *Otkritie* dropped her hook in the inner harbor, King Liholiho himself, sober, and attended by an overwhelming retinue, paid a state call at the mission. He smiled, nodded, shook hands all around, and said affable things. It was pure formality, but it did a lot to bolster the Family's prestige.

On top of that, and only two hours later—oh, it had been a big day!—there arrived at the humble little grass mission hut Commodore Michael Vascilieff together with a Russian Navy chaplain who sported an enormous black beard, and thirteen officers gorgeous in gold lace, besides two interpreters. They reeked of perfume and glittered with diamonds. Their swords clanked, the epaulettes swung. They were noisy, lousy, and punctiliously genial. Vascilieff had just come from an audience with the King, and the implication was that he considered the Yankee mission to be the second most important organization on the islands. He was graciousness itself. He promised to make a flattering report to Governor Reicord of Kamchatka. This again was good for prestige. It was not until later that they learned that by far the greater part of Commodore Vascilieff's visit to Honolulu was spent aboard the *Otkritie,* wining and dining and from time to time dickering with a group of local merchants, among them Johnny Lamb. The Russians might have been sincerely impressed by the effort to spread the Word among the islanders, but they were more immediately interested in buying and arranging for the future purchase of salt for salting fish in their Alaskan settlements. The chiefs got it from salt lakes, and they were delighted to sell it—through the traders on the beach. The Russians finally had to agree to pay three dollars a barrel.

"You have so much more to look at here than we have at Kailua," said Brother Crowell, coming up to where Ann stood.

"Yes," she said. "I suppose we should account ourselves lucky. How did you leave your wife, sir?"

"Not well. I'm worried about her. She was never strong, and this climate's too much for her—though she won't admit it."

"I'm sorry," said Ann, who was fond of Abigail Crowell.

Horace Crowell had been studying theology at Andover when he heard the call to serve in the mission. Within a week he had quit his studies, married, and gone to Boston to present himself. He still hoped to become an ordained minister of the gospel, under the tutelage of Reverend Mr. Bingham and Reverend Mr. Thurston. He and his wife, together with Dr. and Mrs. Holman, had been left to found a mission at Kailua, on the island of Hawaii; and this was Brother Crowell's first visit to Honolulu. He blinked, mopping his brow.

"It was an excuse to view this harbor again, really. They were going to send a boy, but I asked them to send me."

"What's this?" sharply.

"I was to summon you to tea at the mission. Real tea. A gift from the captain of that ship," and he nodded toward the Indiaman. "Reverend Mr. Bingham wishes all to be present. He wishes to consult us, he says, on a very important matter."

"Oh—Now?"

"Yes."

She knew what the very important matter would prove to be. She nodded, and turned to walk by Brother Crowell's side. He was a gentleman, and she admired him and was proud to be seen walking with him; but that was not what she thought of now. She walked with her head down, her hands folded before her.

The Lady Said No   11

There were not enough chairs. The females sat, the men stood behind them, forming a loose circle. It was good that the men did not squat on their heels. It was one of the things about the islands that had most amazed Ann Mathewson, and it continued to amaze her—how almost nobody ever sat down. That they had never known the chair, or troubled themselves to invent it, seemed more astounding than the fact that until recently they had never even known the wheel or any metal. They lay propped on one elbow, Roman fashion, when they feasted, flat on their bellies when they played cards. When they chatted or ate ordinary food, they'd squat.

She was glad that the men of the Family never condescended to squat. It was better to stand. It was more dignified.

They all more or less turned to Hiram Bingham. Before him sat his wife Sybil, she of the large nose, of the eyes that could smile. Sybil not seldom interceded for them with a leader who was scarcely flexible, however patient. Shy, hard to know, surely she was beloved by them all; yet it was to her husband that they looked, Ann Mathewson the most intently of all.

He opened the meeting with a prayer, asking for guidance in any decision they might need to make here this evening. Then, when they had risen and arranged themselves, he told them about the new ship.

They were all there, all listening dutifully, excepting Dr. and Mrs. Holman and Mrs. Horace Crowell, who remained at Kailua. Besides Reverend Mr. Bingham and Sybil, and Reverend Mr. Asa Thurston and Lucy, meek and mild, there were

Mr. and Mrs. Samuel Whitney, Mr. and Mrs. Samuel Ruggles, Ann Mathewson the widow, Horace Crowell, Mr. and Mrs. Elisha Loomis, and the only persons in the Family over thirty, Mr. and Mrs. Daniel Chamberlain. They stood or sat in respectful silence, and never stirred. They were hard workers, and persons of great faith, which they sorely needed.

Mr. Bingham described a visit from the captain of the ship out there, the newly arrived Indiaman. Captain Strook, he said, was a man of God and one who wished the missionaries well. He had praised what he saw, and had agreed to praise it again when he returned to Boston. He would seek out members of the ABCFM there and tell them what the Family was doing and what the Family stood in need of. Meanwhile, and though he was sailing very soon, having stopped only for wood and water, Captain Strook had placed himself at the disposal of the missionaries. He would be glad to carry any letters—or any passengers.

At this point Reverend Mr. Bingham paused, and another man would have cleared his throat; but Mr. Bingham had never suffered from any sort of nervous habit. He was, as always, appallingly forthright. He looked at Ann.

"Sister Mathewson, in your bereavement we have been chary of troubling you. But do you not think that you should consider this opportunity to return home? Your services have been great, and you have been faithful, devout, and uncomplaining, and surely nobody would speak any slight word of blame if, your helpmeet having been drawn back to the bosom of God, you separate from us now and accept passage on this reputable craft commanded by a man we can trust. You will do this, no doubt, Sister Mathewson?"

Ann shook her head, without looking up.

"No," she said in a low but perfectly clear voice.

It flabbergasted her as much as it did the rest of them. Until a moment ago she had not been at all certain what she wanted to do; but she resented being forced into anything:

80

she would not even have Reverend Bingham tell her what she must do. She didn't look up when he came to her. His hand on her wrist was gentle.

"Sister, I do not know what the others think, but for myself let me implore you not to make a hasty decision."

"You said I had to."

"A matter of hours, Sister. That is true. The ship will sail at dawn, but to be sure of catching the tide you should be aboard tonight. But there is still more than an hour until darkness. Please think about it very carefully."

"I have. I'm going to stay here."

The hand on her wrist tightened a mite, though there was no threat in it. The voice was low and resonant.

"Sister Mathewson, your reluctance to seem to quit does you credit. We all realize that, and we will see to it that the folks back home are made to understand it. We others of the Family know that you have done noble work here. There is no shame in turning back when the finger of the Lord has so clearly pointed the way. It is because of no fault of yours that all of us beg you to embrace this opportunity to take back a report of our work."

"Captain Strook or whatever his name is can do that."

"Not the way *you* could, Sister."

Again Ann shook her head.

"I'm going to stay here."

She wondered why Reverend Mr. Bingham was being so stubborn. He must have been able to see that she hadn't the slightest intention of changing her mind. He stepped away from her, and probably regarded her pityingly for a moment. She didn't lift her eyes. Then with his arms raised he walked to the center of the circle, where there was no sort of stand or table, and in a low trembling voice, turning as he did so, he asked them all if they would pray with him to the Lord for guidance in the decision Sister Mathewson was obliged to make. Just *stubborn*, that's all he was, Ann thought angrily.

81

He knew right well that she had already made her decision.

They got down on their knees.

Reverend Mr. Bingham prayed in a slow-paced, even, low, firm voice, and for a fairly long while, maybe twenty-five minutes. It was a moving prayer. His prayers always were. His voice was at all times gentle, not harsh as you would have expected, and sometimes when he prayed there was even a dreaminess in it. There was the sound of buzzing flies, and from outside the thud of tapa mallets. Some sailors ventured into the enclosure and lounged in the doorway, where they said a few half-heartedly scoffing things, being somewhat awed by the scene in spite of themselves. Then one of them cursed and threw something soft that skittered across the mats and came to rest in front of Ann. It was a banana peel, she saw: she had her eyes a little open all the while. The sailors laughed and went off. Reverend Mr. Bingham prayed and prayed.

After they had amened and risen, Ann took the banana peel and dropped it daintily under her stool. She waited with folded hands.

"Sister Mathewson, may we ask you now, since time is so short: Do you find that our petition brought you any light?"

"No."

It was not a part of the nature of the mission's leader to show impatience, no matter what the provocation. Nobody knew better that humility, meekness, and resignation were cardinal virtues. He had never been heard to sniff or to snort; he had steeled himself, trained himself over the years, never to permit the escape of any exclamation, however small, of exasperation or disgust. He lowered his head now, and turned back to his previous place beside the wall, moving slowly, a man crushed.

Ann sat down. The other females sat, too, grateful for something to do, excepting Mrs. Loomis, whose day it was for cooking and serving, and who now, suddenly remembering it, scurried outside for the tea.

82

It was the best tea Ann had ever tasted, a heavy black smoky souchong. They had no milk to go with it, there being no cow on the island, nor could they spare sugar from their scanty stock; but with a tea like that you didn't want sugar or milk anyway.

Reverend Mr. Bingham did not drink his, only stared glumly into it, while nobody said anything and everybody sipped much more rapidly than they would ordinarily have done, in their nervousness burning their tongues, which was a pity, for the tea was worthy of better treatment. At last Reverend Mr. Bingham placed his cup on the ground.

"Sister Mathewson, it must seem to you that we are plaguing you cruelly in the grief which no doubt still lingers in your breast over the passing of your loved one. Please forgive us."

He was not consciously using the regal plural. He said "we" and "us" because he believed with all his heart that he really was speaking for everyone there excepting Ann herself—and, indeed, it could be that he was.

He leaned toward her, hands spread.

"But, Sister Mathewson—"

The sunset gun spoke at the fort. You never could be sure of that gun. Sometimes they forgot to fire it; nor was it always punctual, even when it did go off. It was a symbol rather than an announcement of time. The hour itself you knew from the multitudinous bells of the ships in harbor, if anybody in Honolulu cared. The sunset gun at the fort was rather (when it did go off) an audible assertion of power, authority. It was a noise that the chiefs liked to hear. Sometimes it was the merest "pip," sometimes it roared. Tonight it was especially loud and sudden. The whole hut shook. Such cups as rested in saucers— they didn't have enough saucers to go around—leapt and clicked in alarm. The flies buzzed higher. The insects chiffering in the thatch fell silent.

"Sister Mathewson," said the man, who had been disturbed not nearly so much by the explosion of a cannon as by one touch of opposition to his authority, "could you perhaps find it in your heart to tell us *why* you insist upon staying?"

"Certainly," said Ann, and put her cup down. "I'd be glad to."

It was dark in the hut now, and there was only the faintest far sound of roistering from the waterfront. Ann did not look at the leader but at Horace Crowell, who stood opposite her. She could not see his clothes, which were of course dark, but she could make out his unnaturally pale face, and she believed that he was admiring her, which gave her some courage.

What she was about to say had come to her in a rush, all at once, and she could only believe, she hoped not frivolously, that she had been divinely inspired.

"My duty here is not yet done."

There was a hissing, an outbreathing of protestation. She was not fair to herself! Nobody could have worked more diligently! Nobody could possibly—

Ann stilled this with a *"Please!"* in a voice (for her) downright haughty, imperious. They gasped, and were silent.

"I am not talking about routine at the school, which I daresay I do as well as anybody else. As I see it, I have a more special duty here—or should have."

She hurried on. She could make out Horace Crowell's face only as a wan blob of lightness. She could not see any of the other faces at all.

"We are failing. Let's admit it—we've been here half a yeaı and haven't made a single convert. We've been an unmitigated failure, so far."

She paused only for an instant, wetting her lips. Had she paused any longer she would have broken down.

"We were greatly favored by the Lord when we came and found all the heathen gods overthrown. But even if their old gods are dead, the natives don't seem to be looking for any new ones. They stumble—but they spurn the hand we offer

84

them. The truth is, they don't *want* to be led. They are simply not that kind of folks. Look at them! They want to be *driven, not led!*"

Amid a rusty rustle of clothes, a restless scraping, the voice of Asa Thurston came, pained: "But surely, Sister, this is the opposite to all we have been trying to inculcate into these people. Our Lord Jesus, remember, was a shepherd."

"I am not likely to forget it, sir. But shepherds have to drive their flocks sometimes, too, as well as lead them. You should know that. You're a country man. Now, please! Let me finish! I don't suggest *we* push these people. That'd be ridiculous. They wouldn't follow us. They'd laugh. No, it's their own chiefs who should drive them, as they always have done all the days of their lives. And who drives the chiefs? Not the King, of course. You all known as well as I do that the King is no leader but a slave—he's a slave of his own weakness. No, it isn't the King I mean. It's Kaahumanu."

"I have prayed for her personally." It was Hiram Bingham. "We all have. Many times."

"Perhaps that's not enough. It may be that the Lord God in His wisdom prefers to have us use some more direct action. It would certainly seem so. Now I know the Queen tolerably well. I've made several gowns for her. I think that underneath it all she has a kind heart. But she resents us. There's only one haole on this island for whom she has any respect. You all known who I mean."

When she felt her face grow hot, she was more than ever grateful for the darkness.

"Now I don't know whether they—I mean, whether the two of them—Well, anyway, he certainly has a great influence over her."

Somebody cried, "Shameful!"

"Agreed," said Ann. "But have we not been told that the ways of God are inscrutable, and may it not be that we can turn this—this relationship into a beacon that will light thou-

85

sands the way to salvation? Look: To win the people we have to win the chiefs, and to win the chiefs we have to win Kaahumanu, and to win Kaahumanu we have to win Johnny Lamb. See?"

She dropped her hands, one on each knee, triumphant. There was some silence. Then Hiram Bingham spoke.

"This has been most illuminating, Sister. But have you forgotten that we have prayed, too, for the soul of Captain Lamb, and equally without avail?"

"Maybe he doesn't want prayers. Maybe they can't touch him. He's a worldly man—well, let's approach him in a wordly manner. Here is where my function becomes clear. Here's why I should stay.

"I will go to Captain Lamb—This will sound prideful, and I am as well aware as anybody that we are all equal in the sight of the Lord. But we don't all of us always remember that. I wish there was somebody else from Hartford. If Mr. Mathewson, my late husband—Well, anyway, I was born Ann Buttoner. We live on Prospect Street. The Lambs live down by the river. There is all the difference in the world, as anybody from Hartford could tell you. I will go to John Lamb, and I will tell him to forbid those girls from swimming out to the ships and to stop selling rum and to instruct the sailors that they are not to annoy us.

"He's a brute, but he'll listen to me. He's the bullyboy of the beach, and he can do anything he wants with the Queen, but he'll listen to me because I am a Buttoner—from Prospect Street. He knows perfectly well that we're cousins of the Harpers in New Haven. That may not mean anything to you, but it does to him. After all, he's in business. He isn't here," Ann finished shrilly, "for his health."

They crowded around her, fumbling for her hand, mumbling congratulations and thanks. There was no doubt that they'd been impressed. A new spirit had come to the Family.

When would Sister Mathewson go to this man?

86

"Right now," she answered. "Or at least, right after supper."

Mrs. Loomis, whose day it was, hustled outside. The others followed more sedately.

They ate that night, as they customarily did in clear weather, by the side of the taro pit, in the starlight. It was a cold supper, except for the warmed-over tea. There was usually a breeze at this hour, and they dreaded flying sparks. Also, a fire would attract insects.

It was not a festive occasion; yet though they said little, they were eager and excited, seething with wild hope. They had not until this evening realized how rutted they'd been, how discouraged. The accepted methods of persuasion had failed. This bold new plan exhilarated them, snatching their breath. Ann Mathewson indeed, outwardly at least, was the most composed member of the Family. The others often glanced at her in admiration.

When the meal was over, she went back to the hut and got her shawl, which she fastened with a plain pin. She wished she had the cameo brooch she'd given away when she married Jabez Mathewson. She had no jewelry of any kind now. She sighed.

She moved by feel, there being no light in the hut. She thought of taking her Bible, and she did lift it in her hands and fondle it. It was a small Book, light, leatherbound; when Ann wished to read, customarily she borrowed the preaching Bible, the Family's own, which had large type. One thing, at least, in her own Book she never needed to read, knowing it by heart, and that was the farewell message written just inside the front cover, "To our sister, to my daughter, dearest Ann: Go to the dark places with a heart of light and spread sweetness around you. We will always love you, here." It was signed by her mother and by Helen and Grace; and the signatures, rather wobbly, were not as clear and clean as they might have been had they been put down in tranquillity. Ann would never forget, she knew, how she had felt, how they'd

87

all felt, when, weeping, after that horrid scene of recrimination, they had embraced one another and said goodbye.

She kissed the Bible she couldn't see, and put it back into her chest.

She wished there was a light. She wished she had a looking-glass. She touched her poke, she touched her shawl and her dress here and there. She drew a deep breath. She went outside.

"I'm going to him now."

"Not at night!"

"Why not? God watches over us at night as well as in the daytime."

"But—but he lives down on the beach!"

"In Hartford he lived down by the river—and I lived on Prospect Street," evenly. "No harm will come to me. Don't worry."

"I'll go with you," cried Horace Crowell.

"And I, too," said Hiram Bingham. "We can't let you go down to that horrid place alone."

"No," said Ann. "This is something I must do by myself. Excuse me. Good night."

Steps in the Night 12

A thought sprang up within her as she started along the road toward the beach, and it jolted her, causing her to jump. She recovered herself almost immediately.

There was nobody in sight, though there was a deal of shouting and singing in the fitfully torchlit place toward which she was making her way.

The thought had been: Suppose this sudden-appearing plan had indeed been an inspiration, yes, but not a heavenly one? This chilled her temples and dried her mouth. Everybody knew that the Devil sometimes came in curious guise. His could be a soothing stroke, a honeyed whisper. Why had she wanted so fiercely to go home and yet now was conniving to remain? Partly it could be sheer orneriness: that she admitted, being prepared to grant that if Reverend Mr. Bingham had not insisted upon her departure, she herself might have insisted upon it. That was the way her mind and her will sometimes worked. It was deplorable, and she meant to get rid of it in time; but presently, undeniably, it existed.

Yet—could it not be that perversity itself was a result of the secret prompting of Satan? Surely it was self-indulgence, which should have no part in the make-up of a God-fearing person. It was a weakness, a deviation.

Ann knew little about the ways of the flesh; but she did believe that she knew a great deal about the ways of God, having read and studied much, and thought a heap, too; and she did have a sound understanding of and alert watch over her own instincts. Other persons might rile her; and she could be perverse and willful, true; but not when she was alone. She had a habit of being honest with herself.

She had seen very little of Johnny Lamb since the day after the mokomoko two-three months ago, but she could not deny that she had often thought of him. She hoped that her conduct had been exemplary, and believed that it had been; but assuredly her pulses leapt and her heart quopped whenever she heard his name spoken—and it was spoken a great deal in Honolulu these days—and for an instant on those occasions the book or sewing or lesson, or whatever was before her, jiggled erratically as though her eyes had been thrown out of focus.

Was it this same force which had caused her, amazing herself, to be so outspoken just now back there in the mission house? Was it the same force which was propelling her on her way with swinging strides right this minute?

It might be best if she turned around and ran back to the mission, and threw herself down among them, and confessed the way she felt, humbling herself, opening herself out, begging for help. It might lay this force. It might slacken the strain on her nerves, and ease off the suspicion that bumped gently but insistently against her mind like a piece of rotten fruit at the piling of a dock.

However, she kept going toward the beach.

It could have been that the fright and fear the beach stirred within her were responsible for the way she marched, a woman impelled from within, a woman entranced, powerless to resist. For in spite of her gait she was frightened. Her way was literally not down, for the mission house stood not far from the water, but she distinctly had the feeling of descending into something. This could have been her imagination; but it almost did seem to her that the air grew warmer as she walked, waxing hot against her face. She had never before been to the beach alone, even in daytime.

The name would mislead a mainlander. There was no sand,

no gentle slope, or place for swimming or for picnics. By "the beach" in Honolulu, as in any other Pacific island town, was meant what elsewhere would be called the waterfront. To some it was a rialto, to others a pleasure place. To all right-thinking persons, of course, it was primarily a sink of sin, it being known that sailors seldom stray far from their elected field but when ashore demand their joy in quick violent gulps; so that in a general way, deplorable as this was, it could be said that the nearer you got to the docks the deeper you got into man's depravity. There were no docks in Honolulu, but the principle applied.

The beach at Honolulu wasn't bright, it wasn't gay. The roads, or lanes, were the same casual thoroughfares as the rest of the town showed, mere passages among the huts, ankle-deep in dust or mud, depending on the weather. There was no main street, and no central square or plaza. The huts were similar to those elsewhere, dull, bleached, shapeless, suggesting haystacks. The only difference was that girls squatted in the doorways of most of them. A few of these girls dived back into the protection of full darkness when they beheld the unprecedented sight of a Long Neck on the beach at night; a few spat at her; but most of them only giggled. Ann's heart bled for them. She walked resolutely in the middle of the road.

There were a few stone warehouses, low ones.

Finally there were some shored-up huts, which though floorless were in part constructed of something besides sticks and thatch. Odd boards had been used, and odd beams. Bits from different ships, bits brought from New England. Strips of tin here and there. All of these places had doors, if flimsy ones, unlike the "boarding houses," where there were merely openings. These were the "cafés." They were lighted, more or less. From some came singing and the sound of tables rhythmically slapped.

Out of one, as Ann approached it, hurtled a small sailor with cap awry, stark terror in his eyes. His shirt was ripped half off. Blood streamed down one of his arms and that hand was all bloody. He ran along the lane, away from Ann. Three men, each with a naked sheath knife, tumbled out after him. They disappeared into the darkness, and a moment later there were screams from that direction, pleas for mercy, which were cut off.

Silence fell over the beach at Honolulu then for a little while. The hum of talk, the singing and thumping, died; but these were in a moment resumed. Nobody came to any doorway. Nobody went or even looked in the direction from which the screams had come.

The three men with knives returned, wiping these on their breeches. They did not speak to one another, and none of them noticed Ann. Grimly, but exactly, in single file, as though they had rehearsed it, as though it were a drill, they went back into the café.

Ann moved on. She was shaky in the legs, and had considered turning and running back to the mission. She might have done this—had she not become aware that she was being followed.

She stopped, and the footsteps behind her stopped. She looked back but could see nothing. She started again, and the footsteps started again. There were at least two men back there, probably slinking along in the shadows of the huts, and she knew that they were white men because they wore shoes— the natives, men and women alike, never made a sound when they walked.

There could be natives back there, too, stalking her; but certainly there were at least two white men.

If she broke into a run they would run after her. She walked a little faster, holding her head high.

A man came out of a café and saw her and gaped. He was drunk, swaying. He cried, "Oh, my!" and lurched toward her, and tripped and fell to hands and knees. "Oh, Jesus Christ! Oh, my, my!" he mumbled, and shook his head. He seemed to be striving to get up. He reached for her skirt, but she easily slipped away.

She could hear the footsteps behind her again.

Then came four men from the opposite direction, sailors, at least partly drunk, and they all saw her at once, and stopped. "Blow me down! It's one of them God-damn' missionaries!" They spread across the lane, arms akimbo. "Let's see what she looks like with her clothes off," said one. "You reckon they're put together the same way as other women?" They started toward her.

She might have screamed, but what would a scream mean in this neighborhood? What she did was better. A moment before the appearance of these men, she had seen Johnny Lamb's house on the left of the lane just beyond where they stood now. It was easy to identify, even in the darkness, being the only two-story structure in town. He was doing well for himself, that Lamb lad.

Now she walked directly at the sailors, making a scornful gesture as though they were no more than cobwebs.

"Excuse me," coldly. "I have an appointment. You wouldn't want me to call out to Captain Lamb that you were trying to prevent me from reaching him, now would you?"

They fell away, for the name was magic; but they did not fall far away. They closed in behind her, ready to chase her if she ran, to grab her if she turned. They were almost breathing against the back of her neck when she went up to Johnny Lamb's door.

Yes, decidedly he was doing well for himself. The house was substantial, a rectangular one, of whitewashed stone. The roof, probably for coolness, was made of thatch, but it was good fresh green screw-pine thatch, the best kind, and its edges were trimmed. She had never been near this building, but she had heard that he ran his shop downstairs and lived upstairs. She had heard, too, that a great deal of card playing, with high stakes, was indulged in upstairs.

93

"Better not let the Queen catch you!"

"I thought Johnny liked 'em fat?"

The door touched her heart. It was a dark glossy green, and might have come right out of a doorway in Hartford; perhaps it had. There was a trim brass plate with the name LAMB. There was a brass knocker in the shape of an American eagle, and it brought a lump to Ann's throat when she reached for it.

The biggest man she had ever seen, a veritable Goliath of Gath, opened the door. His jaw hung low. His eyes might have been of average size, but in that huge face they showed tiny and piggish, and they were lit with an expression of perpetual puzzlement. His hair, thin and fluffy, stood up in a sort of scalplock, adding to the appearance of stupefied astonishment.

"You must let me in immediately, and don't let any of these men behind me in." She spoke in Hawaiian, which she could be fairly sure the sailors would not understand. "Captain Lamb will be angry if I am delayed. No, don't announce me."

She pushed past the giant, but the sailors did not dare to do that. The upstairs windows had been lighted, and light now streamed down a stairway against the far wall. Unhesitatingly, though with her mind in a turmoil, Ann went upstairs.

There was one large room, well lighted by a whale-oil lamp on a low table in the center. At this table, sideways to her, Captain Lamb sat in an old-fashioned rocking chair. His feet, in felt bedroom slippers, were on a stool. He wore a stunning silk robe, obviously from China, very rich, glistening and smashing with colors whenever he stirred. There was a drink of rum-and-lemon at his elbow. There was a cigar in his mouth. He was reading a book.

He looked around, then he stood up.

"Hello," he said. "Come in."

94

Bells Across the Bay 13

He acted as though he was used to receiving ladies after dark, Ann thought, furious. He shoved the rocker forward.

Almost without thinking, nervous, she untied and took off her bonnet, the high-standing poke all the Family females wore, to the vast amusement of the natives, and which had won them the nickname of ai oeoe, the Long Necks. It was inexpensive, unpretentious. Fleetingly, as she handed it to him, she thought of that d'Angoulême in her chest; but she never would have dared to wear that anyway, knowing that somebody from the mission would be sure to see her; besides, it would have to be pressed, all the ribbons and ruchings separately.

Johnny Lamb stood there holding the poke rather gingerly, as though he thought it might start spouting streams of acid. It was not until this moment that Ann Mathewson, sitting down, realized that her host, too, was nervous. His suavity went no deeper than that glittering robe. In fact, he was all of a twitteration inside.

She rocked, reveling in the motion. She could not, for a little while, talk business. She had determined upon an attack; but it could wait until her body got used to the feel of this luxurious chamber—just as, when you enter a dim place, you must wait for your eyes to adjust themselves.

Yet even what she had glimpsed dazzled her, so that she murmured, "How goodly are thy tents, O Jacob!" to herself.

The room was big and the ends of it were not well lighted.

There were few articles of furniture, though there were many mats on the teakwood floor, lauhalas and makalous mostly, good mats, thick ones. Over the bed, itself not remarkable except for its great size, had been thrown an exquisite Spanish shawl. Here and there on the whitewashed stone walls hung pieces of Chinese brocade, rich and bright. There was a huge Chinese ceremonial sword, in a crusty scabbard, standing in a corner. Near her elbow, on a table, was a set of carved ivory chessmen, mandarins, pagodas, coolies, fragile things, much too lovely, certainly, to be played with. She wondered if Johnny Lamb had ever been to China, or whether these were gifts from favor-seeking skippers who had.

However, the finest thing in that room, by all odds, in Ann Mathewson's opinion, was the Connecticut rocker in which she sat. It was almost too good to be true, and she rocked fervently.

At last she opened her eyes. If she didn't speak soon, he would; and she had designed to open the attack. He was still standing there, the cigar in one hand, the poke in the other. He looked confused; and that would be a good time to begin.

"I suppose you wonder what I'm doing here?" evenly.

"No trouble at the mission, I hope?"

He started to crush out his cigar; but he changed his mind, and went to the head of the stairs and called softly, and when the giant appeared, head-and-shoulders out of the opening, for all the world like a genie conjured up by the rubbing of a lamp, he handed him the cigar. Vastly delighted, grinning, the giant popped this into his mouth, and sank, miraculously it would seem, out of sight.

"No. We haven't been doing the work we'd expected—but that's because we've been blocked at every turn by certain commercial interests here on the beach."

He had been crossing the room toward the bed, the poke in both hands now, and he stopped and turned his head to regard her. She rocked gently, chin down, watching him through her eyelashes.

96

"People who have more regard for their pocketbooks than they do for the immortal souls of the unfortunates among whom they find themselves," she added.

He said, "Oh," and finished his trip to the bed, and put the bonnet down.

"For instance," she went on, "there's those poor pitiful creatures who swim out to the ships—with no clothes on at all."

He came back to the middle of the room, and sat on the stool, facing her. He nodded slowly. His hands cupped his knees.

"So it was business you came here on, eh?"

She bristled, trying to sit upright, a difficult thing to do in a rocking chair.

"You certainly don't suppose I came here for any other reason, do you?"

"I didn't know. I asked, that's all."

But he was less uneasy now, and was even smiling a bit, more the bold daring-staring fellow she had met at Queen Kaahumanu's palace. She frowned, for this was not the way she had planned it.

"Then there's the sale of gin. That should be stopped."

He opened his eyes very wide, and leaned forward, cocking his head. He shook a remonstrative finger.

"Gin represents a good share of my income," he pointed out. "You wouldn't interfere with a man that was just trying to earn his living, would you?"

She sniffed. As though awakened by the sound, a small black pig rose from a corner, stretched, yawned, and trotted to Johnny Lamb, whose ankles it rubbed against, catlike. He scratched it behind the ears, smiling, then scooped it up and with a bob of apology took it to the trapdoor. He called the giant, whose upper half appeared, smoking a cigar, and handed him the piglet.

"I suppose Kaahumanu gave you that?" Ann said, with much more sourness than she had expected, shocking herself, indeed, by the sound of her own voice.

"Matter of fact, she did. Why?"

Ann shrugged, being unable to think of anything else to do.

Businesslike, Johnny Lamb returned to the point. There was, he said, no law against selling liquor in the islands. Came to that, there was no law at *all* in the islands.

"There's the law of God!"

" 'Tis variously interpreted."

"You should not mock it!"

"I haven't mocked it, ma'am. All I meant was that I'd rather hear the voice of our Maker direct than take Hiram Bingham's word for it."

"You don't like Reverend Mr. Bingham?"

"Not very much. Would you expect me to like a man who sends a woman to do his work for him?"

She sat upright, slamming one hand on an arm of the rocker, the other on the table.

"Just what do you mean by that, Captain?"

He opened his eyes very wide, and there was no hint of a smile on his mouth.

"Ma'am, could there be the slightest doubt of what I meant?"

She stood up, a ramrod.

"I'm going to leave!"

"You're welcome to stay as long as you want." He rose. "You won't get what you came for, of course — what you were sent for—but why not just sit around and act like folks for a while? I'm enjoying the visit. It's been a long spell since I've talked with anybody from Hartford."

"No, Kaahumanu isn't from Connecticut, is she?"

Frowning, he shook a puzzled head.

"I'm swouched if I see what Kate's got to do with it."

"I'm going," she said.

But her hand on the table rested on a book, the book he had been reading. Moving away, she jarred this, and it started

98

to slither off the table. Instinctively, not thinking, she straightened it—and saw what it was. She gasped. All amazement, she looked at Johnny Lamb. She looked at the book again. It was open, and there was a flat black jadeite marker carved in the likeness of K'wan Yin, the Chinese goddess of mercy. Incredulous still, needing to hear herself say the very words in order to bring belief, like a woman in a dream she read:

"The beauty of Israel is slain upon thy high place: how are the mighty fallen!"

"Tell it not in Gath, publish it not in the streets of something-something; lest the daughters of the Philistines rejoice, lest the daughters of the uncircumcised triumph," he finished with a fond grin. "Then there's that part a little further on, where it says something about the shield of the mighty being vilely cast away. I always like that, I don't know why. *Vilely* cast away . . ."

"You—you read this?"

"Oh, yes. I was taught to read, you know. As a boy."

"You sit in a heathen gown, and drink rum, and smoke a cigar—*and* read the Book!"

"It's really easy to do all four of those things at once. Just takes a little practice."

"Captain Lamb, my astonishment may be very amusing to you, but you must grant that it's natural. After all, you *are* an ungodly man."

"Because Hiram Bingham says so?"

"You can't deny that you sell liquor, and force your men to work on the Sabbath, and tolerate all sorts of rowdyism and prostitution."

"I don't have anything to do with prostitution."

"You don't deny that it exists here?"

"Course I don't. It'll exist in any seaport, naturally. But that ain't any part of my concern."

"Yours may not be the *legal* responsibility, no. As you yourself said, there isn't any law here anyway. But the *moral* responsibility's yours. And don't tell me I'm parroting Reverend

Mr. Bingham now, because I'm not. I would have said this and thought it even if Brother Bingham had never been born."

He shrugged.

"Well, maybe you're right. I won't argufy with you. Most of these whaler hands only understand one language, and I speak that pretty good." He looked at his fists. "I reckon I have more influence in this part of town than anybody else. Leastways I can't think of anybody on the island I can't whip — excepting one man, and he works for me." He chuckled. "If you can't lick 'em, hire 'em, eh? Here he comes now."

They heard the street door being shut, and steps across the floor and on the stairs, and Captain Lamb went over and took the piglet from the mighty hands of Humu, who thereupon jack-in-the-boxed back into darkness, leaving a wisp of smoke which surely was that of tobacco, not brimstone.

Johnny Lamb held the little pig in the crook of his left arm and with the fingers of his right hand stroked it behind the ears. The pig whuffled softly, and when he put it on the floor it trotted to its corner and flumped down flat, belly and chin, and lay looking up at him. He smiled at it.

"I call it Clarissa, for no particular reason. I just thought it ought to have a fancy name. They're easy to housebreak, you know."

He was not looking at Ann but at the animal, which was just as well, for she felt her face hot.

"I wonder why folks back home don't have pigs for pets, instead of dogs. Give 'em half a chance and they keep themselves perfectly clean. They'll eat anything. They're quiet. They're smart. And affectionate!—why, Clarissa here follows me everywhere. She even tries to go in after me when I go swimming, though she's scared to death of the water, and I have to rescue her."

"You don't like dogs?"

"Oh, I reckon I do all right. I just never really got to know a dog. Wasn't allowed to have one when I was a boy. And of course nobody could cotton to these poi mutts here. All they keep 'em for is to eat."

She winced.

"I — I actually ate part of one once," she whispered. "I didn't know it at the time, of course. It was when we first landed, at Kailua, and the King had us for a feast. It—it makes me sick to think of it."

"Don't think of it. I've eaten dog lots of times. You just take a swig of whiskey and keep on talking, that's all. It ain't bad."

He squatted beside Clarissa and tickled the back of the pig's neck. Ann noticed how easily he squatted, with an utter lack of self-consciousness. He always had got along well with the natives, no doubt because it flattered them to have a white man stoop to their practices. Eating dog, indeed! Clarissa grunted whooshingly and rolled her eyes.

"What I'd really like is a cat, but you can't get one here for love or money."

"You've tried both, I assume?"

"I've tried everything I know," soberly. "Plenty of them put in here. Hardly a ship ain't got at least one. But try and buy it! I know skippers'd give you anything you want—give you the shirt off their backs—only don't try to get the ship's cat out of them! Maybe it's superstition, I don't know. Maybe they're afraid of a mutiny. Whaler hands'll take most anything—short grub, floggings, wet quarters, practically no wages. But if you start to take the ship's cat away, you're in for trouble!"

And so this strong man, this notorious bully, squatting on his heels, stroking a pig, talked about how much he would like to own a pussycat. Only with difficulty did Ann resist a wild impulse to giggle. The strain caused her voice, when she did speak, to sound harsher than she meant it to.

"There are many unexpected things about you, Captain, but I think the strangest of all is that you read the Good Book and yet refuse to practice it."

101

He had been affable, but here she stepped too far. He flared.

"That's the trouble with you missionaries. You think the Book's your own private property. Religion mustn't be what a man believes inside him. Oh, no! It must be just what you dish out. If it don't come from the Bingham factory, it ain't the authentic article."

He was striding up and down, windmilling his arms. And Ann was sorry. She had in fact been rude. But she didn't know whether she wanted to admit this.

"Because I smoke means I shouldn't read Second Samuel! Because I like liquor means I'm depraved! Because I treat whores like human beings I'm a pimp!"

In anguish she turned away from him; and this brought before her a portion of the room she had not previously seen. Her anguish went. Rage rose inside of her.

Here was Kukailimoku the battle god, with its lank dirty human hair, its sharks' teeth, and empty twisted eyes. All hate and murderous fury, it grinned down from the top of its pole. Ann gave a little cry, and whirled around, breaking the spell with a snap that could almost be heard.

"Throw that thing out! I won't allow you to keep it!"

He stopped, pop-eyed.

"It's indecent! It's sacrilegious! I suppose your friend Kaahumanu gave you that, too?"

He said slowly, in a low bitter voice, "I still can't see what Kate has to do with this. Well, no! Wait! I guess I do, at that— The idea is to get her into the fold and she'd take care of the rest, eh? And by God, she would, too! She'd drive 'em to church with a horsewhip! But when you try a direct approach she laughs at you, right? So you're going to try to get *me* to put the bit in her mouth and fasten on the saddle, right? That means *I've* got to be won over first. So Hiram Bingham picks out the one unmarried woman he's got—which happens to be the only one with a bust that don't look like a knocked-down

102

tent—and he sends her here. He's read his Judith all right, that one! The trouble is, she messes the job by showing that she's flubbergumped to find me reading the Book and by criticizing my taste in decorations, which ain't the right way to go about it when you start to wheedle something out of somebody, ma'am."

She should have been contrite here. She should have defended Reverend Mr. Bingham and taken all the blame for this visit on herself. But he'd riled her, the way he went at it. Her chin tipped up.

"Maybe, Captain," icily, "you'll not be so high-and-mighty when I remind you that there's a murder indictment against you back home in Hartford."

He seemed honestly amazed, not at the news but at her mention of it.

"What's that got to do with it?" he asked.

"You killed a man and ran away."

"Sure. If I hadn't killed him, he'd've killed me. And if I hadn't've run away, the *others* would've killed me, his friends. They were all pretty drunk."

"In that case you should have given yourself up later."

"I should have," he agreed. "But what with the trial and all the hard feeling, I wouldn't have got any business done— and that's what I was back there for, to make connections that I could tie up to my trade here in Honolulu. So I figured I'd have to wait for things to cool off a mite. So when I got a chance to hop a whaler heading out this way, I did." He nodded, as though he had often thought about it and now once more found his conduct correct. "I'll go back some time and get that matter straightened out," he added.

"And in the meanwhile, Captain, suppose I should tell the authorities here that you're wanted for murder?"

He looked at her.

"What authorities?" he said.

The bells on ships in the harbor were being struck, each

103

bell three distinct times, here high and clear, there low, throaty, carrying well across the water. All sorts of bells spoke, some jangling with others, some sending forth sounds free and clear. Three bells—half past nine. After a moment the chorus ceased.

"What authorities?" he said again.

She relented. She was wrong, and she'd admit it. She had moved close to him as she made her threat—the threat that had blown up in her face—and now timidly she put a hand on his forearm. He almost jumped. She herself almost jumped. She stood breathless, not able to speak, looking down, afraid to look at him, afraid to take her hand away or to move or tighten it. Kukailimoku the baleful glared down at them, but she no longer thought of it. She couldn't have stirred had her life hung in the balance. Maybe it did? She trembled.

"Y'know," his voice was lower, quieter, and there was a thread of amusement in it now, "I've just thought of something."

She managed to raise her face, but she didn't otherwise move. Johnny Lamb was grinning at her now, very quietly.

"Y'know, it was *you* that night in that bedroom."

She wanted to shake her head but couldn't. It would not have done any good anyway. She felt her face go hot, and Johnny Lamb's grin broadened. Yet it was not a malicious grin, but rather tender.

"Of course," he whispered. "It was the Buttoner house. Didn't have time to figure that out, then. I just popped in through the first window I saw. But of course. . . past that pear orchard, sure. And it had to be you. Neither of those sisters of yours would've had the spunk to come flying back at me after I'd given 'em a good hard wallop on the ass."

He chuckled fondly. He took her arms.

"I gave you something else, there in the dark. Remember? I enjoyed that—Ann."

He drew her even closer, smiling. She couldn't close her eyes.

104

"We're on the other side of the world now, but it's the same thing here—Ann. Come on."

If they had heard Humu downstairs open and shut the outside door, they paid no attention; but the sounds that followed were not to be ignored. There was an outburst of voices in the street, one high and loud, squealing or screaming, scolding in Hawaiian; another angry; a third, the only intelligible one, booming in an urgent bass: *"Help! Help! Help!"*

Johnny Lamb spun on his heel and made for the trapdoor. "Stay here," he called. He went below.

She disobeyed him promptly, without hesitation. She was only a couple of leaps behind him when he flung open the street door.

Johnny fisted his hips and threw his head back, and you could have heard his laughter halfway to Diamond Head. Ann, behind him, peered under his arm.

The mighty Humu, that mountain of a man, had just pounced upon two skulkers, clad in black and for that reason not as easily seen as he himself was. They struggled violently, twisting, trying to punch; but Humu held them straight out, at arm's length, one on each side, as another man might have held up, by their ears, a couple of kicking rabbits. They were yelling. Humu was screaming—he had a high piping voice—first at them, then at Johnny the Lamb. He shook the men. He screamed that he'd thought he saw somebody lurking in the shadows when he took Clarissa out to make mimi, but he had pretended to see nothing then, and had returned to the house and listened at the door. These haoles, he screeched, had sneaked up to the door, one on each side. He'd heard them. He'd rushed out and grabbed them.

He shook them again.

Horace Crowell had ceased to struggle and hung limp and unresisting in the mighty hand, sobbing a bit in rage. Reverend Mr. Bingham still flapped his arms, and he still shouted in that fine deep resonant voice: *"Help! Help!"*

It was a full minute before Johnny Lamb could recover

105

himself sufficiently to call a command to Humu, who there-upon dropped his prisoners. It was dusty there in the darkness; the men fell into dust. Tut-tutting solicitously, Ann helped to brush them off. So did Johnny Lamb, as well as he could for laughing. It was all Ann herself could do to keep from breaking out.

"You were following me?" she asked at last.

Reverend Mr. Bingham bowed brittle agreement. Horace Crowell managed to smile.

"And then *you* had to rescue *us*," he said ruefully.

"Then that was your footsteps I kept hearing? They scared me half to death."

"You didn't look scared."

"I didn't dare to."

Horace peered around. There was nobody else in sight, but the darkness, you suspected, indeed you knew, had eyes and ears. Certainly this group was being watched and whispered about.

"We couldn't stand by and let you go alone. We, uh, didn't realize that you had a protector."

He looked at Humu.

"No disgrace to be manhandled by him, mister," Johnny said. "I have been, too, comes to that."

Reverend Mr. Bingham by this time had recovered suffi-ciently to trust himself to speak.

"Captain Lamb, this has been most regrettable. We realize that it was no fault of yours. But it will be all over town to-morrow."

"Sure will."

"I wonder if we, uh, if we could induce you to walk back to the mission with us. It's a beautiful night for a walk. Yes?"

"You'll be all right. I'll send Humu along."

"It, uh, it wasn't that, Captain. It was that I thought that your personal presence, which would be sure to be re-marked—"

106

"Oh, now I see!"

Johnny didn't like it. His brows drew low. His mouth tightened. One of those black moods was coming upon him; but Ann Mathewson went to him and put a hand on his forearm as she had done upstairs—the same hand, the same forearm. "Please?" she said.

He glowered a moment, then gave a grin.

"All right. If I can walk with you."

Clarissa and Humu stayed home to guard the store; but even without them this little party had dignity. The widow had put her poke back on, and Johnny had substituted a tail-coat for his Chinese robe and had clapped on a yellow beaver. He had hooked his arm at Ann, who accepted prettily. These two went ahead, Johnny sometimes turning to address one of the others, Reverend Mr. Bingham or Brother Crowell, who followed sedately—and not too close.

From everywhere, as they'd expected, they were watched. They seldom saw anybody, but they were seen—from the inside of huts, from doorways, between spread-apart thatch—and already the word was going around that Johnny the Lamb himself, the great Captain Johnny, had walked out as calm as you please with the Long Necks.

The moon rose with a weary shrug, as though doing the world a favor. The sound of the bells on ships came low and clear across the water as the party reached the mission house. Four bells, ten o'clock. Some of the strokes were high and clear, some throaty, but all were grave. And they were followed by silence.

Work was personal, painful, and it required patience. Those of the Family had to conduct regular services; write regular reports, formal and informal, for the folks back home; keep up the school; care for such natives as applied for spiritual or physical help; and—this was largely the province of the leader—do whatever they could to persuade the chiefs to set a better example. In addition, they had to guard themselves against the attacks of sailors and of jealous traders. Finally, and perhaps most tellingly, they had to do all their own washing, cooking, cleaning. It was this manual work that Ann Mathewson disliked the most, for when she did it she used no part of her mind, and she couldn't keep from thinking about Hartford. She would have given a great deal for a good full old-fashioned cry, with her head in her mother's lap; but these sneaky small scalding tears in the corners of her eyes never brought relief; and when she felt them she would lower her head a little and work on and on.

It was difficult to feel close to Jesus when your back ached. Sometimes, passing from one hut to another, she would pause a moment to stare up at Oahu's red hills, murmuring the while the words of the psalm: " . . . from whence cometh my help." But help *didn't* come. These were not the hills of the Connecticut River valley, but bare, dusty, depressing peaks, angular and stiff; and as she'd look at them Ann, so far from feeling a lift of spirits, could only groan, telling herself: "If I was to die in this place I'd be buried in this place — help me, help me, God!"

As she thought it, thought she might leave her remains in this dusty hot land so far from home, she'd shudder. This was not right, and not even logical. The Sandwich Islands were as much God's land as ever was Connecticut; and anyway it was the soul that counted, not the crass material body. All the same she would shudder. She was never going to forget the time they buried the Binghams' baby. Poor Sybil! She'd had a horrible time of it, and a long time. She very nearly was gathered to the arms of her Maker: for days it was touch-and-go. She got to the funeral, but they had to hold her up, she was so weak, Ann on one side, Jane Chamberlain on the other.

Lucy Parsons Bingham, duly christened, was not much of a baby. She didn't cry. She lacked the strength, poor thing. She lived just sixteen days; and they buried her back near the foot of the hills, at the edge of that dreary plain. Such a little coffin it was! Reverend Mr. Bingham had conducted the first Christian funeral in this part of the world with unfaltering solemnity, not missing a word, while his wife stood as straight as she could, trying not to lean hard on Ann Mathewson's arm. Neither of the Binghams ever referred to that baby again, at least in the presence of others; but Sybil, Ann knew, sometimes snatched time from her work to carry flowers back there to the tiny grave; and once she herself, Ann, going there with some palapalai, had found that baby's father, he of the unbending back, on his knees in prayer—and had tiptoed away without speaking to him, without leaving the ferns.

There was another thought she tried in vain to get rid of, and this was the speculation of what would have happened that night at Captain Lamb's if Horace Crowell and the Reverend Mr. Bingham had not been flushed and captured just when they were. Sometimes, eyeing them, she thought of them as saviors; at other times she was not so sure. Why had she gone there, truly? She often asked herself this. Would Johnny Lamb have kissed her, had they not been interrupted? She

109

was certain of it, certain, too, that she would have permitted it. She refused to lie to herself: she knew how she'd felt. Would he have tried to do more, and would she have permitted that, too? She didn't know. She did not like to think of it. She reminded herself almost savagely that after all the Lamb boy had lived down by the river; but it did no good. When she saw Johnny even at a distance—the only way she ever did see him these days—she would get all chokey and would have to lean against something or sit down. She saw him much more often in her mind's eye, and it was an image reeking with evil, for it was the memory of Johnny as he'd looked all naked on the mats in the Queen's palace after the horua run when natives were fisting him in a lomi-lomi. She remembered how white his skin was, how hard and bunchy his muscles. She remembered how straight he lay—straight-boned, firm.

She knew that such an image could spread poison through her mind, itself corrupting her. She thought that if only she could talk to somebody about the way she felt, it would help. She was so alone! But whom could she talk to? Johnny himself? She'd never dare. Of the white women on the *Thaddeus* she had been closest to Abigail Crowell, Horace's wife, who was on another island now. She loved Sybil Bingham, who was kindness incarnate; but though they lived under the same roof, prayed together, ate together, often worked side by side, and though they were about the same age, she and Sybil in fact had very little time to talk. Always at least one was busy. After all, it wasn't a thing you could blurt under your breath. Then, too, there was always back of Sybil, occasionally literally, the small somber, intensely in-turned figure of her husband, head of the Family. Most of all, Ann hated the thought of wounding Sybil, who would certainly be shocked to learn that one of her sisters, one of the Lord's Anointed, was or had recently been thinking thoughts like that. It would be cruel to hurt so gentle, so good a woman, all for the sake of getting some vulgar relief. Ann kept silent.

110

She tried in various ways, then, to cure herself. She tried to recall to memory the Lamb house in Hartford, Johnny, his playmates, that end of town generally. It did little good. She had never been a part of the life down by the river, had never wanted to be. Johnny as a boy? It was not now conceivable. So she would try a more positive approach, and do what she could to fetch back to her mind and memory the image of Jabez Mathewson, her late husband. This, too, was difficult. It had never occurred to her, until the time they chuted his poor sewed-up body into the sea, how little after all she had known her husband. He'd had a gentle voice, kind. He'd been a reader, always with a book. There was not much else. Though she bore the man's name, she could not rightly remember what he looked like.

Most revolting of all her thoughts, yet persistent, not to be denied, was this: Is it possible that some secret longing for this man Lamb brought me here? He had told me he was making for the Sandwich Islands. Would I have accepted Jabez if I had not known that? Would I have been as willing to do the Lord's work in some other part of the world?

She knew that the Devil sometimes took strange forms. Was she possessed, his pawn? For all her frantic protestations, was it after all sheer carnal desire that had driven her into this thing? Was she at bottom that most despicable of all sinners, the hypocrite?

The only time she met Johnny face to face in this period, she was rude to him.

That was when the King had come down with delirium tremens out at Waikiki. Members of the Family had decided that they should wait upon his Majesty night and day, taking turns. This was not to be a change but extra work, an added labor: they took it out of their sleeping time. They agreed to nurse the King physically as much as this might be permitted, to pray for him without pause, and to be prepared to give him instruction any time he asked for it.

111

Liholiho, though badly scared, never did ask for instruction. "Later, perhaps," he would murmur.

The member of the Family on duty was allowed a place at the royal bedside, but there was no nursing for them to do. Liholiho never had fewer than fifty body servants; and at least four or five times that many persons were outside, night and day, eager to be of help; for several weeks there, it was difficult even to get near the Waikiki palace.

As for praying, there was nothing against this, and so they prayed most of the time they were in attendance.

Possibly as a result of these prayers, the King recovered. He thanked the Lord's Anointed for their good wishes and their attention; but he (though still polite) deferred indefinitely a proffered explanation of the Word. "Later," he pleaded, smiling. Along with his wives and several hundred chiefs and slaves, he forthwith departed, by the royal yacht *Cleopatra's Barge* and sundry commandeered schooners, for a tour of the other islands. It was thought well to get him away from Honolulu and its too accessible liquor.

Just before he sailed he graciously and most unexpectedly granted permission to the missionaries to erect their house.

The house was to be a proper New England one. Part of it they'd brought with them; the rest, sent by the ABCFM people in Boston, had arrived aboard the ship *Tartar* on Christmas day, their first Christmas in the islands, though it was their second away from home. Rejoicing, praising the Lord, then, they had made preparations to erect it inside of their enclosure about half a mile from the village on the road to Waikiki. This was a flat hot dusty plain, a thoroughly uncomfortable place, and the three grass huts were already coming apart. It would be so good to have a real house with a real roof, a floor! It would be good to clean it, and to keep it clean. It would be, as they all knew, the first frame house between the Rocky Mountains and China, a decent white clapboard structure, and it would have windows, and the dust wouldn't

112

drift in through its walls, which would not need constant patching. Ecstatic, they dug a cellar.

Here they were stopped. It was pointed out that they had not obtained the King's permission to erect this fort. Fort? This wasn't to be a *fort!* Well then, they were asked, why did they dig a hole for the storage of gunpowder? What nonsense! Oh, no, they were told: Captain Charlton himself, the British consul, and several others, mostly English traders, had publicly explained that this proposed "house" was to be neither more nor less than the headquarters in which a revolution was to be hatched and from which the rebels would sally forth in order to annex the Sandwich Islands to the United States. That much was certain, attested, as everybody, including the King, knew. If they really wanted to put up their house, they had better see the King.

Fuming, they did. They demanded to be told whether Liholiho, Kamehameha II, believed that preposterous story; and he changed the subject, smiling apologetically. It is doubtful that he did believe it. Sober, Liho was nobody's fool. He himself, when he was originally urged not to permit the newcomers aboard the *Thaddeus* to land and to colonize, lest they prove to be no more than adventurers intent upon annexation—he himself had, very quietly, put forth an argument of crushing convincingness: "If they meant war," he had pointed out, "they wouldn't have brought their women."

All the same, the King was evasive and wouldn't speak out. He studied plans, nodding portentously, pursing his lips. He smiled deprecatingly whenever the gunpowder-in-the-cellar story was mentioned; and he was more gracious than ever in his manner, treating the missionaries as though they were chiefs; but he did not give them permission to build.

It was amazing that a man ordinarily so straighforward, and of so frank a personality, could quibble so successfully. There must have been some reason they couldn't see, the members of the Family decided; nor did they see it until their

113

friend James Hunnewell, he who had been mate of the *Thaddeus* and was a trader in Honolulu now, pointed it out to them.

"This is to be a two-story house," he said, "and big, at least compared with the huts around here, and white, and made of wood. Well, his Majesty just doesn't like the notion of anybody having a house bigger and grander than any of his palaces, that's all."

The simplicity of it—they were seated in one of the three grass huts, the one Ann Mathewson shared with the Binghams—the simplicity of it stunned them; and Reverend Mr. Thurston, after a moment, sighed and took refuge in quotation.

" 'Vanity of vanities . . . all is vanity and vexation of spirit.' "

"Not a bit," said Mr. Hunnewell. "It's plain business—the business of being a monarch. Liho's got to protect his position. Even in civilized countries the king's got to have the biggest house. That is, if he wants to go on being king."

"The House of the Lord *should* be the biggest house," said Reverend Mr. Bingham, "anywhere."

"Agreed, sir," said Mr. Hunnewell. "But Liholiho may not see it that way. To him it is what the Chinese'd call a matter of face."

The proceedings dragged, until the King's collapse put them entirely to one side; and his Majesty's decision to permit the building—a decision announced after he had already boarded his yacht—caused joy in the Family.

There were two explanations of the grant. One was that it was an answer to their prayers. The other was that it was in part an answer to their prayers and in part was due to the fact that the King had been touched by their devotion to him in his illness. Ann Mathewson had an opinion of her own, but she did not voice it. She believed that Liholiho had had practically nothing to do with the matter, and that the real relenting had been on the part of Kaahumanu the dowager as a result of the importunities of Johnny Lamb; and Ann secretly exulted that she was the cause of it.

114

In another way, however, she was not so pleased. This meant that Johnny Lamb really did have great influence over the Queen. Was this influence the outcome of an unspeakable connection, a sin against God? She did not want to think about it, though she did think about it, and often, and it made her sick.

Undeniably, and whatever the reason, there had been a change in the relations between the Family on one side, and the bullyboy of the beach on the other. He was scornful in his manner, as before, and in many ways remained aloof. He refused even to listen to pleas that he cease to sell rum, nor would he shut up shop on the Sabbath if there were any customers in sight; but he did pass out word that the girls were no longer to swim to ships. That was all he needed to do—pass out the word. His power in those parts was prodigious. There was a great deal of hard feeling, and Johnny was threatened many times, even his life being threatened; but he only laughed. When they accused him of truckling to the missionaries, he laughed again.

"Better for business this way. Let 'em come ashore for it. Where else in the world would you expect to have it delivered on board? Those girls! Why, they must have given away thousands of dollars' worth before they even knew they could sell it!"

The whalers departed, sore; but in the spring they returned in greater numbers than ever, and it was then, so they heard at the mission, that Captain Lamb met real opposition. Well, he stood firm. There was a deal of spluttering and swearing; voices were raised, fists, too; but the girls did not swim out to the ships.

Johnny seldom left the beach, and when he did it was usually for a surfboarding party at Waikiki or a picnic back in the Manoa Valley with Kaahumanu and her following, when, as they of the Family heard, the gambling was shameless and lasted far into the night. Since their own business seldom took them to the beach, they saw little of their curious

115

champion there. Sometimes late in the afternoon he would ride past the mission compound, and if the children were cantillating, as they customarily were at that hour, he would stop his horse and listen awhile, smiling, his head to one side, his lips moving as he recited the remembered words. He even used to swing his hand a bit, as though keeping time to music.

> Cross words and angry names require
> To be chastised at school;
> And he's in danger of hell-fire
> That calls his brother, Fool.
> But lips that dare to be profane,
> To mock and jeer and scoff
> At holy things or holy men,
> The Lord shall cut them off.

He would not dismount, and after a while, still smiling, he'd ride on. He liked children. There were always children around his shop, some of them children who were supposed to be learning Dr. Watts's verses in school. Children trailed him when he moved about the waterfront, and they were permitted to play, hilarious and innocent, among the kegs and cordage in his warehouse. He fed them gumdrops.

When the whaling fleet came back in the spring, the missionaries did not see him at all, yet even then they sometimes heard from him unexpectedly—and indirectly. For instance, nobody attributed it to prayer when some servants of Kaahumanu appeared at the mission one day with a dozen small halas, the fastest-growing kind of shade tree. Members of the Family suffered from the heat, the dust, the glare, in that windswept plain; but they'd been too busy, this past almost-a-year, to give thought to their own comfort. Hala trees would help wonderfully. The Queen was thanked, which thanks she received with studied disdain; and the trees were planted and watered. Of course, Kaahumanu *might* have thought of them herself. It *might* have been she who noticed how exposed to the sun the mission huts were. Whoever it was, it was good to have the halas.

116

The time of Liholiho's collapse was the time when Johnny Lamb was busiest, both inner and outer harbors being crammed with ships and the waterfront alive with men; but he managed every day either to ride out to the palace at Waikiki or send a servant out to inquire after the condition of the King.

When Ann encountered him, she had just been relieved after one of the longest and most terrible of the vigils; and this was why she was unfair. Her heart thudded laboriously, dammed by blood, as her throat was choked by grief, her eyes wet with tears. She wasn't herself.

There is a notion among certain nitwits, who are without experience in the matter and have formed their opinions from the talk or drawings or writings of other nitwits concerning pink elephants and such, that there is something funny about delirium tremens. There isn't. It is one of the most horrible of all ailments to watch; it is worse even than hydrophobia, which stiffens the patient and turns him black while it kills him slowly; worse than yellowjack, which makes him ache all over, and vomit up black stuff, and bleed at the gums, and have the whites of his eyes turn yellow, his skin turn orange-yellow and later a nasty green . . . . Delirium tremens is worse than these, and worse than others. And his Majesty Liholiho, King Kamehameha II, suffered an especially severe attack.

Ann thought, kneeling there, that she would never survive that vigil. She was afraid she'd swoon. She kept her head averted, her hands clasped under her chin; but though she could keep herself from seeing the poor man a few feet away, she could not help hearing him, for his cries filled the palace, or smelling him. He thrashed about, knowing nobody, afraid of everybody and everything, shrieking in fear when anybody touched him in an effort to restrain him. Sometimes his voice sank to a thin whimpering; more often it rose to a scream. Occasionally for a little while he would simply groan, for the pain gave him no rest.

Delirium tremens patients do not suggest the gardenia.

Large though the bedchamber was, it was crowded with natives who themselves sweated in sympathetic agony with their monarch; and of course there were no windows. The direct smell of the King himself was compounded chiefly of sweat—for he sweated profusely—and the sharper, more pungent odor of urine. Evidently he could not control his bladder, even in moments of comparative lucidity. For five days he had been passing water almost without pause, a thin persistent dribble. He burned with fever, and when he could be induced to touch them, drained large number of coconuts.

When Lucy Thurston, seven months' pregnant, slipped into place beside her, Ann knew that it was none too soon. She rose without a whisper—it wouldn't have been heard anyway, for the King was screaming—and forced herself to look at him a moment. He was arched high, as though in paralysis, so that his buttocks did not touch the mats, and sweat rolled off every part of his great fat oily body. He held his hands before his face, trying to ward off some evil thing. He screamed with amazing strength. Ann shuddered. She had been kneeling for more than three hours, and her legs were stiff, her knees were sore, besides which her stomach whambled warningly, so that she was dizzy, unsteady. She not only brushed against but actually lurched against several natives on the way out, and this dismayed her. She was afraid that she might not make the door.

Just outside, gasping in relief, she encountered Johnny Lamb, who was about to enter the bedchamber. He came toward her, lifting his hat, looking properly grave; but she flared at him.

"*I hope you're happy. I hope you're proud of what you've done.*"

She jerked her head toward the room the screams came from; and then she swept away.

118

View of a House 15

If Johnny was offended, if he held it against her, there was no sign of this. It was only three days after the incident that there arrived at the mission house that same old-fashioned Connecticut rocking chair she had sat in the night of her visit to him, and with it a note that said that Captain Lamb was too busy these days to use the chair and wouldn't she care to do so? He finished by wishing her, very formally, a happy birthday.

How in the world he had known that it was her birthday, she couldn't guess. Nobody else knew it, on this side of the world. She had not expected anything. It made her cry a good deal all through that afternoon and into the night, which was bad, for she needed the sleep.

She loved the chair. She thought of sending it back, but she didn't think of this long: it was too precious to renounce. She knew from the beginning that it would be a temptation to be at all times resisted, for it could easily lead her into ways of sloth; and she only permitted herself to sit in it when it was absolutely certain that there was no work remaining on hand for her to do, so that she surely wasn't shirking anything, and even then she would not permit herself to sit there *long*. The others, and especially the women, were like her delighted with the chair — and afraid of its possible influence. They would not sit in it when Ann was present — or at least not unless she pressed them to do so. Even Reverend Mr. Bingham himself once sat in the chair and rocked back and forth several times; he got up from it with a start, as though it had burned him, or as though he had begun to enjoy himself; but he did pronounce it to be very comfortable, very comfortable indeed.

It was Ann's chair, her very own, the most valuable worldly possession she had, she reckoned—though the d'Angoulême poke in many ways meant more to her, perhaps just because it was a secret.

She wrote Johnny Lamb a long and somewhat effusive letter of thanks, but she tore this up. She wrote a shorter, much more formal note; and she almost tore this up, too, but she sent it.

So now she had a material reminder of Johnny Lamb, as though she had needed anything of the sort! She told herself with firmness and great good sense that she was only making herself miserable by permitting herself to think of him. The thing was hopeless. She was no longer a free agent, if she ever had been; she was a dedicated woman now. It was not like being a Roman Catholic nun; but in one important respect perhaps it wasn't so different, at that. Marriage was not prohibited, but it was a mighty remote possibility; and if she should be married it would surely not be to anybody at all like Captain Lamb. He wouldn't want her, in the first place. He liked fat dark women. And she wouldn't have him if he did want her. It was true that he had a lovely smile, and his manners could be really quite polished when he wished 'em to be, and it was true, too, that he was doing very well with that commission business of his; but who could dream of marrying a man who drank and gambled, who worked on the Sabbath?

So she would tell herself, waxing stern. But then a few minutes later she would walk past the rocking chair, and see it there, maybe even brush against it; and the next thing she knew it was hard to give attention to her work because of the tears in her eyes.

As soon as permission was granted, they started raising the house, everybody helping, even the school children. They lined the cellar with adobe bricks made of mud and dried grass;

120

they laid the floor; they lifted beams into place. It was trying work, chiefly because the natives who assisted refused to take it seriously, treating the whole matter as a lark. There were screams of laughter at the most inappropriate times; and when anything fell, or conspicuously failed to fit, that was considered hilariously funny.

Also, there were too many visitors. The islanders made a party of it. They slipped into the enclosure. They cheered and applauded. Soon for every man or woman actually working there were at least four or five friends stretched full-length, chatting, laughing, eating bananas. It was confusing, and it was hardly the proper spirit in which to go about the Lord's labor.

Nevertheless in time the house was assembled, a wonderful thing.

It was larger than Johnny Lamb's house, though not as large as either of the houses Kaahumanu and Liholiho were causing to be built inside the royal enclosure in Honolulu, plans for which had been approved and the lumber obtained before permission to build the mission house was granted. Yet though the new palaces were downtown, near the fort, their construction did not attract as much attention as did that of the mission building. For one thing, the mission building had been so much more discussed, and there were hundreds who still believed that explosives-in-the-cellar story. Then, too, the royal palisade was high, and the gate was guarded, so that not many persons managed to slip inside, most of the curious being obliged to satisfy themselves with peeks through the gateway. *Anybody* could get through the gateway of the mission enclosure, or else over or through the flimsy low palisade, and almost everybody did. The building of the two palaces might have been a grander and more awe-inspiring job, but the raising of the mission house was a greater social success.

Still, eventually the building was there, almost complete.

121

Only one room was finished inside, or finished enough for occupancy, and that was a large room downstairs which it had been agreed should be turned over to the Chamberlains and their six children, a decision applauded by the workers and their friends the spectators, by whom the children, the only ones in the Family, were greatly beloved.

The Chamberlains would not be much more comfortable there, for the present, than they had been in their grass house, but they would assuredly be safer from the danger of fire.

Yet from the outside it was a complete house, a proper house. If you stood a little distance away and looked at it from under half-lowered eyelids, as Ann Mathewson was fond of doing whenever she got a chance, you could sometimes, for a minute, almost fool yourself into thinking that you were back home.

There were no palm trees or banana trees immediately around, to spoil the illusion, and the hala trees still didn't amount to much.

What it most needed, to be sure, was snow, and those windows sealed-shut, the way they would be at home. But there are limits to the imagination. Ann had seen the white stuff on Mauna Kea, on the island of Hawaii, when they first arrived. She doubted that she would ever see it again, unless it was in the same place. She would never, she reflected as she shaded her eyes, as she squinted appraisingly at the new building—she would never again stand at a rime-edged window and look out at the hurly-burly of falling snow. She would never again spread arms and legs and fall backward into new snow, to make an "angel." She would never laugh in sheer exuberance as she kicked snow off her shoes before going indoors.

She sighed, and strove to bring her thoughts to bear upon a less lugubrious subject.

The house was a good house all right. It was square and gabled, of two stories, plain, as a house should be, clapboarded, painted white. There was no fanlight over the door—

that would have been asking too much—but the door itself was green and trim and plain, making no concession to fashion. It lacked a knocker, and she envied Captain Lamb his. There was, true, no need for a knocker, for the door would seldom be closed, much less locked; but it would be a comforting thing to have. She might ask Captain Lamb, next time she happened to see him, if he would try to get them a knocker: he had contact with so many New England ship captains. But no, she wouldn't do that. She owed him too much already. Shading her eyes, frowning, annoyed with herself for even at a time like this thinking about Johnny Lamb, she determined then and there to have nothing more to do with him—aside, of course, from whatever association actual politeness demanded. She would forget him; she'd put him out of her mind.

What *was* it that the house lacked, really? What always punctured the illusion?

"A handsome edifice, señora. I make no doubt that you have great pride in it, eh?"

"Good morning, Señor Marin. We have been taught that pride is a feeling to be shunned. 'Though thou exalt thyself as the eagle, and though thou set thy nest among the stars, thence will I bring thee down, saith the Lord.'"

The Spaniard was startled, for he had not yet become accustomed to the way these newcomers quoted the Bible, a book of Latin to him, one better left to the priests. He made a little outward motion of deprecation. He was old and small.

"Ah, true, señora! Still, is it not true also that at such a time as this you feel a lee-tle smitch of it in your heart, eh?"

"Oh, a little smitch maybe," she said, and smiled.

She was fond of Don Francisco de Paula Marin, a trader who had been living on this island long before the arrival of the Family. He was called "Manini," that being as near as the natives could get to "Marin." Unfailingly amiable, calm, well informed, the master of half a dozen languages, he knew all the ins and outs of the court, all the intricacies of rank and

123

precedent; and despite the fact that he was himself an admitted Roman Catholic—he made no bones about it—he had been helpful as an interpreter and go-between.

Nobody knew—it didn't do any good to ask *him!*—how Marin had got to the islands in the first place. An incorrigible gossip, he yet wrapped his personal affairs in secrecy. He had no partners, no associates. He lived in a small house near the mission, a house with a high wall around it. Now and then a ship's captain might be invited to that house; but no resident had ever been there. Few had ever even seen past the gate to the fabulous garden in which Don Francisco spent so much time. It was said that he raised in that garden a kind of poppy unknown elsewhere in the world, and that it was because of narcotics that he was able to get such good terms from the skippers. But then, a great many things like this were said about Don Francisco, who would smile blandly, neither affirming nor denying them.

Ann liked him, but she never did see any need to pay him much mind. He carried manners to the point where they became artificial and meaningless, so that when he talked to you he was doing so only from a sense of duty and didn't really expect you to listen.

"I know!" she cried. "It's the rocks!"

"I ask your pardon, señora?"

"I'm sorry. Excuse me, señor. Do go on with what you were saying—it's so interesting."

Yes, the rocks. That was the big difference. At home, snow or no snow, night or day, there were always, everywhere, rocks. Rocks were the foundations of houses, and slabs of rock were paths. Rocks were walls and doorsteps. Rocks in fields untended thrust themselves up through the crust of the earth, more and more each spring, as though they were some sort of tribute offered by the forces below, so that the good gray granite was everywhere. Here there was nothing like that, no gneiss or trap, no quartzite (a respectable substance), or Stockbridge limestone, or Canaan marble, stuff which would last . . . . How

124

she longed for the rocks of Connecticut, bleak but hard, grim, glum, rocks with nothing frivolous about them, that were fixing to stay in place a long, long while. Why, this crumbled red porous flaky flaccid lava here, and the coral from the reef, unstable, unreliable, soft—you couldn't make a fence out of that, you couldn't make *anything* out of it!

And where were the gravestones? What manner of people was this, that had no burying-grounds? As much as any other occupation Ann Mathewson missed the little lazy walks she used to take through Connecticut cemeteries. Surely there had been nothing morbid in that, nor had she ever, in those places, felt sad — a poetic melancholy sometimes, perhaps, but real sadness never. The graveyards she had known were good graveyards, well positioned, carefully kept, respected. What was there to sniffle over in the sight of those fine unslanting slabs of slate commemorating the names of men and women who had waited upright for death, scorning to cringe away from it, and who at last were laid by the side of their ancestors? In her mind's eye Ann right now could see the sedate stones, the correct unimpassioned lettering, the winged skulls (most of these had no lower jaws, and she had often wondered whether this was meant to show that when the soul ascends to Heaven the baser parts fall away and are lost), the cherubs with their fat serious faces, and the hourglasses and cornucopias and Gabriel's trumps, the urns over which weeping willows wept without real grief but gracefully and well. Nothing dolorous there.

But these islanders, they had no tombs, no monuments to the beloved dead. Often, when they didn't want 'em, they killed their babies and buried these, but they never marked the spot. When an adult died it was thought a fearful portent, a disgrace as well, and his body or hers was hustled away furtively, in the dark of night, to be dismembered in some undisclosed place, amid the greatest secrecy, and the parts scattered and well hidden, as much as possible destroyed, after which

125

the whole business was never mentioned again. Why were they so afraid of death, these poor benighted creatures?

Well, it would be different when they had received the Word, when they listened—if they ever did. Ann sighed.

" . . . so you do not think so, señora?"

"Eh? Oh, I beg your pardon. What was it you said?"

"I said that Capitan Lamb, he should know the men of the beach. He should know what to expect. I think he did. He showed a fool's courage when he insisted that the swimming-out should cease."

"What's this? . . . What? . . . Señor, is Johnny Lamb hurt?"

She was shaking him, a circumstance he pretended to ignore. She shook him like a doll, so that his few remaining teeth clattered together. She had her face down close to his.

"Did you not hear me, perhaps, señora?" He remained dignified, even while being shaken. "I had been saying that they set upon Captain Lamb last night. There were five or six of them, and they surprised him in a dark place when he was alone."

"Did they—did they—?"

"I believe that he was not killed. Not quite. I am told that he had been, uh, indulging rather heavily, and that this was another reason why they ventured to assault him. I am told, though, that he put up a magnificent fight, in spite of this. He would. But they certainly thought he was dead when they left him. But, señora—"

Don Francisco was alone. This did not seem to amaze him. He fingered his nose, and shrugged ever so slightly, as with a bemused smile he watched Ann Mathewson, her skirts hitched high, run down toward the beach. He clucked his tongue, shook his head.

"I had heard it . . . I'd heard it," he whispered to himself. "But I never believed it, until now."

He went into the mission house. Here was a tale worth telling.

126

The Hire of the Harlot　　16

There was a man outside, a gawky big sailor, and he turned when he heard footsteps, and spread his arms as though to catch her.

It could be that he meant the gesture in mere playfulness, intending no harm or insult. She did not pause to find out. He was in her way, that was all she cared about, and with no hesitation she slapped his face—hard. He roared with rage or amazement, and she slipped under his arm and darted through the doorway.

A tall man faced her, a pistol in his hand. The pistol was pointed at her. It was cocked.

"Oh," she said, and stopped stock-still; and for a small part of a moment everything in the world was motionless. "Oh."

The gawky sailor pounded into the shop, and like her stopped short at the sight of the pistol, and at the same time Humu came tumbling downstairs.

The man with the pistol, the tall one, uncocked it; and he, too, said, "Oh." He put the pistol down on a counter.

"So it's you?" he said. "Excuse the greeting. I was expecting somebody else, somebody that's *not* a mission worker. But sit down. Can I fetch you some tea?"

To be sure, it was dim in the shop, but even then, how could she have failed, even for an instant, to recognize Johnny Lamb? The shock, she supposed. And she must unconsciously have expected to find him upstairs in bed.

He sold the sailor a plug of tobacco and shooed him out, and brusquely, almost contemptuously, he sent Humu upstairs to make tea. He looked frightful, and he knew it and was embarrassed. He carried himself with all the old-time jauntiness: he still looked prepared to thumb his nose at the whole wide world, and his clothes were trig—cream-colored kerseymere breeches, a white waistcoat powdered with silver, a wine-colored cravat, and when Ann arrived he slipped on a blue coat with steel buttons. It was his face that fascinated, the way some squashed animal might, so that Ann, all but screaming, could not take her eyes from it. It was hideously puffed, seeming to be at least twice its ordinary size, and between the bandages it showed a pulped red. His hands, too, were swollen and red, the knuckles enormous.

He slipped a keg under her, and lowered her gently onto this.

"You'll be all right in just a minute. I'll try to keep my head turned away."

"I — I thought you were hurt."

"Anything about my looks to make you think I'm not?"

"But—I mean—"

"I got no assistant," dryly, "to trust the business to. And besides, I want to be on hand to find out who my playmates last night were. I'm aiming to have another tussle with them— one by one."

She smoothed an already smooth skirt with hands that trembled.

" 'It is wrong to put on the garments of vengeance for clothing.' "

"It wasn't when Isaiah wrote that. Or Amos. Whichever it was."

" 'Vengeance is mine, saith the Lord.' "

"It's going to be mine, too, soon as I get set. I know three of 'em already, and I'll learn the others, don't worry!"

She hated herself for the way she talked, but she did not mean anything like that at all. She had intended to commiserate with him, to offer to nurse him and pray for him. How-

128

ever wicked the violence itself, it had been brought about by his willingness to co-operate with the members of the mission. Ann herself, indeed, was probably more responsible than any other person for his present condition. She was contrite. But the words that came out of her were prudish and disapproving, and sounded self-righteous. Why was it that he so often affected her that way?

"You should have turned the other cheek."

"They didn't give me a chance to turn either cheek. They were lamming me from both sides at once, and from the front and back at the same time. Besides, I always did hold more with the Old Testament than with the New. An eye for an eye, you know. That's Exodus."

"Yes, I know."

It was not until then that she realized that she must almost have swooned, a little before, when she first saw him. The blood must have left her head: her face still felt cold. He replaced her upon another keg, not so near the door. He himself faced the door across a counter, on which, aimed toward the door, was the pistol. It was a shadowy place, and he kept his head turned away from her. Even then, she was shocked. His voice alone, low, bitter, harsh, and just the memory of that face, shocked her. Here was the real Johnny Lamb. Now she was seeing him at his worst, which perhaps would be a good thing for her, who previously had not seen enough of him to chase away a dream. This was what he truly was—a low man, a ruffian, vengeful, vindictive. She was glad that she had been granted a chance to see him like this.

"And it ain't only personal, either," he said unexpectedly. It was odd, having him talk with his face turned away. "If I don't get those boys who got me last night, I might just as well shut up shop and go out of business. That's the kind of place this place is. You may not understand it, living back there at the mission, but that's the kind of place it is all right. Yes."

"Bestial—" she whispered.

129

"I didn't make it that way, remember. But if you want to do business you got to take things like you find them. Here's Humu. Have some tea."

It was excellent tea. And there were sweet crackers to go with it, a treat.

Clarissa came out from behind the counter, and Johnny Lamb gave it a cracker and tickled it behind the ears, talking to it, seeming to be glad of something to do. His voice was low and gentle when he talked to the pig. ....

"She's a sunbeam. Oh, she's a perfect sunbeam . . . . Now clean up those crumbs."

Clarissa farted thoughtfully, and trundled off to a corner, not having finished the crumbs. Soon it was asleep.

Some customers came in, obviously sailors, and Johnny Lamb waited on them. They were gruff men, but sober and low-spoken. They glanced at Ann, where she sat on a keg holding a teacup, and clearly they were flabbergasted; but they touched their caps and mumbled something meant to be manners, and Ann managed a smile. They showed no expression when they looked into Johnny's face, though it was probably what they had come to see. The things they bought were small personal things, shipboard articles, not all of which Ann knew the use of; and Johnny waited on them with cool detachment, neither curt nor obsequious. Ann tried to feel contempt for him. She had not the slightest scorn of trade itself, and never could understand why anybody should have, the way the English were said to. Her own father had been a merchant, dead these three years now, and had worked in his own store in Hartford. Jabez Mathewson's people were shopkeepers, which was why Jabez had been able to go to Yale College. Still, a man *can* look contemptible when he is waiting on somebody across a counter. Johnny Lamb didn't.

Ann began to look around. She had never before seen the inside of this shop, having only passed through it in darkness the night she called on Johnny upstairs. It was a large cool dim place, crowded with bulky objects, somewhat shapeless objects, and suggested at once a warehouse and a rigging loft. There were many large barrels and crates, many coils of rope, and from the walls hung reeves and blocks and dead-eyes. Nothing was labeled or marked, but Johnny Lamb unhesitatingly knew where everything was and what it cost.

On the way out, one of the sailors spotted a case of French brandy, and drew forth and examined a bottle of this.

"How much?"

"Ain't for sale."

The man put the bottle back, and they went out, as Ann turned a tremulous smile on Captain Lamb. He shook his head.

"Not what you're thinking. That don't mean I'm giving up handling spirits. That brandy happens to belong to my best customer, Liholiho."

"The King!"

"Yes. Before he went on tour he swore he was never going to touch another drop. Didn't even want the stuff around the palace. So he asked me if I'd take back all he had, six cases of brandy. So of course I said sure. He owes me a heap of money already, or at least he owes the parties I represent, so all I had to do was credit his account. I didn't charge for the service."

"Then why don't you sell the brandy?"

"Because he'll want it back. And if I haven't got it in stock he'll buy it somewhere else. I don't want to lose my best customer. Especially when he owes me so much money."

"I think that's— Haven't you any respect for the King's word?"

"About other things, yes. Not about rum. I've known drunks before."

"I think that's base!"

"Maybe. But it's business."

"Couldn't you refuse to sell to him?"

"Sure. And I could also throw money into the lagoon, to

131

watch it sink. He'll get all he wants. He might as well get it from me. Kate knows that—Kaahumanu. She's asked me not to drink with him, or anyway not *start* drinking with him, and I said I wouldn't. But even she knows better than to ask me not to sell him the stuff."

"When *I* asked you not to drink with him you went right ahead."

"He was well started then. Besides, that was some months ago, before I saw how bad he could be when he gets to really hitting it up. He's a humdinger all right."

"*We* pray for him."

"Well, that's one way, I guess."

Some men came in, and priced things, and went. Clearly they had not wanted to buy anything, only to get a look at Johnny — or perhaps at Ann, whose presence in the shop by this time undoubtedly had been reported up and down the beach. Ann had already learned that waterfront folks are among the most gossipy in the world. The native Sandwich Islanders, too, having nothing much else to do, loved to talk about people. This did not disgust Ann Mathewson, only puzzled her. At the mission they had no time for gossip. They were seldom together, for one thing, before the evening meal, supper, by which time they were tired and not inclined to be chatty. At supper, too, it was their custom to talk over plans for the following day, and immediately after supper, and after evening prayers, they would go to bed.

Johnny got rid of the men easily, and Ann looked at him. She had better get control of herself now.

"I'm sorry I acted so sharp, a little while back," she said. "I declare, I don't know what gets into me sometimes."

"I know how you feel. I get that way myself sometimes. And particularly with you."

"You do?"

She rose, and went to him. He did not turn his head. She paused, her hands laid on her breast.

132

"I—I wanted to thank you. I came here to find out how wounded you were, but it's a good chance to thank you for helping us."

"All right," he said, not looking at her.

She went closer, stepping around back of the counter. She stood very near him, bending forward.

She would never understand this man. He straightened, from leaning on the counter, and faced her. He even put out his hands a little, and it was then that she closed her eyes and raised her face. Did he take the closing of the eyes amiss, thinking that she could not bear the sight of him? Whatever the reason, if there was one, when he spoke his voice was a cutlass.

"I see," he said. "I'm about to get paid, eh?" He rubbered out his lips. "I reckon this is what Micah the Morasthite would have called the hire of the harlot, eh?"

She felt her face go hot, as though somebody had slapped it with a hot wet towel. She was acquainted with Biblical words which out of their texts would have been unrespectable among decent folks. Many a time she had read "whoredom" and "harlot" and "damn" and "hell" and even that horrid word that occurred so often (and to Ann unaccountably) in the latter part of Ist Kings. She had heard these, too. But it was one thing when the Reverend Mr. Bingham uttered such a word from the pulpit in his rich, resonant, scrupulously sexless baritone; it was quite another when Johnny Lamb of River Street said it.

Besides, the implication was that she had been about to let him kiss her, and this of course infuriated her.

"You are mistaken, Captain," she said after a careful moment. "No sort of payment was even thought of. Good day, sir."

"Don't go. I get like that sometimes. Ornery. When I'm kind of worked up about a fight . . . . I didn't mean it."

"Good day."

133

There was a small crowd outside. They made way for her readily enough. They didn't appear to be doing anything, just standing there. They broke up with an almost audible movement of separation, a "click," a "ping," when Johnny the Lamb appeared in the doorway.

"Please don't go," Johnny said, not to the loafers.

She did not answer. Her back was rigid, her head high, and though from habit she clasped her hands before her, there was no touch of humility in the position. She walked away.

Johnny stood in the doorway, heedless of glances that calculated the extent of his bruises and cuts, and he shook a sad head as he gazed after her. Touchy. Well, he couldn't say as he blamed her. He ought to've been more soft-talked, ought to've sung small.

He watched her go.

She had a damn' pretty behind. Nothing *robust* about it maybe, but it was firm and had a good shape.

He sighed, and turned back into the shop.

A Talk of Two Women   17

Seated on a high stool, then, the pistol within reach, and cocked, Johnny Lamb got out the ledgers. Johnny could keep things in his head, but he preferred to see them on paper. The sight of the figures themselves invigorated him. When he was a boy and had to split wood all afternoon, from time to time he would pause for a look at the pile. It helped, to see how high it was. He felt that way about his figures. He loved to check and double-check them, all but caressing them like handle-able things, as a Chinese collector, say, turns his prized jades over and over, running his fingers across them. Nobody had ever taught Johnny how to keep accounts in a book. He had worked it out by himself. The system, if such it could be called, was unique, his own, and nobody else could have made head or tail of it. Johnny gloried in it. And he knew nothing better for taking his mind off things—such as, right now, for example, the memory of that Buttoner girl's backside as she walked up the lane. He opened a ledger.

In a little while he fell to shaking his head. It was the old story. He was making money sure enough, but making it for other men, men who weren't even here on this side of the earth. Like the way he'd told Kaahumanu it was with whaling—the only ones who got rich were the owners. He was tired of doing other men's work for them and passing on most of the cash. Tarnation! He was as much of a servant on land as he had been at sea. It was more lucrative here, but it came to the same thing. It would take a long, long while to get wealthy, the way he was operating now.

Half closing his eyes, he raised his head, and his lips were still moving, as though from momemtum, with figures that no longer meant anything in his mind. What he needed, then, was to be an owner. He needed to get back and tighten his connections in Boston, Hartford, Providence, Newport, and meet these moneyed men face to face, and hammer on the table, demanding a larger share. He'd get it, too! They would have to listen to him.

So he would go back home and buy a small ship. He'd sail that ship back. With the organization he had here, and with his own reputation, with the work he had already done, he could arrange that the ship owned by him would make fair buckets of money right here in Honolulu—in part out of the whalers, even more out of the Chinese ships that were touching here in increasing numbers. *Then* he would finally go home, rich.

What he needed first was a stake. His own cash was tied

up in the shop. Nor would he take money from Kaahumanu. Anything else—but not money. A man had to draw the line somewhere.

He shut his eyes entirely. And it was then that he became conscious of a curious sound from upstairs, a sound he might well have been hearing all this time without noting it, for it was not unfamiliar. Humu up there was singing, probably to the piglet Clarissa, of which Humu was incredibly fond, for it was a lullaby, though an obscene one. Humu had a high, piping, shrilly thin voice, a voice that sounded as though it needed oil; and though he did show a certain rhythm, and did not lack enthusiasm, he had no sense of pitch.

Johnny the Lamb opened his eyes. He began to smile.

He was extremely happy in that moment, having thought of something brilliant; but he was still alert, if not as twitchy as he'd been a little earlier; and when he heard a crowd approaching, he rose. The pistol behind him, he went to the door.

They were baiting Reverend Mr. Bingham, seven or eight of them, grown men, rough men, behaving like badly brought-up boys, mischievous, malicious, cruel. They were throwing chunks of coral at him, poking him with sticks. He ignored them as best he could. Though in some danger—not immediately but it could develop into that—he showed no glint of irritation, much less of anger. When somebody knocked off his hat, he picked it up and replaced it. Even when a man tripped him from behind and he sprawled to hands and knees in the dust, he rose, brushed himself, and walked on without a word or glance.

"That'll do," Johnny said from the doorway.

He did not display the pistol, but he was obeyed. This made him feel good. He didn't smile—he had to be careful about moving any part of his bandaged face—but he felt warm and tingly inside. His authority was still sound. He'd been mauled; but while he was alive he was lethal. They jumped when he spoke. Good.

136

"Come in, Parson. I'd sort of been expecting you. Sit down. That keg of nails is about the best place, I guess."

"Thank you."

They studied one another, not warily, not furtively, for these were forthright men, guileless, direct.

Johnny was much the larger. It was not only a matter of inches and pounds: Johnny was bigger all over, and looked even bigger than he was; and the opposite was true of Hiram Bingham, who had small hands, small wrists, small feet. Johnny the Lamb was high-colored. In all except his face, truly in all except his deep-set compelling eyes, Hiram Bingham was medium, carefully moderate. Nothing about his clothes stood out. Neat, he was by no means dapper. He looked as though he might absorb light yet never reflect it. His hair was moldy hay. His clothes, though clean, were drab. But when once you had looked into his eyes, it was difficult to look anywhere else.

The two men were the same age, twenty-seven.

"I come in peace."

"I'm sure of it, Pastor. I just keep this thing here in case— well, we've been having some trouble down here on the beach. Nothing that need bother you, though."

Reverend Mr. Bingham placed his stovepipe on the floor, brim-up. He put his hands on his knees. He did not flinch at the sight of the face Johnny Lamb did not turn from him. After a moment he looked around slowly, with deliberation, nodding his head.

"You are doing well here, Captain."

"Very well indeed, thank you."

"Money means a great deal to you, doesn't it?"

"Sure does. The longer I live the more I get to know that money's just about the most important thing a man can have."

"A clear conscience?"

"You know what I mean. I can take care of my own conscience."

"I wasn't offering help, Captain. However, if ever you

137

should feel the need of some, call on me at any hour, day or night."

"Thanks."

The missionary looked around again. No light of contempt touched his eyes, but his thin sallow lips, though untwitching, tipped up a bit at the ends. Johnny Lamb, watching him, began to feel black and bitter as gall, though a moment earlier Johnny had been feeling fine.

"Oh, sure, I know where it says in Matthew that you can't serve God and Mammon. But I'm not going to. That's just the point. I want to fix it for Mammon to serve *me*. But you got to get the goods first. You got to stock up."

The missionary made no comment, but continued to look around. Johnny glowered. This man, with his fancy college education—it was all very well for him to pontificate on the wickedness of wealth and to quote that passage about the desire for riches being the root of all evil; but had *he* ever lived for weeks and weeks, working fifteen-sixteen hours a day, with nothing to eat but salt cod and an occasional turnip? Had *his* coffee for years been made of parched rye and chestnuts roasted and ground, his only pepper pounded prickly ash bark, his tea dried blackberry leaves? How many nights had *he* been so cold he couldn't sleep, no matter how close he huddled to his brothers and sisters? What experience had *he* had in wearing only slopchest clothes for months on end, and them wet three-quarters of the time, in antarctic latitudes?

Johnny Lamb wasn't complaining — he never did — but he wasn't going back to that life again either. "Honor thy father and thy mother," all right. But after this at a distance.

"You came to see me about a woman, Parson?"

"About two women."

"Oh."

"Surely even you could not take offense if I told you what you must already know — that all over the island your name is being linked with that of Queen Kaahumanu?"

138

"Take offense? Hell, no. I'm proud of it."

"She is, uh, an extraordinary woman."

"She sure is! The most extraordinary woman you're ever likely to meet. You missionaries want to get anywhere in this part of the world you'd better start with Kaahumanu."

"Precisely. We realize that. But we wonder, we can't help wondering, whether the Queen's soul would be receptive of the true teachings when she is so wound up in, well, when she's so much, uh, interested in you?"

Johnny Lamb laughed. He felt like suggesting to the Reverend Mr. Bingham that he mind his own business; but he knew the answer he'd get: That the Lord's business was truly his, as it was everybody else's. There was never any profit trying to argue with a man like that. So Johnny laughed.

"Don't you worry about Kate not keeping her mind on her work. She could take care of half a dozen men like me, and still never miss a trick in politics. Matter of fact, she's got three or four husbands somewhere around the islands right now, I think—unless she's divorced 'em by royal decree."

"I hadn't known that."

"You ought to keep up with matters better. Save yourself a lot of trouble that way. Now, for instance, maybe you don't know that Kate—Kaahumanu—she's going to marry the King of Kauai here pretty soon. She's got him as good as a prisoner. Tricked him to coming here. Kaumualii. He's a handsome man, which Kate don't mind. Kate's got a claim to that island, you know. She came from there. Kaumualii's got a wife there already, but that don't make any difference to Kate. Just to play safe, while she's at it she's going to marry Kaumualii's oldest son, too. Lad named Kealiiahonui. She's going to take 'em both on at the same ceremony."

This brought the Reverend Mr. Bingham to his feet.

"You mean to say you'll tolerate such a thing?"

"Why should I squawk? And what good would it do if I did? Kaahumanu's got a mind of her own. Besides, it's perfectly all right, the way they feel about things out here. It's not like it is with us. Love and marriage ain't necessarily the same thing. All depends on your point of view."

"But that's blasphemous!"

"Well, maybe. But they don't *know* it's blasphemous, and I reckon what they don't know won't hurt 'em."

The Reverend Mr. Bingham, shaken, took a turn around the room. When he sat down again it was gingerly, as though he half expected the keg of nails to explode on contact.

"As far as Kate goes," Johnny went on, "she ain't taking orders from anybody any more. The only man she ever did take orders from was her original husband, Kamehameha. You know, the old fellow. The Conqueror. And what a tough nut *he* must have been, Parson! He beat her something dreadful, they say. He only married her to get a claim on Kauai. But he loved her all right, once they got acquainted. He loved her more than any of his other wives. She didn't mind them so much—though there were twenty or so of 'em—but it made her sore when old Kamehameha turned around and married her own two sisters, just to make sure of that title to Kauai. She was young, and she must have had a might of gravel. She raised hell. He knocked her down. He locked her up. She broke loose and ran away. She stole a canoe somewhere and started back for Kauai where she'd come from. All alone, mind you! It's a hundred miles, if it's a foot. If she'd ever got there, they would have refused to give her up, sure. And that would have meant another war, just as Kamehameha was getting the islands rightly consolidated. It would have meant a big slaughter. They played for keeps when they fought wars here in those days, Parson. There didn't used to be any losing side left, ever.

"So the old King sent every canoe he could find after her. War canoes. He had hundreds of 'em in those days, Parson. Can you picture them, the whole Hawaiian Navy in pursuit of one spunky little girl who was trying to get home?"

140

Johnny grinned in embarrassment. He knew he must look and sound like a fatuous father who sings the praises of his child; and as a matter of fact, that's exactly the way he did feel toward the young Kaahumanu, the Kaahumanu he had never known.

"They caught up to her, of course. She was so high-born that they didn't dare lay a hand on her. Anybody so much as touched her, old Kamehameha would have had every bone in his body broken, one by one. The old King was powerful fond of that gal, Parson.

"What they did, they got all around her in their canoes and just forced her back, pushing her canoe, dozens of them. She went to work on them with a paddle, the only weapon she had, and from what I hear tell she laid plenty of 'em out while her strength lasted, but there were always others to take their places. And after a while they got her back here to Oahu—and the King.

"Well, sir, when *he* died you can imagine how Kate felt. She wasn't going to take anything from anybody after that, never." Johnny spread his hands. "So that's the kind of woman you're dealing with. You just think of her that way—think of the girl battling the whole Hawaiian Navy single-handed. So if you expect *I'm* going to squawk if a lady like that takes on a few extra husbands—well, you're greatly mistaken. That Queen's morals are her own affair, Parson, not mine."

Reverend Mr. Bingham swallowed.

"I trust, at least, Captain, that you don't extend that reprehensible attitude toward the other female to whom I have reference—Sister Mathewson?"

Johnny felt his face tighten, which hurt. In fact, as he well enough knew, this hollow-eyed fanatic was much better acquainted with Ann than he was; he had been close to her for more than a year now; and there could be no doubt that he thought he was acting in her best interests. Johnny paused a moment. Then: "Ain't it a bit late to bring that up?"

"What do you mean?" sharply.

141

"Not what you're thinking. She hadn't ought to be here at all, was what I meant. You'd ought to've sent her back by that Indiaman."

"You're right, Captain. I should have. And I'm sorry I didn't."

"She needs a husband."

"Captain, would there be another Indiaman like that?"

"Might. Not likely though. Looks like there'll be more Chinamen as time goes by, if only because of the sandalwood. And they'll most likely go clear on around. Best winds that way."

"Would any one of those be fit for a white woman alone to sail on?"

"Probably not. Could be. It'd depend entirely on the skipper."

"You are agent for most of the ships that put in here, ain't you, Captain?"

"Most of 'em, yes." Johnny studied the backs of his hands, horribly swollen. He closed his fists as far as he could, looking at the knuckles. "I—I sort of insist on it."

The minister rose. He leaned a little on the counter.

"Captain, would you tell us if any such ship came in?"

"Glad to."

"And would you be good enough to tell us whether, in your opinion, it would be a safe ship for Mrs. Mathewson to take?"

"I'll do that on one condition, Reverend, and that is that she comes and asks me herself, at the time, and tells me that she really wants to go away."

"That seems fair enough. And in the meantime, Captain, may I ask you to abstain from seeing Mrs. Mathewson?"

"You can ask that, yes, if you want to. But it ain't going to do you a particle of good."

Mr. Bingham shook a finger at him.

"Captain, you be careful with that lady."

"Reverend, I'll be just exactly as careful with her as I God-

142

damn well happen to feel like at the time."

Johnny drew out his ledgers, and went back to work.

Ann had known it was coming, Don Francisco de Paula Marin, prim and precise, with a mincing step, had been leaving the mission house when she returned; and it was clear that he had been talking with Reverend Mr. Bingham, the only person home just then. The head of the Family looked uncommonly thoughtful, even for him, and his eyes were as dark as down a well, when a few minutes later he left the house, making for the beach.

Ann had turned to her journal in the hope of chasing anxiety away. Unless it interfered with the regular work, this was esteemed a commendable occupation at the mission. But she was unable to write. She could not even write personal letters to her sisters, to her mother—at least, not letters that were worth reading, aloud or otherwise. How could anyone possibly describe a place that was as strange, as fantastic, as this? It had to be seen to be believed. Any ordinary description would sound extravagant. "Tell of our work, what we've done, our rewards," they had been urged. Well, the work was drudgery of the dullest sort. If she wrote of that, honestly, she would only depress her well-wishers and frighten off potential recruits. If she told about what they'd done, it would hardly gain many contributions. For they hadn't yet made a single convert, not one. Their rewards? Oh, they would of course be rewarded after death—of that Ann Mathewson had not the slightest doubt—but it could hardly be said that they had earned much from a worldly point of view. Lucy Thurston and Sybil Bingham and the others might know a gush of pure holy joy on their knees at night; but not Ann. Ann indeed—and this frightened her—could not even pray well any more, much less write.

Not a word had been put into the journal when the Reverend Mr. Bingham returned from the beach; and then it was time for supper.

143

Having known that it was going to come was bad; and when it actually did come it was almost a relief.

This time the Reverend Mr. Bingham did not make any pretense of taking a vote. He simply issued a command.

He addressed himself first to Horace Crowell, who had only an hour before received by inter-island schooner a letter from his wife in Kailua, on the island of Hawaii. Mr. Bingham asked about her health, in detail. The report was not cheery. Mr. Bingham shook his head.

"It is next week that you return to Kailua, Brother Crowell?"

"Yes. Wednesday, Thursday. Whenever they get around to sailing. You know how they are."

"I think that it would be well if Sister Mathewson went with you. She could do your wife's work for a while, and give your wife a chance to rest and regain her strength."

He turned to Ann, who had stopped eating but did not look up from her plate.

"We will miss you greatly here, Sister."

"Yes," said Ann.

"But the Lord's will be done."

"Yes."

How To Be Happy

One coat was scarlet with blue facings, one was lilac with vermilion facings, one was black and red slashed with canary yellow. Gold braid and gold embroidery in massy chunks, ropes, and coils were sewn on each. Each was heavy silk. Two had swords.

One coat had been given by His Majesty George IV of Great Britain and Ireland; one had been given by His Majesty Louis XVIII of France; the third was the gracious gift of His Imperial Majesty Alexander I, Czar of All the Russias.

None of these personages had ever even heard of Johnny Lamb of Hartford, Connecticut.

Johnny hung the coats on a row of hooks, and from time to time he'd turn them over, or rearrange them, smiling quizzically.

"Fair give you a conniption fit, wouldn't they, Humu?"

The mokomoko fighter was entoiled, his mouth open.

"You'll have a chance. Just keep your britches dry."

One coat had been handed to Johnny by Commodore Michael Vascilieff of His Imperial Majesty's Ship *Otkritie*, with the understanding that it be passed on, formally, to King Liho at a moment Johnny-on-the-spot might deem propitious to the Russian interests on the islands—an understanding Johnny had not the slightest intention of living up to, for he loved souvenirs.

One coat, the one from London, had been given to Johnny by Liho himself as security for a case of gin. As far as Johnny was concerned, it wasn't worth a case of gin—in cash. And

Johnny knew that he'd never collect. It had been given to Liho, in King George's name, by the British commercial agent in Honolulu, Charlton.

The Bourbon's contribution had been ceremoniously presented to Queen Kaahumanu for her stepson Kamehameha II by the captain of a visiting French warship, in the name of his monarch, Liho himself being just then prone under a table. Kaahumanu afterward had refused to turn it over to Liho, who she said didn't deserve anything so pretty. Instead she had given it into the custody of Captain Lamb.

"It's a European custom, Humu, to net you dark-skinned boys with coats. I don't suppose there's a warship in these parts that don't keep a good-sized locker full of 'em, ready to whip one out whenever they meet a new chief—and each one absolutely guaranteed to come straight from a genuine crowned head, sure. Catch on? If the chief wears the royal colors, it might make him a kind of vassal—they hope. It won't do any harm anyway. And if later on the different countries get to squabbling about who's going to protect the place, it's something of a claim—and a cheap one."

He waved expansively at the coats.

"When d'ye suppose some nation's going to present a potentate out in these parts with a pair of *pants*? I predict that my own fellow countrymen'll be the first to think of that, Humu. Maybe. Whoever it is, *they*'ll do the heavy annexing. Who's that knocking down there?"

Humu went below, and Johnny put the coats into the seachest, spreading some shirts over them to complete the packing. He felt good. His face was virtually healed, his hands were their normal size. He no longer started, however slightly, at the sound of a knock at the door, as he'd done when still afraid that his five assailants would return en masse to finish him off before he could get a chance to seek them out one by one. The episode was closed now—or as closed as it could be, here. Three of the men had been separately "rearranged,"

146

as Johnny liked to put it, and the whole beach, of course, had heard about this. The remaining two, leaving more than eight months' pay due them, as everybody knew, had skipped to another ship; if they ever dared to make Honolulu again they too would be "rearranged," each in his own time.

Johnny Lamb was not proud of this exploit, but he knew its need. By the time he'd reached the third man he was tired, disgusted, and his hands hurt worse than ever. Nevertheless he had made a thorough job of it.

Now he was glad it was over, and that he could get away and make some money. He reckoned he'd have fun doing it, too.

There were noisy attempts to be quiet downstairs, and a sound he recognized immediately: Kaahumanu's whisper was anybody else's shout. He knew a moment of annoyance, for he had forbidden her to come to his home; but soon he smiled, the fact being that it was going to be good to see her again.

Messages—verbal messages, of course, since the Queen could not write—had been coming from the palace with increased frequency of late; and he might have expected, having left them unanswered or having answered them only evasively, that Kaahumanu herself would climax this series. She wasn't a woman to be put off with excuses. She wanted to see him.

Well, that was all right. He wanted to see her.

Smiling, he went to the stairs.

The reason he had forbidden her to come here (knowing damn' well she'd disobey him whenever she felt like it) was not one to do with public shame. Everybody in Honolulu and the surrounding countryside, indeed everybody in the Sandwich Islands, knew what was going on. The dowager queen was built for love, yes, as none knew better than Johnny; but assuredly she was not built for amorous intrigue. There was no guile in her. The circuitous, the sly, she simply did not understand. And when she went anywhere, habitually, from

147

earliest childhood, she went at the head of a procession. There might be three hundred or more persons in her train, her punahele, when she paid regal if routine visits to the outlying islands. When she called on Johnny the Lamb, then, and permitted no more than twenty-odd followers to follow her, she considered that she was doing very well indeed, being virtually incognito.

Of course everybody knew her! That wasn't the point. The point was that Kaahumanu, a woman of whims and moods, a woman of sudden impulses, was likely to appear at any hour of the day or night, demanding attention. It was bad for business. It amused and perhaps to some extent attracted the whites; but the natives, though entertained, though gathering by the score, by the hundred, when Kaahumanu was calling upon Captain Lamb, didn't thereafter go to the shop, which they took to be automatically kapu, tabu. To be sure, by the King's own decree nothing was kapu any more; but you can't squash a custom of hundreds of generations, standing by just saying that you have.

The time he went to China—on a proper ship, not a whaler— Johnny had been second mate, acting first mate for a while, and as such, when it was learned that they'd have to stay at the Whampoa anchorage for a couple of months, he had rated certain shore liberties. Theoretically it was forbidden that any foreign devil go ashore, all business to be conducted by hong merchants or their agents, who went out in launches; but in fact it could be and often was arranged. So Johnny, with time on his hands, money in his pocket, too, had hired himself a Chinese chick and enjoyed that which a sailor spends so much time dreaming of. To take her aboard would have been bad for discipline, so he used to have himself rowed ashore almost every night to visit her; and the whole arrangement, made through their own compradore, had been most satisfactory— and not as expensive as you might suppose, either.

Now Johnny Lamb had never rightly got to know this

148

Chink girl—she was no more than a girl, hardly in her teens, as he realized after a while—for she couldn't talk a word of his language any more than he could speak a word of hers. He was never even sure that he'd got her name right. Still and all, he had come to be very fond of her, somehow. He never could quite believe that she was real; for she seemed a doll, a thing of tinsel, delightsome surely, but not a human being. Yet when sailing day came, and he told her as best he could, placing a gift on the bed, that this time he would not return, admittedly Johnny the Lamb had a lump in his throat. She understood. For a moment tears flickered in her slanty eyes; but she was well trained, and instantly she got control of herself, and began to smile, then to laugh. This laugh was not hysterical. It was well modulated, carefully pitched, deliberate, loud. She looked square at him when she laughed.

Outraged, Johnny had stamped out; and it was not until he was in the street that the truth came to him. Of course! The Chinese are a strange people, who believed that you should not show any emotion you felt. As far as that goes, a plenty of folks in New England believed the same, sure. But the Chinese went further, and believed, and taught, that out of consideration for any person who might be embarrassed by a knowledge of the emotion you felt you should show an opposite emotion. If you were hurt, then smile. If you knew real grief, laugh. Their funerals were hilarious always. It was politeness.

He had started to turn back, but it would do no good; there were merely minutes to spare at best. So he had hurried down the street hearing that laugh, hearing it as he jumped into the gig, all the way across the roads to the ship, hearing it (he thought) even after he was aboard—that loud merry high laugh of the tiny girl who lay on silk, the small soft yellow girl who had loved him so much and whose heart was breaking.

There were times even now, when he was low, that he thought he heard the far faint sound of that laughter.

149

At the head of the steps he remembered this incident only because the guest he would greet was so different. There was nothing Chinese or upside-down about Kaahumanu. When *she* felt bad she wept; when she was angry she roared; and when Kaahumanu was happy she laughed, so that everybody knew it—everybody for a long ways around.

Johnny was fond of Kaahumanu, but there was no question that she kept customers away.

Well, it wouldn't matter tonight.

She fairly bounded up the steps, as light as any girl, and threw her arms around him, and they rubbed noses passionately. But a moment later she pushed him away. In a voice of thunder she accused him of spurning her summons, of trying to avoid her. He grinned, and shook her tenderly. He had only wanted for his face to get back to its usual shape and size, he said. He was a vain one. Also, he didn't like to cause her pain.

"But you look beautiful, Tony!"

"Well, it's the first time anybody ever called me that."

"You were not hurt? You weren't punched?"

"Not to amount to anything. And the business's all over with now."

"Now you won't fight any more?"

"Not unless I have to."

"But"—she had seen the packed chest—"you are going away?"

"Just to one of the other islands. I won't be long. Have to raise money."

"I would give you money."

"Sure, but we don't need to go into that again. Sit down, Kate. Matter of fact, *you* look pretty damn beautiful yourself."

She giggled. She wore Nile green velvet, a great deal of it, in magnificent rolls and swags. From under this from time to time her feet, absurdly small for the rest of her, peeped like tiny brown birds.

150

Half a minute later, while he was mixing a rum-and-lime, she started to berate him for receiving other women in this room. She was so human about it, and so explosive, that he jumped, spilling rum. It was good rum, too. He could hardly believe his ears. Kate admitting the existence of a rival—in anything! He shook his head.

"Don't know what you're talking about."

"That Long Neck who makes dresses! Twice she has been here!"

That was Honolulu for you. No secrets. It was one vast whispering gallery. No doubt the only reason why the Queen hadn't heard much earlier of the Buttoner girl's two visits was because they were all afraid to tell her.

Now she slapped her chest.

"The one who is like a papa hé náru, a surf board. Why was she here?"

"Oh, I wouldn't say a papa hé náru, Kate."

"*I* would!"

He handed her a drink, picked up his own, strolled to a window.

"That was fun, that time we rode the surf boards. We must do that again some time."

In the lane outside, thirty-five or forty men stood in small groups, talking low, repeatedly glancing up toward this and the other front window. Johnny swallowed. It always fussed him to know that there were so many people just outside, or just in the next room, waiting, breathless, for him to get through.

"Why was she here?"

"Business, Kate. Her business. She was trying to win me over to the One True Faith."

"But, Tony, you *are* a Christian!"

"Not their kind."

"There are different kinds, then?"

"Yes. Ain't suppose to be, but there are."

151

"But why does not your Jesus command them all to be the same?"

Johnny shrugged.

"I guess nobody's thought to consult him lately. It's hard to explain, Kate, even if I really knew, which I don't. But with you not understanding English . . . You'd really ought to learn English, Kate."

"So that I can understand the Long Necks?"

"So that you can understand me."

"I understand you all right, Tony. I understand you too well."

She glanced at the chest, and her patrician features fell and were even twisted a moment in pain. It hurt Johnny to see her that way.

"You see, if you knew about God—"

"We used to have gods, too."

"We have only One."

"Then you can't know much about them. We used to have hundreds. Thousands. More than forty thousand."

"That's a heap of gods, Kate."

"Too many. But they're all dead now, and I'm glad of it. They used to make things hard. They'd keep things away from you. For a woman, even a queen, almost everything was kapu. That was the gods. Do you know that until only two years ago I'd never even eaten a banana or a coconut? At least, only when I was sure nobody was watching me. And it isn't often that somebody isn't watching me. You know that yourself, Tony."

Johnny bowed grave assent.

"That was the gods," the Queen said again. "And what did they give you for it? Nothing. You'd make sacrifices, you'd build hieaus—and no answer. I'm glad they're dead. Now I eat anything I want, no matter how many people are looking at me."

"I can see your point. But—don't you sometimes feel that

152

maybe it'd be good to have Something to take their place?"

"No."

She looked up at Kukailimoku, the battle god, the god-on-a-stick. She hawked, and spat.

"What good did *he* do? He was the favorite of my husband all his life. My husband the Conqueror. So many sacrifices he made, so much fruit and rice and awa, so many men killed! And the hieaus he built for that Kukailimoku! On every island. Hieaus big as mountains, where there were great slaughters. You should see the one on Hawaii, Tony. On the Kona coast, back of Kailua. That is the most wonderful of them all."

Again she scowled at the idol.

"But look at him up there! What did he do for my husband? He let him suffer terrible pain for many days. He let him die."

"We all got to die sooner or later, Kate."

"No!"

She meant it. She shook her head positively.

Johnny Lamb did not smile. He was impressed, as always, by the firmness of this people's *disbelief* in natural death. It was something the missionaries would never understand. A man might be killed in fight, he might be drowned, or fall over a cliff; a man might be deliberately sacrificed on an altar, as until a few years ago so many were; but if a man died a "natural" death, a death for which there was no apparent explanation, it could only mean that something was wrong— that the gods had killed him, the gods having been offended by him, hating him, and by implication hating all his family and everybody connected with him. The gods were never good, always bad. Love was human, not divine. This was the reason that a "natural" death was a disgrace and everything about it should be hushed up. If only the Long Necks would understand this . . . .

Johnny was not as scornful of the missionaries as once he had been. He had no thought of playing their game, but in spite of himself, in spite, too, of the way he talked about them,

153

he had come to have a sneaking admiration for that little band of workers. They weren't going to quit. They were here to stay. Moreover they were not as stupid as at first they had seemed. They were getting things done, laying the groundwork.

"I am never going to die," cried the Queen.

"By gum, you know, Kate, there are times when I almost believe that."

But she glanced at him suspiciously. What was all this talk of gods and death anyway? What was Tony getting at? She hadn't come here to talk.

"Are you trying to *convert* me, Tony?"

"Not exactly," and he smiled. "But maybe it's worth taking a look at. And if you could only read English, it'd sure help. Give you something to do when I'm not around. Keep you from getting too lonesome." He shook his head. "Because you *are* lonesome a heap of the time, ain't that right, Kate?"

"Ae, ae," she whispered. "Yes, Tony. Much."

"Good old Kate. I'm sorry."

"Would—would *you* teach me English, Tony?"

"Might. When I come back."

"All right. If you teach me, I'll read about your God. I have spoken. But never mind that now." She was tearing off the Nile green gown, and it developed that she wore nothing underneath. She held out her arms, wriggling the fingers. "Come on, Tony. We make panipani."

"Kate," he said as he unbuttoned his shirt, "I've got to give you credit for one thing anyway—you sure are outspoken."

When he whuffed out the lamp, a long-drawn sigh of bliss rose from the lane below. They were happy, those who waited down there, because they knew that soon their Queen would be.

See Snow from a Stove 19

" . . . and there are times when I think that Our Father must be testing us here at Kailua, testing our faith in Him and in His Beloved Son," Ann wrote to her sister Helen, "by the process of tossing us into a skillet which He jiggles over a Celestial fire, much as you and dear Grace and I used to take a pan (but one with a long handle!) and put Injun into it, with a mite of goose grease, and jiggle this in the fireplace. And as those kernels of Injun used to do, dear sister, we here in this remote blistered place, we, Dr. and Mrs. Holman, Mr. and Mrs. Crowell, and your humble sister, now leap and jump, to keep from being scorched entirely and indeed quite burned to blackness. I wonder if it truly is a part of God's all-embracing plan?"

She tore up this letter not merely because it was flip, conceivably even irreverent, but because it was true.

The place where she found herself, a village on the west coast of Hawaii, the biggest and most southernly of the islands, was sometimes spoken of as being in the shadow of Mauna Hualalai; but the phrase was purely poetic. Kailua was not in the shadow of anything. Buried long ago under hot ashes from Hualalai, the last time that volcano spoke, with an obstinacy not easy to divine the village had been rebuilt on the site of the ruin, all cooled lava and relentless blue-gray cinders. Kailua, then, did not rest upon earth, but rather on what might have been the very floor of Hell. It seethed; it shimmered. For four miles back from the beach no tree or bush grew. Honolulu, at least near the shore, had coconuts—those gawky prim trees that always caused Ann to think of old maids out for a walk. They cast little enough shade, but they did

155

rattle in a friendly if foolish way, and they glistered in the sunlight, twittering. There was nothing of the sort at Kailua, where whatever slits of earth had accumulated between rocks were planted only with taro. There was no fresh water. It was necessary to send a man four miles to the edge of the forest for water and for wood.

It was pitilessly hot out there. This was some two hundred miles south of Honolulu, and the climate was much different. Moreover, it was now summer; the trades had fallen off, and when any wind did blow, it was the languid hot kona out of the south: the Hawaiians called it the wind of sickness.

Yet this was not unexpected, nor was Ann unprepared for it. She had seen Kailua previously, and she had heard much about it from Lucy and the Reverend Mr. Thurston, who had been stationed here for some time. Kailua indeed was the first place where the Lord's Anointed had stepped ashore, following five weary months, eighteen thousand miles, at sea. After Boston—here. Even then it had not seemed inviting. What manner of people had they come amongst, who wore no clothes, did not respect the Sabbath, and persisted in living in such a place as this?

For some obscure religious reason—presumably something to do with the fire goddess Pele, who controlled volcanos—the rebuilt Kailua, though uncomfortable and inconvenient even by Hawaiian standards, remained not only inhabited but the site of a royal palace, visited for so-many weeks of the year by the great Kamehameha himself, more recently by his widows and his son. Those aboard the brig *Thaddeus*, having raised the northern coast of this island, had learned from canoeists that the King was at Kailua, so that it was here they had come, not venturing to put foot on shore without royal permission. It was here that they had met Liho, the haughty Kaahumanu, and sundry others. It was here, too, Ann remembered with a shudder, that without knowing it they had tasted dog. Oh, she hated Kailua! They of the Family had wished to press on to Honolulu, which they'd heard was one of the largest of the villages as well as the one most often visited by white men and therefore the most blatantly corrupt; but the King had cried that all haoles wished to live on Oahu. The King had commanded that they leave one man of medicine as well as one priest at Kailua, possibly against the time when he, the monarch, would have to come back. Dr. Holman, then, their only physician, together with Lucia Holman and Reverend and Lucy Thurston, had been left at Kailua. Soon afterward the Crowells had been sent out, to replace the Thurstons, called to Honolulu, Horace Crowell rating as a "priest" in the eyes of the islanders.

The gods had been declared dead, and no doubt Liho had long since forgotten his whim, but it was unthinkable that the station at Kailua be abandoned. You must not turn back, once you have taken up the Lord's work. It's bad for prestige.

Hualalai was nearer, more immediate, true; but at any hour of the day and on any tolerably clear night you could also see Mauna Loa from the village, and that was a noble sight, to be sure. The highest peak rose majestic, awesome—at certain hours and especially early in the morning and late in the afternoon, seeming not solid at all but rather a trick of lighting, a tinted shadow that in a moment would vanish. Its white cone against a sky of lilac seemed fairly to shiver then, sometimes even to swing back and forth a little.

Snow above the massed tropical ferns and palms—it never failed to transfix Ann Mathewson, that sight. When she felt low, when she could have cried, as Habakkuk did, "Oh Lord, how long?" she would stop working for a minute or two and go to the back doorway and stand there staring at Mauna Loa, taking heart.

"I reckon this is the closest I'll ever get to snow again," she would whisper; and then she'd think of the little white houses at home, and the little white fences around them, and the brass knockers against green doors; and in her mind's ear sometimes she would even catch a tinkle of sleigh bells.

But soon she'd have to go back to work.

Perhaps the most pointed difference between this stove-town and Honolulu was that of *pace*. The northern port, even when the whaling fleet was in, though crowded was hardly bustling; but it might have been New Haven, or even Boston, compared with Kailua. Oh, work was done in Kailua! The women made tapa and cultivated their taro; the men went fishing or hauled wood and water from the forest. But there was less movement, and what there was lagged. There were fewer fires, many families cooking at one to save wood, so that fewer spirals of smoke stood up, and these were weak, lackadaisical, wavering as they rose. The very thud of tapa mallets, though rhythmic, was excruciatingly slow. Fresh water being so hard to get, there was little washing. The men who fished with spears and throw-nets, and were sometimes in and out of the lagoon, were bad enough. The women were almost unbearable. When one pressed close to you, it was difficult to hide your repugnance. And as at Honolulu, though more insistently, they crowded around the Long Necks, especially the women. They fingered clothing, the lousy things. When they spat, it made blue-silver spearheads in the cindery dust. They sweated prodigiously; and their hair was rancid with sweet sticky coconut oil. Their fingernails were fecaloid. Their breath was like low tide.

Even those at the mission, though surely not complacent, and having little leisure, did not drive themselves. There was the feeling, and it was inescapable, that they constituted after all no more than a gesture, a forgotten fancy. Their souls were filled with faith, in their hearts they held no doubt; yet it was not to be expected that the King and court would soon again visit these lugubrious precincts; and by this time they all knew, what Ann had pointed out at a meeting of the Family, that these Polynesians were not to be converted from the bottom up but from the top down. That might be deplorable; it was also true. But they endured. Without enthusiasm, lacking the drive, the galvanic impulse, that the presence of Hiram Bingham would have given, still they went on working.

Of the Holmans, Ann saw little. He made many trips into

the interior or up and down the coast or around to Hilo, being gone for days together, even weeks, and his wife invariably went with him. They worked hard and in silence, but their hearts were not with this mission. From the beginning the fact had been apparent: the Holmans wanted to go home. It was not any wavering of their religious faith; it was not revulsion from the sere land, the stench and discomfort; but these two, though seldom mentioning it, believed that they were not sufficiently useful to justify a lifetime in this outlandish place. They wanted to have a child, and how could they have a child here? Nobody argued with them, nobody tried to dissuade them. Soon they would go. This was accepted.

Since Abigail, Horace's wife, was vehemently opposed to this attitude, and indeed esteemed the Holmans to be nothing less than traitors, though she never said so to their faces, the atmosphere at the mission house when the physician and his wife were not traveling was seriously strained. Horace himself, blinking his watery blue eyes, would shake his head whenever Abigail would splutter about the Holmans; and he'd assert, mildly, that doubtless they knew what was best and it was all God's will. Horace was definite enough in certain other matters—he never failed to protest against the lighting of fires on the Sabbath, for instance, and went around stamping them out, often at great personal peril—but regarding the Holmans he could say nothing more disapproving than that he sometimes wished that Dr. Holman could afford to give more time and attention to Abigail, who was a mighty sick woman, seven months with child, too.

"I don't care so much about that. I'll probably die soon anyway—"

"Abigail!"

"—but I do consider it's shameful to quit. What will the folks back home think? You didn't see Ann Mathewson here scamper off on the next boat after her husband was recalled to Our Father's bosom, now did you?"

Horace said nothing, looking at Ann. Ann, too, was silent,

and she was thinking of how horribly homesick she'd been and most of the time still was. She wondered if she was remaining on this side of the world for sheerly fleshly reasons. As much as possible she kept from thinking about it.

Abigail was a joy. Ann had known her tolerably well in the close quarters of the *Thaddeus* all those dragging months, at least had known her better than she had known any other members of the Family, but here at Kailua, after a separation of almost a year, these two grew a real friendship.

Abigail was ailing. What was wrong with her nobody knew—not even, Ann suspected, they all suspected, Dr. Holman. Certainly she suffered; but you'd never get her to tell how much. Her face, which a year and a half ago had been pretty, was drawn with pain, just as her once smooth pale hands were calloused and reddened and all scuffed from work. Her pregnancy was only part of it, and probably not an important part. She had already had two miscarriages. She looked to be getting on to forty, who was barely twenty-two. There was always agony in her eyes, as though she were looking up at you, a free person, through the murk of some private unspeakable Hell. Yet she could smile: athwart the surge of fever that face smiled. It was a slightly acidulous smile sometimes, as her voice tended to be tart, for Abigail Crowell was an outspoken female; it was a thin and somewhat thorny smile; but it was genuine.

She and Ann found a great deal to talk about; and Ann knew early, and with a gush of warmth within, that she was welcome here, for Abigail too had been lonesome. They talked of the voyage, and of their fellow passengers, Abigail being outspoken as usual, Ann inclining rather to giggle. They talked, with indignation, about conditions aboard the inter-island schooners. They talked about the Polynesians, whom they were trying to like, and wondered whether any white person ever would come to understand them, if, as Ann pointed out, even Reverend Mr. Bingham himself could not always be counted upon to do so. They talked of Horace and

160

his ideas of how the mission ought to be run. Occasionally, when they had the hut to themselves, they even talked of clothes.

Abigail was not of a cheery disposition, yet there was something mighty comforting about her, something that soothed. Ann felt like confiding in her. Once or twice they even wept together, though neither could have said why.

Some day, Ann thought, I will tell her about Captain Lamb. Some day. Maybe.

It startled Ann to learn that Abigail Crowell, for all her disapproval of the Holmans, had little confidence in the mission. Oh, eventually they'd succeed! For, as everybody knows, truth will inevitably prevail. But immediately, she thought, they were doing a poor job. This seemed disloyal to Ann, who however said nothing.

"If you were to go back and tell folks—" Ann suggested. "How can they know, from our letters, what kind of place this is here? If you went back, to where you could get a good doctor—"

"I'd never do that. It'd wound Horace."

Sometimes she patronized her husband, and in his presence she could be vinegarish—a circumstance both Horace and Ann meekly accounted for on the ground of her suffering—but in the long run she admired him. She was all for his way of thinking in the matter of how the natives should be treated. Abigail seldom went far from the hut, some days could not even get out of bed, and she and Ann, while the Holmans traveled, conducted the school. Horace, on the other hand, was much abroad. He preached frequently, whenever an occasion offered. He preached well, too, with feeling; and often the Hawaiians, though they hadn't known a word he said, cheered him. It was Horace who had the most contact with the natives, and he was pronounced in his ideas. He kept after the chiefs. He had the persistence of an unwanted insect, and simply would not be brushed off. He rallied them about their promiscuity. He scolded them for their drunkenness. When a

161

hulahula was danced, one night in a grove back at the edge of the forest, he marched the full four miles there, by the pale blink of the moon, and single-handed tried to break it up. He was the sternest of the stern in matters of Sabbath observance.

Horace believed that the natives should be taught that the white man is superior. Horace did not believe that the white man *was* superior—in the eyes of God, at least—but surely he *seemed* so, and advantage should be taken of this appearance, even though it was false. He was agreed that conversion would have to proceed from the top down, and he proposed that the missionaries themselves constitute that top. Until this was done, he argued, they would not be respected. And if they weren't respected, how could they hope to win any souls to salvation?

Abigail said that this was absolutely right.

Ann wasn't sure. There were moments when Ann wondered whether the Hawaiians weren't maybe a whit smarter than they looked. But Ann admired Horace.

She had always liked him, on the *Thaddeus*, for his manners. The other members of the Family were thoughtful and mild, commendably industrious, utterly sincere, and filled with a courage it was breath-taking to contemplate; but not every one of them was truly well-bred, at least not so much so as a girl from Prospect Street, a Buttoner, who was related to the Harpers of New Haven, might wish. But Horace Crowell, without being pushy about it, was indisputably a gentleman. It helped.

She was grateful to Horace, too, and always would be, for his kindness and attention throughout that horrible, perilous schooner trip from Honolulu to Kailua, when again and again, in misery among the natives, the pigs, the dogs, and chickens, the greasy fishbones and bits of rotten fruit awash in the scuppers, it seemed as though they must sink. Ann would never forget that trip. The schooner itself, a slight, narrow, cranky vessel, was unbelievably dirty. There were no cabins, and they slept, when they were able to sleep, on deck. On the other hand, the sailors, if they could be called that, Hawaiians who were happy-go-lucky to the point of suicide, were rather more likely to be asleep than awake; and since they kept no regular watches there were times when they were all asleep at once, unmindful of the nearness of a reef. During that horrible voyage, then, eight days and nights of grinding discomfort and embarrassment, Horace Crowell, himself certainly suffering, had been a pillar of strength. And he'd been more than strong: he had been gentle, sympathetic.

But she still wasn't sure that he had the right attitude toward the natives.

"They don't even *see* things our way," she wailed once, after Horace had departed to preach. "I was talking to Lili today, when she was making the fire. Even with the clothes we've got her to wear I could see that she's, uh, in a family way. She admitted it as chirk as you please. She's got a big belly, was the way she put it."

"Well, she made herself clear anyway."

"But what are you going to do with people like that? I tried to point out that she shouldn't be in that condition when she was not married, not even married the way these Hawaiians are sometimes. She just laughed. She admitted it would be a nuisance, but she said she'd had fun getting that way. That was the very word she used, as near as I could make it out—fun."

Abigail looked out the way Horace had gone, but said nothing.

"I told her I wasn't interested in that phase of the matter. What I was interested in, I said, was her immortal soul. And was she impressed? Not at all. She saluted and said, Aye, aye, sir, like that, in English, and then she burst into gales of laughter. Now what *are* you going to do with people like that?"

Abigail chuckled.

"Well, I won't have to puzzle about it much longer anyway. I'm going to die soon."

163

"You shouldn't talk like that!"

"I don't know why not. Don't know who has a better right to. I'm going to die soon, and then you'll marry Horace."

"*Abigail!*"

"That's all right. I can see the way he's been looking at you. But it's all right. Be a good thing for both of you."

"I don't think you ought to talk that way! It—It's—"

"Here come the children," said Abigail.

Out of the Sea Rose He   20

Of the two greatest differences between this and the Honolulu station, one was in front, one in back. In back rose the peaks, and particularly far Mauna Loa; but there were also lesser hills, all smeared with green-black foliage. The leeward side of Oahu, the Honolulu side, except for some coconut and hau trees at the shore and some koa trees in the creases that were the Moana and Nuuana valleys, were brashly bare, having been stripped by sandalwooders, and they stood red, stark, crumbling, the cause of the dust that gritted into everything. These hills back of Kailua, however, looked the way tropical hills, it's assumed, should look. They were shadowy places, forests concealing their flanks: they were places of mystery. More than once, standing in the back doorway, Ann wished that she had time to take a walk in those hills. She had never been more than half a mile from shore.

In front there was something different. Not the harbor of Honolulu, splotched with slatternly whalers, its water oily, its air slick with the fumes of boiling blubber; but a reef-fringed lagoon like that at Waikiki, only smaller, the reef being closer inshore, and notably more colorful.

164

The hut they lived in was large, as such huts went, and they had it reasonably well furnished. Each had a bed. There were no rugs, only mats, but they were good mats, made of lauhala. There were two straight-back chairs, in addition to the rocking chair Ann had brought from Honolulu. The hut was near the water, and caught whatever breeze there was. A walk ran clear around the outside, a walk four or five feet wide, made of white coral and crushed white seashell. It was a good place from which to watch either the mountains or the sea, to watch a sunset, or just to sit with your eyes closed, thinking, if possible, of nothing at all. Some part of it was always in shade.

Ann Mathewson and Abigail Crowell used to sit out on this walk whenever they had a chance.

Who could it have been who started the sheeplike procession of those who speak or think of the "monotonous" sounds of the sea? Surely nobody who had ever lived at the edge of a tropical lagoon. The sea, Ann came to know, has a great many voices. It's by no means monotonous, quite the contrary. It is forever speaking, whether thoughtfully, or carelessly, or in a rage, and as constantly changing its tempo, its pitch, its rhythm, and accent. There was no hour of the day or night, not even a minute, when they who lived in the hut couldn't pause, cocking the head, and hear a whole multitude of mysterious noises issuing from the nearby lagoon. There were the pettish gulls, and the fish that leapt out of the water, to fall back sideways with a resounding spank. There were the waves' tiny love-slaps at the marge, which sometimes when the seas were running high outside rose almost to a tinkling; and at such times, too, they could hear the spray spitting and hissing along the ridges, and hear the spindrift hum like taut vibrating wire. The reef in particular gave forth a variety of sounds—boomings, hollow deep roarings, thudding, vast throaty watery tramping and tumbling, sometimes a pistol-crack, sometimes a long high steamy shriek, and furtive splashes and whispers, the grinding of small smooth stones,

165

the spick of foam as the water struggled back to its right level. The reef, itself seldom seen, gave forth here in geysers, there in great uplifting masses of water which broke into billions of iridescent specks, to float reluctantly down. Even in the mildest weather there was a film of jeweled spray catching the light over the reef. It made Ann think of a bridal veil.

In the matter of color, too, and of light, the lagoon was a much-changing place. Apart from the bijouterie of the spray, the water proper, the lagoon's surface, was incessantly winking, blinking, shifting, renewing itself in a polychromatic pandemonium, so that it teased the imagination quite away, leaving nothing but gauzy dream. Ann reflected that it was like looking into a fireplace. You shouldn't do it—it was a dreadful waste of time—and probably bad for your eyes—but it fascinated.

"You shouldn't have said it. You shouldn't talk that way."

Abigail smiled, shading her eyes.

"There's the schooner. Can't seem to make up their mind whether to come in."

"It's wicked! And I'm sure Mr. Crowell never even thinks of me at all, except in a gentlemanly way."

"It is a narrow pass. If they don't do it right soon they're going to have to stay outside all night, which means we won't get our letters until at least noon tomorrow—assuming that some mail's reached Honolulu lately, which is assuming a lot. Why shouldn't Horace marry you after I'm dead?"

"Because you're not going to die."

"Oh, yes, I am. And so are you. Only I'll die first. And Horace is human. Why? You haven't got anybody else in mind, have you?"

Ann caught up her breath, turning her head away, and she felt the blood pound into her head. Wildly she thought: Here's the time to tell her about Captain Lamb! She waited, not daring to look at Abigail. She was sure that Abigail would sense her distress and ask a leading question, and the rest would be easy. Once she started talking about Captain Lamb,

166

Ann knew, she would talk on and on . . . . She had wanted to, for so long! She waited.

But Abigail was watching the schooner, which again had balked at the pass. Abigail shaded her eyes, shook her head.

"They're scared, that's what. This rate, they'll never get here today. Appears as if somebody got tired and is swimming in."

Ann looked.

"That's a coconut, I think."

There was so much sunlight that she could not be sure, and she assuredly did not care. The fishermen often carried coconuts out in their canoes, ripe ones for eating, green ones for water.

Should she tell Abigail? Would it banish Captain Lamb from her mind if she could talk about him? Or would it only make her feel worse? Not knowing what to do, she did nothing, just sat there staring out over the water, where the sunset slammed down pastels, making it resemble the neck of some gigantic pigeon. There were no canoes in sight. The bobbing spot, coconut or whatever it was, was getting closer.

Abigail's hand fell, lightly enough, on her shoulder. Ann fairly jumped. It was as though she had been caught doing something dirty.

"You've been thinking about Horace, and you feel guilty. You mustn't, dear."

Ann tried to say something, and stammered. Abigail shook her gently, fondly.

"There's nothing wrong with being human, way I see it. And you wouldn't be human if you didn't think sometimes about marrying him after I'm gone. Naturally. After all, you need a husband. Anybody can see that."

"It—It's disgusting!"

"Well, yes, a heap of the time it is. But I reckon there's nothing we can do about it. But don't feel as if you're being sneaky, thinking such thoughts, Ann. You're not. I understand. Horace will, too—except of course it'll take longer for him to."

167

A long time passed, or it seemed a long time. Ann was all right now, quieter. Soon, she knew, they would go inside. Sunsets were barbarously brief and abrupt in this land of no twilight. Meanwhile Ann knew some relief. The question had not been asked; she had not blurted the tale of how she felt; and perhaps this was for the best. After all, she was away from Captain Lamb now, and well away, some two hundred miles. She was grateful to Reverend Mr. Bingham for this. They could say what they pleased about Mr. Bingham, but he had a clear head and a kind heart, let nobody deny it.

"Pity about your husband, Ann. I haven't ever spoke of it because I don't reckon you're anxious to talk about it?"

"I don't care, now."

"You were like all the rest of us females there, excepting Hattie Chamberlain, weren't you? I mean—you'd just got married for the occasion, just before we sailed."

"Two days before."

"And then Mr. Mathewson fell sick right off. That was hard, Ann. Specially with you feeling the way you must have felt, right then. So you couldn't—you couldn't have done it often?"

"Never did it at all," said Ann. "The two nights we slept together before we sailed, Mr. Mathewson said both our souls ought to've been so lifted up in exaltation at the great task before us that it would be almost wicked to perform any fleshly act then."

"Well, yes and no," Abigail murmured. "But it's true, we were all mighty swole up with our feelings right at that time."

"I said all right. I didn't know what to make out of it, but I was scared enough anyway, so I said all right. We said we'd do it later. But of course we never got a chance. We ought to go in and see about supper, Abigail."

"You're right. And we shouldn't ought to talk about things like this."

"I didn't say that."

"No, but you were thinking it. Well—No, that's all right, dear. I can get up alone."

Ann rose. It had done some good, and she felt better. There were compensations, even out here. She was getting nearer, in spirit, to what she rightly should be, what she once had thought she was. She felt stronger. She could conquer.

This made her feel suddenly all warm inside, this conviction, all tingly at the extremities, and light-headed, the way she'd been told you felt if you drank a glass of wine. So it might have been wrong. But anyway it was a relief.

There was a slight splashing, and at the edge of the lagoon only a few feet from where they stood, the coconut proved to be a man after all, and he, too, rose, and he stepped evenly out of the waves as if they belonged to him. He grinned.

"Hello," said Johnny Lamb. "Saw you through a glass, and I didn't hanker after waiting till tomorrow morning, so I swum it. Anything for supper?"

A Walk in the Woods 21

The dry blue-black brittle stones, or ashes, clinked and splintered when they were trod on. The jungle, as the two walkers neared it, loomed enormous, black, a monstrous maw. Ann found that she had stopped, a hand against her breast.

Johnny Lamb turned solicitously. Was there anything the matter? A touch of sun? He had been talking in an offhand way, almost gayly, giving her the gossip of Honolulu, and had she paid polite attention she might have been amazed that the two of them had so much in common, who lived such different lives. But she hadn't been paying attention. She knew that Captain Lamb had come to this island on business, and that besides his servant he had brought a chest crammed with goods and stuffs. She knew that soon he would start for the interior, presumably to ply his trade. She was not at all sure that this was the only reason why he'd come, but when she asked him point-blank he answered evasively, turning away, coloring. But this, too, Ann had dismissed from her mind now, as she crossed the volcano bed. She was thinking only of that upreaching, outreaching forest—it showed arched, concave, like a comber about to break—and of the darkness of it, and of the fact that she was going there with Captain Lamb.

"I—I don't think we ought to," she whispered.

"Why not?"

It flummoxed her, and she was sure she looked silly; but indeed she fought panic again, standing high on her toes now, both hands pressed to her breast. Why did she have these terrible moments of fear? Did other women sometimes feel like this? But other women had husbands to turn to, or mothers. Ann's mouth had fallen open—she felt it—and she swung her lower jaw back and forth slowly, carefully, deliberately, in order to keep a scream from coming.

"Thought you said you wanted to take a walk in the woods? The right day for it, too. Though you never can tell, this time of year," and Johnny glanced back past the village, past the lagoon, to the bland afternoon sky, "about rain."

"The Holmans are away—And leaving Mrs. Crowell alone— She's been so ailing."

"She herself said it was all right, didn't she?"

"It doesn't seem—right."

"You take a little rest now and then, you do something just for the fun of it, and that makes you so you can work better afterward. I know. I've been working too hard myself lately."

Ann exhaled cautiously. She closed her mouth, and let her heels return to the cinders. She even made a smile.

"Well—But if it rains, what'll we do?"

"Get wet, I reckon. Come on."

The captain today was a good companion. He chatted lightly, even frivolously; and he did not appear to have thought there was anything unusual about her hesitation.

170

From his landing, two days ago, from his emergence, Neptune-like, out of the sea, he had been all affability. Though much of the time busy in the village seeing to the storage of his chest and the housing of himself and his mountainous attendant, and with confabs of a secret nature with sundry chiefs, nevertheless he had managed to eat with the Anointed. He had been prodigal of news about the Family, every member of which he seemed to know astonishingly well. Though not infrequently harsh and even unchristian in his opinions, and making no pretense that he liked Reverend Mr. Bingham, he had not been quarrelsome, or even sarcastic. The Holmans were away, as usual; but Abigail had liked Captain Lamb—Ann noted this instantly—and even Horace, though of course disapproving of him, was entertained.

"Always did like hills, when I was a boy. I'd think I wanted to go down to the sea, but it was hills I got the most fun out of, really. There's—there's something— It makes you feel, well, *all wopsed up,* don't you reckon?"

"Yes."

"All in a wopse, so to speak."

"Yes."

" 'Let the hills be joyful together.' That's Proverbs. Or Psalms. Yes, I guess it is Psalms, come to think of it."

"Yes."

If he makes any proposal, or if he touches me (Ann thought), a scream wouldn't do any good. And he's not to be reasoned with—you don't reason with a beast. If he does anything like that, or says anything, I'll just turn around without a word and start walking back. It wouldn't do any good to run (she thought). He could overtake me easy. So if he comes after me I won't run, I'll just get down on my knees and pray (she thought).

"Here we are," said Johnny Lamb.

As though they were about to enter another world—as indeed they were!—they turned for a last gaze at the glittering blue-black plain, the huddle of shacks each of which looked

171

so absurdly like a haypile, the opalescent lagoon, the far faint wavering white line of reef, the sky.

That sky was ominous. Rain was coming their way low on a kona: they could see columns of it thrust straight down from the clouds, the outside of the columns lighted by the sun. It was moving slowly. It might swing to north or south and never reach their shore, or it might be attracted by the peaks, which had a pull for rain—or so the natives said—and come directly at them.

There was no way of knowing; so they shrugged—or at any rate Captain Lamb shrugged—and they entered the jungle.

It was like that—like going *into* something, like lifting a blanket or tent flap and passing from one place to a totally different place. Elsewhere along this strip of forest-and-plain the break might well have been more gradual, for there were groves of tossing coconut palms and some koa and ohia trees, even a few bushes; but at the point where Ann Mathewson and Captain Lamb entered the jungle the quitting of the sun-splashed plain was as abrupt and sudden, and as dramatic, as the poofing out of a candle.

Thunder rumbled far behind them.

Everything had been hot and bright, a heat that was like a million tiny pinpricks. Now everything was hot and wet. They stood a moment, panting in the close air, gasping, afraid to move. Blind, their eyes throbbed.

After a while they stirred self-consciously.

"Spooksy at first, ain't it?" he said, and though she could not yet see his face she knew he was grinning.

"I don't see anything to be afraid of."

"Well, no. Not now. Come on."

No longer did the ground splinter as they stepped on it: here in the gloom it sighed soggily, and when you lifted your foot out it gave a gluey glugg. They slid as they walked, bracing themselves against creepers and unseen trees. Leaves slished them wetly, a sly salute. Small spiked plants tugged at their ankles.

172

He went ahead, she close behind him, and soon they came to know that this place after all was not pitilessly dark—though it was dark enough compared with the glare outside. They could see one another, and they could see the vine-drugged trees sometimes now, though the ground itself was hidden by a three-inch carpet of sensitive-plant and later as they climbed by ferns knee-deep. Exotic flowers stared blankly at them, like beautiful faces without eyes: they were lovely beyond anything Ann had ever seen, but they were frightful at the same time, for she couldn't help but believe, despite the scolding of common sense, that these blooms would prove poisonous even to the touch. Sunlight that was glittering golden javelins pierced the jungle. They heard no birds or insects, indeed no sound at all save that made by their feet in the muck.

They came to a clearing, and he turned.

"You all right?"

"Of course."

It was a murky place at best, vapory; and the overhanging foliage showed as though afraid of the sunlight, striving to keep it out, jealously guarding its own flat dark wet shadows like a fussy hen wing-covering its chicks. Overhead nothing but sky was visible, and not much of that. There was another and nearer mumble of thunder.

"Sit down?"

They were whispering. This was a conspiratorial spot, where it was hard to breathe. The creepers, the branches of the trees, leaned low. Nature held a forefinger to its mouth, shushing.

Captain Lamb was as uneasy as she was, Ann noted. For the same reason? He, too, was unaccustomed to jungle. For all his wanderings over the face of the earth, when could he ever have been in a place like this?

"Sit down?" he asked again.

She looked at the fallen tree—and maggoty it seemed, rotten, spongy, matted with bile-colored moss.

"No, thank you."

173

Her voice remained a whisper, but he laughed. She had noted that he had the ability to laugh himself out of fear or uneasiness. It was as though he had trained himself. The laugh was not at all artificial; if it had been, it wouldn't have irked Ann Mathewson. The captain was not merely being polite: he was asserting his physical superiority. Alert for such a move, she straightened her shoulders.

He seemed not to notice this. He had been remarkably good-natured ever since his arrival from Honolulu, and had not once mentioned the last time they'd met, much less hinted that he was ready to apologize for his language then. This nettled her.

"When I woke up this morning," he started conversationally. "That is, when Humu woke me up— Say, ain't it pleasant the way these Hawaiians have of waking you up? Don't you reckon it's a chirk way to start any day?"

"I'm afraid I don't know how they waken you," Ann said. "We don't need servants for that, at the station."

"Oh . . . Well, they got a way, they shake you very, very easy, never hard. Make no difference if the hut was on fire, they wouldn't fetch you up fast. One of the things about 'em I like."

"Why do they do that?"

"Well, I asked, here lately, and it seems they believe you got three souls—or as far as I can figure they're souls—something like that anyway—and these might be roaming around, or flying, and if you was to be woke up sudden they might not all get a chance to get back in time. Which would be very bad."

"Captain, I think that's outrageous!"

"Why? Sounds sort of pretty to me. Quaint."

"You should never encourage pagan beliefs like that! You should try to stamp them out!"

"I'm swouched if I see why. Can't do any harm, far as I can make out. And I like to be woke up that way, myself. Only thing I like better is not to be woke up at all."

174

He hooked his thumbs into the top of his breeches. He rocked on his heels, reminiscent.

"If you could see the way I *have* been woke up, most of the mornings of my life—"

"I think that we had better not talk about this any more, Captain. *I* consider it sacrilegious."

(Why was she ranting this way? she wondered. She did not mean to hurt him, or rile him.)

"All right," he drawled. "I don't side with you, but we won't argue. Too hot a day."

Thunder spoke again, directly overhead this time, and the sun went out as though somebody had pulled a tarpaulin over the top of the clearing. Impulsively Ann put out a hand, and it touched his arm, and she withdrew it as though from a dank wall or a snake. If this offended him he gave no sign.

"I think we ought to go back, Captain," she whispered.

"Start back now and we might catch the rain halfway to the village. We're better off here than we would be there."

There was no gainsaying this.

"Besides, there's a big hieau up this way somewheres, so I'm told, and I'd like to look it over."

"Hieau—isn't that an ancient heathen temple?"

"Sort of. I've never rightly seen one." He paused, and she knew that he was looking down at her. When he spoke again his voice was lower. "Why? You ain't frighted, are you?"

"Why should I be afraid of a temple to false gods?"

"Don't know, I'm sure, ma'am. Only thing is, you missionaries appear so superstitious sometimes. Attach so much importance to things you can touch and lift up and all like that."

"I assure you, Captain, that I am not in the least superstitious."

"All right. Let's go there then."

She gathered her skirt.

"Very well," she said. "Let's go there."

Place of Sacrifice 22

So they went on and on, stumbling, dogged and determined, their heads down. They did not talk, for the air was too close and hot for talk, and anyway they needed their breath for the climb. The way, previously a gradual slope, now was steep. Ann could see no manner of path nor indeed anything to indicate that human beings or even animals had ever passed here; but evidently Captain Lamb did, for he sometimes turned a bit this way, sometimes a bit that, while she plugged along after him with resolution, conscious, usually, only of his feet and the lower part of his legs.

She no longer even wondered at herself, or asked herself why she was here. It didn't matter. She felt that she was being drawn onward and up by a force that could not be measured, or even named. To try to resist, the way she felt, would have been foolish. It would only have caused her to miss a step.

She did slip several times, and fell, the heels of her hands slithering through slime she could not see under the ferns. Each time Captain Lamb turned and gravely helped her to her feet, and they went on without a word.

Ann observed no change in light, and when her companion stopped and she stopped behind him, she was startled to find that they had emerged from the jungle and were on top of a hill.

The clouds were low, and it was as dark here, almost, as under the trees.

Before them was the hieau, and Ann Mathewson's first impression was one of disappointment.

So far from suggesting a church, however idolatrous, it rose rather as a fortress, yet even as such not strong. It was moldy.

176

It sagged. The rocks, put together without cement, were peeling off the tops of the walls, as she had seen neglected stone fences peel at home, and there was nothing bright or upstanding, nothing dramatic about the hieau as Ann first saw it.

Here was no building at all, but a large cleared space of perhaps three hundred by one hundred fifty feet, enclosed on three sides by walls made of loose black stone or lava, walls possibly fifteen feet high, ten feet thick at the base, five or six feet thick at the top. There was no decoration on these walls, but their very size and regularity struck the beholder with awe.

There was no gate. The fourth side, the downhill side, facing them as it faced the sea, consisted of a series of ascending terraces shored up by the same sort of stone, one above the other, all shallow. The main floor of the hieau itself was set with tall grim monolithic boulders, upright, without ornamentation, even without any but the crudest shape, though obviously these were idols of some sort. Beyond, farthest from them, just inside the back wall, was a roofed structure made of huge flat rocks laid across upright ones, forming a high bare platform over a sort of cave or grotto. This clearly was the most sacred spot, the holy of holies, the altar itself, where sacrifices were made. The sight of it sent a shiver through Ann.

Captain Lamb at her side exhaled feelingly. She reconnoitered him with a glance. His mouth was a trifle open, his eyes were shining. When he started to turn his head toward her, she looked again at the hieau, for she didn't want to face him.

The place entoiled her now, and frightened her. The early disappointment slipped away; and she came to know that for all the lack of tinsel and twist, here was a temple of massed magnificence, a site surely dedicated, though dedicated only to noisome unnamed rites. For there was evil here; she felt it. Evil lurked in those upright Druidical stones, and crouched beneath that black lowering altar where for generations beyond count screaming men, impaled on sticks, had been

177

hoisted for sacrifice. The place was a very dwelling of malice and evil.

Silence pressed down upon it, even lower than the clouds. The leaves of nearby trees and bushes hung motionless, but not limp, stiff rather with expectancy. The storm was coming.

The only things that moved, anywhere, were the lizards. A little earlier they had been sunning themselves on the rocks; now they scampered for crevices in which to hide. It was not the arrival of the humans which had caused this, but instinct. The lizards knew when to hide. Soon not one of them was in sight.

Then the rain came. They could hear it marching up the hill behind them, clattering furiously on the foliage, louder and louder. A drop fell near them, and it made a sharp sibilant sound, a snake's hiss. Another drop fell, hitting as hard as might a pellet of lead. The roar of the rain came closer.

He grabbed her wrist and started to drag her up the terraces.

"No, no! Not there!"

"Got to! Only place! 'S going to be a humdinger!"

It was dark as night now, and as they hurried across the main court the rugged gaunt rocks rose on all sides, some shadow-thin, others immediate and menacing. Lightning spoke; and Ann screamed. She had seen in the flash that a few at least of these upended boulders had flowers and fruit at their feet, offerings. The fruit was rotten, the flowers dead, but still they were proof that this was more than a picturesque ruins to the villagers far below: it was a shrine, where the old-time gods called for propitiation, where the old-time magic still worked.

The sight of those simple offerings unnerved her. She stumbled. A drop of rain, tepid, oily, spatted against her cheek. It felt like a whole cupful of water. She started to fall. Captain Lamb, dropping her wrist, grabbing her arms, lifted her.

The lightning spoke again. The sky was very low, and thunder filled the air.

178

"No! I won't stay in a place that's—"

He stooped under the altar, and put her full-length on a bench. It was dry there. It was even soft, the stone being covered with leaves and moss. The leaves rustled apologetically as she struggled.

"No! I won't stay in a place that's—"

He got in beside her, and put his arms around her.

Abruptly they were dungeoned by the tempest. It was as though a steel cage had been clamped around them. The world was filled with the noise of water.

Captain Lamb held her tight, an arm underneath her, and he started to kiss her. She whimpered, moving her head from side to side, at first. Then she knew a sudden surge of joy. She had often wondered how she would feel if this happened to her. Horror was what she had expected. Happiness was what came.

There was lightning, a splintering crash. She felt it sting her eyelids; but she did not open her eyes.

Johnny was hers! He wanted her! She pressed against him, and began to return the kisses. "No—no—" she heard herself moan when she felt his free hand fumbling with her skirt and petticoats. Yet she helped him. "Not there—Let me do it." Johnny was hers!

It was hot on the altar, and close, hard to breathe. It was a small place, but dry, while the rain, wielding a maniac's lash, shrieking, flayed all the world outside; and water gurgled and sucked and splattered, and it shushed in sudden spates; and the thunder mumbled low.

Red Eyes in the Dark

23

It might never have rained, when they quit the forest and started across the plain toward a flamboyant sunset. Back in the hills the air had been wet, as before, the ground too; and when they came down, speaking never a word, they heard a high continuous after-dribble of rain among the leaves. Sometimes, too, a large warm drop fell on them. But the plain was unchanged, utterly dry, scorched, baked, as though about to curl at the edges from the force of heat. No hint, no glint of rain remained. The porous lava had taken as much as it could hold; the sun drank the rest.

The ground hurt their feet. It crick-crinkled and crunched with a bitter, faintly tinny sound.

Ann marveled most at her own acquiescence. Why, she'd not really struggled a bit! All the teaching of a lifetime, all the decency her soul was supposed to treasure, had gone so easily! A half-minute of relaxation, of consent, and everything in the world was changed, never to be as it had been before. And she still didn't care. With Johnny always by her side everything would be all right.

Her heart sang and she held her head high, not daring to glance again at her sweetheart for fear that she would weep and embrace him. The ground might have been pneumatic, the way she walked.

Three times she wetted her lips before she ventured to speak.

"There's a passel you must promise before we get back and tell 'em we're married."

"Eh?"

"First and foremost, I am not going to put up with any more

180

of this barbarous behavior, as if you were almost the same thing as an untutored savage yourself. What we're going to have is a Christian home."

"Oh, I see."

"No truckling to them, like riding on their surfboards and squatting down without a chair and keeping a pet pig and — and — well, no more of that being awakened a little at a time."

"After this I got to be woke up all at once, is that it?"

"Yes."

She strove to think of other details, for she wished to cover the subject before they reached the mission. She had no idea how she would announce the news. Maybe she'd let Captain Lamb do that. Or maybe she would whisper it to Abigail, and let Abigail tell Horace later on, and Horace could tell the Holmans. But she was too happy to worry about this now.

"And that heathen idol on a stick, too," she said, suddenly remembering it. "That must go. We'll burn it."

"Kukailimoku? Oh, so we're going to burn him?"

"Certainly."

"Why?"

"Because of what I told you. I won't have a thing like that in my home. It may have been all very well for you, with your friends down to the beach, and maybe it was very funny and all that — the way you look at it — but it's a quite different thing for a decent respectable married lady."

They walked a while in silence. They had the plain-desert to themselves, and the sun, though westering low, still was hot. Ann could not see Captain Lamb, who was half a step behind, but she sensed that he was massaging the right side of his nose in that way he had when he was thoughtful — when he was getting set to be stubborn about something.

"Listen, ma'am, I wouldn't want in any way to seem to contradict a female," mildly, "but don't you think maybe you're taking a lot for granted?"

"What do you mean?"

"Well, about this idea of us getting married. I'm flattered, sure. But after all, don't you reckon it'd be better if when you ask me to marry you, you at least wait for an answer before you start laying down the law about how we're going to live afterward?"

She stumbled, but caught her balance instantly, and went right on walking toward those haystacks, Kailua.

After a while: "Just what do you mean by that, Captain?"

"Well, you *did* ask me to marry you, didn't you? Or did I mishear?"

"Sir, it is not a lady's place to take part in any such discussion as this."

"Well, you started it. I was just trying to get the thing straight in my mind."

"If you must know, Captain, I — I assumed that *you* had proposed marriage to *me*."

"I don't remember it. When was that?"

"Why, just now. Back there. When you — when you did what you just did, under that altar."

"It was two of us did that, ma'am."

She colored, but held to the attack. Not planning to, she had ceased to walk.

"I have heard of men like you, Captain," evenly, "but I never expected to meet one. Do you really mean to say that you'd throw me over — leave me to face the world alone with my shame."

"No. Not if there's any shame connected with it. We don't know about that yet. I suggest we wait and find out."

"I don't understand you, sir."

"Sure you do. How long before we'll know?"

Blood flamed in her face, and she couldn't look at him. She longed to run, to hide somewhere; but this was important, and she must stand her ground.

"I — I would never have mistaken you for a gentleman, Captain, but I'd supposed you wanted to be one?"

"Not at all. Never said that. I do aim to get rich, but that ain't the same thing. Or maybe it is."

182

"It isn't."

"All right. But you ain't answered my question yet. When'll we know?"

"Two weeks from Tuesday, Wednesday. In there somewhere."

"I'll remember it. You do, too."

"I am not likely to forget." She swallowed. "And if — if I'm going to have a baby?"

"Then I reckon we better get married, yes. It'd be pretty bad for both of us if we didn't."

"And if I'm not? If I'm — well, all right? That's a dreadful way to put it."

"Well, I reckon that's something we can figure out later, when we're both not so tired."

"And pray tell me, Captain, how am I to explain this to my fellow workers?"

"Why explain anything, unless you got to?"

She flared. "And live a lie?"

"I wouldn't call it that, necessarily. I'd call it just keeping your mouth shut. Thousands of women do, all the time. Millions maybe."

She took half a step toward him, and her chin was high.

"Captain, I refuse to accept that answer. You are responsible for the position we find ourselves in. And even if you're not a gentleman you're a Christian — or you're supposed to be anyway. Now, I'm not going to plead with you, sir. All I'm going to do is *demand* that you do your duty in the eyes of God."

Suddenly he grinned. It covered his whole face.

"You know, I never made mention of this before," he said, "but you really got right lovely eyes. Especially when you're graveled up like this. It makes 'em even greener."

She whirled away, started to run, was afraid that she couldn't, and sat with a bump on a piece of lava. She gave up. She slammed her face into her two cupped hands, and wept and wept. It felt good. It hurt, but it cleared her out. She shook, and swayed. Certainly she sobbed aloud: she might even have wailed.

After a while she looked up. Captain Lamb sat on another

183

slab of lava some fifty feet away. He was not looking at her. He was smoking a cigar.

She was glad that he'd had sense enough to refrain from trying to comfort her. He wasn't all bad. She noted, too, that he had so placed himself that the stench of his cigar would not be carried to her.

"Reckon we ought to be getting on?" he asked.

"Let's wait a while. My eyes. They're not green now, they're red," wanly. "But it'll be night soon."

"All right."

They stared across the darkening plain and said nothing. From time to time Ann blinked, but she was careful not to rub her eyes. Once a hand went instinctively to her abdomen. She snatched it away. She must do everything possible to keep from thinking about that. If she was going to have a baby, well and good. She wasn't frightened by the thought of labor and birth. She'd seen her share of it. On the other hand, if she *wasn't* going to have a baby —

She glanced sideways at Captain Lamb. Had he come here, to this island, primarily to see her? She was sure of it. He had wanted her, desired her, even though it was in a lustful way. And now he'd had her. Had she pleased him? Would he want her again — enough to marry her?

Here she was, thinking such thoughts already! She was not on her knees, praying for forgiveness, as she should have been; instead she was wondering if her betrayer could be induced to wed her. Shameful! *He* didn't stir, just sat there smoking.

What she should have been thinking about was her own immortal soul. And that reminded her of the maid Lili. Whom the Lord would chastise, she reckoned, He first puffed up with pride. Here it was not much more than a week ago that she was scolding Lili — she! — for getting herself pregnant without being married. Well, Lili could laugh now. And Lili probably would, if Ann knew her. There was a great deal more excuse for the poor ignorant native girl, upon whom the light of God's

184

knowledge had never shone, than there could ever be for a Buttoner brought up in civilized Hartford. Ann sighed.

One thing at least was certain, and that was that she must tell Abigail Crowell directly she got back to the mission house. Abigail was her best friend — her only friend, really, on this side of the world. Ann reckoned that maybe some women were able to stand alone, but she knew right well that she wasn't. She could endure almost anything — but not by herself. She felt like one half of a pair of scissors, sharp enough, strong enough, but utterly useless without the other half.

Well, it was dark now. Folks wouldn't see her eyes. She would go to Abigail. She rose.

Captain Lamb rose politely, and tossed away his cigar. He did not offer her his arm. He had that much decency anyway.

They skirted the huts, the fires, and the lighted strings of kukui nuts, and came to the hissing edge of the bay. Without a word they went to the mission station.

There was a light inside, a lamp, but the table was not set for supper. Horace Crowell met them just outside the doorway. He looked frightened. His mouth was open, fishlike, and he blinked his weak watery blue eyes. He had been tending his wife, Abigail. In one hand he held a bedpan, which he had come outside to empty. Ann had never seen him look so pitiful.

Horace waggled both hands, including the one with the bedpan, from which however nothing was spilled.

"I'm afraid she's — she's had some sort of stroke. She's very bad, Mrs. Mathewson. I — I'm afraid maybe she's — dying."

They went in through the common room, the "parlor," and past a makaloa mat that marked off the Crowells' "bedroom." Abigail lay there almost naked. She was pale to chalkiness; and aside from her pregnancy, so much more evident now than it had been only a little while ago, she was hideously puffed and swollen, suggesting indeed a corpse that has been too long in water. Her eyes were closed. She didn't move. She did not even appear to be breathing.

185

Captain Lamb went to her swiftly. He felt her pulse, felt her heart. He stooped, and put an ear at her chest. He held a wetted finger before the open mouth.

"A mirror," he ordered.

"There isn't any."

He looked up. He shook his head in wonder.

"You mean you don't even own a mirror? Not even a *little* one?"

"I haven't had one since I took it upon myself to do the Lord's work."

Again he shook his head. He even fetched a sigh.

"You'd ought to," he said.

He worked the bottom of his cravat out of his waistcoat. The cravat was burnt-orange, and made of silk. The waistcoat, velveteen, was the color of a lemon; and its buttons were bright steel. Captain Lamb with a thumbnail tore some threads from the bottom of the cravat. It almost hurt Ann physically to see him do this. It was a beautiful piece of goods, that cravat. But she should not be thinking about worldly things.

Captain Lamb dangled some silk threads before Abigail's open mouth. Then he laid them across the lips.

Horace had entered, and stood beside the transfixed Ann.

They watched the threads, which were motionless.

"She ain't dying," said Captain Lamb. "She's dead."

Horace did nothing, just stood there holding the bedpan. Captain Lamb folded the limp pale arms over the poor breast, and then he clasped his own hands together and lowered his head, closing his eyes. He did not kneel, but just stood there, his lips moving.

Ann went out to her own "bedroom" to get her Book. On the way she met Lili, whose eyes were filled with tears. Lili looked a question at her, and Ann rolled her eyes heavenward, sighing. Lili burst into wails, and ran out.

And a little while ago, Ann thought, I was afraid to come back here and give her a chance to see that my eyes were red.

The little leather Bible was a comfort in her hands, and she

186

held it tight against her. She said over, in her mind: "To our sister, to my daughter, dearest Ann: Go to the dark places with a heart of light and spread sweetness around you. We will always love you, here." And what would Grace and Helen think, what would Mother think, if they knew what Ann had done?

She went back to the deathbed, and got on her knees.

She heard Captain Lamb go out after a while, on tiptoe. He had been unexpectedly dignified and thoughtful, and she was grateful to him.

Outside, the village was still. No natives came near. Warned by Lili, they avoided the mission; for death, as everybody knew, was a shameful thing.

Ann opened her eyes a little. Horace, also on his knees, but not praying, was looking at her. He was looking right across his wife's body at her.

Invitation to the Brawl   24

Clarissa was unhappy. She had to do kukae. She did not dare to move, but lay bellyflat, her chin squodged on the floor, and rolled her eyes now this way and now that as she sought a sight, any sight, to get her mind off the other end of her body. The bells of the bay bonged and clinged from time to time, but they did that anyway all night through, at regular intervals. Clarissa had very little sense of time. She did know, however, that until the windows waxed white she could not expect the Nasty Kanaka; and they weren't white yet; and if they didn't get that way soon, and if the Nasty Kanaka didn't come within a little while, there was going to be a mess, for which Clarissa herself, as usual, would be blamed.

Trying to shove the thought away, she rolled her eyes once

again — and gave a sharp grunt. The tiny hairs along the middle of her back jerked as the skin there twitched. No matter how you looked at it, that fiend-faced thing at the top of the pole always appeared to be scowling right down at you. Clarissa had been afraid of it all her life. She did not know what it was. She did not think that it was a kanaka; at any rate, she had never seen it move or heard it make a sound, though hatred black as gall glowed in its blank-space eyes. She tried never to toddle near it. Now she looked away, which was hard.

She wriggled, sighing, so that her flanks shook. She did not know how much longer she could hold out. There was no white at the windows. She knew the corner she'd go to, if she had to, and if she could make it. The Nasty Kanaka was lazy about cleaning — the Stinky Kanaka would have pitched him downstairs and the Big Kanaka would have chased him away, if they'd been here and had seen how he swept the room — but sooner or later even he would find what Clarissa had done, if she finally had to do it here. And she'd be whopped again.

She was often whopped these days, not like in the old times when the Big Kanaka and the Stinky Kanaka were here, her friends. She loved both of those; but they'd gone away. She loved the Big Kanaka the more, but she loved the Stinky Kanaka, too, everything but his smell. It was not those brown sticks he stuck into his mouth, the smoke coming out the end: it was not them. The Big Kanaka — the biggest Clarissa had ever seen — sometimes had one of those sticks projecting from his mouth, too; but in his case Clarissa didn't mind it, for she loved the Big Kanaka dearly, and completely; she yearned for him. On the other hand, she loved everything else about the Stinky Kanaka excepting the odor that came from his body. She loved his laugh, his feet, the way he tickled her behind the ears. It was too bad he stank so.

It was not the whopping itself Clarissa minded — she had plenty of fat still, even though the Nasty Kanaka did not give her as much to eat as the other two had used to give her. It was the humiliation. In the old days, when the two kanakas she loved

188

were around, a human like that would not even have been permitted to touch her, let alone wallop her. Clarissa stubbornly refused to squeal when she was punished; but all the same, she didn't like it; it hurt her feelings.

The worst of it was, that afterward, after it was too late, the Nasty Kanaka would only put her outside for a while anyway. Clarissa disliked to be outside. It was so dirty.

She sighed again, reflecting that life sure was a bitter pill.

When she could just lie still, thinking of nothing, it was good. Sometimes there was rain on the roof, and that she liked. She would lie motionless, listening. If it stopped in a way that caused her to know it was going to start again soon, she would shuffle thoughtfully, with one eye — she was customarily lying on a side at these times — watching the dust spiral and spin and then settle in fantastic frozen shapes on the floor. There was always dust, ever since the two kanakas she loved had gone away. The Nasty Kanaka seldom swept, and never swept well. It was the only thing Clarissa liked about him.

When the windows were white there would be all sorts of sounds outside; and then Clarissa would snuggle hard against the floor and be glad she was there.

But the windows were whitening now, and there was no sense trying to hold out any longer: already she felt as if she was going to burst. All caution, she heaved herself up. She held her snout down, snuffling the floor in the hope of finding some stray, hitherto unclassified smell that would take her attention from her state of strain. Thus with head low, eyes downcast, she started with great rectitude to cross to the most remote corner. She did not trot. She barely moved. The snuffling was not instinctual but rather desperate. She went direct for the far corner, which in ordinary circumstances she would have approached circuitously.

She nudged something she had not seen, and there was a scraping sound, and she jumped aside, screeching, and looked up — to see the idol with its hideous face falling upon her, pole

189

and all. It landed with a crash. She got out of the way barely in time. But the damage had been done. Now she'd get whopped for certain.

Clarissa stood shaking her head, shuffling sadly, rolling her eyes, her hind legs still spread wide. She glanced askance at the fallen god, terrible even though horizontal. She glanced at the windows, which were white.

She heard somebody open the street door downstairs, and her heart went sick within her.

A moment later, though, she heard the steps of two men on the stairs. She lept in delight, scree-ing wildly. They were coming back, after all this time! She knew those steps!

Wriggling, fairly squirming in ecstasy, her love almost insufferable, Clarissa went to the trap door and jiggled there, waiting for it to be opened. Sweat stood out all over her bland body, so hot was her joy. She could scarcely breathe. Her tail quivered.

Johnny Lamb went up the steps three at a time, batted the trapdoor open with his head, whooped a greeting, uprighted and replaced the stick-god, and raised the pig in both hands. *"Ah, she's my sunbeam! That's just what she is — my little sunbeam!"* He held her high, chuckling at her. Suddenly he remembered that there were sometimes sloppy results when Clarissa was thus hoisted after having snoozed in peace and alone for many hours; but as he put her on the floor he saw that it was too late to worry about that anyway. But no scolding! Here was too happy an occasion for reprimands.

"The room's filthy," he said without heat. "That cousin of yours — what's his name? — Hoopono? —"

"Aye, aye, sir," cried Humu, and roared with laughter.

"You tell him what I think of him. Bet he didn't even give Clarissa half the food we left."

"I'll break one of his arms," Humu promised. "Tomorrow afternoon."

Humu, having emerged into the room, was pounced upon by the piglet. Johnny smiled, perhaps a trifle wistfully — it had always saddened him to see how Clarissa preferred his servant to

190

himself — and started to clean up the mess on the floor. He made a mental note, however, of the need to reinstruct Humu, a literal-minded person who, unless restrained, *would* break one of his cousin's arms the following afternoon.

It was barely dawn, but he would be waited upon soon, he knew, and summoned to the Waikiki palace grounds where a luau was being held. They had heard about the luau from canoeists encountered outside the reef. It had been going on all the previous day and might last several more days and nights. The King was back — that was the reason. The King had forgotten his vow of abstinence. He'd left the *Cleopatra's Barge* two nights ago to climb right on a borrowed horse — Johnny's own, as it happened — and with his attendants, most of them as drunk as he was, had galloped back and forth through the village shooting off pistols. Then he had called for a luau. A real one. A big one.

Johnny shook his head, as no doubt many another had done at the news. About now, after some twenty hours of it, the luau would be going strong. It was certain that he'd be invited, which meant commanded, to attend; and it was equally certain that he could not afford to refuse. Illness was never any excuse for staying away from a royal feast. You could be carried there, couldn't you? Some were. More were carried away.

Not that Johnny was ill. He had never felt better; and ordinarily he would have looked forward to seeing Kaahumanu and other friends again and drinking some real liquor, after so many weeks in remote villages on the island of Hawaii, where awa, which he didn't like, was the only drink regularly served, the okulehau, when it was available at all, being raw. But Johnny was worried. He had not heard from Ann Mathewson in more than a month. All he knew was that she had been assigned back to Honolulu — and he had not learned even that until his return to Kailua a week ago. He would have gone directly to the mission from the beach if it hadn't been so very early, before dawn, when he landed — and if he had not been sporting a week's supply of whiskers, shaving having been impossible on

191

the cranky inter-island schooner. Now he fidgeted, happy to be back, but still nervous.

It was odd how much he missed that Buttoner girl, once he was away from her. Here in Honolulu he might have gone a week or more without a glimpse of her; but he always knew that she was nearby; he knew he could saddle up and go calling. Now, after all those weeks away from her, and far away, and after what had happened that day up in the hieua, he was all but panicky; he twitched.

Nor was it merely concern for her physical condition, though that pricked him, too. He felt a heap different toward her these days. The realization that he was going away, and soon, for a much longer time — all the way to Connecticut; it might take a year before he'd get back here — this, too, influenced and troubled him. Everything was changed now. If only, when they were face to face, she wouldn't be so confoundedly stubborn about some things, wanting her own way. But Johnny this morning inclined to lenience. He could hardly wait to change his clothes to get to the mission house.

He ordered Humu to bring around the horse, and explained again, using his hands, even drawing a little picture, how the saddle went on. More than once the gigantic groom had fastened the saddle on backward.

Now the fighter jogged off, Clarissa in his arms nuzzling him. Johnny scissored his beard and shaved. He was as nervous as a boy. He scowled at his reflection in the little mirror. He considered taking that very mirror along with him as a gift, a peace offering; but he feared that such a symbol of worldly vanity would be ruled out by the mission heads, drat them. He put on a conventional bottle-green coat over a peach-down velvet waistcoat with tiny brass buttons. He displayed two fobs, one on each side. His pantaloons, fawn-colored, were extremely light. His Wellingtons came high. He cocked his beaver. He even, self-consciously, slipped a quizzing glass into a waistcoat pocket, looping its ribbon around his neck. He had never peered through such a device, and probably never would in these parts; but it

192

was comforting to know that it was there; it hinted of affluence elsewhere in the world, a background of fashion and wealth.

He lit a cigar; but immediately afterward, recollecting where he was going, he put it out.

He thrust a scarlet silk pocket handkerchief into his left sleeve.

He had fussed a minute too long. Outside, the horse was ready — but so, alas, was Kamakau, a young chief who was close to the King. Kamakau, approaching now, with hand extended, rated a considerable punahele, or tail, of his own — fourteen or fifteen youths and maidens. He was feeling good.

"Aloha oe! Aye, aye, sir!"

"Aloha! I ola oe ia Johowa in Jesu! How's the party going?"

Kamakau was proud of his westernism and insisted on shaking hands before they even rubbed noses. He had certainly come straight from the luau in Waikiki, where the word had already arrived that Johnny the Lamb was back in town. There was nothing for it but to ask him in for a drink. At this stage of his business Johnny did not dare to offend any important Hawaiian.

At least the tail remained outside. That was something.

The French brandy was unviolated. His own reputation, or else that of the mighty Humu, he guessed, had been enough to offset the temptation. Now he opened a bottle, got glasses.

They were both polite, though Kamakau was vague and his eyes did not always focus properly. They exchanged gossip. Kamakau praised the brandy — as well he might! — whereupon Johnny presented him with the rest of the bottle and also the rest of the case. Kamakau accepted negligently and shouted for six followers, who bore the case away. Two would have been more convenient but would not have made the gift seem worth as much.

A murmur of awe went up from the crowd when the liquor was carried outside; and Johnny and his guest, after bowing to one another, had another drink.

It would pollute Johnny's breath, but what could he do?

193

It was perfectly understood, without anything having been said, that Kamakau, back at the luau, would make a gift of the brandy to the King, who would then as ostentatiously give it back to him — and that Liho would pay for it in the end anyway, if Johnny could collect.

For all his condition, Kamakau had not lost the courtesy instinctive in his race and his rank. He sensed Johnny Lamb's uneasiness; and so, though it was done with sincere regret, he turned away Johnny's proffer of another drink, and instead issued, as he'd been sent to do, the invitation to the feast. This invitation was ceremonious and very long, a set piece; and Kamakau, standing for the occasion, did it justice without caressing it.

And at last, holding the half-empty bottle, and followed in their agreed-upon order by the members of his punahele, Kamakau went away. Chafing, for even yet he was obliged to linger, though all his muscles tugged at him to go — it would scarcely have done to distract attention from Kamakau's departure by mounting the horse, a creature surer to catch eyes in Honolulu than any man, howsoever exalted or splendiferous — Johnny Lamb stood and smiled a false smile after the procession.

When he did mount, Johnny mounted carefully. He rode slowly. Head high, striving to look well, nevertheless he surreptitiously breathed through his mouth.

The House Was Quiet   25

     As he rode he reflected that he ought to be happy, and wondered why he wasn't.

     Dawn had always been his favorite time of day, ever since he could remember, whether afloat or ashore, in fair weather or foul: even back in Hartford, where he had been miserable most of the time, where each dawn had heralded a day of drudgery, he had yet enjoyed getting up, stretching, belching, outing his chin at whatever was going to come. Most emphatically in the tropics was dawn a joyous, glorious time, the brightest hour of all, when everyone smiled, when nobody was lumpy with sleep, a time before the day with its million stickers had been given a chance to attach trouble. *This* day was going to be a lollapalooser, too. The sun all but shouted as it rose, and it javelined the peaks with glee and twittered saucily all across the water of the bay. Honolulu harbor, though it was as you might say his front yard, his workshop, ordinarily depressed Johnny Lamb. It was not so this morning. The whaling fleet had gone; and the few small native craft in this opalescent kindly light showed almost clean and not a bit lubberly as they rocked at anchor in childish contentment. The fronds of the palms that lined the shore clicked and clittered together like thin slats of wood, a musical sound.

     He made a fine figure of a man. He was greeted with fond grins and "Aloha's" from every cooking pit, every doorway; and he knew that these people were proud of him, and, in their way, loved and even adored him. Yes, adored. The tales of his drinking bouts with the King, of his gambling sessions and other sessions with Kaahumanu, most of all the story, already accounted as a legend, of his battle with Humu, and, what was as dear to the Hawaiian heart, their beautiful friendship afterward — these made him a great man. It was not too much to say indeed that he ranked among the gods. This would be esteemed sacrilege, aside from being bad taste, in the establishment to which he was now riding; but it was true all the same. Johnny the Lamb, if more recent, was hardly more real, especially to the outer islanders, than the shark-god Ukanipo, or Pele, or the ferocious reptile-god Keakuamoo, or that great warrior Kiha, or Laamaomao of the wind, not to mention Kalaipahoa, Kuluiau, Punuamoewai, Mu.

Well, to be a god was good, but it didn't butter any parsnips. They paid you, these worshippers, with gratifying glances rather than cash. Immortality was the last thing Johnny would have sought. He was amused and mildly flattered by the way the islanders treated him; but the only time he gave serious thought to this attitude was when he saw a chance to exploit it, as he recently had. His pockets, as he rode, were almost empty; but his ledgers back in the store contained some fascinating figures.

So he should have been happy, though he wasn't.

He had made up his mind. On the schooner trip from the Big Island, on that rocky, racketty, perilous voyage in a contaminated cockleshell, he had made up his mind that, ashore, he would immediately inform Ann Mathewson of his willingness to marry her. It was not only that it seemed decent: it seemed desirable as well. He needed a wife, or would soon, and just that kind of wife, a Connecticut one, well connected, no nonsense about her, yet juicy and round, a girl with glow. She could help him heaps. And he'd sure as snakes keep that glow on her, and keep her juicy! He wanted no worried, worn-out women of the kind he had seen around him all his life, regardless of age, and saw even here among the missionaries—Lucy Thurston, Mrs. Whitney, Mrs. Loomis, Mrs. Chamberlain, Mrs. Ruggles; even Hi Bingham's young wife, who didn't have a bad shape sometimes, if she would ever walk with a spring again and get over being tired; even Mrs. Dr. Holman, still a not unattrac-

196

tive gal, though she was slipping fast. No, Johnny Lamb's wife would keep the bloom. That he swore: he'd see to it. He would buy the right clothes for her, and plenty of 'em, too, by gum; and she would not have to work like the other women, not nearly so much.

Yet, two terrifying thoughts had assailed him. The first — that Ann might say "no" — he brushed aside with little fret. Conceivably if she did, it would be for show; and of a certainty when she learned how much money he would be worth soon, she'd have him and jump at the chance. Johnny wasn't intending to propose marriage for right now anyway. He meant it for when he came back. All he wanted today was the promise. He liked to get things ready, in place. This was a new part of his plan, of the life he had mapped out for himself; but it was going to prove an important part, he reckoned, so that he wanted to be sure of it. As the man says in Luke: "Which of you, intending to build a tower, sitteth not down first and counteth the cost whether he have sufficient to finish it?" Well, Johnny Lamb had counted. He was ready to start.

He shuddered under the impact of the second thought, which was that Ann Mathewson might say "yes" — without hesitation.

He had lived long enough and traveled far enough, met enough folks too, to know that a woman's virtue is seldom worth all that it is customary among the right people, male and female, to pretend to believe it is. Just the same, it was worth *something*. Unless you were a halfwit you didn't just *throw* it away. That Johnny had been the first man into Ann Mathewson had been evident, up there in that hieau, afterward. It was not such a doubt that prodded him. It was an uneasy wonderment, born of the promptitude of her submission, whether she had wanted them to do what they did, and perhaps had wanted it hard, for a long time.

It was indelicate, that's what it was. Johnny himself, even, had been shocked. If he had not happened to be so excited, what with the thunder and lightning and everything, he might have backed away, or at least have held off for a little while.

197

Christ knows, he was no prude! But he did have *some* sense of decency.

He sighed. Well, he'd know, he reckoned, in a little while. He was afraid of finding out.

The sight of the mission gave him a start. He had forgotten how humble the small square white clapboard house looked — and how much like home. Right away, staring at it, he got chokey; and he felt that his eyes were warm and maybe even a mite wet. He reined in.

Even to the little green door — Yes, all it needed was a low white fence around it. They could sure use a knocker on that door, though. It would lend the correct touch. He'd send them one. *That,* at least, the Reverend Mr. Bingham would not be likely to spurn as a luxury! And they'd keep it well polished, too, folks like that.

The house was remarkably quiet. Most daytimes, he calculated, it must be about the busiest place on this side of the globe. No matter how many converts they didn't make — and he understood that they had yet to make their first — these Long Necks were spunky, sure enough, and kept on the move. They were not the curiosities they once had been, and the hubbub concerning the raising of this house had long since died, but they were still worth a good rubber now and then, even on the part of sophisticated Honoluluans. Visitors from other islands, if they hadn't seen it before, or even if they had, customarily upon landing on Oahu made a beeline for this very mission house.

But now there wasn't a soul in sight.

Many a time Johnny Lamb in passing had watched children and grown-ups come and go here, or had paused in saddle, as he paused now, to listen to voices from the schoolhouse:

> Away from fools I'll turn mine eyes;
> Nor with the scoffers go;
> I would be walking with the wise,
> That I may wiser grow.

198

That verse was all right, and so were the hell-fire ones, of which were so many; but he'd wager he could think of a few old Dr. Watts' songs that Sybil Bingham and the others wouldn't teach these tots. One came to his mind, and he chanted it, swinging a forefinger to keep time:

Lord, I ascribe it to Thy grace,
And not to chance, as others do,
That I was born of Christian race,
And not a Heathen or a Jew.

He wondered if Ann Buttoner, Ann Mathewson, had ever recited that? He reckoned she had. They all of them used to have to, back in Hartford.

But where was she? Where was anybody? The place began to give him the crawlovers, so still. Nobody showed at the windows. No smoke rose from the kitchen kiosk behind, no cantillation came from the school. The door stood ajar. He dismounted, and went to it, his heart beating fast.

He rapped, then yoo-hoo-ed. Nobody answered.

He pushed inside, purposely stamping. Everything was in order, though indeed there was little enough to be askew. The door opened directly upon a large room which must have served as parlor, dining room, chapel, and office combined. There was a long rough wooden table, utterly bare, scrubbed, unpainted; and two benches to match. There was an exquisite little hooked rug Johnny himself would have liked to own. There was the rocking chair he had given Ann. Except for an obviously home-made desk, there was little else.

He picked a door at large, rapped on it, and when nobody responded went in.

He knew instantly that he was in her place. He could not have said why. The room, a tiny one, as severe, as spare as any nun's cell, seemed almost intent upon asserting that its rightful occupant lacked personality of any kind. There was a chest, without label. There was no rug. There were a small window, a small bed, a small chair. Even the chamberpot under the bed

199

was small — and plain. There was no ornamentation or decoration of any sort, no feminine touch. Yet he knew that this place was hers. Somehow he knew that.

The only thing on the chair was a small leatherbound Bible. He forefingered up the cover — gingerly, as though afraid that it might explode. He read what had been written inside.

Yes, this was her room. The mother? Sure. She used to chase them when they'd go up to Prospect Street to steal pears. The other two would be the younger sisters, he figured. He wouldn't have remembered their names. Snarsey little skirts, as he recalled 'em. One with a big birthmark on the side of her neck.

The Bible certainly had been given to Ann when she married that wavering wisp of smoke Mathewson and set out for the other side of the world. What a thing to do, after all! Suddenly Johnny's chest got tight. He had never approved the missionaries, and expected he never would; but it took sand to do what they had done, no denying that.

It took more than a mite of sand to scribble these words and signatures into the Book, as far as that goes. From what Johnny had heard, Mrs. Buttoner and the younger girls had been all cut up when Ann married and sailed. They had carried on something dreadful.

He felt guilty here, an intruder. He backed out. The last thing his eyes fell on was the chest; and what a low short shallow thing it was! All her goods, everything she owned in the world, no doubt, excepting the Bible, and the clothes on her back, would be in that wee chest. Pitiful! She deserved better. She had a figure that could fill 'em, and she ought to have silks.

He touched nothing, but went out, leaving the door as he had found it.

"Calling on Mr. Bingham, Captain? Or could it be the Señora Mathewson?"

Johnny did not like Don Francisco de Paula Marin, though he respected him. The men, dramatically different in outward aspect — the Spaniard was tiny, wrinkled, ascetic, bald, as

200

wise as an old spider and probably as wicked—were commercial rivals, though their fields did not truly overlap. They were wary of one another, Marin fearing that Captain Lamb would slam his way into his own long-established business, Johnny leery of the Spaniard's venomous tongue and his influence at court. Oh, they were always polite when they met! But they were cautious.

Now, however, Johnny was glad to see Marin. Whatever else Don Francisco might be, he was the most assiduous gossip on the island, and it was said of him, and avowed, that he knew an event before it had happened. He was walking now, strolling rather, and seemed to have plenty of time. But, then, Don Francisco always seemed to have plenty of time. No matter how occupied he was.

"Aloha, señor! Where the hell are they?"

"Those of the mission, Captain? They were not home last night, eh? No, they are at the luau."

"*At the luau!*"

"Assuredly, Captain." The little man eyed him with admiration. "It comes to my ears that you did well in the group, Captain? Every conceivable picul, eh? It is marvelous!"

"But why should they — Tell me — When did they go there?"

"Last night. Could you tell me how you chanced to think of such a scheme for getting concessions? If you first — "

"Had they been invited?"

Don Francisco de Paula Marin, who always smiled but never laughed, very nearly laughed now.

"Invited? Oh, no, señor."

"Damn it, Marin, this means trouble!"

"Assuredly it does, Captain. Oh, assuredly."

Johnny made the horse gallop all the way to Waikiki.

Make a Curtsey to the Court 26

Everything was on a grand scale. Whatever it was, there was a lot of it — great piles, mounds, masses. The food could be measured in mountains, the drink in hundreds of gallons; and there were millions of flowers. The palace was surrounded by an enormous park that sloped gently to the beach, and every square foot of this was occupied by somebody participating in some way in the feast. More, there were thousands who could not get in but stood around gaping at the swells, and sniffing, their eyes apop, their ears buffeted by the pounding and throbbing of drums, the stamp of feet, and most of all by the multitudinous cackle of servitors and celebrants alike. You could hear it a mile and a half away.

The horse got Johnny Lamb immediate attention, but even with a horse he could not get into the grounds proper. This was not because it was considered ungentlemanly to ride into a royal luau, but purely because there wasn't enough room. He dismounted, therefore, found a man he knew and could trust, and after announcing the sacred nature of this man's charge, not only to him but to everybody else within hearing, handed over the reins and dove into the crowd.

Though the sun was out, there was something murky about the palace grounds, a suggestion of the subterranean. The grass was littered with breadfruit leaves, fish heads, smashed calabashes, bones that had been sucked and gnawed, flowers, melon rinds, shrimp shells, banana peels. . . . From the bodies rose the rank, almost *visible* odor of sweat and coconut oil. It was hot there, but not dry. Flies that were black and large filled the air. Everything was greasy and noisy. Stuck into the ground at irregular intervals were poles of bamboo or of hau wood, to the top of which torches consisting of cotton soaked in whale-oil had been fastened. Many of these torches still spluttered — smudgily, stodgily — while others had recently burned themselves out as far as flame went but still were giving forth heavy thick black smoke which hung low. There were eight or nine large imos, or cooking pits, each much like the pit at a clambake Johnny had attended once in Newport, Rhode Island, only larger. Some were covered, and smoke rose from these through the porous coral rock and the loose-piled dirt. Others were open, and the kahus and their assistants, working among scattered smoking steamy butts of wood and chunks of heated stone, were separating pigs, dogs, and chickens, and heaping them upon large wooden trays. Not all of the diners who had food were eating it. Some squatted, holding it close to them so that it would not be spilled while it grew cool. Your Polynesian does not like his food hot. There was also a sharp odor of urine there on the palace grounds that morning, for so thick was the crowd that it was difficult to fight your way to a tree, and if you were so fastidious as to leave the grounds you stood a chance of losing your place.

The pits were ranged, roughly, in a circle, there being plenty of room between them for attendants. It was inside this circle, a large one directly in front of the palace, that the chiefs of the first and second rank sat. There was a clear space there, too, the only one for a mile or more around, for the drummers and the hula dancers. In this space were the missionaries.

They stood aloof, stern with disapproval, stiff, in an unimaginative row. They were silent, except with their eyes.

They looked, as a matter of fact, sensationally silly. Even Ann, to whom Johnny's gaze went first, looked silly. It was a pity she couldn't be rightly dressed. She wore, as always, gray. She stood rigid. They all did.

What the Devil was the matter with them, anyway? Couldn't they ever let anybody have a good time? It was only natural that they did not enjoy seeing Liholiho drunk again; who did?

203

But it was *his* kingdom, after all. And this was *his* party. The Long Necks had always objected vehemently to the hulahula, a slow, complicated, extremely wearisome ceremonial dance, a hangover from the old days, a tedious business performed carefully and without zest, and it seemed almost interminably, by professionals. For some reason Johnny Lamb could not understand, Hiram Bingham and his flock thought it lascivious. Perhaps this was because he had never stayed long enough at a formal feast to witness the hula. It had been his practice to depart, ostentatiously, as the dance was beginning — a piece of privileged rudeness which many a convention-bound chief envied him. It had also been Reverend Mr. Bingham's habit to protest vigorously before every feast — whether he'd been invited or not — at which it was proposed to have dancing in any form. But previously he had done this in advance, and alone, though asserting to speak for all godly persons in the islands. Now he had his whole crowd out. Moreover, they had obviously been there all night, standing. They drooped with fatigue; but the light of battle still glittered in their eyes, and their spines were taut.

It was then, looking at them, clucking his tongue, feeling embarrassed, that Johnny Lamb remembered that this was a Sunday. *There* was the explanation! Of all the thou-shalt-nots, this skinny Yale man most fervently honored the fourth, attaching the greatest importance to it, though Johnny would be hanged if he could see why. As Johnny got it, in the world of Hiram Bingham you might worship other gods, bear false witness, steal, murder, commit adultery, and do any amount of coveting; and these things, though bad, could be forgiven; but you were irretrievably lost, sunk beyond rescue in sin, if you took a walk or kissed your wife or read anything but the Bible or hummed a tune or smiled a smile — on the Sabbath.

The Long Necks were the more conspicuous because everybody else inside the circle of cooking pits, excepting only the King himself, a few of the queens, and of course the waiters and attendants, either was hunkered down on his hams or else lay full-length. There was a profusion of mats around the "table," which was no more than a rectangle of ground covered with banana fronds, on which had been placed wooden platters and trenchers of roasted pig and dog stuffed with bananas, sweet potatos, yams, taro-tops, seaweed, mountain apples, guavas, and sometimes fish; and drinking coconuts, and bottles of gin and rum, gourds of awa, jugs of claret, Moselle, and okulehau, which is a ti-root distillation somewhat resembling Bourbon; and with umeks or bowls of live shrimps, chunks of boiled octopus, raw sea urchins, steaming breadfruit, roasted kukui nuts mixed with red salt from Kauai, raw livers, yams cooked in coconut cream, and limu, a seaweed suggesting parsley, though more astringent to the taste; and all sorts of containers of the starchy paste called poi, fresh and fermented, one-finger, two-finger, three-finger poi; and bundles of sugar cane for such as wanted to chew; and piles of turtle, both cooked and raw; and buckets of fish pickled in lime juice; and laulau, which was bonita cooked with taro tops and seaweed; and pipi, which were small black shellfish prised off rocks, to be picked out of their shells and eaten raw, like snails; and haupia, which was made of arrow-root and might have been cornstarch pudding, and also koele palau, much the same only stickier, not so sweet, and in color a somewhat disagreeable gray; and, to be sure, many other strange, fragrant, enticing, or in some cases terrifying dishes.

The King sat in an armchair, a substantial walnut piece some ship's captain no doubt had given him. He was drunk. Behind him, in addition to the usual array of kahili carriers, were at least a dozen spittoon and fan bearers. Two of the fan bearers, one on each side, alternated in holding the King, as discreetly as possible, so that he would not slide out of his chair to the ground. Another attendant carried a cuspidor in one hand, a bottle of champagne in the other.

Four or five of the queens, too, were seated, though not so luxuriously. One indeed, the gracious Kahulunuikaamoku, sat on the very brandy case Johnny had a little while before turned over to the invitation-bringer Kamakau. Nobody there was dressed completely in the mainland manner, but all, men and

205

women, excepting only Kaahumanu herself, who scorned haole tricks and appurtenances, wore at least some article of Western clothes. Liholiho's legs were naked, and around his middle he wore only a skimpy though greatly begauded malo, or loincloth, but the upper part of his body was encased in a stiff-starched shirt, with a high collar, a scarlet silk cravat in which a diamond blazed, and a yellow-and-heliotrope striped velvet waistcoat: the stripes were vertical. Keopuolani herself, the queen mother, the highest born of all the widows — even Kaahumanu habitually made the motion of uncovering to the waist when she addressed Keopuolani — though an intelligent woman and, astoundingly, not fat, even she had seemingly supposed that her position called for buttons tonight, and hooks and eyes. But good old Kate, she'd have none of that nonsense. She was dignified in a rich tradition- al pau, wearing nothing else — except flowers. Her head was bare, as were her legs and feet, and her arms and one shoulder Motionless, a thing made of bronze, she lay staring at something, or possibly at nothing. Her husbands, just behind her, King Kaumualii of Kauai and his son Kealiiahonui, the crown prince, she ignored. In one hand she held a raw fish, on which she had been nibbling; in the other a bottle of squareface gin. "Huhu roa," muttered Johnny. "She's sore about something." If she saw him she did not wave to him; but then, she would not have done this anyway until he had duly greeted the others and reached her, for Kaahumanu, though informal in many respects, on public occasions could be highly conscious of her rank and of what was expected of her, particularly if there were haoles present.

Meanwhile, it was required of Johnny, as he well knew, that before he partook of food he should greet and say certain set things to every male celebrant within the circle, starting with the one of lowest rank an ending with the King. This was all right, as far as it went; he knew them all, and liked most of them. The trick was, he had to take at least a sip of awa with each.

Awa looks like dishwater, and often tastes rather like that. It is a mild narcotic. It won't make you drunk; but Johnny Lamb had heard tell that if you drink enough of it you'll be temporarily paralyzed from the waist down. He didn't know for sure. He drank as little of the stuff as he could. It was compounded of the twigs of a certain pepper shrub, chewed for some time by girls, preferably virgins, who after a while spat it into a bowl, where it was mixed with slightly fermented coconut water. Though once it had been a chiefly drink, the chiefs didn't care much for it now that they could get liquor; but it retained its importance as a symbol in the complicated etiquette of the court.

Johnny straightened his leis. Coming through the crowd he had been repeatedly recognized and decorated in passing; so that now he had flowers around his head, over his eyes, around his neck, stuck behind his ears, in the loose of his shirt, and even half-in-half-out of his trousers pockets. He fairly dripped flowers — roses, gardenias, tuberoses, lehuas, fragipanis, hibiscus, taporo, and blooms he didn't even know the names of. He took a deep breath, squared his shoulders — and started across the open space.

Hiram Bingham stepped out of line, raising a hand.

"Are you going to join us, Brother Lamb?"

"I certainly am not, and you've got a Hell of a nerve suggesting it! Anyway, don't you know I'm not supposed to talk to anybody till I'm through greeting? Where're your manners?"

"Where are your morals, Captain? Don't you realize that this is the Holy Sabbath?"

"Sure I do. But there's nothing in that commandment says we can't take a drink on the Sabbath, is there? or eat a pig? or listen to music — if you could call it music?"

He leaned a little toward Ann, who had seemed not to see him, for she stood with her eyes downcast. Johnny knew how she could do that — appear to be gazing only at the ground before her feet but in fact not miss a thing that was going on.

He said under his breath, "Could I see you alone, in a little while?"

"I'll be here," she murmured, not looking up, "if the Lord wills it."

He wished he could ask her about her condition, but he didn't dare do that with Hi Bingham and the others so close at hand. Instead he took a calabash of awa from one of the waiters, and marched to the lowest of the highest-circle chiefs, and made a bow, and clapped his hands, and drank.

He wondered if all those chewers really had been virgins. The stuff tasted more sour than usual. He moved to another chief.

There were only two haoles present, besides himself, and the missionaries, and for these, Charlton the Englishman and Jean Rivas, a singularly unsavory little Frenchman of uncertain background, Johnny had no more than a curt nod. Nor was it necessary that he greet and be greeted by any female, howsoever exalted; that is, he didn't have to sip awa with them; but he knew them all, and felt called upon to stop a little while with each and pass the time of day.

There were a lot of chiefs, even so.

There was John II, the admiral; and Hewahewa, the former high priest, a mummy of a man with the face of a malicious old monkey; and Karaimoku, always called Billy Pitt by the haoles, the premier or something, who technically shared supreme authority with Kaahumanu, though in fact he did pretty much what she said; and Naihekukui, father of one of the queens, a scheming man but not a shrewd one; and Boki, another schemer, the governor of Oahu, who hated Kaahumanu and like everybody else was afraid of her.

Boki was sometimes hailed by sailors as the only Hawaiian with a pronounceable name; but those who knew him called him Okulenui, which is to say, Fat Ass. He was not a fool, ordinarily. His nose was venous and very thick, his eyes had a vulperine brightness. Now he was drunk. Beside him, hunkered down rather than lolling full-length, as Boki was, was his wife Liliha, a discontented ambitious girl, good-looking, too, all got up in lilac sarsenet covered with some transparent white stuff: she even wore slippers.

Boki had been trying for a long while to wean Captain Lamb away from Kaahumanu, and now he made much of him, calling for a song Johnny had once taught him, the only English Boki knew. Laughing, after the awa they did it together:

Hokey, pokey, winky, wum —
How d'ye want your 'taters done?
Boiled or with their jackets on?
Said the King of the Cann-i-bal Islands.

Liliha scowled in wifely disgust, and Boki roared his delight. There was a murmur of amusement from the chiefs nearby; but from behind Johnny Lamb came, sharply, the voice of Reverend Mr. Bingham: "Pupuka! Pupuka!" It started a chorus, so that in a moment all the missionaries were chanting: "Pupuka! Shameful!"

Johnny wheeled, cursing. This thing had gone far enough. If he and the governor couldn't sing a ditty without having a pack of skinny-headed sniveling —

Johnny intended, as he turned, to go right up to Reverend Mr. Bingham and punch his face.

He saw, however, that he had been mistaken. The Long Necks were expressing disapproval — but of the hula to come, not of his and Boki's vocalization. For the hula girls were beginning to appear.

They were serious girls, not notably pretty. A girl of comeliness, able to have a good time, would hardly tie herself to such an exacting profession. Now, clumsy in their costumes, nervous, twittering and tweeching like birds about the positions they should take at the start — it always took them a long time to get started, and even longer, folks grumbled, to get finished— they were thrown into something like a panic by the behavior of the missionaries, who stood in a row, each with an accusing finger pointed at the girls, croaking, ravenlike, again and again, in doleful voices, "Pupuka! Pupuka!" It was disconcerting. The girls fluttered off, back beyond the smoke and steam of the cooking pits. The Long Neck subsided.

Johnny shrugged. Maybe it would have been better if he *had* punched Hi Bingham in the nose, he thought. They were sure not getting themselves liked. How'd they ever expect to spread the Word if they were going to start in by spoiling everybody's fun?

Boki, soberer, was studying him with bright boar's eyes.

"You did well in the other islands, Captain?"

"Very well, thank you."

"You should be rich, if all those pledges hold."

"They'll hold."

"*And* if you can get the wood here, where ships can pick it up. The regular schooners could never handle that."

"I'll get it. I'm fetching my own schooner, from home."

"I didn't know that you owned a schooner, Captain."

"I don't — yet."

He passed on, with the confounded awa. He clapped hands, said the proper things, and had a drink with this personage and with that; and at last he reached Kaahumanu. She was a thundercloud, and paid him not the slightest attention while he greeted her husbands. King Kaumualii and Prince Kealiiahonui, on the other hand, had beautiful manners. Each of course rated a drink of awa. Then there would be only one more drink, thank Heaven — the one with the King. He did not need to drink awa in greeting to Kate, who didn't offer him any of her gin either.

"You promised me you would not fight in the mokomoko again!"

She did not look at him, and significantly didn't call him Tony.

"Humu did that, not me."

"But you arranged all those fights!"

"I never promised you I wouldn't *arrange* a mokomoko."

"And you took part in some yourself. I heard of it. I hear everything here. Everything that happens."

"You sure do," Johnny conceded cordially. "So you must have heard, too, that when I took part in some of them, all I did was fool with Humu — make-believe fighting, just to show them how it was done and get them excited. There is always

210

one man in every village who thinks he can beat anybody, but sometimes he's a mite shy about stepping up and saying so. We did that to encourage him. Those were exhibitions, that's all. Not real fights. We didn't hit hard. Why, Humu wouldn't hurt me for anything in the world."

"He'd better not," muttered the Queen.

"Tell me," King Kaumualii interposed, "how did you persuade each time some local champion to meet such a giant? How did you do that, Captain?"

"Well, it's like I said, your Highness. There always is such a man, in every village, if you can only get him to speak up. And then Humu and I make-believing like that — that got 'em stirred. They'd all heard so much about the time when we really fought."

"Ah, yes," said Kaumualii. "I have heard about that, too."

"Everybody has," said the Prince.

"Then if everything else failed," Johnny went on, "I'd get Humu all rigged up in one or another of the three fancy coats I'd lugged along for just that purpose, see?"

"Good coats?" asked Kaumualii, who always took a great interest in matters of clothes.

"Fit to knock your eye out, your Highness! Real macaroni! Get a gent like Humu into one of them things and nobody could resist the temptation to try to knock him down. And then the betting would begin. The trouble was, Humu himself would be so happy in one of those coats that he tended to strut instead of watching his work, and he damn' near *did* get knocked down a couple of times there. I had to speak right smart to him."

"Take your calabash over to the King, and then come back here," said Kaahumanu. "I want to talk to you." And she added, without turning her head, "Alone."

Kaumualii and Kealiiahonui tut-tutted soothingly, thanked Captain Lamb for his interesting discourse, and with dignity rolled to the far end of their respective mats.

Johnny grinned at his Kate. She sure was feeling ornery today.

211

"Go on," she said. "And come right back."

"I want to speak to one of the Long Necks first, as soon as Liho's through with me."

"Why?"

Of course he could not tell her, and she probably guessed the worst. She gave him a dark look. Then suddenly she smiled. Kaahumanu was like that. Even Johnny Lamb never had become accustomed to her lightning-swift changes of mood. She had, it seemed, just thought of something, remembered something. She leaned toward him, a conspirator. Back and forth across the inner circle made by the ring of cooking pits, heads were being put together as the action of this pair was watched, and men, women too, were whispering their belief that so public a conference of the kuhinanui, the greatest of the dowagers, the most powerful politician in these parts, with her accepted lover, a man who had recently cornered virtually all the sandalwood left in the islands — this conference, the whisperers were sure, intimately involved grave and serious affairs of state.

"Listen, Tony," whispered the Queen. "Do I say this right — " Then, amazingly, she switched to English. "Go with God, God is good." She had a time with those "g's" but stuck to it. "The big black bear shit on the small fast fox. How is that, Tony? For the love of our dear Jesus Christ, amen. Maitai?"

"You've been practicing!" He shook his head, while his eyes misted. "Kate, by God, you're wonderful!"

"Reverend Bingham's wahine, she gives me lessons now."

"Sybil Bingham never taught you that one about the bear and the fox."

She took a pull of gin, and giggled.

"Go see the King," she said. "But come right back."

Will You Marry Me?   27

His Royal Highness Kelaninuiliholiho, King Kamehameha II, wore a smile that was made of suet. He was very drunk indeed, and Johnny Lamb, sipping awa, felt downright sorry for this problem child of the Pacific, a fat young man, gentle, never harsh.

"It comes to me that you have gathered much sandalwood?"

"I've been lucky. Course, it all hangs on the pledged words of different chiefs."

"The pledged word of any of my chiefs should be good."

"Exactly what I figure, your Highness."

"The gracious Kaahumanu is not pleased by this?"

"That's right. But she wasn't thinking about the sandalwood. She was just afraid I might get my face broken in a mokomoko."

Liho smiled. Sleepily he took a sip of champagne; then he asked forgiveness, offered Johnny a drink, and called for another glass. Johnny had to accept. The wine was warm and sweet: he would almost as soon have gone on drinking awa. He smiled, smacking his lips. "Delicious!"

Liho swiveled his eyes toward the missionaries, and wrinkles sprang to his brow. Clearly he didn't know what to do. He did not want to hurt the feelings of these haoles by having them thrown out: his sense of hospitality and his innate gentleness alike revolted from that prospect. On the other hand, the hula must be danced. Liho himself was bored by the thought; but he knew his responsibilities; and because scores of generations of his ancestors had watched the hula, he must. He stirred. He looked almost beseechingly at Johnny Lamb, who had read these thoughts and who sensed that the King was about to ask his advice. But Liho changed his mind, to Johnny's relief. Liho elected, characteristically, to do nothing, to postpone decision. He waved negligently to Johnny.

"Partake, partake of our plenty, that the gods may smile."

It was the traditional phrase for ending a feast greeting, meaningless now that the gods were dead, but still used. Johnny bowed low. Afterward Johnny went over to Ann.

She stood with her hands clasped before her, her head low. The position angered him. It was too damned submissive. Why didn't she look up, at least for a second? She didn't have to smile — if she'd just look up, instead of standing there as if waiting to be axed. She was not a sheep, or shouldn't be; nor was he any butcher.

He swallowed. He took a deep breath. It was half a minute before he could trust himself to speak.

"May I see you alone for a little while?"

She did not stir.

"My duty is here," she answered in a clear low voice.

Well, he felt like snapping back that there were plenty of psalm-singing dimwits here without her feeling called upon to keep them company, and also that it might just barely be possible that she had a duty to him, too, besides the Reverend Mr. Bingham. But he didn't say anything like that. What good would it do? Matter of fact, how could he speak to her alone here anyway, except the way he was doing — in a whisper? For them to get off the grounds, away from the crowd, might take half an hour.

So he kept control of himself, wetting his lips, swallowing again. Reverend Mr. Bingham approached.

"Changed your mind, Captain? Going to join us?"

"I certainly am not!"

"Uh, I hoped that in any event you are not going to try to dissuade Sister Mathewson from doing her clear duty?"

"You can hope anything you please." Johnny swung toward Horace Crowell, who had come up from the other side. He didn't like Horace, didn't care for the way the man eyed Ann. "That

214

applies to you, too. Would it be too much to ask both of you that for once in your life you mind your own business?"

Horace started to bluster, and Reverend Mr. Bingham opened his mouth as though to pray, but Ann shook her head a little — it was only a little — and they were silent, and moved back.

"Now maybe I'll have a chance to ask you something. Are — are you — are we going to have a baby?"

She shook her head.

"You sure?"

"Yes," she whispered, "I'm sure."

It was difficult to keep from exhaling in one long swee-ee, which would hardly have been good manners. Besides, he had to think of his face as well as his voice, for he was being watched. He did not lift his head, any more than she did hers, but he sensed that many eyes were upon him. The measure of the hubbub remained unchanged: waiters hurried here and there, drinks were downed, another pit was opened and the great piping rocks were rolled and levered away, steaming packages lifted out; the flies buzzed indefatigibly, the torches spluttered; through it all the drummers were trying out their drums while they waited for the hula girls, and the jibber-jabber of a thousand voices never faltered. But the missionaries all were watching these two, and maybe the King was, perhaps crafty old Boki, certainly Kaahumanu.

"There's another question I have to ask you," Johnny whispered.

He had sometimes wondered, on night watches, whether he would ever propose marriage to anybody. He was not worried much about it, women, in those days, being far away, wealth even farther. One thing was certain: In his wildest dreams he had never thought of whispering a proposal against the top of a poke bonnet in the midst of a babbling disorderly throng at seven o'clock in the morning — to the beat of tomtoms.

"I'd've asked you this question when I got back to Kailua, only you weren't there any more."

215

"I could hardly stay in that mission house alone with — with Mr. Crowell. The Holmans were away."

"You folks certainly have dirty minds."

"It isn't us," sharply. "It's for the benefit of the natives, what they might think. Mr. Crowell, as far as that goes, I'm sure he never had an impure thought in his life."

"You are, eh? I wish *I* was sure of that."

There was a pause. When she spoke again he had to lean over closer in order to hear her.

"What was the other question you wished to ask, Captain?"

"To ask you to marry me."

Now she did lift her head. A gust of gladness took him, and his arms went out. But then he saw her eyes — and it was as though she had dashed a pan of water into his face.

She was not melting, not raising her mouth for a kiss. She was wrathful. That mouth worked. The eyes flashed.

"You should have asked me that a month ago, sir!"

"Sh-sh!"

"You told me you were visiting the Big Island just to see me, when you really weren't at all!"

"Ma'am, I never told you I went there just because of you. I went there *first* because you were there, before I went to Molokai and Lanai and Maui and Kauai. And I *did* jump overboard and swim the lagoon because I'd seen you on the beach. That's all."

"All you were there for, really, was to take your poor slave out and exhibit him like a gamecock!"

"Humu loved it. Don't you think you ought to keep your voice down a little?"

"And you gambled, and cheated those poor chiefs out of the only real thing they had — their sandalwood."

"I did not. There was no cheating, all fair fight."

"You'll strip the islands of sandalwood!"

"Well, I can't for the life of me see why I shouldn't. If I don't, somebody else will. The only thing that gravels the others

216

is that they didn't think of it first." He put a hand on her shoulder. She didn't wince, but he felt her go tense under his fingers. "Listen, I'm going home soon, and when I come back I'm going to have my own schooner, and then I'm going to get really rich."

"You think of nothing but money."

"I've been thinking about you a lot lately. I'd like for you to go back with me, when I go back for good. We could build a house — on Prospect Street."

"A man like you!"

"I'm changing. I can afford to, now. I ain't staying the same."

"You're a murderer!"

"That don't mean I'd be a bad husband. Anyway I'll fix that. When I come back here I won't be a murderer any more."

"And that — that connection with Kaahumanu?"

"You always manage to drag Kate into it somehow, don't you? What's she got to do with it? She didn't help me get that sandalwood. Matter of fact, she's sore about the whole business."

"The—the connection. The affair. It's—*unspeakable!*"

"Oh, now, I wouldn't have called it that. Seems to me folks have been speaking about it for some time."

"That's just the point! Everybody knows about it!"

"Would it have been better if I was sneaky about it? If I did it and then denied it? After all, I'm not a hypocrite. You got to give me credit for that."

"I'll give you credit for one thing only—a colossal audacity."

"Well, that's something." He could feel the hairs on the back of his hands tingle. A droplet of oily sweat meandered down his back. "So then—will you marry me?"

She hesitated, not for lack of words but rather for lack of confidence in her ability to pronounce them. She swayed.

"Listen, Ann," softly. "We both'd have to give something up. That's what marriage is, from what I hear. It's asking a right lot, I admit, for a pure and good widow like you, a godly woman, to take a hardened old sinner like me. But I'll be getting some

217

things I maybe don't like so much, too. Well, I'm willing. I'll take the chance. Looks to me like the percentage was about right."

"We are not talking about gambling."

"Well, we're talking about marrying. Comes to pretty much the same thing."

"Don't jest, please, Captain."

"I ain't jesting." But he was losing his temper. Another tadpole of sweat coursed a leisurely tickling way down his back, and another; and then one started to zigzag down his chest. "I mean what I say."

"You might at least refrain from shouting it."

"I wasn't making as much noise as you were."

In fact, they were both trying, not always with success, to keep their voices down. They rasped. They stood very close, glaring at one another. He would have taken his hand off her shoulder except that he feared she might fall.

Certainly there were plenty of people looking at them. The missionaries edged closer.

More quietly, "When you called me a pure and good widow, a while back, Captain, were you being ironic?"

"Don't know what that word means, but as far as I'm concerned you are pure and good, yes."

"But don't you realize that you're asking me to believe in a miracle, practically?"

"Well, why not? You believe in plenty of others, in the Book."

"I consider that sacrilegious."

"I don't. But anyway why shouldn't I change? Why shouldn't I become respectable, once I can afford it? Nobody in Hartford's going to know what I used to do down on the beach here."

"You're prevaricating, Captain. I am talking about higher things. You ask me to believe that you are worthy of being the husband of a godly woman, but what evidence do you show?"

"Well, what evidence do you expect?"

"I don't know. A sign of some kind. Something solid."

"Money's solid. Won't that do?"

218

"Please be serious, Captain."

"I was never more serious in my life. But God-damn it, here you stand telling me that you want some sign or something —"

"I certainly do! Before I even consent to hear your proposal I ought to be given some evidence — some really tangible evidence — that you are at least beginning to renounce your wicked ways. I'm entitled to that much, at the very least."

"Well — *what*, then?"

"Well —" Then it came to her. She was frightened and confused, and afraid of going on looking up into his face, but at the same time afraid of turning away, as if his face, pushed down so close to her own, was like his hand on her shoulder, a thing of support, indispensable. But it came to her. "That heathen idol you keep in your room."

He gasped.

"Kaili?"

"You know the one I mean. The one on the pole. Any man who harbors a monstrosity like that is not fit to ask me to marry him."

"You expect me to give that to you?"

"I do. Before we go any further in this conversation I expect you to hand over that idol to me, so that I can destroy it."

"Now God-damn it, this is carrying things too far! It's bad enough you should treat me like a beggar when I come up to you with a perfectly decent offer, but now you want me to crawl on my belly, is that it?"

He was shouting, and he knew it, but he couldn't help himself.

"Well, God-damn it, I'm not going to! I'm willing to go halfway, any time, but I damned if I'll wear any callouses on my knees groveling in front of a dirty little slut that don't even know her own mind!"

He took his hand away, and Ann sat on the ground, pop-eyed, and then toppled sideways, giving a little moan.

Reverend Mr. Bingham was there promptly, and that Crowell fellow, and Elisha Loomis, and some others. They propped her up.

"You ought to be thrashed," cried Horace Crowell.

"You aim to try it?"

But Johnny did not want to stay. His rage was still upon him, shaking him, and if he stayed he'd start smashing faces.

"Give her some gin," he snarled. "It won't kill her."

He saw Kaahumanu get up from her mat and start toward him, and he plunged into the crowd. At the edge of the grounds he recovered his horse, and he rode wildly back to Honolulu. He got a hammer and some nails downstairs in the store, and when he went up to his living quarters he frightened Humu and Clarissa. He didn't speak to them. He went right to the corner where the god of battles, bloodthirsty Kukailimoku, leered from his pole. The building was made of stone, but there were beams of hao wood in each corner, twelve-by-twelves; and he went to one of these. Firmly, working fast, cursing the while, he nailed Kukailimoku to the beam. Humu, who cowered in a corner, later was to swear that he heard the god shriek while this was being done. He was afraid of Kukailimoku. So was Clarissa.

For several hours after that, coddling his rage, letting it seethe and simmer, Johnny busied himself with ledgers, going over and over the figures. The work gave him no delight, as normally it would, but it served to quiet him, almost hypnotizing him. Not until afternoon did he return to the feast at Waikiki. By then he was hungry, thirsty too, and since he had already been greeted and had formally paid his respects to the court, it was not necessary for him to drink any more awa. He was accompanied by Humu, who carried another case of brandy; and he was welcomed and made much of by virtually everybody in the inner circle excepting the one person he did want to talk to — Kaahumanu. *She* sulked. The party otherwise was gay, the weaker drinkers having long since fallen asleep, adding their snores to the sounds of celebration. The Long Necks had gone away, exhausted, discouraged, using Ann's swoon as an excuse, in this manner saving face; and the hula, thank Heaven, had been finished.

The sun sank with tropical abruptness, and the moon, as though it had been awaiting this as a signal, rose full and fine, fleering on the tops of the coconut trees, filling the glades with silver. Soon somebody said, "Let's go swimming," and the party tumbled down to the beach.

The beach at Waikiki was reserved for those of chiefly rank; but there was no objection — there never was — to an audience, provided the commoners kept their distance. Thousands then watched the court go splashing, and when the wiliwilis were produced, the surfboards, excitement ran high, and the betting began, those penniless men putting up whatever they had — their mats, their taro, their services even to the point of slavery, often their wives—on who should come in first. The nobles also, while they undressed, were betting. Kaahumanu, in good spirits again, roaring with laughter, backed herself magnificently.

"Fifty dollars, my Tony! You're rich now!"

"I'm not much good at this," Johnny muttered.

"You're afraid!"

"Fifty dollars, you said? All right."

"Come on!"

Johnny Lamb had been on a surfboard only once. It was a trick not easy to learn, he knew. It *looked* absurdly simple; but it wasn't. A board was eight or ten feet long, two or three broad

221

at the broadest point, several inches thick, and, being hollow and made of very thin wood, unexpectedly light to lift. Kaahumanu literally tossed hers into the air and caught it, in sheer exuberance. Johnny Lamb did not try anything like that.

About twenty of them paddled out toward the reef, to the place where the waves make up. The waves at Waikiki, being inside, do not break until they reach the beach — which is why the surfboarding there is so good.

It was a long way out, and you had to lie flat on your wiliwili and paddle with your hands on each side, an unnatural effort. The others, accustomed to it, chattered and laughed all the while. Johnny Lamb for the most part was silent. He did maneuver to bring his board alongside of that of Kaahumanu, and he tried to get her to tell him why she had agreed to take lessons in English; but it was no time for serious talk, as he should have known, and he was ignored; and after that he saved his wind.

Surfboarding, or at any rate learning to surfboard, is an extremely strenuous sport. The others cavorted, which made Johnny, plugging grimly, feel old. He was not used to this. He was tired, his muscles were tight, he'd been living hard and was feeling the strain. He was used to being the best in every sport, always had been. He hated the thought of losing that fifty dollars. He never would have taken the bet if it hadn't been offered so publicly.

They kept their line, and when they had reached the place where the waves made up, about three-quarters of a mile out, they turned in unison, smartly, making something of a military drill of it — except that Johnny the clumsy was, as it were, out of step. They all laughed at him, though goodnaturedly enough.

Now they waited for the right wave. No sailing man, only a landlubber, would ever believe that seventh-wave silliness; but it was unquestionably true that all waves were not the same size. On a wiliwili, facing in toward shore, but glancing behind you from time to time, ready to ride, you wanted the biggest wave you could get. It might be the first to come along; or it might be the fifteenth. You wanted to be ready for it, in any case, so before it could reach you and lift you up you started paddling wildly.

You would start to go up, as it overtook you, and right there was the split-second upon which everything depended. You had to slide to the back of your board, rasing the nose a little, and slant down the front of the wave. Maybe you only got to hands and knees back there, or maybe you rose right to your feet, the way the experts did; but in either event you had to shift the whole balance of the board. If you did this too soon, too near the bottom of the wave, the nose wouldn't come up but instead would dig into the water, so that all the rest of the board bucked behind you like a wild horse and sent you flying ten-fifteen-twenty feet through the air. The water was shallow, and if the breath was knocked out of you and you weren't careful to make the dive flat when you struck, you might be cruelly slashed by the coral of the bottom. On the other hand, if you slid to the back of your board a wee instant too late, so that you were riding near the top of the wave, you might not get it slanted right. In that event the board might readily rise up and slam you in the face, and almost certainly, even if the board behaved, the wave would pass right underneath you, leaving you rocking gently in a trough, while the others sped shoreward, yelling, laughing, singing. You could feel almighty silly when you were left like that. Johnny knew.

Now they let one, two, three go by. They were yelling, clowning, as carefree as puppies.

Johnny Lamb studied the shore, the white sand, the coconut trees, the hills beyond, all soaked in unbelievable moonlight; and as he had done more than once before, he marveled at the dreamlike quality of this land. It was difficult to believe it, even when you'd rubbed your eyes. You expected to wake up at any moment. Nothing that could possibly happen here, you were sure, could have any real meaning, much less importance; nothing would last.

"*Here it comes! Maikai! Maikai nui!*"

They all began to thrash the water. They started in a row, spewing the air with drops that glistened like quicksilver, leaping and flashing. The wave reached them, lazily lifted them. . . .

Johnny Lamb never did learn what he had done wrong. Whatever it was, it happened very swiftly. He slid back; he got to his knees, and at that time he was even with the others, going fast, too, nicely tilted down the front of the wave; and then — he was in the water, his ears ringing, and the board floating idle ten or twelve feet away. The water immediately about him was still; he might have been in a pond. The others were streaking toward the shore, where thousands cheered. They were standing on their boards in a lather of spray, windmilling their arms, laughing, yelling, having a wonderful time.

Johnny swam to his board, and climbed on. Wearily he paddled to shore, getting small listless rides down a wave now and then, but for the most part muscling it.

He felt forlorn. He moved slowly, head down.

He had expected the beach to be deserted, but Kaahumanu was there, standing alone, waiting for him. She went right up to him and kissed him mainland-fashion on the mouth.

"Forget the fifty dollars, my Tony. It was not fair."

"No, no. You'll be paid."

It was good to see her again and to hear her laugh, and it truly touched him that she had waited, with a mere handful of attendants. He slipped an arm around her waist, a considerable distance, and she chuckled, snuggling close to him. Then, with her punahele of thirty-odd falling in behind, they started back for the palace grounds.

"Kate, bless you," he said. "Why *did* you come to listen to Sybil Bingham? You're not going to get yourself converted now, are you?"

"I might." Stark naked, wet, holding him as close as he was holding her, she spat expertly. "Maybe I must meet this God of yours? Maybe my Tony will never really be mine unless I do?"

"Did Sybil Bingham sell you that idea?"

Kate nodded, rubbing her cheek against his shoulder, rolling her eyes.

"The woman's got more sense than I gave her credit for," muttered Johnny.

The Queen slipped an arm loose and goosed him, caused him to jump. He slapped her behind. The attendants cheered.

"Tony," she said sideways, when they had quieted a bit and were walking again, "what does it mean — 'immortal soul'?"

"That's something you better ask Mrs. Bingham about, not me. I will give you a Bible, I'll do that, to read while I'm away. But right now, to tell the truth, I'm more interested in a drink."

It was that night that the party really got under way. It lasted until Thursday.

Simply Say Good-bye   29

The cabin was immense, nineteen by twenty, and so high that you did not even have to stoop much. It was done in gold and red; and at the ports hung velvet curtains with long, dangling, somewhat tarnished gold-braid tassels; while there was a Turkey-red rug on the floor. This was in the style already coming to be known as Empire — though when you stopped to think of it, as few did, it was some years since the incorrigible Boney had been shipped off to spend his last dreary disagreeable days on St. Helena. The pillows, the rug, the curtains and tapestries, and all the rest, were pretty well smirched and blotched; yet in certain lights they could still show elegant.

Kings had caroused here, dukes had been drunk. Cannibals from unnamed islands, and khaftaned nomads from deserts far away, had stood, all awe, gaping at the splendiferousness of this cabin.

Forward, atop the capstan, there was a life-sized American Indian made of wood brightly painted. The Polynesian sailors were still afraid of it. Visitors from the outer islands invariably uncovered down to the waist in that direction—or made the motions, if they weren't wearing anything—before venturing into this dazzling fabulous cabin.

Cleopatra's Barge had been built by Retire Becket at Salem, Massachusetts, some eight-nine years ago, on the order of George Crowninshield, Jr. In its time it had been the most luxurious private pleasure vessel afloat; and when Crowninshield took it around the world, exalted passengers had fought for a glimpse of this cabin where Johnny the Lamb sat scowling now.

He slammed a fist on the table, and the bottles jumped, while streamers of blue tobacco smoke bestirred themselves languidly.

"God-damn it, gentlemen, that's the way it is! You can take it or leave it!"

"I guess we'll leave it," said one.

"Yes," said another, "leave it."

Johnny blinked at them. They were not cowering, not a one. Some few looked a shade uneasy; but they didn't turn away when he glared. Rivas the Frenchman even went so far as to sneer.

"Monsieur, I fear, takes upon himself all the prerogatives of majesty. Is that why we're on the royal yacht? But others know Liho."

"Is that a threat?" stormed Johnny.

"No, monsieur. Only a comment on one. *You* made the threat."

Johnny pounded the table.

"I did no such thing! I promised to cut you in on some of the profits provided you kept the stuff moving while I was away."

226

"But you implied, monsieur, that if we did not do it on your terms we would not bet a single picul all the time you were gone—or even after you came back."

"That's right, Johnny," said Jim Hunnewell. "That's what you practically said. You didn't *say* it, but you practically did."

Johnny stared at him aghast. There were some of these men he didn't care for; but he liked Hunnewell, an American, an honest careful trader, a seaman once.

There were others. There was young Jones, who represented Marshall and Wildes of Boston; and Don Francisco de Paula Marin, never saying a word but sitting in a corner watching each speaker with small bright reptilian eyes; and Woodland, and Beckley, and Harbottle, Englishmen, each controlling a certain amount of trade; and Butler of Maui, and old Parker of the Big Island, Americans.

Johnny had supposed that he controlled these men. Excepting Marin, an interested party anyway, he was in direct competition with all of them; and the only reason he had not pushed them out, one by one, as he figured it, was because in the long run it would have been a bad thing for his business—for the port of Honolulu and the islands generally. Hell, he was certainly broadminded, wasn't he?

Yet here they were, staring back at him. Had this been a crowd of bullyboys on the beach—even a much bigger crowd —Johnny would not have hesitated. He would have flung himself upon them single-handed; but such violence had seldom been needed, for the sailors knew that they would get no women, and they'd get no rum, and likely enough no wages at the end of the voyage, if they talked back to Johnny the Lamb. With the traders if was different. They just sat and looked at him, not blinking. After all, they were in this part of the world for the same reason he was—to make money. They didn't scare easily.

"The trouble with you, Johnny," spoke up young Jones, who at that probably was only a few years older than Johnny but who would never before have ventured to speak to him like this, "you seem to think you're the real king. We all know Liho ain't. But that don't prove you are. No, nor Hiram Bingham either."

This left Johnny like a sail in a scanting wind. He had never before been put into a class, any kind of class, with the Reverend Mr. Bingham; and he had never expected to be.

After a while he shook his head, unbelieving, and cleared his throat. He knew he was doing the wrong thing; but, flustered, he didn't know now how to find out what the right thing was.

"All right, gentlemen. You've heard my offer. And you prefer to reject it. Very well: I'll keep all the stuff for myself. And when I come back, gentlemen"—and here he leaned his right elbow on the table and pointed a long red-haired finger now at this one and now at that — "I expect to find things the way I left them. If they ain't, I'll raise hell. And you all know I can do it, too." He picked up his ledgers. "I won't be gone longer than I have to."

"Don't hurry," somebody said.

Johnny looked up quickly; but the faces were blank. He didn't splutter. He'd spluttered too much as it was. He rose.

"These proceedings are closed. Good day, gentlemen."

It threw his confidence out of kilter. He was suddenly alone. He had been left behind.

He was not afraid of a loss of trade. He had, he believed, anticipated everything. He had all the sandalwood of the outer islands so sewed up that none could be handled or even cut by anybody not working under his own, Johnny's, orders. The pledges had been solemnly made, before many witnesses. The fact that they represented prize-fight losses could mean nothing to the honor of the chiefs. Johnny had supposed he was doing the other traders a favor when he offered to let them start the haulage. And they'd laughed at him—well, maybe not actually laughed, but it came to the same thing. Oh, they'd learn! They would find out soon enough that the only way they could get to that sandalwood was if Johnny died, in which case it was to go, by the pledges, to the issue of his body, which in fact did not have any issue—yet. So only if Johnny did not come back could these sharp-eyed men pounce upon what he (with the aid of Humu) had won. But he *would* come back. Damn it, he'd come back if for no other reason than that.

All the same, it had put him into a twitteration. And added to this was the fact that he could not say good-bye to Ann. There was no sense trying. After that feast at Waikiki a couple of weeks ago, and after the fumes had evaporated, so that his head was clear again, he had written her an apology for his rudeness. He had not been abject, naturally. He'd been formal, even maybe a mite uppish, but perfectly plain. He had, in fact, reproposed. And by Jesus, he'd been turned down again! Her answer, which reached him less than an hour afterward, had, like his proposal, been somewhat stiff—but plain. Mrs. Mathewson appreciated the great honor paid to her by Captain Lamb, whom she thanked with all her heart, but she felt obliged to make it clear that the situation in her eyes had not changed at all and that she could not in any circumstances tolerate a continuation of this discussion unless and until Captain Lamb had seen fit to meet her preliminary provision—in other words, until he'd handed over Kukailimoku.

Well, Kaili would stay nailed to the wall. A man had to keep his self-respect or what good was he? But it had shaken Johnny. He had her letter in his pocket right now. He had read it many times, and each time something hurt him, soft but insistent, inside.

Not since boyhood had he been uncertain of himself like this—and he didn't like it.

On the way in—and Johnny had his own varnished gig, one of the sights of the harbor—he passed under the counter of this new Indiaman, *Parnassus*. It had arrived only that morning, a beauty. He eyed its lines now, and remarked each spar canted at the proper angle, every inch of canvas furled; and he thought of the well-scrubbed decks he couldn't see, the cables neatly coiled, lines all tarred, the fixtures polished. *That* was the way to go to sea, if you had to go at all!

Back in his bedroom—he never thought of it as "home"—he smiled a whit grimly at Kukailimoku. He touched the letter in his pocket.

But Johnny Lamb was not a weak man, whatever else he was.

"And that's where you're going to stay," he told the idol.

A visitor was announced a few minutes later, and it came as no surprise to hear his name. Johnny made a bow, which he hoped was not mocking, not too mocking anyway.

"Come in, Reverend. Didn't know we'd been bracketed together, did you?"

"Eh?"

"Not worth explaining. Sit down."

Mr. Bingham did not sit down. He had never been up here —their previous interview had been downstairs in the store— and his eyes flicked around the room, seeing everything, showing nothing.

"That ship that just came in?"

"A humdinger, Reverend. From Whampoa. She's going back around the Horn. It'll be bouncy. Good time o' year, though."

"Would you say she was a safe ship? Seaworthy?"

"Sure as snakes, Reverend."

"And clean?"

"Spotless. I've been all over her already."

"And her captain and officers, are they of good moral character?"

"You're thinking of Mrs. Mathewson, I expect?"

"Why, of course. You promised that you would give your opinion on the next ship by which she might conceivably sail."

"That's right, I did."

"You seem to know a great deal about this ship out there already. Had it any passenger accommodations?"

"It has one free cabin, Reverend. Right next to the third mate's. I'll arrange if for Mrs. Mathewson, if you want. The only thing is—maybe it's only fair to tell you who the third mate is."

"And who is he?"

"Me. I just signed on. Save the fare."

Reverend Mr. Bingham closed his eyes and then opened them again, but still there was no expression in his face. He gave a slight bow. Johnny, too, bowed.

"Perhaps we had better forget the matter, Captain."

"Just as you say. You're sure you won't have a drink, now. . . ? No. . . ? Well, don't slam the door when you go out."

No Smoke Stood in the Sky   30

It was that kind of night you could hardly see your hand before your face.

Alvin Lofts, the second, was undismayed when the Captain came topside and took a place behind the helm, but he was flabbergasted when the Captain curtly countermanded an order to lower.

"We're going *in,* sir?"

"Yes."

Alvin slid a sideways look at him. There was no gainsaying the Captain; and Alvin, who fairly worshipped him, was the last person in the world to question his decisions. All the same, Alvin wondered what it was that drove the Captain back to this village he'd quit exactly ten months ago. The spell-of-the-tropics some men raved about? But Johnny Lamb must be nigh onto twenty-eight now, and he'd been just about every place you could think of. Why should he be eager to return to a land he knew so well? Somebody there? Some dusky damsel? She'd have to be right soncy then, Alvin reckoned; for the Captain was not a man to lose his head over just any old female who came along. Yes, Alvin reckoned that's what it was. Back in Hartford they said of Johnny Lamb that he had a whole swarm of brown babies in Hawaii, where he maintained a harem. But then, there had always been whisperings about Johnny Lamb, ever since Alvin could remember. Nor had the Captain, with that manner of his, done anything to stomp them out.

The *Heavenly Hope* was a forty-five-tonner, sixty-eight feet over-all, beamy, and she didn't draw much. By no means new, she was in good condition. Johnny Lamb was reported to have paid considerable of a sum for her, in cash. The Captain had a heap of commissions but very little gold. He had some kind of sandalwood concession or monopoly in the islands; but of solid point-at-able property, as far as Alvin Lofts knew, the Captain had only this schooner, which was altogether his— and which wasn't insured. Nevertheless the Captain drove her: he was a driver. In any kind of weather at all he would crack on everything but the cook's shirt. Heaving-to for the night was unknown, even coming around the Horn; and clearly it was to remain unknown. Not once in all the thousands of miles they'd logged between Saybrook, Connecticut, here to Makapuu Point—not one time, for water, for wood, or anything—had they put in anywhere.

Yes, sir, this Captain Lamb was sure in a tarnation big hurry to get back. Well, that was all right to Alvin, who, as soon as he got the hang of the islands, was to have the schooner for his own command: the first, the only other mate, dour slab-sided old Crimmons, was slated to go into trade under Captain Lamb ashore. The crew then would all be kanakas. Alvin had never seen a kanaka. So, understandably, he, too, was eager to make Honolulu.

232

At the same time, it was going to call for a power of luck. Alvin esteemed Johnny Lamb the finest sailing man he had ever met; but to face a prospect like this without so much as a quiver called for perfect confidence in both Johnny Lamb *and* God.

They couldn't see a thing. They had to estimate their leeway by the sound of breakers, and Alvin at least estimated it as mighty little. The wind was puffy, and there was a ground swell. Sometimes the breakers seemed to be on one side, sometimes on the other, and more than once they could have been on both. The size of the pass Alvin didn't know, though surely the Captain did. They had no chart of the coast: likely enough none existed. The harbor of course was unlighted, the channel unmarked.

Worst of all, at this time of year both inner and outer harbors—the Captain had described them—would be jam-packed with whalers. Still other whaling vessels, small, lubberly, not alert, would be loafing outside the pass, waiting for day to break. It wasn't safe even to be near Honolulu Bay on a night like this, much less go into it.

"Better call all hands," Johnny Lamb said.

That seemed an excellent idea to Alvin Lofts, who sent the helmsman below to holler.

All hands consisted of Crimmons; Eb Hatton, a good seasoned bosun; and six others, not a foreigner among them, all decent men, Connecticut and Rhode Island men.

There were leadsmen at the chains, both starboard and larboard, but the vessel was moving too fast to permit sending a boat ahead. There was a lookout at the forepeak. And a man lay along the bowsprit. Captain Lamb did order a little canvas taken in, but all the same they moved fast through that silent night, the prow speaking sharply with a good sibilant hiss, while the wake was a cream of tiny twisting whirlpools.

"Hard a-starboard! Steer smart, man!"

Most of them squealed or gasped involuntarily when they

swung so close to the sudden-appearing brig that you could have spat from one deck to the other, and somebody on the brig actually screamed before she passed as suddenly from sight; but Captain Lamb only gave a grunt of annoyance and shoved the helmsman aside to take the wheel himself.

He was granitic, that man. He just didn't have nerves. Alvin, supposed to be listening and peering, as they were all supposed to be, again and again found himself stealing glances at his superior. Despite day-by-day, almost hour-by-hour contact throughout the voyage, the second still found it difficult to believe that he stood in the very presence of Captain Lamb—the Johnny the Lamb of the Hartford riverfront, the boy little Alvin had adored from afar so many years ago, grown into a giant now, a phenomenon, virtually a myth in his own lifetime. And he was a Hell of a sight more than just a crack sailor, too. Alvin knew that. He didn't know why it was; he did not even try to analyze that extra something that made Johnny Lamb in his eyes great, not merely sensational; but he knew it was there. Alvin Lofts was a matter-of-fact youth ordinarily, and not easily moved. But he stood entranced, entoiled, this night. He forgot that his own life was at stake. By God, he'd go anywhere with that man! By God, if he ever wrote a letter home, or if he ever got back there, he'd sure have something to tell them!

Alvin was always to remember that making-port, as indeed they all were. That Captain Lamb knew both harbors the way a man knows his own bedroom, a woman her kitchen, was obvious; but here was a miracle, even so. It was a damn-fool thing to do; but it was magnificent.

When at last they let go the hook, in the first faint shimmer of a dawn flagrantly opalescent, they were surrounded by shipping—and not more than a couple of hundred yards from the beach. You wouldn't have thought a rowboat could do it. Yet they had all their paint, and hadn't so much as brushed a cable.

All around them bells started to ring. Some of the strokes

were high and thin, some were somber. Each bell rang eight times.

"Break out the Moses. Mr. Crimmons, you're in command. I'm going ashore. Now."

He was below only a few minutes, yet when he returned he was shaved and fresh, not at all like a man who had been up all night. He wore a peaked cap, a blue coat, fawn-colored breeches, all exceedingly smart. His boots glittered. A quizzing glass hung from his neck by a red silk ribbon.

Under his arm was the large square gray ledger over which, throughout the voyage, he had been bent for so many hours, the book in which he had recorded with precision every penny spent. Also, he held something in his hand. When Alvin saw what the Captain held in his hand, he began to tremble and wish he hadn't come. He disliked even to be near such a contraption. It made him jumpy.

For this was one of those new-fangled Instantaneous Light Boxes, containing sulphuric acid, sugar, gum arabic, potassium chlorate, and the Lord only knew what else, besides some sticks of treated wood they called oxymuriated matches. Alvin would as soon have shared the Moses boat with a live rattlesnake. In fact, sooner.

"You're taking me yourself?"

"I, uh, I need the exercise."

"All right."

The Captain was affable, if a trifle absent, watching the shore. He held the Light Box negligently, as though it was just anything.

The Captain was a driver, yes; but he wasn't one to waste his breath on cussing to no purpose. If you did your trick, that was all he asked. He wasn't disagreeable, but he was not chatty either. As sociable a man as you'd care to meet on land, at sea he was inclined to be glum; and he was a stickler for nautical etiquette, who ashore was informality itself. He was by no means the first such skipper Alvin had ever known, though he was the best. Many a sea captain appeared to change his whole nature the moment he came aboard, to wax easygoing again, as naturally as a man slips off a coat, when he stepped ashore months later. Those were the ones who could never take the sea for granted: they hated the sea, most of them, resented it, possibly feared it, and were looking forward to the time when they could be shut of it and ashore, where a decent man belongs. But as long as they had to do some skippering they'd do the best job they could, no doubt reckoning that the harder they worked the sooner it would all be over.

Just now, however, the Captain was easy, gracious. He even seemed inclined to jaw, though he didn't pay Alvin much mind: his eyes were on the beach.

"Funny there ain't any smoke," he said suddenly. "Usually this time of morning they'd be lighting up all over the island."

"It's the Sabbath, sir, remember."

"That wouldn't make any difference to them. Looks funny the way it is, with no smoke."

The Grass Tabernacle   31

Now more natives were appearing between the huts, but if they'd had breakfast they'd had it cold, for Johnny saw not a fire. On the other hand, he saw six more hats. And no flowers! He couldn't get used to the sight of Hawaiians without flowers.

A second absence-of-sound now struck the ears of his memory. Not only was nobody singing: nobody was making tapa. The clicketty-thud of the wooden mallets they used when they beat the bark from which to form clothing—a sound persistent, pauseless, and everywhere, from sunrise to sundown—

was as fixed in the Honolulu scene as the rattle of coconut fronds. If at home on a summer night the crickets ceased to chirp, all at once, it would scare you. If you lived on a breakers-beaten beach, and that familiar unnoticed roar stopped for a moment in the middle of the night, it would wake you with a start. So it was with Johnny Lamb, this morning of his return to Honolulu. Though it was full daylight now, nobody was making tapa. Nobody at all.

An uneasy fear came upon him as he roamed the lanes. Was everything all right out at the mission house? What in Hell had happened to God's Anointed anyway? The natives were all heading that way.

Johnny was greeted, and often with smiles, but surely this was nothing like what he had expected. He had looked forward to a stir. It had always been like that: he had been a public personage, hailed, cheered. Now he was not ignored, but he was treated with a strange reserve. This was not like the islanders, who had not previously in Johnny's acquaintance of them known anything about reserve.

Nor were they preparing for the whaler hands, who soon would be pouring ashore. Johnny saw no groggeries. Nobody had anything to sell. No girls stood in doorways, simpering.

These people seemed glad to see him. That much he could tell from their eyes. But they did not give expression to their pleasure, seeming to think that there was something wrong in feeling it.

"Brimstone, Auae," he cried when a third-rank chief, having so far forgot himself as to give a cry of joy and rub his nose against Johnny's, apologized, "What *is* all this, anyway? Why's everybody so persnickety all of a sudden? Tell you what: Let's you and I get ourselves a bottle of squareface and talk it over, eh? Like old times."

Auae shook his head, looking off, as though the mere sight of the man who had proposed such a thing might contaminate him.

"Gin is forbidden," and he hurried away.

Even when Johnny produced his Instantaneous Light Box he did not hold a crowd.

He did it with a flourish, taking a cigar from his vest pocket and slapping it aslant into his mouth, making himself look more like the old Johnny Lamb they had known. He opened the box and took out one of the oxymuriated matches.

Men and women, children, too, fascinated, stopped, the ones in front shrinking back in fear, the ones behind pushing forward. They seemed to know what the box was. They must have heard of oxymuriated matches, though they could hardly have seen one.

Johnny treated a stick, and grandly struck it. The explosion was not great, not notably loud either, but it caused a churning of the crowd, which began to move toward Waikiki, its members resolutely refraining from looking back, though frightened.

Johnny was left standing there, feeling foolish, like some little boy whose tricks no longer work and who cannot attract attention.

Yet, damn it, they would have loved that, and laughed and jabbered about it for days on end, for weeks, a year ago.

They were going to church: there was the reason. Now he could hear the bell—he had himself been drifting out toward the mission house—but even before he heard it he had suspicioned its existence.

They were going to church; and this was something new, so they were deadly serious about it. You had to be serious about the gods, especially this new one, Jehovah. When you went to church you didn't skip along; you didn't laugh and talk; you did not even permit yourself to enjoy the sight and fragrance of the flowers, the spring cleanness of the air. That's the way it had always been in Connecticut, Johnny remembered, and he reckoned that was the way it was going to be in Hawaii.

He went along with them, for everybody in town appeared

to be headed in the same direction and it was easy to become engulfed in the movement. In the past, to walk with a group of Hawaiians was like walking in the midst of a bevy of gay tropical birds, scrawking, scritching, spreading their feathers. With their flashing teeth, their flowers, and laughter, they used to make a picnic of the commonest chore.

Now it was like going to meetinghouse at home—the same studied lack-of-expression, the same self-conscious good manners, holding yourself in all the while, afraid of what people might say.

Alvin rested on his oars, and turned.

"Looks funny anyway, to me," he confessed. "Looks like a lot of haystacks."

"They do, that's right. First thing everybody thinks when he sees them. Only thing is, they're hollow, so you let one of 'em catch fire and—pom! all of a sudden it ain't there any more. That's why they build their cooking pits away from the house. They try to keep the fire going all night. This time in the morning they're usually poking 'em up. There ought to be fifty-sixty strips of smoke in the sky there. I don't know— Looks kind of spooky, the way it is."

But he grinned suddenly. In all the months aboard the *Heavenly Hope* the second had never seen Captain Lamb grin like that, or indeed grin at all. It was a fine glowing grin, and lit up his whole face. It made him handsome as the Devil.

He jiggled the Instantaneous Light Box.

"Maybe they had rain last night? Maybe this is what they need? I'm going to have a heap of fun showing it to them anyway."

Alvin bent to the oars again, leaning low to conceal his fear.

"That's all right," said Captain Lamb. "It won't explode."

"Leastways," he added, "I don't think it will."

The beach was literally that: there was no sort of dock or seawall. It was full daylight by the time Alvin pulled the Moses boat up and Captain Lamb, the ledger under his arm, stepped out. There was nobody in sight. Indeed, there was more activity aboard the fleet of thirty-odd whalers than here on shore. Fires were being lighted in galleys, out there in the harbor. On land no fire showed. Smoke rose from the ships, but not from the cooking pits. Bells sounded out there, telling the time; but there was no sound of any sort on the beach where Captain Lamb and his second mate stood.

"Can't make it out," the Captain muttered. "Nobody *sing- ing*—Used to be, no matter what time it was, somebody would be singing something. They're the singingest people you ever met."

He looked out at the whalers, a slovenly lot, disreputable, dirty. More would be coming in all day. He looked again at the silent village, and shook his head.

"There'll be big doin's here tonight. I hope they're all right over to the mission. These whaler hands can get right rough, if they don't have somebody around to kick the skin off their asses every now and then."

A man and a woman came along the beach, walking care- fully. They were side by side, which was not the custom in the islands. Innate dignity, a racial characteristic, alone kept them from appearing ridiculous. The man's legs were bare, but he wore a peajacket evidently given him by some sailor. There were no buttons on the jacket, which was clean, if threadbare. The woman, who was very fat, was draped from chin to toe in a loose gray nightgowny frock, with long sleeves. You couldn't even see her feet, and she had to walk very slowly in order to keep from tripping over the gown. She wore a hat, the first Hawaiian woman Johnny had ever seen under one. It was a flimsy home-made thing of straw, and it sat atop her head like a bird's nest, but she held that head high.

"Good God! They—they're practically *naked!* "

Alvin ventured: "Look pretty well covered to me. More'n I'd expected."

"But don't you see, man—*they haven't got on a single flower!*"

Nevertheless he straightened himself as the couple ap-

240

proached, and he raised an arm, and gave them his best grin, crying, "Aloha!"

They responded politely, bowing a bit from the waist, but kept on their way. Oh, they recognized him all right! He could tell that from their eyes. But they didn't cheer; they didn't laugh, or even giggle; nor did they run off to spread the tidings that Johnny the Lamb had returned. No. They only bowed, and passed on, walking in the direction of Waikiki. They didn't even look back, though it must have been torture.

Alvin Lofts was alarmed.

"There's something wrong, sir?"

"There sure as thunderation is."

"Maybe, uh, maybe I'd better stay here with you?"

Captain Lamb looked at him, and Alvin felt his face go hot. The Captain smiled a little—not sardonically but kindly.

"No, that's all right. I can take care of myself. I'll hire a gig when I want to go back. Tell Mr. Crimmons to keep that anchorage."

"What if the port captain orders us off?"

"Mister, there ain't any port captain here. Or maybe," he added, wonderment upon him, "maybe there is, now. *Something's* certainly happened."

"Then if anybody should try to make us shift, I'll just tell 'em this is Johnny Lamb's vessel, is that right, sir?"

"That's right. You just tell them that."

Returning, Alvin rowed slowly. He was hailed from sundry vessels he passed, but he paid no attention, for he was watching the Captain. He saw another couple come along the beach, and he saw the Captain greet them with a raised arm, and they bowed slightly and passed on, not looking back. He saw the Captain take off his cap and scratch his head. The second couple, like the first, was walking in the direction of Waikiki.

Alvin looked at the sky. Not one column of smoke stood up from Honolulu.

241

When Alvin looked down again, the Captain was gone.

Johnny cocked his cap, and he toothed the cigar so that it jutted up at a sharper angle. He dug his hands into his breeches pockets. He blew smoke through his nose. But though many glanced at him askance, nobody giggled.

" 'How art thou fallen from heaven, O Lucifer, son of the morning!' " he murmured.

The church was enormous. Just behind the mission house itself, it was bigger even than the royal palace. But it was not made of wood. It was made of grass in bunches mounted on hau poles. It was one of those haystacks, the biggest.

As for the crowd, Johnny Lamb had never before seen so many persons in one place, not even in New Haven, or in Providence. Pretty near everybody on the island must be there, he reckoned.

The crowd was seemly. There was no waving and calling. In twos and threes mostly, they would smile fleetingly at one another or perhaps bow. Nobody laughed. Then they would pass with measured pace into the immensity of the grass tabernacle, from which, though it must already have been filled, came only a faint buzz of whispering and the shrill indefatigible peep of Sybil Bingham's harmonium.

Johnny slipped out of the crowd, and, prompted by he didn't know what instinct, walked around to the rear of this huge building. There he found Ann Mathewson.

It was she who was tolling the bell. There was no belfry in the church proper: it wouldn't have been possible to build one without real timbers. The bell, an oversized ship's bell with a fine clear juicy tone that would carry for many miles when the wind was right, was suspended from a wigwamming of three hau poles nine or ten feet above the ground. It could be that the reason they had it in back instead of up front was that they feared it might get knocked down by the worshippers there. Or, more likely, it was here because that made it easy for the toller, when tolling time was over, to slip into the plat-

242

form end, the preaching end, of this long church by means of a small low doorway. Yes, that would be it.

Anyway, and for whatever reason, Ann was ringing the bell.

He was some thirty feet away when he caught sight of her, and he stopped in his tracks. She did not see him, he was sure of it. She stood with her head down, moving only her arms to pull the rope steadily, slowly, again and again. Her eyes were cast down: they really were. She seemed entranced, standing there, a woman who hears voices from some other world, yet not exhalted, not inspired; and in fact she tolled dully, as though in the grip of terrific supernatural forces against which she had long since ceased to struggle. She looked tired, beaten.

Johnny's heart gave a bound when he saw her, and there was a gush of pity that rose like blood to his head, tingling the top of his mouth, and bringing tears quickly to his eyes.

Yet before he could cry out, or take even one step toward her, she was joined by a man who came out of the church— Horace Crowell. Say, *he* ought to be over on the Big Island, at Kailua! It could be that there was going to be a conference and he'd been called in; but it didn't look so, the way he acted. Right to Ann he went, and took her arm. There was something about the way he did it that made Johnny boil. He wasn't rough, or abrupt, but he was God-damn' possessive. He acted as if she belonged to him; and she did not resist either, but quit her tolling and submissively went into the church with him.

So Crowell was here, watching her with those desiring eyes? How long had he been here? Johnny could smell the hand of the Reverend Hiram Bingham. Unwed persons were not desired in the Family, where now, because of death, there were two such. Why shouldn't those two get together? It would settle all sorts of complications, and the Word of God could continue. They did not know when reinforcements would arrive; and meanwhile they were reluctant to send anybody back to Boston. So give these two every chance to become intimately acquainted. Encourage the affair. Drop hints. Belittle a long widowhood. Speak now and then of the manifest will of the Creator. And leave the room every time these two were in it.

Oh, sure, get her married! Get her married before ever that dreadful man Lamb came back to the islands! Never mind what she thought about it personally. Twang on that will-of-God string. Keep twanging on it. If Sister Mathewson could be made to believe that it was her clear duty, she'd do it. Forget the rest.

Halfway back to the front of the church, to the road, still fuming, he was seared by a thought, and once again he stopped in his tracks. Good God! suppose they were *already* married?

Johnny had been gone ten months, to the day. In that time, he had gone to Hartford, surrendered himself to the authorities, stood trial on a charge of manslaughter, won an acquittal, and on a fast schooner, purchased and refitted by himself, had returned to Honolulu. For what he had accomplished, ten months seemed a short time, but here in Honolulu, among the packed, stifled personalities of the mission house, it might be a very long time. Ten months: yes, Reverend Mr. Bingham could get in a heap of pressure-bringing in ten months. So— had it happened?

On the heels of that thought came another, which shook him even more violently: Suppose they were getting married *right now?* Suppose that's what all this fuss was about, and that Crowell, right this instant, a good grip on her arm, was relentlessly leading Ann to the sacrifice?

This was absurd, as he'd have realized had he thought about it; but Johnny the Lamb was not in good thinking shape just then. He resisted an impulse to run back to that little low doorway and burst into the church through the rear, confronting them. Instead he ran for the front, the main entrance.

244

Jostling recklessly, caring nothing for decorum, in a moment he was inside.

One look at Ann, even the length of that bleak building, steadied him. Of course she wasn't going to get married now! Common sense reasserted itself, more or less, and he thought of half a dozen reasons why he could be sure this was no wedding.

First, Ann herself. She just didn't *look* like a woman about to be married. A bride should show radiant, or, if not that, though preferably that, then at least firmly fixed in her purpose. Ann, arranging hymn books, looked only tired, resigned.

Also she wore drab clothes. He had never seen her in anything else; but these were the *usual* drab clothes. Surely a woman about to march to the altar, even a psalm-singing missionary, would find something new or fancy to pin or tie on somewhere. Why, thunderation, Johnny didn't think that even Hi Bingham would object to a touch of color in those circumstances—though admittedly you never could be sure what Hi Bingham might object to, especially on the Sabbath.

There was another point—this *was* the Sabbath. Would Bingham stage such a spectacle as a marriage ceremony, presumably the first ever to be performed in this part of the world, on a Sunday, the day when—under the new dispensation, apparently—he would draw a good crowd anyway? No. He was too good a showman for that.

Again, there is about a wedding, any wedding, however subdued, an air of festivity. It is essentially a joyous occasion. These Polynesians would have sensed that. Even under the gaze of the vinegarish Long Necks, they would have shown gay. They didn't. They were intense, deadly serious, like children who are afraid they'll be punished if they do anything the least bit wrong.

So she wasn't going to be hitched right now? Good.

That didn't answer his first fear, though. *Was* she married already? She could have been. That worn and weary sag of

245

the shoulders, that lack of luster, that droop: she would have looked that way if she had been married to Crowell, never fear.

He was attracting attention. His height, his clothes, the ledger, the Instantaneous Light Box, most of all the cigar which still jutted, forgotten by him, from between clenched teeth—these turned heads, caused murmurs.

He glanced around. Inside, in the gloom, the tabernacle looked even more enormous. The only light was supplied by the early morning sun, which here and there hurled spears through breeze-blown openings in the grass. These openings changed position as the breeze shifted back and forth, an effect not conducive to reverence.

There was no floor, though the ground was well trampled. There were no pews, only a few benches at the upper end, benches no doubt reserved for haoles and chiefs. There was a low platform, a preaching stand, Sybil Bingham's harmonium, a table with hymn books. There wasn't much else.

Johnny was not invited to sit on one of the haole benches. Instead men and women were frowning at him, shaking their heads.

He slammed the cigar to the ground.

"Oh, go to—to blazes!" he cried, not able, even then, to speak a profane word in what after all was a House of the Lord, if an odd one.

A man sidled toward him, cautiously, picked up the cigar between thumb and a crooked finger, and carried it outside at arm's length, as though it were a wriggling slimy lizard.

Disgusted, Johnny elbowed his way to the door. And when he had come again into the blasting sunlight he found himself alone, for the way had been cleared—not for him but for a newcomer.

It was then that Johnny saw what all this business was about.

Kaahumanu was arriving in her carriage.

The First Time Since Moses   32

It was the same pair of wagon wheels with a rickety board platform that she had ridden that day when they went to the top of the Punchbowl for the horua; but the wheels, bright blue and yellow then, now were a steadfast black, as was the platform itself; and the men who drew it, and who had been naked and loud with laughter on the day Johnny and his Kate raced for a stake of twenty Spanish dollars, this morning wore expressions of determined solemnity — wore also shirts, pants, hats.

It was not the same Kaahumanu. She sat erect, unsmiling, almost rigid, as though fastened in place, on the back of the dray; and though her feet dangled, as before, she did not swing them; while if she wriggled her toes, the way she once had done, you would never know it anyway, for Kaahumanu wore shoes.

She wore also a natural straw Rutland poke, very tall, than which, on her, nothing could possibly have been less becoming; and the ribbons, plain white, were tied under her chin.

Between shoes and poke, virtually the whole distance, she wore a shapeless white sarsenet frock—it was good material, and immaculate, but there wasn't a speck of decoration on it —with long sleeves and a high neck.

She was sedate, even for a queen. When the pullers had so manipulated the ropes that the back of the dray faced the front of the church, and had brought it to a stop, she did not leap off: she slid down with care, her feet together, still holding herself erect, while her hands prevented her skirt from riding up her legs.

She started for the church.

She must have seen Johnny, though he had quickly stepped into the crowd, knowing that when Kate was on her dignity it was best to keep out of her way, seeking, too, a chance to gasp without being greeted. She must have seen him; but she gave no sign.

She was as lovely as ever, if you could disregard the preposterous poke, the shapeless frock. She walked carefully, but she walked well: the heels were not high. She had lost weight.

All the same, there was a curious stiffness about her. It was not just the imperiousness she could and usually did show on state occasions. It was not her newly assumed air of austerity, of piety. It was a physical thing—something in the very way she moved.

Still she remained the beloved of her people. Though she never glanced at them, right and left they fell down before her—here smacketty-dab in front of the tabernacle, too—fell on their faces, making the ancient conventional motion of baring themselves to the waist, though in fact no flesh was exposed. And there rose from them as she passed, not a cheer but a deeper, lower, more sincere susurrus sound of awe, of adoration.

So she passed into the church.

Though it had not taken long, Johnny Lamb was aware that a very great event has just occurred.

The others passed in after her, maintaining a respectful distance. The piping of Sybil Bingham's harmonium died. The service had begun.

Johnny walked away.

It was a beautiful morning, no breeze. It would be a hot day. The fronds of the banana plants, glossy and dark, hung limp as though discouraged; those of the coconut palms, nervous, thin, light, alert, tried hard to tremble. The sun smote the bay.

Soon boats would be putting out from the vessels in the harbor, the town would be filling. Johnny didn't think he

248

wanted to meet any whalers. Halfway to the village he paused.

Somebody behind him hawked apologetically, and he wheeled, edgy as a racehorse.

"Forgive me, señor."

"Hello. Why aren't you in church?"

Don Francisco de Paula Marin, known locally as Manini, chuckled. He always had had, Johnny remembered, the appearance and manner of a man who stands on one side, watching with amusement a show in which he had no wish to take part.

"It was a something to see, eh, Captain?"

"It sure was. But why aren't you there? Everybody else is, seems like."

Manini wore white, and wore it well. He was small, small-featured, fragile.

"You forget that I am a despised Papist. It may be that I am exempt from the law. I risk this. I have never liked to be close to others, crammed in. I—I do not enjoy the odor of my fellow men."

"I don't either. What law?"

"You have been away for a long time, señor. You have not yet learned that the islands have a constitution."

"Huh! A real constitution?"

"Indeed, a model one."

"But how could they, in that time? Who wrote it?"

"God, señor. No other. The Almighty God."

"Now listen, Manini. I may not always do the things certain folks I could name think I ought to do maybe. But I'm a Christian, I'm no heathen. And what you said just now sounds to me like blasphemy."

The Spaniard took a tiny backward step, as if he feared a blow, though it was unthinkable that anybody should whop such a slight, such a delicately put-together man.

"It was not meant to be, I assure you, señor. It is the truth, exactly. No, no, not blasphemy! Only the truth."

249

A smile flicked the corners of his mouth, and he stepped forward again, raising a finger so waxy you could all but see through it.

"It is my confession, señor, that I followed you from the church, yes. I sought to see how you reacted to the new state of affairs."

"You always was a great one for prying into other people's business."

"But you must understand, I was coming this way anyway, señor. To my own home. One throng has gone indoors. Another is about to come ashore. I care for the second even less than for the first, so I had thought to shut myself in behind my walls. It is wise, do you not think?"

Johnny nodded. Incurably interested in the affairs of others, this diminutive Spaniard guarded with great jealousy his own. He was a rich man, as men went on the beach at Honolulu, richer even than Johnny Lamb in immediate, touchable, get-at-able goods; but he conceded no obligations brought about by his possessions, and clung to his seclusion. Few had ever got inside the wall around his much-talked-about house, much less inside the house itself. His Chinese servants, when they went marketing, did not gossip.

"Señor, it is early, but—would you care to drink a glass of wine with me, perhaps? I could tell you about the new constitution."

Johnny raised his eyebrows.

"Well, sure. You put it that way, all right."

"My home is near here, señor. You are to consider all that is in it your own."

Johnny knew tarnation well that he hadn't meant that, except as a fancy way of speaking, and soon afterward Johnny was wishing with all his heart that he had.

Inside the wall they found themselves in a lush yet orderly garden, a sort of cross, it struck Johnny, between Polynesian helter-skelter and New England primness. That is, the blooms were brash, exotic, brilliant of color, and they strove to writhe,

250

scatter, stretch; but they had been kept firmly in hand, so that they stood in rigid if reluctant rows. The walks, too, consisting of black and white sand polychromatic with pebbles, were miracles of neatness, each grain, it seemed, in a predetermined place.

The Spaniard was watching him.

"You like it, señor?"

"It's beautiful!"

"I had not known that you fancied flowers."

"Always had a hankering after them."

Marin had paused, as though to admire a circular bed of some scarlet flowers Johnny had never even seen before.

"Such a place, it takes long work, señor. Money, too. But you have much money today, eh?"

"Expect to have, soon."

"You have just landed, señor. May I be the first to tell you that an attempt has been made to persuade the chiefs on the outer islands to break their pledges to you?"

"I expected that."

"But it did not succeed. The pledges hold."

"I expected that, too."

"You are now in the same position you were when you left. If you could only handle all the wood—"

"I can handle it, now."

"You could not, then, be induced to repropose your original plan, the one you outlined on the *Cleopatra's Barge?*"

"Too late for that. But tell me about this constitution."

"Ah, but the wine first, señor! Wine before business!"

You didn't think that way a minute ago, reflected Johnny as he followed the little man into the house.

The house was small and it was low: it could not even be seen from outside the wall. It was not in the least like a tropical dwelling. It was built of heavy dark wood, with no bamboo, and not even a hint of thatch. There was no veranda.

Inside it could scarcely be called attractive, for it was not well windowed and despite the brightness of the morning it

251

was dim. Also it was oppressively close. But undeniably it was elegant; and Johnny Lamb sure admired elegance, always had.

The furniture, such as he could see of it, was dark and heavy, and very rich, and the same could be said of the rugs, the oil paintings, and tapestries. The stuff looked European, Johnny thought, though he didn't know for sure, not being educated in such matters. At least it was not Chinese.

The chair into which he sank was deep, if not very soft. The arms were massive.

Don Francisco de Paula Marin, scarcely to be seen, even after Johnny's eyes had become accustomed to the dimness, clapped his hands. A Chinese, appearing, never so much as glanced at Johnny, which proved his training. Marin ordered the wine brought, and it was brought.

Johnny reckoned that the glass must have been the most expensive he had ever held. He wished he could examine it in a real light.

The wine was dry and tart, and it went down easily, without bite. Claret, he reckoned, though he was not sure—something red, anyway.

"Somebody gave Kaahumanu a Bible," the Spaniard said, after a while. "These missionaries, from the time they came, two years ago, they've been trying to give her one—but she'd never accept it. But she took one from somebody. I wonder who it could be."

"I wonder," said Johnny, and sipped.

"Some more wine, señor?"

"Not finished with this yet, thanks."

"Some fruit?"

"Now there's an idea."

He felt better after he had eaten. They did not talk. Johnny finished his drink, and the Chinese refilled his glass.

"Queen Kaahumanu is no fool, señor."

"Yes. I knew that."

"Of course. I'd thought only that you might, uh, you might

252

perhaps be rather better acquainted with her emotional nature—"

"I know that pretty good, too. As good as anybody can, I guess."

"But she has a fine brain. She's shrewd. I think she must have known more English than any of us realized, all along."

"I used to wonder about that."

"She began asking questions about that Bible. Not of the Long Necks, no. Others. Señor Hunnewell especially. And me. They were searching questions, I can tell you."

"They would be." Johnny held his glass up to what light there was, and squinted at the clear lovely wine. "You know," he said portentously, "I've just thought of something. The way she walked a little while ago, when she went into that church—you know, damn it, Manini, I got an idea she had corsets on!"

"To be sure she did, señor. She has been wearing them for a month."

Johnny shook his head.

"I oughtn't to have gone. I oughtn't to have let her out of my sight."

"Some of us wish you never had."

"This means that every woman of rank in the islands is going to want a pair of corsets, God help us."

"It does. Already they are doing everything they can to get them. They talk with sailors, who give them promises."

"And what do they give the sailors?" Don't tell me—maybe I can guess." His laugh was short and held no mirth. "That's a twistical way to get a set of stays, Manini. Or rather a promise. Still, I suppose millions of women have given it for a promise. And will."

They were silent for a spell.

"About a month ago," the Spaniard resumed, just as if there had been no interruption, "she sent for Hiram Bingham. She didn't go to him, she sent for him."

"Of course."

"Three days after that the constitution was proclaimed."

"Ah, now we're getting around to that constitution. So there really are laws here, Manini? Is that why there are no fires?"

"Yes. It is the Sabbath. No fires on the Sabbath. No games. Nothing but church. That is one of the laws. The fourth."

"But how could they have framed a whole constitution—Hi Bingham and Kate—I mean Queen Kaahumanu—in three days?"

"They did not frame it, they took it over whole. As I told you, in all earnestness, señor, it was God who wrote this particular constitution. It was the one brought down from Sinai. But in those days it was on stone."

Johnny sat up so smart he almost spilled his wine.

"You mean—"

"I refer, you understand, to the Decalogue."

"The Ten Commandments! Those're it?"

The Spaniard gravely inclined his head.

"We live, sir, in a country unique in history. The Ten Commandments are the actual law of the land. They will no doubt be supplemented from time to time, as I believe the original ones were. But they remain the corpus of the law, the constitution, and anybody who says they don't had better not let Queen Kaahumanu hear him. So far as I know, señor, this is the first time a people has been so governed since the days of Moses."

"Well, I'll be a club-footed cockroach," said Johnny.

He remained in this convenient haven, sometimes chatting a bit, mostly sitting in silence, thinking, for the rest of the morning and a good part of the afternoon. From time to time, circuitously, Don Francisco would bring up again the matter of the sandalwood concessions; but Johnny refused to discuss this.

At length he took his leave, which was ceremonious.

"You must come and see me some time, Manini."

"It would give the most exquisite pleasure. For indeed, it's

254

a pity we have not become better acquainted before this. Now conceivably if our business interests were in some way united—"

"No," said Johnny. "Well, good-bye. And thanks for the drinks."

The streets or lanes of Honolulu were thronged with sailors. There must have been two hundred of them. No door was open, but many of the huts did not have doors, and the sailors poked boldly in. There was not a woman in sight.

There were some bottles, not many.

The crowd was in a nasty mood. Even Johnny the Lamb did not attempt to push through it. He went around the edges of groups, striving to be inconspicuous. He had an errand.

Before his store-warehouse, still the only two-story building in the islands, he found another crowd. The door was open. Troubled, he hurried.

Only three keys to the lock of that door existed. He had one in his pocket. One he had left with Humu, who would live out in the bush with his beloved Clarissa—Honolulu was too noisy for him, he couldn't sleep well there—but who had agreed to air out the place now and then, and check against burglary, and sweep it. The third key, at her request, Johnny had given to the late Kamehameha's favorite wife, who thought she might like to go there some times and just sit a while and be lonesome.

"He's got brandy that's been left in there, I tell you I heard it straight he has," a man was telling another.

"We'll get it all right," the other said.

"Like Hell you will," said Johnny, and clouted him over the ear from behind.

The first man spun around.

"Say, that's a friend of mine!"

"You should never admit it," said Johnny, and broke his nose.

He pushed past the rest. He turned in the doorway.

255

"You beefwits! Don't you know who I am?"

They did, by that time. They hovered; but it is not likely that they planned a rush.

"And what's more, you stick to the beach tonight, understand? I catch any of you out Waikiki way and you're going to have a hard time chewing afterward. That clear?"

"What are *you* getting at that mission house, Captain?"

He ignored this, for he had long ago learned the futility of trying to identify one heckler in a crowd; and he went into the store.

There were three Hawaiians, all members of Kate's entourage. They bowed. Johnny bowed; and as he did so he noticed from a corner of his eye an all-but-empty bottle of French brandy on the floor behind a packing case, and deduced that the couriers had been surreptitiously consoling themselves for the long wait.

"Love and happiness fly to you."

"Happiness and love fly to thee, brave Captain."

Then, just as he was getting set to mouth some additional banalities, as had been the custom, they presented him with a letter. It flummoxed him. The fact that there were only three messengers in the first place was extraordinary. Hawaiian chiefs were punctilious about things like this, and Kate in the old days would have sent at least eight or nine. Nor would they have had anything but a verbal message; and now there was a letter. Dazed, he opened it.

It was in an uncertain but at the same time strong hand, a large hand. Kate's own? Had she learned to write too, then?

"Her Imperial Highness Kaahumanu sends flying love and happiness to Captain John Lamb and cries joy for his safe return to Her Imperial Highness's realm, and commands him to appear before her"—here there was a break where she had evidently tried to write either "'instantly" or "immediately" and had crossed it out. The letter went on "—at once. K."

Johnny bowed again.

"It is necessary that I make some slight preparation. But I

256

do not wish to hold you gentlemen up. Pray assure her Highness that I will be there—at once."

And he called after them: "Another thing. If I was you, I wouldn't stand too close to her. Kaahumanu knows that smell."

Death Right Below   33

A comber would come marching in from far out there beyond the reef, a long wavering line like a line drawn with chalk on a sea of silk incredibly blue. Behind one, before another, it would march; and they'd keep themselves properly spaced. Miles away, twelve hundred feet below, they would sweep in as though to embrace the whole of the island and smother it with foam.

The comber would strike the reef, and it would pause a moment, baffled, outraged, spitting and spewing itself high, sometimes in veritable geysers, catching the sunlight: it would heave itself, all confused, angry, its whole length. Then it would be over, and into the lagoon, a subdued wave now, without ferocity as formerly, white still but sending forth no spray. And so it would march again, less certain of itself, wobbling, until it fell, weary and without smash, grateful for the release, upon the beach—like a tired woman falling into the arms of her lover.

And all the while, from as far out as you could see across the blue Pacific, they kept coming in that way, arrayed in stately rows, enraged by the reef, leaping, spitting, but limp and languid as they finished the thousands-of-miles journey, creaming flat with grateful hisses across the sands of Kaneohe under an unstained sky.

Kaahumanu dropped from the dray, laughing a little, for

she was glad to be here: the pali was one of her favorite places, and this day had been wearisome until now. But a shadow creased her face; and Johnny, approaching, surmised that she had felt again the restraining pinch of the corset. He grinned, toiling up the last slope. Kaahumanu clapped her hands, and immediately was surrounded by female attendants who hiked up her holoku, or Mother Hubbard, and made her more comfortable, afterward retiring with the corset held high as though it were a prize of war, a captured standard. Kaahumanu beamed upon Johnny when he reached her.

"You might have let me do that," he said reproachfully.

For an instant, seeing her eyes darken, he feared that he had gone too far. The Queen of the formal reception had indeed been as queenly as all-get-out, seated on a chair, giving him two fingers, with a bric-a-brac politeness inquiring after his fortunes and assuring him of the gladness felt by her and her people at his safe return. But he had known this pomposity before, on certain public occasions, and was not put out about it. The invitation to go up the Nuuana Valley with her and watch the sun set from the top of the pali had followed naturally and easily; and the expedition itself, as soon as it started, promised to be a jolly one—there were fewer than fifty attendants, for one thing, and some of these were told off to form a rear guard and prevent any trailing population: Kaahumanu more than once had emptied Honolulu merely by going for a picnic back in the hills.

While they climbed through the forest of ironwood and hoa trees, and across the old battlefield, there had been no chit-chat, as there would have been in the old days, for after all this was the Sabbath; but things had been easier and looser than at the palace, with the Queen downright amiable much of the time and getting more and more pleasant as they neared the top. (As soon as the audience was over she had taken off that damned poke bonnet and also the shoes.)

Now her shoulders went back, and that dark look came into her eyes, and Johnny's intestines tightened, for he knew how terrible she could be in her wrath. But suddenly she smiled.

"You know how to do it, then, Tony? You have had much experience, taking them off, eh?"

Relief flushed his face, but the flush remained and even intensified, burning him; and with a start he realized that her remark had embarrassed him, and that he was blushing—and this realization of course made him blush the more.

Kaahumanu slapped his shoulder, staggering him, and she roared with laughter.

Even above the wind that always blows past the Nuuanu Pali—the trades funneled furiously between grim basaltic Lanihuli on one side, gaunt basaltic Konahuanui on the other —even above that, Kate's laughter rang full and free, round, rich. The attendants, retired to a discreet distance, looked at one another, and nudged one another, and they too tittered and laughed, happy because the Queen was happy again.

To change the subject, and to cover his embarrassment, Johnny produced his trump card. The Instantaneous Light Box caused an instantaneous sensation. Unfortunately the wind was such that even though attendants formed a human windbreak he had to treat the stick time after time before he could light it. They were frightened, but fascinated, the Queen most of all. "Maikai nui!" she cried. When the flame appeared they fled a short distance—and of course the flame was blown out.

It had been his first thought to light a match and flip it over the edge of the cliff, the pali. They stood, here, on a celebrated spot, a place that marked the end of the last, bloodiest, and most decisive battle in the history of the islands. The plain down there, drowsy Palikoolau with its huts, its palms, its kalo beds, hemmed in by hills, gilded by the late afternoon sun, was more than a thousand feet below them; and some seven hundred feet of this was sheer drop, perpendicular, without slant, plant, or projection. It was at this place that various gods of the old days, cornered by their enemies—for the gods were forever fighting among themselves—had been by magic transformed into birds of one sort or another, a feat the followers of Kalanikupule, the last king of Oahu, no doubt wished they could emulate when they found themselves in similar circumstances only a few years back. The Oahuans had met the invaders a mile or so down the valley toward Honolulu. The scene that ensued was messy. Largely it was said because of the power of the god-on-a-stick Kukailimoku, which was carried at all times in the forefront of the fighting, the Hawaiians, under Kaahumanu's husband, Kamehameha I, prevailed. The Oahuans were driven back, up here, where they had their choice of dying in fight, their backs against the drop; or jumping; or being pushed over. Not one survived.

But Johnny had forgotten the wind that always blows up there. It is said that if you open your mouth while on top of the Nuuanu Pali you'll never manage to close it again until you get behind something. One by one, after the human windbreak had dissolved, the matches were whuffed out.

However, the matches smoked voluminously. Kate, delighted, demanded that he throw over at least a smoking stick, so that she could watch it fall. He went right to the edge, and knelt, and did this; and Kate threw herself flat on her belly, her whole head over the verge, and screamed with joy as she traced the tumble.

There was other smoke in sight. From the sleepy coastal plain down there, where the natives, cut off from Honolulu by a mountain range, risked a violation of the fourth law in the new constitution, twenty or more columns rose. The Queen frowned when she saw these, but only fleetingly. Soon she was smiling again; and this was not because she herself was breaking the fourth law—for wasn't she above all law?—but simply because she was in good humor.

She called for leis, which were promptly forthcoming, having been brought along, like the Light Box, for just such an emergency. She herself was draped in half a dozen of them —of lehua mostly, and awapuhi, the flower of the wild ginger, and pikake, which is jasmine. They went out horizontally

260

from her neck, flipping and flapping flirtatiously, as did Johnny's when attendants had decorated him, too.

Kate stood then with arms and legs spread, flowers flying behind her, her hair flying just above the flowers; and the wind flattened the sarsenet against her, so that every curve of that superb dis-stayed figure was clear and plain. My God! she was a gorgeous thing! They'd had some wonderful times together! Johnny swallowed hard, turning away. He could always blame the tears in his eyes on the wind, but Kate wasn't an easy gal to fool.

She sat down—right spang on the edge, her lower legs hanging over. The woman had no nerves at all.

"Sit beside me, Tony."

She could say "Johnny" now, if she said it carefully; but she preferred "Tony."

He sat gingerly, his feet hanging over. He watched her, not daring to look down at the plain, out at the white-striped sea.

She put her hands behind her and leaned back, her chin uptilted. In that position, and with her hair flying, she looked positively girlish. But she was grave.

"It is beautiful down there, Tony."

"It sure is. This whole country's beautiful."

"You like it better than your own country?"

"Well, it's different."

She was watching him intently. They spoke in Hawaiian. Part of the time during the audience at the palace Kate had insisted upon English, for she sought to show off; but Hawaiian was easier and more natural now. She kept watching him.

He did not look directly at her, but neither did he look down at the breathtaking view. It still unsettled him a mite to reflect that if one of his boots happened to fall off, it would drop seven hundred feet without touching a thing.

The members of the punahele stayed out of earshot, though within sight; and they were silent.

"Tony?"

"Yes, Kate."

261

"I—I have been so lonesome!"

"Ah, poor Kate."

"And after a time you will go away, and then I'll be lonesome again. I don't want to be that way ever again, Tony."

He said nothing, for he reckoned that there was nothing he could say. He felt bad. Somehow he felt that this was all his fault.

"There is so much more work. So much business. We have to gather more money. Did you know that we have a port captain now, Tony, in Honolulu?"

No, he hadn't known that.

"We charge them forty dollars for the outer harbor, sixty dollars for the inner harbor. And I am thinking of proclaiming —what is it you call them?—taxes?"

She had to say the word in English.

Johnny nodded.

"You have them in your country, too, Tony. Those—taxes?"

"Oh, sure. I reckon they have them just about anywhere you go nowadays."

"I need somebody to take those things, here. It is hard to know who—My people, you could always trust them with anything, Tony. Always. But it's different now. Look at me, Tony."

He looked at her. He felt himself trembling under the force of her gaze.

"Listen, Tony: I do not regret what I have done, to bring my people under the command of your god Jehovah. That is good. I love Jesus. And they will all love him, too. I'll make them. But—but it's hard sometimes, Tony. And it gets harder. I need somebody to help me. Somebody I trust — and love."

She leaned closer, her big brown eyes bright, lips a little parted.

"Tony," she said evenly, low, "Tony, will you marry me?"

He looked away, though not quickly. His heart hurt him. Tears were rolling down his cheeks; he didn't even try to wipe them away.

262

After a while he cleared his throat.

"You—you have some husbands already, Kate."

She shook her head impatiently.

"I will pass another law. The people of Kauai would follow me anyway. You—listen, Tony—you know I only married Kaumualii and Kealiiahonui for that island, don't you?" She touched his sleeve. "You don't think I do panipani with either of them, do you, Tony?"

"Well, I don't know. A man and wife usually do."

"Well, I don't. Only with you. And the people would follow you, too, Tony. The people of Kauai and Maui and Hawaii and everywhere. My people love you. And if we were married we would get rich, Tony. You like money. You always said you liked money."

She pointed. The sun was setting, but it was behind a mountain, so you could not see it, only the mountain-shadows it caused to steal across the plain of Palikoolau, and the glint and glitter with which it struck the oncoming rollers. For they faced the east here, the direction of home.

"You said this is a beautiful land of mine, Tony. It is. Why don't you take it, all of it? And all of me?"

He stared at the combers rushing in.

"Answer me, Tony."

He hung his head. The twittering among the attendants had ceased, as though they had sensed something tragic taking place. There was no sound now but that of the wind.

"Y'see, Kate, it's hard to explain. When you asked me a little while ago whether I liked this land better than my own, all I could say was that they're different. They are. And we're different, too, Kate, you and I. God knows I love you! Make no mistake about that! But—Y'see, when I was away, just lately here, I had a lot of time for thinking, and it came to me that I ain't got any right and never did have to go roaming the seven seas and setting up a trading business. I'm a Connecticut boy, and Connecticut's where I belong. That don't mean this place ain't wonderful, and it certainly don't mean that

263

you ain't wonderful, too, Kate. I'd whop any man dared say that. But—we're different. In a lot of ways. Y'see, your folks—how can I say it?—Well, your folks, they were all kings and queens, and they were different from my folks in the first place. And that applies to even 'way back. It's a shame, I guess. But that's the way it is, Kate." He cleared his throat again. "So that's the reason I don't think we ought to get married, if you'll excuse me for saying so. It wouldn't be really fair."

There was a silence. When Kaahumanu did move, Johnny looked up with a start. He was afraid, for a split-second there, that she was going to slide over the edge of the pali, maybe taking him along.

But she rose easily, quietly, holding down her skirt. She brushed herself off.

"We had better start or it will be dark before we get back." She spoke in English, meticulously. "I'll put my corset back on."

She clapped her hands.

The women surrounded her; and when a moment later she was exposed again it was as a queen well strapped and stayed.

"Good night, Captain. You go ahead. It is harder for them to draw my carriage downhill than up. We'll be slow. But you go ahead. You must have many things to do in Honolulu."

He looked at her, ignoring the hand she extended. And suddenly he was weeping again. And she was weeping.

"*Kate!*"

"*Tony!*"

They rushed together, arms outstretched. Each put hands on the other's shoulders, and they leaned close, and passionately rubbed noses, first on one side, then on the other.

"Aloha oe, my Tony."

"Good-bye, Kate. Good-bye."

He tore himself away, and he fairly ran down the slope. He turned only once, for a moment. They were helping Queen Kaahumanu up onto the dray. She looked old.

264

A Sinless Sunday 34

She would have to tell Horace. She had been dreading it for months, ever since the time when she came to know that sooner or later she was going to have to give in to him. If Horace was weak, he was dogged; and he had been bat-bat-battering at her every day with all the soft insistence of a miller moth thumping against a window. Only, the moth would never win through. Horace would.

That the others were back of Horace, that there was a conspiracy, was obvious: nobody even tried to conceal it. But Ann did not trouble herself about the others. She didn't have to tell them what she and Captain Lamb had done that afternoon in the hieau back of Kailua. There was little doubt in Ann's mind that she would have succumbed to Horace months before—so soon as ever she had come to admit to herself that she'd lost Captain Lamb—if it wasn't for the need to tell him about what had happened that day. She had aimed to tell Abigail Crowell, but Abigail died too soon. The thought of telling anybody else was scarcely bearable; and the thought of telling Horace was the worst of all. Nevertheless it had to be done.

In a mild well-mannered way she was fond of Horace Crowell. She hated to hurt him, as she was going to have to do if she married him. And she reckoned she would marry him. They all seemed so set on it, not just Horace but everybody in the Family; and Ann knew her own limitations; she could hold out only just so long.

She had known but one last-minute surge of rebellion, and that petty, a matter of vanity. She had promised Horace that she would give him her answer, at last, immediately after the Sabbath services. They both knew what that answer would be; but Ann also knew, and Horace probably sensed, that it would be necessary also to say more than just "yes." Horace, however, pretended to take the answer for granted. He who had been so obsequious as a suitor, fawning on her, now waxed self-confident, or pretended to do so. He became unbearably possessive, and even patronized her.

At another time she might have flared up. Who did he think he was, anyway? But she seemed to have no spunk left any more, ever since Captain Lamb's stubbornness in refusing to surrender that heathen idol had kept them apart. She couldn't care. She was listless. The others were animated, for this was a great occasion, this Sabbath service, and never since the earliest days of the mission had it known such excitement. But not Ann Mathewson.

Two things it seemed were about to reach separate climaxes simultaneously.

Everybody in the islands knew that the church could not have been built without Kaahumanu's approval, and that indeed she actually assisted by sending materials and workers. Everybody knew, too, that she had conferred with Hiram Bingham before she issued a proclamation declaring the Ten Commandments to be the national constitution. These were great victories. But a greater was to follow, to cap them. Kaahumanu had promised to attend the service this Sabbath morning in person. That was all she *had* promised; but it was a great deal. They were agreed in the Family that this would prove the most important single service they had given.

At the same time there was the matter of the whalers. With the great dowager herself behind the mission, and the law of man and the Law of God for once synonymous, it was decided that the time had come to enforce the Fourth Commandment. This would not be easy. The officers of the whaling ships, for the most part Yankees, were God-fearing men,

266

many of them; but the hands were largely foreigners, to whom the Sabbath was no more than a day to drink and carouse. The Lord's Anointed had made every effort to clear the town of gin and rum that day, though they knew that a certain amount of it was sure to be peddled by unscrupulous traders. Of the women, however, they were certain. By Queen Kaahumanu's own order all the women of Honolulu were to go to other parts of the island immediately after the church service. Arrangements had been made to house them for the day and night. Not even Kaahumanu could expect to keep the women back in the bush all the time the ships were in; but it was hoped that one sinless Sunday would establish a precedent. Hiram Bingham was not greedy. He would settle for one day in seven devoted to the Lord, right now.

All this spelled trouble. It was conceivable that the sailors, finding rum prices high, and no girls, would return grumbling to their ships. That was possible, yes. Much more likely was that they would head for the mission house.

The ladies had been urged to depart with the rest of the female population, but they'd said "no" without hesitation. Nothing would induce them to leave the mission.

This was an additional reason why the service at church was of such great importance.

Ann's moment of near-revolt came just before the service. Sickened by the air in the overcrowded church, at Sybil Bingham's suggestion she had relieved Horace at the bell, while he did her work inside. When it was time to start, when the Family was to be assembled, Horace had come back for her. That was all. It was the *way* he had come up to her then, they way he'd taken her arm, that enraged Ann. In his most impassioned moments previously he had not dared to touch her. And now here he was striding up to her and leading her off as if she was already his wife.

But where was the profit in resistance? She was going to succumb sooner or later anyway. She just didn't have the heart to do anything about it now. Let Horace have his little show, if it made him feel good. She shrugged, having given no sign of her anger; and she went meekly with him, a led lamb.

There were already sailors loitering near the mission house when they returned at noon, and some things were shouted that made the ladies' faces flush, but nothing was thrown. "Come in," Reverend Mr. Bingham urged them. "Come and visit with us." But all they did was jeer.

After the midday meal, which of course was cold, Ann and Horace retired to her room, leaving the door open. This was permitted and even encouraged. It was difficult to find privacy at the mission; and everybody trusted Horace Crowell. It wasn't proper, granted; it would have horrified folks back home; but some concession had to be made to the circumstances.

It was there, sitting on the bed, that she told Horace. She said that there was something she thought he ought to know before she answered his proposal, and then she just plain told it. It was as simple as that. She was even, she supposed, glib. She didn't look at him, but neither did she hang her head: rather she sat like a girl in school, her hands folded in her lap, and when she told him what she had done with Captain Lamb that afternoon in the hills back of Kailua she did so, again, rather like a school girl reciting, in a singsongy voice, without expression.

Indeed, when she was finished she actually had to suppress an impulse to giggle. This was wicked, and she reproved herself for it, promising herself that she would remember to ask forgiveness for it tonight in her prayers.

She looked at Horace.

He was staring at her so wildly that she started, truly afraid that the man had gone mad. His eyes, always inclined to be protuberant, now bugged out an appalling distance, and looked as if they might at any moment burst, like overstrained bubbles. Sweat gleamed on his forehead. A vein throbbed

268

darkly—though for the rest his face was chalk—at his right temple. His mouth was working.

When words did come they were a torrent.

"Fornicator! Whore of Babylon!"

"I won't be talked to like that. Get out of this room."

" 'Know ye not that your body is the temple of the Holy Ghost?' Oh, corruption! How—How could you have done it? And with that great shambling uncouth man!"

"Better not let Captain Lamb hear you say that. And please keep your voice lower."

She was seated on the bed, and he was standing. They were necessarily close, for the room was narrow. Elsewhere in the mission house there was silence. Horace's voice had been heard. Ann could only hope that nobody had distinguished the words.

He raised both fists, leaning over her. She just sat looking up. He trembled. Suddenly he began to weep. He ran out of the room.

She heard him cross the main room, where the others would be writing letters and reading, and go into his own bedroom, slamming the door. She could hear his sobs even then.

She got up and closed the door, and went back and sat on the bed again. She would have liked to pray, but she didn't know how soon Horace would be back and she did not want him to surprise her on her knees. So she just sat there.

She seethed inside, however. Calling her names like that! She'd make him pay for it. She supposed she should be merciful and take into consideration how unstrung he'd been, not himself. Men attached so much importance to such matters. Horace had been shocked even more than she had expected. But all the same, he didn't need to call her dirty names.

Horace's outcry had brought silence not only to the mission house itself but also to the road outside, where the original group of loafing sailors, considerably enlarged, had been singing obscene songs in loud voices. This form of torment was

269

by no means new and it was only mildly annoying to the Lord's Anointed, who, indeed, because of this smallboyishness, and in spite of their own tastes, had over the months become extremely well acquainted with the more unspeakable chanteys and grogshop ballads.

Today the silence out there was unsettling. As Reverend Mr. Bingham used to say, the poor lost creatures were harmless so long as they were singing. Now, the newcomers might have insisted upon something more than childish insults. It had been agreed in the Family, and enunciated by Reverend Mr. Bingham, that good policy would be to remain indoors all afternoon, even keeping away from windows. The situation was surely explosive, and if there was violence there would be a great deal of it. Nor did they have any defense. Mr. Hunnewell was at his busiest now, what with so many ships in harbor, and couldn't take the time to help them. Captain Lamb had been away only ten months and could scarcely be expected back yet. There was no watch, as there was no army. They had made some converts by this time—they were taking them in carefully, refusing to hurry, since all of them, and especially Reverend Mr. Bingham, knew what a disastrous effect a general backsliding would have—and they had among these some men who were both sincere and able-bodied, and good friends. These would have helped to protect them against the sailors, so far as they were able; but it happened that they were all back in the bush now, taking care of their hustled-out womenfolks.

Yes, if Captain Lamb were back it would be different. Or would it? He could do anything he wanted with those men, even a mob like the one in Honolulu now, the biggest yet. But would he? She had given herself to him once without having first exacted any sort of promise from him. He was a hard-headed businessman, and proud.

The door was flung open. Horace threw himself on his knees. He buried his face in his hands, sobbing.

It was pitiful, and she was sorry for him. She reached out

270

and stroked the fine mouse-colored hair. She murmured that she understood.

"I don't know how I ever could have said such things!"

"You were het up. You weren't yourself."

"You're so good! You're so kind!"

He closed the door. He took her by the shoulders.

"I don't think we ought to talk about it now," she said. "You're upset."

"If I'm upset it's because of you."

She nodded grave agreement. He got closer, and put his face down toward hers, until she realized in amazement that he was about to try to kiss her. At any time this would have been extraordinary behavior in Horace Crowell. On the Sabbath it was astounding. Yet she decided, in that split-second, gasping, that she would let him. She decided that because she was so sorry for him.

He kissed her on the mouth. She closed her eyes, unwilling to see his own eyes so close at hand. After the kiss she lowered her head. He tried to kiss her again, but she pushed him away; but she was gentle. She did not look at him as he stood over near the window. She was afraid that he might start to cry again. He was a whipped spaniel. Yet he retained some touch of dignity. Simply he held out a hand.

"That was beastly, what I said," he whispered. "I love you, Ann. It's the only excuse I have. Is—is it enough?"

She almost smiled.

"I think it is enough."

"I didn't mean it. I couldn't possibly have meant it! That you told me what happened that day, that terrible afternoon, it's the more reason why I admire you and love you. You didn't have to tell me."

"I know that, Horace."

"It shows your goodness." His voice, very low, trembled. "By the living God that made me, Ann, I swear that I'll never again mention it or allude to it in any way. I mean, whether you'll have me or not. Because I still want you for my wife."

271

"No, Horace."

He made never a protest, though his shoulders drooped.

"But you do forgive me? Say that."

"I forgive you."

He sighed. He turned away. But not toward the door: he turned toward the window. In his own muffled mothlike way he would still fight. He would keep trying. He had time on his side, and he knew it.

"Ann, if only you'd—"

"Please, Horace."

"—try to see it from my point of view. From the bottom of my heart—"

"There's one of the bastards now!"

The window was smashed. Glass in slivers and small pieces flew into the room, tinkled to the floor. Some stones fell to the floor, too.

Horace screamed. He bolted for the door, ran out.

Ann looked at the shattered glass, at the stones. She went to the window, and her lip curled.

"Haven't you anything better to do?" she cried.

Another stone was thrown, and it struck the glass just over her head, sprinkling her with small bright particles.

She sighed, shrugged a little, and turned away. Reverend Mr. Bingham stood in the doorway. He showed no trace of fear.

"Sister Mathewson, I think they are about to make a rush on the house. You'd best come out to the main room."

She went immediately and unquestioningly.

Horace was there but he did not look up. They were all there, on their knees. Mr. Bingham raised his hands, and he prayed for a short time, and they all said "Amen." Then he asked them to remain as they were.

They could hear voices outside, getting closer. Another window was smashed.

"I will go and speak to them," said Reverend Mr. Bingham.

272

Whom Shall I Send?   35

They could hear him out there for a long time, his voice rising and falling. Sometimes they'd hear the others, too, scoffing at him, or snarling like dogs; and then the voice of Reverend Mr. Bingham would swell to a stronger note, and the others would subside—for a little while.

Several times they heard sharp grunts or cries; or the stamp of feet; once a sort of cheer. Several times, too, stones cracked against the door.

At first Ann Mathewson was too scared really to pray, though she did try. She wondered if this was going to be the end of everything, and she wondered in particular if these ruffians would rape the ladies. She would fight, of course; but she didn't have much confidence in her strength: she was afraid she'd faint even when they just got close to her.

She trembled, and tried again to pray.

She peeked at Horace, on the other side of the circle. His eyes were closed, his head averted, but Ann thought that she'd caught a downward flick of the lashes when she peeked, as though he had previously been peeking at her. Well, he probably had. And probably he had been thinking lascivious thoughts. She was sure he had never had such thoughts before —that is, about her. But as soon as he'd learned that a man had had her, if only once, a man not her husband, then immediately lewdness took and shook him, and he supposed that he could do anything he liked with her. Men! All right, it's true that she was no longer virtuous. She had lost something she could never get back. But why should any man suppose that because a door had once been entered the lock was destroyed, that it could never be closed again. Why should they think that, the—the loathsome beasts! She closed her eyes hard, so as not to see Horace any longer, and fairly shuddered with the intensity of her rage. She opened her eyes, and glanced sideways at Sybil Bingham. That quieted her.

This was no time to be in a rage, if there was ever such a time; her heat should be drained away, if only for decency's sake; and Sybil Bingham was the perfect febrifuge.

There was dignity in her posture. She did not grovel. Her head was bent low, and her eyes were closed, though not *squeezed* shut; but her back was straight. Some of her hair had escaped the comb and hung down the sides of her face. Her nose shone. Her lips moved.

Quietness came over Ann when she peeked at her, and soon she closed her eyes again, and then she really was able to talk to the Lord, and she lost herself in this.

After a spell the leader came back.

His coat was torn, his shoes were scuffed. His hair, ordinarily prim, was in disarray. There was a cut high on his left cheekbone—he had high cheekbones anyway—and blood moved sullenly out of this and down his cheek. His large eyes swam in sadness; his face was set that way, too, no touch of anger there.

"I think they will be still for a while. How long I don't know. Only the Redeemer knows that. May I join you?"

And he got to his knees.

It was arranged readily enough, in low but carefully not-hushed voices, that each should go about his ordinary Sabbath business as though nothing was wrong, except that they would take the precaution to keep back from windows and they would not go outside.

Of a normal Sunday afternoon those of the Family, except such as might have special errands or duties elsewhere on the island, habitually relaxed. Some read, or rather re-read, either letters from home or the Book, or both. Some sewed, for this was esteemed the Lord's work and not labor in the usual sense of that word. Some even lay down and slept, for they could always use sleep. Most of them, however, wrote letters or caught up on their journals.

There was seldom any general conversation. They were too tired for that. Today in addition they were too frightened.

Everybody was conscious of the fact that Sister Mathewson and Brother Crowell had reached some sort of crisis, had had if not a quarrel then at least a scene of shattering emotion; and that for the present they did not wish to make any announcement. But this situation, of all but unbearable importance ordinarily, was nearly forgotten in the thought of the violence outside. This relieved the pressure of embarrassment on the two of them, a circumstance for which they were grateful. They avoided one another's eyes.

Ann went to her room, and swept up the fragments of glass, bending low when she was near the window. She closed the door and sat on the far end of the bed, and she wrote a little of a letter she'd been writing for two weeks: it was not unusual for these busy persons to take a month or more on a single letter, there being so few ships to carry mail home by way of China, India, the Cape of Good Hope, fewer still around the Horn.

But Ann's heart was not in this, and soon she ceased. Neither did she feel like praying, right now. So she just sat and thought.

This letter in her lap—would it ever reach Hartford—or would it be shredded and burned when the mob swarmed over the mission house? She wished that she could go with it. She was, just then, sitting there, passionately homesick. This was not the homesickness of the early months in the islands, which had been a definite ache, a pain inside of her, as dull but persistent, as undeniable, as hunger. But the homesickness of the early days had been unthought-out. Now she *knew* that

275

she should not have come. She did not belong among the Lord's Anointed. She was not of the stuff of which good missionaries are made.

Her Book was on the little table close at hand, and she took it and opened it to a favorite passage. Mr. Mathewson had quoted this when, eyes aglow, heart too aglow, he had asked her to go to the other side of the world with him:

"I heard the voice of the Lord, saying, Whom shall I send, and who will go for us? Then said I, Here am I; send me."

Those were the words that had done it. The words of old Isaiah, dead more than two thousand years, had seared her soul there in the parlor of the house on Prospect Street. It was not her own unquenchable spirit suddenly become articulate. Nor was it the personality of Mr. Mathewson, dim at best. It was the words. With those in her ears, ringing and ringing, the way the thunder of surf is said to keep going in infinitesimal echoes deep in the heart of a seashell, she had gone mad. She had swept all reason aside; spurned, and stormily, the pleas of mother, sisters, friends; married a man she scarcely knew; dedicated her life to the enlightenment and uplifting of savages she'd never heard of; and started to pack.

"Declare his glory among the heathen, his wonders among all people. . ."

"Go ye into all the world, and preach the gospel to every creature. . ."

" . . . to open their eyes, and to turn them from darkness to light, and from the power of Satan unto God. . . ."

Years ago men had said these things, and written them, or other men had written them. Centuries ago, in a land far away. And so Ann Buttoner, reputedly a hard-headed Yankee, daughter of a merchant, had lost her head. And here she was.

"I heard the voice of the Lord, saying, Whom shall I send. . . ."

Something—she didn't know what—yet it was as definite

as a hand under her chin—lifted her face and turned it, so that she was staring at the window. And the breath went out of her.

A man was there. His face was close to one of the lower unbroken panes: his nose actually touched the glass. He wore a dark cotton cap, and he was bearded high, his hair being black. He was a big man. His mouth, the lips red, slobbered with saliva, was foolishly agape—it was an idiot's grin. Idiocy was in his eyes, too, which shone brightly.

Motionless, Ann felt cold all over, her skin prickling. Would it be one like this when the rush came? Would it be this very man? Who was there to protect her? She would not be able to run, or fight, not any more than she was able to move right now: she sat frozen in place, staring wildly at the man, who stared back.

She was never to know how long the two of them stayed like that, only a few feet apart—a few feet and a whole world. She found tongue suddenly, not otherwise moving. She was downright startled to hear her own voice.

"Get out of here! Go away!"

She sounded like any old housewife. She sounded indeed like her own mother when she chased away the boys from River Street who had come up to steal pears.

"Go on, now!"

The man went. He did not seem to retreat, nor yet to move aside. He simply faded, and was not there any longer.

Ann continued to stare at the window. No, there was nobody to protect her. She put aside the letter she'd been writing, in her lap all this time. She had never been so miserably alone. All over the country, back home, congregations of the faithful were praying for the success of this pioneer mission—thousands of devout persons. Again and again, in public appeal and in private, God was implored to watch over them. But Ann Mathewson sat more alone than ever, because of her secret.

There was a knock on the door.

"Evening prayers, Sister."

She realized with a start that it was dark. Night arrives suddenly in those latitudes, where there is almost no dusk, and darkness swoops down with eagerness; but Ann had not noticed a change. She rose, brushing her skirt.

"Coming."

Reverend Mr. Thurston, who conducted the prayers that night, was mercifully brief. The sounds outside had increased; and Ann at least could not pretend that she was in communication with her Creator, or even pay much mind to what Mr. Thurston said. She wondered if the others felt that same way. She wondered if like her they were *wishing*, almost, that the sailors would rush the house. What ailed those men out there? Did they need to bolster their spirits? Were they sending for more of their vile alcoholic drink, in order to work up the courage to storm a frame house defended by seven unarmed men, seven women, five children? They knew that there was nothing to stop them, nobody to hold them back. The monstrous thing of which they were the parts, and which was greater than all of them put together—greater, more ignorant, more vicious—the mob—owned the island. What was it waiting for? Darkness? But darkness had come.

Ann's lip curled. She squeezed her clasped hands together hard, so that the nails went white.

They had a whale-oil lamp, but they did not light it, nor did they light a candle. It was thought better to remain in darkness.

They talked in whispers, when they talked at all, but they strove to keep their voices slow, or at least not fast. If any of them had screeched, or even sobbed, it might have been too much for the rest.

Supper was silent, a mumbled business, and they passed one another things by feel. Sunday night supper in the Family always was cold anyway, though ordinarily after sundown they permitted themselves tea. There was no tea this night.

278

There was no stove in the house, and it was judged best not to go out to the cooking pit. They drank only water, and not much of that, though they were all inordinately thirsty. They had no well; and after the church service they had stocked the house with all the water they could, the men carrying it from the nearest stream in every container available, even calabashes, which stood in rows around the walls now. But they drank sparingly, suffering. And when supper was finished, though it went against all their training, the women agreed that the dishes should not be washed. Every drop must be guarded.

It was a little after eight o'clock—it must have been about five minutes after—when there came a terrific explosion and the air was filled with light.

When a God Is Killed 36

Ann, cringing, for a split-second wondered whether the Lord had come out of His Heaven to hurl a thunderbolt upon those drunken impious beasts. Others must have thought this, too, or hoped it; for a moment later, despite their fear, and their agreement, they rushed to the windows.

No, it had been the work not of God, but of Satan. The church was on fire. There was a mighty hissing, a spitting, a great roar. In a matter of minutes all the compound was lit up, and all the ground, so that the trees and bushes stood red on one side, black on the other, while billions of sparks swarmed toward the sky.

Though sweat rolled slow and cold down their backs, as they stood at the windows their faces and hands, all the front part of their bodies, were pricked as if by hot pins; and their eyes smarted, gushing tears.

"So it must be," Reverend Mr. Bingham mused aloud, "when poor damned souls first face the Everlasting Torment. Pity them."

Pity *us*, was Ann's wild thought. She retreated, as the others did, to the far wall. Even there they could feel the force of the fire. The roar was stupendous, filling the world. The sparks multiplied, leaping higher, faster.

They were lucky in one respect. There was no breeze, as most nights at this time of the year there would be. Tongue after tongue of reaching straining flame, each bounding with a burst out of a side of the church, making a *"poo-oom!"* audible even above the roar, stripped upward, spewing sparks. Sometimes these tongues wavered, wobbled; but they straightened.

The walls went first. They were no more than dried grass, and licks of flame scurried across them like lizards, never needing to pause. The hau poles which formed most of the framework were green, recently cut. The roof—it was hard to distinguish it from the walls, except by color—was made of coconut thatch, a material less likely to admit rain than the dried grass, less likely to blow away, too. This thatch was comparatively green. But neither thatch nor poles was going to be able to resist the heat of the blazing walls.

In that crimsoned room, crammed against the far wall, as though the very finger of fate had pinned them there, they stood and watched the mob gather itself to charge.

For the sailors were visible now. No longer were they mere voices out there in the darkness. They no longer skulked. Emboldened by the fire, as though they had done a notably valorous thing when they lit it, perhaps maddened by its intensity and the thunder of the flames and the spitting of sparks, they ran here and there, or danced drunkenly, waving things, screaming. In this way they made the scene seem even more hellish, for their twisting leaping figures, grotesque in silhouette against the fire, had all the lineaments of fiends; and their shadows, as they cavorted, swooped and stretched fantastically, and contracted, and shuttled back and forth, blue-black upon the red earth.

Yet it was real enough, this scene. Those were real men out there, and for all their curious capers they were gathering to attack. If there was no leadership among them there was a common hatred, unifying in itself: they all wanted to crush the mission house, the missionaries. They must have sensed that it was tonight or never. Once let the Lord's Anointed get the upper hand in Honolulu, and the whalers would whistle in vain for women. Well—women? There were none in the village, but there were sure enough some in that white frame house over yonder. And a blaze would drive them out on the run, squealing, to be caught and thrown on the ground. What if they were psalm-singers? Psalm-singing females looked the same as any others, didn't they, when you got their clothes off?

The one thing that had kept the sailors back—the rumor that there was something to that powder-stored-in-the-cellar story after all, and that a rush on the mission house might be the signal for a suicidal explosion — was swamped by the arrival of newcomers from the village, lust-crazed men, and thirsty. Many hung back, but there were volunteers to spread the fire.

Trembling, the Lord's Anointed saw the torches lighted, and saw them passed around. There must have been a dozen torches, spitting, spluttering. The men who held them began to walk toward the house.

"Let us pray," said the Reverend Mr. Bingham.

There seemed nothing else to do, and they got down on their knees, there on a floor littered with rocks and bits of broken glass—all except Ann Mathewson, who remained standing.

281

Ann reckoned that there'd been enough praying. If God was not going to help them the way things were already, well, then she reckoned that God wasn't going to help them at all; and if that was blasphemous it would just have to be blasphemous.

Anyway, *she* was not going to get down on the floor. She was going to wait for them upright. She even took a step forward the advancing men.

It was for this reason that she was the first to see the miracle.

Part of the church roof fell in; an immense cloud of sparks shot up; and the glare, terrible before, was heightened.

Ann faced the direction of Honolulu, where the crowd had come from. The flimsy low palisade of bamboo which surrounded all the mission buildings, including the church, had long before been trampled down. The mob was no more than a hundred yards away, and it swayed, moving back and forth a little as though pushed from behind. Ann could see the mob clearly now, in the increasing glow.

Suddenly it was turbulent. Some mighty thing behind it was churning it. Men turned, then fell aside, yelling, covering their heads with their arms.

Captain Lamb ran into the cleared space, and he had a long pole as thick as your wrist. He held it in both hands. He turned, swinging the pole in a circle. Three men went down.

Captain Lamb was laughing, and presently he began to sing. But he wasted no time, asked no questions. He went right after the men with the torches. He twirled the great stick, and one man, the torch tumbling from his hands, went down with a broken hip. The others backed away. Three drew knives. Captain Lamb charged them.

Oh, the boys and the girls went a-huckleberry hunting,
To me way-aye-aye-aye-aye-i-yah!

282

"And *stay* there, you bastard, or I'll rip the balls off you and cram 'em down your throat!" Johnny Lamb added.

Ann must have cried out, for the others had scrambled to their feet and were by her side.

"He's back! We're all right now!"

The ones with the torches had dropped these and rejoined their fellows, instinctively crowding together. Knives were drawn. There were many men with clubs, too.

"We've got to help him!"

She would have run out there; for Captain Lamb, so far from taking advantage of the retreat of the torch-men, and scampering for the house, had turned to face the mob itself, and was even shuffling toward it, swinging the great stick above his head. She would have run to his side, but they held her back.

"Let me go! Can't you see—"

> Oh, the boys and the girls went a-huckleberry hunting,
> And sing high-low, my Ranzo Ray!

Bare-headed, chin high, feet wide-spread, Johnny the Lamb moved in. If they'd thought to get around behind him they could have brought him down, but they were afraid of the weapon he held. He swung it as lightly as though it were a mere stick of bamboo, and wherever it struck it broke a bone.

Windmilling that thing, charging, singing, in the light of the burning church he must have looked twice his real size.

A mob has no courage, in itself. Neither does it have the ability to reason. Terror tapped those men. In a moment the road to Honolulu swarmed with fugitives—and Johnny the Lamb was alone, except for those who lay groaning on the ground. He turned toward the mission house.

It was then that Ann Mathewson stopped struggling, and they released her, and she went into her bedroom, shutting the door behind her.

283

Captain Lamb came in. He did not knock, he did not call out, but simply flung open the door and stalked in.

The rest of the church roof fell, sending up an even greater cloud of sparks, so that the room was a light as day.

He looked around.

"Where is she?"

Nobody answered. Captain Lamb nodded, as though the silence itself was an answer, and he strode straight to the door of Sister Mathewson's bedroom. He did not ask where it was: he just went there. This act was much commented upon afterward. At the time, it seemed perfectly natural.

Ann had straightened her dress and smoothed her hair, when he knocked once and entered. He threw on the floor the thing he had been holding.

"I was bringing this to you. Happened it came in handy."

Kukailimoku, the god of battles, had fought its last fight. Battered and broken, the feathers stripped off or burnt, the wickerwork squashed, the once-ferocious scowl knocked foolishly lopsided, it would scream no more. The hair that once had surmounted it in loose dirt-crusty hanks was torn off. The sharks' teeth had been slammed out of the mouth, still open in rage but impotent now.

Smoke rose uncertainly from the mashed, smashed idol, and struck the underside of the table's edge, and coiled up past it, not touching the leatherbound Bible that rested there, chaste, serene, above Kukailimoku.

Johnny Lamb moved his chin.

"You marry that man out there?"

"No."

"You promise him to?"

"No."

He let out a great deal of breath very slowly. He lifted his arms.

"Come here," he said.

284

Thoughts Under a Stovepipe

Their friends would not have known them from the hats they wore; but they were the only persons at the taffrail; and so great was the clamor on shore, a short distance away, that the voices of the hands forward, who were having up the hook with a chantey, scarcely reached them.

For him a stovepipe, for her a d'Angoulême poke: it was a reversal of their previous roles.

Oh, Johnny still had beavers! But he considered it more in keeping with the dignity of the occasion, and his own dignity as a wealthy public benefactor, to don a solemner hat. He must get used to a stovepipe anyway. He was not a bullyboy any longer, but a business man. He was a friend of the missionaries, too, which would help him back home. Hadn't he paid a record fee to the Reverend Mr. Bingham for performing the first marriage service in this part of the world, that fee taking the form of a new church? They'd even proposed to name it after him, the John Lamb Memorial Church; but he demurred. "They got enough other things around here to remember me by."

The rest of Captain Lamb, too, was garbed becomingly. He wore a tailed coat of broadcloth, royal blue in color, with plain silver buttons, a black velvet collar. His pantaloons were a severe jonquil yellow, and not tight. His waistcoat, though scarlet and white with stripes, and sprinkled with silver, nevertheless contrived to be conservative. He sported no fobs or rings, and neither were there any ornaments in his ears. His gloves, a concession, were lilac in color; but he did not carry his quizzing glass.

Captain Lamb was a shade heavier in the jowls than he had been when first he came to the islands three years ago. He was a trifle more deliberate in his movements. Now he stood stiff at the taffrail, acknowledging the cheers of the throng; but his thoughts were on his ledgers down in the cabin: he could hardly wait to get his hands on them.

Came to that, there was something else he could hardly wait to get his hands on; and now, while holding his head straight for the benefit of those who cheered, he glanced sideways at her.

That had been a good pick. Never before had she looked so lovely, a world of difference from the way she used to look when she wore that damned dead gray all the time. Now her green eyes sparkled, and wisps of dark brown hair straying from under the d'Angoulême crackled. Her lips were a bit parted. She was happy; and there was color in her cheeks.

The poke itself was a burst of ribbons and ruchings, very big, the brim bright peach to match the trimmings, hung in front with frills of Mechlin lace which formed a sort of mask over the eyes. Ann Mathewson Lamb wore peach and scarlet bombazine covered with patent net and trimmed with swansdown. A lavaliere hung around her neck. There were pearl pendants in her ears. When she waved, her bracelet and bangles flashed in the sun.

The beach was crowded: just about everybody on the island was there. It was not of course the Sabbath—they wouldn't have sailed on the Sabbath—and work on the church, which took hundreds of men, had been suspended for the occasion, following the marriage service at which Reverend Mr. Bingham had preached on a text from Galatians: "Let us not be weary in well doing: for in due season we shall reap, if we faint not."

"I'm not going to faint," Ann had whispered, her cheek against her husband's shoulder.

"You'd better not!"

286

Reverend Mr. Bingham and all the others were there, sedately waving farewell. Johnny studied the leader.

"He's a fool in a lot of ways, but I guess we all are," he told his bride. "Anyway the islands are his, now. They used to call me King John. I reckon they'll be calling him King Hiram pretty soon."

Humu was there, cheering in his shrill high silly voice. Humu wore the coat that had been presented to the King of the Sandwich Islands by the Czar of All the Russias, and he also wore a loincloth. He held Clarissa high, like a baby, so that it could see over the crowd.

The King was there, to be sure, tolerably sober, and all the court, and especially the kuhina nui, the great Queen Kaahumanu.

The business man's eyes misted a mite. Good old Kate!

Sybil Bingham had brought her harmonium down, and the Family struck up a hymn.

At the same time the hands forward, while they walked the capstan, were having themselves a chantey, a notably bawdy one.

Johnny looked at Humu, with his fond foolish grin, and that absurd upstanding tuft of hair on the top of his head. He looked again at Kate, bless her heart. He swallowed.

His wife snuggled against his shoulder as they stood there, in a manner perhaps not altogether proper, but he was too overcome with emotion to reprove her.

"The ways of God are inscrutable," she said.

"They sure are," said Johnny Lamb.

287